click.date.repeat.

a novel

K. J. Farnham

Click Date Repeat
Copyright © 2014 by K. J. Farnham
All rights reserved.

Cover design © QDesign
Edited by Leah Campbell and Julie Collins
Formatting by Karan & Co. Author Solutions

No part of this book may be reproduced or transmitted in any form without permission in writing from the author. The only exception is by a reviewer, who may quote short excerpts in a review.

This is a work of fiction. Names, businesses, places and events are either products of the author's imagination or used in a fictitious manner.

more.*books*.by k. j.

Click Date Repeat Again

Don't Call Me Kit Kat

A Case of Serendipity

Visit kjfarnham.com for more information.

dedication

To my husband, who I met after a year and a half of online dating.

chapter one

Chloe – 25
Location: Milwaukee
Could We Be a Perfect Match?

Relationship Status: Never Married
Kids: No
Want kids: Yes
Ethnicity: White / Asian
Body type: Petite, Slim
Height: 5' 2"
Religion: Christian
Politics: Middle of the Road
Smoke: No
Drink: Social Drinker
Pets: Cats
Education: Bachelor's +
Employment: Education
Income: 30,000-40,000

I've been a teacher for three years and am currently working on my master's degree. I enjoy staying active and spending time with family and friends. A few of my favorite activities include biking, hiking, and running. I enjoy travel and a variety of music and food. I'm looking for someone who is family oriented with a good sense of humor. I have photos to share by email if interested.

∽

"I can't believe you're finally going on a date." Even through the phone lines, I know my friend Jess is rolling her eyes. I can feel it in her tone.

The phone is cradled against my right shoulder as I scrutinize myself in the mirror. "I know. I think it'll end up being worth the wait though. This guy seems pretty perfect." I hope some of my enthusiasm rubs off on her.

So far, online dating seems like a good fit for me. It's easy to find guys who have all of the attributes I'm looking for, and I can prevent wasting time on the rest. Like everything else in my life, I'm trying to make the whole process as efficient as possible. If I sift through my matches carefully enough, I'm sure to find someone worthwhile. Right? That's what I keep telling myself anyway. Jess thinks I'm wasting my time. If it were up to her, I would still be searching for someone in a bar where, let's face it, prospects are slim. I've seen them all: too old, too drunk, too full of themselves, too eager, or already in a relationship. The list goes on. Heck, some don't even hide the fact that they have a wife or girlfriend.

"So, where are you meeting him? And which one is it? The dark and handsome one or the guy with no photo?"

"It's Scott. The dark and handsome one."

Seeing his photo for the first time brought a smile to my face. It was the day I created my account. Such a handsome face on my list of potential matches prompted me to spend nearly two hours learning how to use the Yahoo! Personals site when my only intention initially had been to browse through a few profiles. It seemed urgent to send Scott a message that day though, just in case his profile wasn't on my list the next time I logged in. I had no idea how these things worked, after all. For all I knew, he could be matched up with someone else and stolen away from my list of possibilities before I even got the chance to say "hi."

Unfortunately, every time I typed a line or two, the words just felt wrong. *How are you supposed to start a conversation like this*, I wondered. It all felt so foreign to me, and over and over I kept typing the sentences only to delete them. I finally decided to send an icebreaker, the Yahoo! Personals equivalent of sending over a drink at the bar. It was a way to let him know I liked his profile without having to think of something to say. I convinced myself there was far less pressure with this option, and that if he looked at my profile and decided he wasn't interested, at least knowing I had not painstakingly bared my soul via e-mail would soften the blow of rejection.

I check out my backside in the mirror. "We're meeting at Applebee's." I close my eyes and brace myself for Jess's response.

"Applebee's? Why? You hate Applebee's!" she says.

"I know, but it's an equal distance for both of us." I don't want to tell her that Scott sounded pretty adamant about meeting at Applebee's. In fact, he mentioned something about loving Applebee's. Even though my stomach turned when he suggested it, I didn't want to come across as pushy by suggesting somewhere else.

"Who suggested it?" She isn't going to let it go.

I pause for a second and consider lying to her. "He did."

She laughs. "So you've waited this long to go on your first date, and the guy you're meeting up with picks Applebee's? Sounds like a sign to me."

Uneasiness settles in the pit of my stomach. Maybe it is a sign. Or maybe Jess is just getting into my head. I can't help but be a little bit pissed at her for not being more supportive. Who cares if he likes Applebee's? He has a good job, makes a decent amount of money, has a sense of humor, and he's *really* attractive. I never say anything about that controlling, weaselly, coke-sniffing, car-salesman boyfriend of hers. I take a deep breath. "Whatever, Jess."

"Honestly, Chloe, I still don't get why you're spending money to meet people online when there are more than enough guys to choose from at nearly every corner bar. Remember Lily, my redheaded co-worker? She said her sister tried online dating and every guy she met was a total weirdo. Think about it. There's something fishy about a guy who sits at home on his computer looking for women." She laughs.

"Well, I sit at home on a computer looking for men, and I'm not a weirdo." Jess doesn't respond. "Hello?"

"Oh. Sorry. I was pondering what you just said." I envision her smirk, and for a split second, I wonder why we're even friends.

"Very funny. Not everyone who attempts online dating is weird. That's like saying that everyone on the prowl in a bar is normal. If Internet dating sites were full of crazies, there's no way they would stay in business. Online dating is new to us, but Yahoo! Personals has been around since like 1998. C'mon Jess. It's 2003. It must be a successful way to meet people if it's still around. And there are other sites, too, like eHarmony and Match.com. eHarmony even advertises on TV."

"I don't know, Chloe. It still seems bizarre to me. Tell you what—when I see a ring on your finger, I'll change my tune. In the meantime, please try not to go out with any axe murderers." I assume she must be smirking again. "Anyway, I hope your date goes well tonight. Call me as soon as you're done. Maybe you guys can meet up with me and Ned at Jannigan's."

Yeah, because that's exactly what I want to do—meet up with Jess and her boyfriend so they can tell Scott how much I hate Applebee's. "Sure, maybe. I'll give you a call."

"Sounds good. Have fun!"

"You too."

Fife forty-five. Shit. I have to get going. I take one last look in the mirror. Snug, low-rise jeans, black V-neck sweater, and black mid-heel ankle boots. I actually feel overdressed for Applebee's. My hair, slightly longer than shoulder length, is sleek, medium-brown and parted slightly to the left. I've had the same hairstyle since my junior year in high school. Prior to settling on a semi-Marcia Brady 'do, I went through the nineties perm phase and had bangs off and on, but nothing ever felt as comfortable as straight hair with no bangs.

I rarely wear makeup because my skin is sensitive to breakouts, but I have a little on tonight at the urging of the co-worker whose online-dating success story convinced me to try this whole thing out in the first place. As I study my lightly mascaraed lashes, I can hear Cassie Thurman's innocent and just-trying-to-be-helpful voice. *"How come you never wear makeup, hon? You're pretty but would be a lot prettier with a little color."* Typically, only a bitch would say something like that, but Cassie isn't a bitch at all. She's a sweetheart who simply was not raised to have a filter. Sometimes I think of her as a Caucasian version of my Asian mother, someone who occasionally says things so socially inept that everyone within earshot stares at her and wonders, *"Did she just say what I think she said?"*

I consider putting on a brighter top, but decide to stick with black, as usual. I grab my purse and head out the door. Cassie was filling in as a long-term substitute for a third-grade teacher on medical leave. I didn't know her all that well, but we ended up going out to lunch with a big group of teachers. As she dominated each mini-conversation, I imagined how naturally pretty she might be underneath all of that makeup, flawlessly applied every day. She wore tailored J. Crew pantsuits and stylish jewelry and seemed like the kind of person who would be too worried about reapplying her lipstick every fifteen minutes or breaking a nail to work with children, but she was kind and genuine in her own way.

Somehow, the conversation shifted to how Cassie met her fiancé on a popular online dating site. Over the course of three months, she had made connections with three great prospects through Soulmate.com. One of her matches was Ted, a sports writer for a local newspaper. She dated Ted exclusively for two months before he proposed. As Cassie told her story, my married co-workers—pretty much everyone but me—started raising their eyebrows in my direction. Then Jan Bowman, who was sitting next to me, traded seats with Cassie. That's how I ended up with her in my ear throughout the rest of that lunch.

"Chloe, you really need to try it. Honestly, you'll never meet the man of your dreams in a filthy bar! Plus, you probably don't know your type the way you think you do." She paused to reapply her lipstick as she peered at herself in a compact mirror. "After all, I never would have chosen Ted on my own. He's not as good looking or cultured as the guys I've dated in the past, but he's harder working and has a bigger heart than all of them put together."

Once I had heard enough to piece together the complete history of her online dating journey and storybook romance with Ted, I figured that if someone as high maintenance as Cassie could find the love of her life online, then I should have no problem at all. After doing a bit of research, I opted for Yahoo! Personals, the less pricey version of Soulmate.com.

I've been so self-conscious about this whole process up to now that all I've done is send out icebreakers, which have mostly gone unanswered. But Scott had replied immediately with a friendly email, and two weeks and six emails back and forth later, we took our relationship to the next level when he offered his phone number. Not only was I pleased with his profile picture, but his stats were exactly what I had been searching for.

Scott – 30
Location: South Milwaukee
Searching for that Special Someone

Relationship Status: Never Married
Kids: No
Want Kids: Maybe
Ethnicity: White / Caucasian
Body type: Athletic
Height: 6' 0"
Religion: Christian
Politics: Middle of the Road
Smoke: No Way

Drink: Social Drinker
Pets: No
Education: Bachelor's
Employment: Professional
Income: 50,000-60,000

∽

I pull up to Applebee's at six oh five, a bit late as usual. The parking lot is packed, so it takes me a few minutes to find a spot. The fall air is brisk, and I'm glad to have a warm jacket in case we decide to meet up with Jess and Ned.

I enter the crowded foyer, and a hostess with a black pixie haircut and a small, nearly invisible diamond nose ring greets me. With a ruby red grin she asks, "How many?"

"Two, but I don't know if my date is here yet."

I look around nervously for Scott's vaguely memorized face to emerge from the crowd. As I do so, I envision his profile photo, in which he is wearing a cobalt blue, open-collar dress shirt. His dark brown eyes are intense, and his smile is confident, yet modest. And his thick, dark brown hair is short in the back and a little longer on top.

"I can check. What's his name?"

"Scott."

"Hmm. Let's see." The hostess scrolls her finger down the waitlist. "Nope, I don't see a Scott." I can sense her mounting impatience as she eyes the group of four waiting behind me.

"Would you like me to add his name to the list?"

"Please use mine. It's Chloe."

I thank the hostess and then scan for an open spot as I move toward the bar. As soon as I settle onto an empty stool, I search for Scott again, wondering if he might have slipped past the hostess without giving her his name. Still no sign of him, but the entrance is to my right and just out of my immediate gaze, so I consider switching spots.

"Hi there. What can I get for ya?" A bartender with that I-know-I'm-hot demeanor asks, postponing my move. He's shaking a silver tumbler over his right shoulder.

"Umm . . ." My nerves *could* use some numbing. "A tall Mandarin and seltzer would be great. Thanks," I say smiling.

"Coming right up," he says with a nod.

I retrieve a five from my wallet and watch as he finishes up with the customers ahead of me. Moments later, I'm sipping my drink and checking the time. Six twenty-one. Scott and I haven't exchanged cell numbers yet, so if he's running late or stuck in traffic he won't be able to let me know. After about ten minutes, I'm tempted to call Jess, but decide it won't look good if I'm on the phone when Scott arrives. So, I continue to people watch.

Two women are sitting on my left with their backs to the bar. They're facing two guys who are standing—must be a double date. One of the guys leans toward me and reaches for the menu on the bar. He smiles. "You don't need this, do you?"

I lean back and politely return the grin. "Nope. Go right ahead."

The woman next to me—I assume it's his girlfriend—looks me up and down, then stares for a few seconds too long. What the hell? A wave of insecurity settles in my gut. If I had more liquid courage, I would probably ask what her problem is. Instead, I raise my eyebrows and look away.

That's when I see him. A guy is making his way through the crowded foyer to the bar. I check the time again. Six forty-five. We make eye contact, and in that moment, I know it's Scott and immediately wish it wasn't. He quickly looks away and continues walking through the crowd. This guy isn't tall, dark, or handsome. He's five-nine, at best, and pasty white against the dimly lit backdrop of the dining area. Part of me wishes he'll stop next to someone else at the bar or return to an empty stool next to some other woman. Instead, he continues in my direction, curving around the far end of the bar to my left. With the exception of when we first made eye contact, he doesn't look at me again, not to smile or even to let on that he's heading my way. *Oh well. Might as well get this over with.* I swivel left and hop off my stool to greet him.

"Hi, I-I'm Scott," he stammers as he extends his left hand and looks directly at my right earlobe.

For a brief second, I optimistically consider the fact that he isn't staring at my barely-there chest. But then my heart begins to race, and I feel as though every ounce of blood in my body is rushing to my face. I've had this feeling before in the presence of people I've been attracted to, but these same physiological symptoms are occurring for a completely different reason now. Based on Scott's online dating profile, I expected him to be extremely good-looking, well-dressed (since he mentioned a love for shopping), and in good shape because he claims to be an avid gym goer. In reality, he's a balding, watered-down version of the man in his profile picture. To make matters worse, the double-daters appear to be listening as we commence with our awkward introductions.

"Hi. It's nice to finally meet you." I extend my hand and attempt to grip his, but his palm falls slack and melts away to his side the second we touch. I cringe and consider scurrying through the crowd and out the door, yearning to be at home in my PJs watching a rerun of *Sex and the City*.

Again, without making eye contact, he replies, "Yeah, I put in my name. I guess we have a forty-five-minute wait."

Is he serious? I've been waiting for nearly an hour. Just then, the red lights of my Applebee's pager illuminate, and we both glance over at it. I pick it up along with my drink and smile weakly. "Actually, they're ready for us now."

As the hostess escorts us to our booth, I sense she's scrutinizing us. I can't imagine what she must be thinking. I'm no super model, but at least my clothes are from the current decade. Scott, on the other hand, is wearing acid-washed jeans, a canary yellow polo shirt, and a light gray Member's Only jacket that's two sizes too big. Rounding out his ensemble is a pair of brown penny loafers.

Actually, the penny loafers aren't that bad. They remind me of the pair I had when I was in eighth grade, back when they were cool. So, I suppose he can have a pass on the loafers. But there's no excuse for the rest of his getup.

The hostess hands us our menus and says, "Benjamin will be here shortly to take your order. Enjoy your dinner." With that, she smiles politely and raises an inconspicuous eyebrow at me before she turns to leave.

As I browse through my menu, Scott peers out the window and drums his fingers on the table, his menu still lying where the hostess left it. "Did you already decide?" I ask.

"No need to decide. I always get the chicken tenders," he mumbles with a lazy shrug.

I nod and go back to my menu. Who *is* this guy? The Scott I've been getting to know is well-spoken. He's a man of many words and is capable of carrying on a decent conversation. To my surprise, he speaks again.

"So, were you waiting long?"

I try to mask my disbelief. "Uh, yeah, for about forty-five minutes. But . . . I suppose I was a bit late myself."

Why am I telling him I was late? Compared to him, I was early. I pause, wondering if he plans to tell me why he was late or apologize or . . . something, but he says nothing. And just when I'm beginning to wonder if he's fallen asleep with his eyes open, the waiter arrives.

"Hi, I'm Benjamin. Can I start you off with some drinks?" He peers at my glass, and then grins at me. "Looks like you're ready for another!"

"I'll just have a Coke and the chicken tenders," Scott says loudly.

Benjamin looks over at Scott, then gives me a quick, apologetic glance before raising a pen to his notepad. "Coke aaand chicken tenders," he recites slowly as he writes.

I guess being late and ordering before the lady are part of Scott's dating repertoire. And, a Coke and chicken tenders? I feel like I'm on a date with my four-year-old nephew.

Scott hands his menu to the waiter then stares at me as if to say, "*My order is in. Now it's your turn, and make it snappy.*"

"And for you, miss?" Benjamin asks.

"I'll have another Absolut Mandarin and seltzer and the Oriental Chicken Salad please."

I hand my menu to Benjamin with a tight smile. Not only am I disappointed because I'm on a date with someone who's a completely different person than I thought he was, but I'm also uncomfortable because he has the worst dating etiquette I've ever encountered.

As I take a sip of my drink, I realize Scott is still looking at me. Correction: staring. He has gone from hardly being able to make eye contact to eyeing me like a lunatic.

"So, how was work today?" I ask, hoping to strike up some much-needed conversation.

"It was okay, nothing new really. What are you drinking there?"

"Absolut Mandarin and seltzer. Do you want to try it?"

He shakes his head adamantly. "Oh, I don't drink hard liquor. I didn't know you did either."

I know for a fact that he spent the majority of last Sunday with a hangover, so this claim perplexes me, especially since his hangover was supposedly the result of too many shots.

"Oh. Well, are you sure you don't want a beer?" I don't mind drinking alone, but maybe the date would be less painful if neither one of us was completely sober.

"No way. I'm still recovering from last weekend."

Okey doke. I take an extra-long sip to finish off my drink as Benjamin arrives with the new one. He smiles and says, "A Mandarin and seltzer and a Coke. And your food should be up in a sec."

I smile back at Benjamin and wonder why he can't be my date instead. "Thanks."

Meanwhile, Scott is pounding one end of his straw onto the table, trying to get the other end to pop out of the wrapper. Instead, the straw bends sideways. He tries two more times without luck.

Ahhhhhhh. I want to rip the straw from his hand and remove the wrapper for him, but he finally gives up and decides it's time to simply tear the wrapper off like a grownup. Then, he inserts the straw into his drink and takes the longest guzzle I've ever seen in my life. By the time his lips part and back away from the straw, only about a quarter of the glass is still filled with soda. I examine the petite hand he has wrapped around the glass and wonder how it's even possible for the athletic-looking man pictured in Scott's profile photo to have such dainty fingers. I suppose now is as good a time as any for me to ask about the picture.

"Hey, there's something I'm curious about." I hesitate, worried that my inquiry might offend him, but decide an explanation is in order. I can live with not knowing why he was late, but the discrepancy in his appearance has to be explained. "You look different in person than you do in your profile picture." I expect him to either shift nervously or blush with embarrassment, but he doesn't seem the least bit uncomfortable.

"Yeah, that picture is pretty old."

"Oh. How old?"

"Hmmm." He cups his chin and looks to the ceiling, as if the question is a real stumper. "Well, it's my senior picture, so I guess it's about thirteen years old."

His senior picture? Does he mean college or high school? Who am I kidding? I know what he means. He says it so nonchalantly, and then proceeds to slurp down the rest of his Coke. I stare at him, mouth ajar, not sure how to respond. He doesn't even seem to notice.

Like a gift from above, Benjamin arrives with our food. In the same fashion that he delivered our drinks, he names our dishes as he places them in front of us.

"Oriental Chicken Salad and chicken tenders. Can I get either of you anything else before I leave you to enjoy your meals?"

"Another Coke please, and I'm pretty sure that'll do it," Scott says.

Benjamin nods and turns to leave.

"Actually," I call out, "I could use a glass of water when you get a second."

The waiter acknowledges by pointing an index finger at me with his thumb up.

"How rude," Scott mumbles.

"Excuse me?" I can't wait to hear what this man considers rude.

"Oh, just the way he gestured."

With that lesson in manners, Scott excuses himself to the bathroom. As I watch him get up to leave, I consider slipping out to escape this miserable date. However, my conscience won't allow me to act on such an impulse.

When Scott finally returns, we begin eating, and there's another uncomfortable break in conversation. Maybe it's only uncomfortable for me, though, because he eats his food and grins as if the date is going just as he had planned. I can make out bits and pieces of conversations going on around us. I'm not trying to eavesdrop, but the silence that plagues our table leaves me with nothing else to do.

"So, your friend's wedding is next weekend?" I already know the answer, but clearly I need to spearhead any conversation we're going to have. Scott surprises me with a response that contains more than two sentences.

"Yeah, Saturday afternoon. Hopefully it doesn't rain. It rained on his first wedding day. I just saw him before I got here. He was wondering who I was bringing as a date. Do you have plans for next Saturday?"

Oh, my God. Is he on the same date that I'm on? Does he know how awkward this is? Could this actually be going well for him?

"I mean, it seems like we've really hit it off here." Yes, the date is going well for him.

My heart rate quickens as my level of discomfort rises to an all-time high for the evening. "Um, I'm sorry. I already have plans."

He responds with a shrug and proceeds to down his second Coke.

During the next twenty minutes, we finish our meals and engage in intermittent, shallow conversation about nothing. Scott also finishes two more Cokes, bringing his total to four, and he uses the bathroom two more times.

When I begin to feel a twinge of pressure against my bladder, I decide it's time to wrap things up—not only because I refuse to use the Applebee's bathroom out of fear that someone I know might recognize me and wonder who I'm with, but also because this is the worst date I've ever been on.

"Can I get either of you anything else?" I like Benjamin. His timing is impeccable.

I eagerly reply, "No, just the check. Thank you."

As Benjamin reaches into one of his pouches to retrieve our bill, I fight the urge to hand him a credit card right away. That's how desperate I am for this to be over.

"Here you go." He hands the bill to Scott. "You can pay me when you're ready."

Oh, I'm ready.

Scott examines the bill. Then, he takes out his phone and begins making calculations. "So, it looks like your half of the bill comes to nineteen dollars and seventeen cents." I know he's an accountant, but this is ridiculous. Not only are we going Dutch, but he figured out our portions of the bill down to the penny.

"That's with a tip, by the way."

As we stand outside, I think about how badly I need to use the bathroom and how chilly the air has become. I put on my sweater, extend a hand, and say in my most pleasant voice, "Well, it was really nice to meet you, Scott."

This time, he shakes my hand and replies with a surprising amount of gusto, "Yeah, I agree. I had a great time."

I'm shocked by his sudden change in energy. "Okay, well..."

"So, do you want to get together again?" he asks with more enthusiasm in his voice than I've heard all evening long.

Maybe Jess is right. Online dating might be a bad idea. After all the weeks I spent getting to know this man, I still know absolutely nothing about who he really is. I only learned surface details, most of which looked great in print. Maybe I just have my hopes set way too high. Damn that Cassie Thurman and her unrealistic fairytale.

"Um, sure." Shit. What I should have said is *no, thank you*. Heck, I should just walk away, but I don't. "It's just that I'm going to be super busy with work and grad school, so I'm not sure when I'll have time. You know?" I feel like such a coward lying to him.

"Okay, well, should I give you a call next Sunday?" he replies cheerily, cluelessness written all over his face.

"All right, sounds . . . good," I say, taking a few steps backward. "Well, bye, then." A wave of relief washes over me as I turn and speed walk toward my car.

But then I hear quick footsteps behind me and Scott half-yells, "Do you like bowling?" I turn around only to come face-to-face with him. Startled, I stumble backward.

"Bowling? Um, yeah." My bladder is about to burst, but I can't risk going back inside only to begin our goodbyes all over again.

Scott smiles. "Me too. My friends and I go every few weeks." He's shivering and clear snot is running down his upper lip. This chilly November air isn't conducive to his Member's Only jacket or even the sweater and jacket I'm wearing, but at least my nose isn't running. I have to end this.

Desperation forces me to lie again. "Okay, well, give me a call next week and we can make plans to meet up for bowling."

"Really? Okay, I will for sure."

With that little bit of encouragement, he quickly leans in and gives me an overzealous hug. I cringe because I know his snot is now in my hair. I give him a series of quick pats on the back and break free. Then with one last polite smile, I turn, allowing the feeling of sheer terror over what has just happened to wash over my face as I race to my car.

"Bye, Chloe! I'll give you a call next week!" Scott waves

enthusiastically as he continues to stand on the sidewalk in front of Applebee's.

chapter two

"His nose was running and he didn't even realize it?" Jess repeats at the other end of the line for Ned's sake. There's an eruption of laughter. "I'm sorry Chlo, but this is too much!" Another eruption of laughter.

"I'm glad someone is able to get a good laugh out of my date." Not one thing about the date was funny, but I can't help chuckling as I listen to their reactions.

"So, are you coming out? After what you've just been through, I'm sure you need a drink."

"No, I'm heading over to my parents' right now. I might as well get some work done." I'm in the middle of a master's degree program, so I spend a lot of time in my parents' basement, where they have a small office. Until I dig myself out from under my student loans, I refuse to spend money on a computer when I can just use theirs.

"Aw, come on, Chloe. You're letting this master's program take over your life. And don't you think it's time you got a computer of your own?" Jess asks.

"I'll get right on that." We've had this conversation before. No use getting into it again.

"You're going to check your messages, aren't you?" Jess knows me too well.

I *am* going to check my messages, but I'm not about to admit that to Miss Anti-online Dating. My first date has already given her enough ammunition for poo-pooing my new dating scene, but I'm not ready to give up just yet. After all, I'm only a month into my subscription.

"*No*, I'm not. Look, I'll see you tomorrow night anyway. The plan is still The Forum, right?" I know a wisecrack is on its way. The Forum is a bar, arcade, and bowling alley all in one.

"Of course. And since Scott is such an avid bowler, maybe you can surprise him and invite him along too." Jess laughs.

"Very funny. See you tomorrow." I hang up before she has a chance to respond.

I pull into the driveway of my mom and stepdad's yellow Cape Cod. It's nine fifteen, so they're most likely in their default positions—my mom on the paisley couch watching television and my stepdad half-asleep in the La-Z-Boy.

"Hello," I say in a loud whisper as I enter their living room, finding them exactly as expected.

My mom looks at me, surprised. "What? Your date's over?"

"Yeah. It didn't go so well."

In most cases, this one in particular, it's best to avoid sharing too much information with my mother. Her view of my personal life is a dichotomy. She always warns me to be more cautious—make that suspicious—of men. However, whenever I get into a more serious relationship, I'm also supposed to be more trusting and tolerant. My boyfriend becomes the one who should be cautious of me. And when I call it quits with someone, she says I'm too picky and debunks any flaw I may have found. In her mind, I'm likely the cause for a failed date and most certainly the cause for failed relationships. Yet warnings regarding the trustworthiness of men, in general, never wane.

"Yeah, what happened? I thought this guy was perfect." Her voice has a twinge of I-told-you-so in it, but then again, it usually does.

I showed her the Yahoo! Personals site back when I was still pondering whether or not to give online dating a try. She watched as I scrolled through profile after profile and then asked, "All of these people think they're going to find love at first sight? Yeah, sure." This was followed by a "Hmph!" which is one of my mother's most characteristic means of communication. I clicked on a profile and tried to explain to her how it worked. When I got to the part where the guy listed his income, she laughed and said, "I wouldn't believe anybody on here. They can type whatever they want."

"Someone can say whatever they want to say in person, too," I said. "These are just basic details. Why would someone lie on here when he would eventually be found out? Who would go through the trouble of paying and setting up a profile full of lies? I think most people on here are serious about finding someone."

Standing before my mother, I recall the painful date I've just been on and question my initial beliefs about the intentions of other online daters.

"He just wasn't what I thought he'd be like. Our chemistry was way different in person than it was when we were emailing and talking on the phone." *Not to mention, he posted a photograph from when he was seventeen and turned out to be socially appalling.*

"You hear that, Glen? Another guy that wasn't what Chloe expected."

My stepdad shifts in his chair and says, "What?"

"Oh, never mind. Go back to sleep!" My mother shakes her head and refocuses her attention on me. "I didn't think this yoohoo thing was going to work. You have to be more careful. So now what? You wasted your money?"

Having come to the United States from Taiwan with hardly any English and having gone through a bitter divorce from my father when I was seven, my mother has been through a lot. As a result, this petite Asian woman often speaks with a bluntness that takes most people by surprise and requires some getting used to.

"Yahoo!, Mom. It's called Yahoo! Personals, and no, I didn't waste my money. I can meet as many people as I want until I cancel my subscription."

"You never should have broken up with Matt in the first place," she snips and turns back to the television.

"That was two years ago, Mom."

"I know, and you ditched him so you could go and waste your time for a year with that loser." She's referring to my most recent boyfriend, Cliff.

She doesn't even bother to turn from the TV. But her pouting doesn't affect me in the least, because it's not the first or even the fifty-first time I've heard these statements. Until I find her a suitable replacement for Matt, who she has made clear I should have chosen as her son-in-law when I had the chance, there will never be closure for her.

"Okay, well, I'm going downstairs to get some work done."

My account indicates three new messages. I'm excited and appalled at the same time when I see who the messages are from.

The first, which I was expecting, is from another guy I've been communicating with regularly from the start. Drew initiated communications with me the day I signed up. If he hadn't introduced himself, I never would have found him because my filter was set up so that I could only see profiles with pictures. According to Drew, his scanner wasn't working, so he couldn't post a photo. Even though I was leery about responding to someone without a photo, the truth was I didn't have a photo posted either because I didn't want to risk any of my students or their parents coming across my profile. After perusing Drew's stats, I realized that he met all of the qualifications I was looking for, so I responded to him despite not knowing what he looked like. To my surprise, we had even more in common than expected. We started sending each other lengthy emails on a daily basis, and a great new friendship began blossoming. After he requested to see photos of me and I obliged, he let me know how pleasantly surprised he was and tastefully explained exactly what he liked about each of the three photos I had sent. I was flattered and felt compelled to share the message with

Jess. She thought he sounded long-winded and came across as an ass-kisser. "I don't know, Chlo. He sounds like a nerdy brownnoser to me." I disagreed. I thought he sounded more like a sweetheart.

In my last message to Drew, I inquired about whether or not he had had any luck fixing his scanner. I've had butterflies of anticipation ever since. However, I've also been consumed by paranoia over the possibility that I might not find him attractive. My date with Scott has only increased that paranoia.

I skip Drew's message and move on to the second, figuring his will require the most time for me to read and respond to.

The second message is from someone new with the screen name Firefighter66.

Hey, Chloe.

My name is Todd. Enjoyed reading your profile. Seems like we have a lot in common. I'd really like to get to know you better so check out my profile and if your interested, I'd love to hear back from you soon.

The first thing I notice, of course, is his use of the word *your* when it should have been *you're*. I teach the difference between these words to first graders, so it really irritates me when grown adults can't get it right. I decide to click on his profile link anyway and am pleasantly surprised to see a handsome man in a tuxedo. The photo appears to have been taken at a wedding since he's in a sideways pose and the shoulders of men in tuxedos are on either side of him. The photo's date stamp can even be made out: 2002. At least it's current. I'm hit by a wave of nausea as a fleeting memory of my date with Scott washes over me. I decide to remain leery of Firefighter66's photo and move on to his profile data.

Firefighter66 – 28
Location: Milwaukee
Can You Light My Fire?

Relationship Status: Divorced
Have kids: Yes
Want more kids: Maybe
Ethnicity: White / Caucasian
Body type: Athletic
Height: 5' 11"
Religion: Attends Services on Holidays
Politics: Middle of the Road
Smoke: Only when I'm drinking
Drink: Social Drinker
Pets: No
Education: Bachelor's
Employment: City Employee
Income: 40,000-50,000

∽

This guy is divorced, has at least one child and smokes. And he thinks we have a lot in common? These are typically three major deal breakers for me, but who knows. I'm starting to wonder if online stats are enough to determine compatibility.

This is a good example of the problem with most of the men who have responded to my profile. For some reason, the specifications that highlight what I'm looking for in a mate are of no concern to them. Could this be why these men are still single? Then again, I'm still single, so who am I to judge? Furthermore, my date with Scott has me thinking that maybe I should explore every possibility, since he turned out to be the exact opposite of what I expected. What do I have to lose by dating outside my own predetermined parameters?

I type out a quick response to Firefighter66, letting him know that I'm open to communicating with him. I also attach a recent photo of myself because no one deserves to have their time wasted the way Scott wasted mine.

Now I have the third message to deal with before I can get back to Drew. It was sent at nine thirty this evening, just after I arrived at my parents' house. Sender: Scott. Again, I feel nauseous. I reluctantly open the message.

Dear Chloe,

I wanted to let you know again what a great time I had with you tonight. My friends are looking forward to meeting you. I told them that you'd be going bowling with us in a couple of weeks. I don't know if I can wait to talk to you until next Sunday, so I was hoping that maybe we could get together one night this week for dinner. If I don't hear from you soon, I'll give you a jingle tomorrow.

Love, Scott

Dinner creeps its way back up my throat. *Love, Scott?* He'll call me tomorrow if I don't get back to him soon? What is wrong with this man's sense of reality? This imaginary love affair Scott is all of a sudden having with me has to stop. I click the icon to respond.

Scott,

I'm sorry, but . . .

I back out of the email screen. I never want to see, speak with or email this man again, but I can't bring myself to tell him. For the second time tonight, I feel like a coward. Yet I still click to block any future messages from Scott.

My pangs of guilt begin to dissipate as I move on to Drew's

email. My favorite thing about Drew is I feel comfortable sharing just about anything with him. Well, maybe not anything, but enough so that I feel like we're old friends. He's so easy to talk to, and I never feel as though he's judging me or being disingenuous. He's an open book, which makes me open up to him as well. He even knows details about the other men I've met online and the progression of our communications. Drew shares his stories with me, too. As far as I know, he's only talking with a few others and has only been on a few dates in the couple of months that he has been using Yahoo! Personals. We're kind of learning the ins and outs of online dating together. I'm nervous and excited to see what he has to say in response to my scanner inquiry.

Hey Chloe!

First of all, did you watch Survivor yet? I won't say anything revealing in case you haven't, except HOLY TRIBAL COUNCIL!

Secondly, how did your date go tonight? Of course, I hope it didn't go well because pretty soon you'll only have enough free time to go on dates with me. :)

Now, moving on to the most important reason for this message: My scanner still isn't working! I've done everything I can, but unfortunately, I think I need to buy a new one. I know you're getting antsy to see what I look like, which is completely understandable. So, how about if I send you some pictures by snail mail? Email me your address, and I can put them in the mail tomorrow or Monday.

Until we type again,
Drew

My first reaction is to be suspicious. So far, Drew and I have only been communicating through email. We don't even know each other's phone numbers. I know he lives in Oak Creek, a suburb just south of Milwaukee, and he knows that I live in Bay View, a small community within the city of Milwaukee. I hear my mother's voice warning me about strangers after an episode of *Dateline*: *"He looked perfectly normal. Handsome even. You just never know. You have to be careful. A lot of crazy people are nice looking!"* Even though my mom watches way too much TV, I decide to take her advice into consideration this time. I give Drew my parents' address instead of mine and explain that he's sending the pictures to West Allis instead of Milwaukee because I still haven't decided if he could be an axe murderer or not.

As I work on an assignment about controversial children's literature, I receive a response from Drew. It's been about an hour since I sent him the address. He gives me an LOL and promises to put the photos in the next day's mail, so I can expect them by Monday or Tuesday. I'm aflutter with excitement yet on edge because I don't want my budding relationship with Drew to end. I'm not a superficial person, but what if I don't find him attractive? Or, what if his photos are fine, but he looks completely different in person? I know it's what's on the inside of a person that truly matters, but let's face it: there has to be some physical attraction. All I have to do is wait out the rest of the weekend before I can decide where our relationship might be headed.

chapter three

A beeping answering machine greets me when I arrive home. It's nearly one a.m. but not uncommon for me to be awake and full of energy during the wee hours of the night. On the flip side, mornings have never been my strong suit. It took a while for me to adjust to entering the "real world" when I began my teaching career. I'm not so sure "adjust" is even the right word though. My routine consists of late nights and late starts during the weekend and semi-late nights and early starts during the week. My mom always reminds me how unhealthy it is to keep such a sporadic sleep schedule, but for as long as I can remember, I've always gotten this second wind as soon as the sun sets.

Waiting for me when I enter my small, one-bedroom upper flat are my three cats: Hugh, Butler and Clover. Clover is a kitten, but I got Hugh and Butler three years ago when my life was full of new beginnings. I had a new teaching career, a new apartment with my friend Shelly, and a new boyfriend, Matt. He was always showering me with unexpected gifts, one of which happened to be Hugh. Butler came later, after Matt moved in and Shelly moved out. Now here I am, two years later, with three cats and no boyfriend. The quintessential old maid cliché.

After Matt and I separated, we kept in touch for a few weeks. But eventually, he started to pull away, seeming to reach the understanding that our "break" was really more of a breakup. I knew it was really over when I realized it didn't bother me that he stopped calling. I just didn't miss him the way I had thought I might. So with that, I stopped calling him as well. And everything we once had sort of just faded into the background of life.

Aside from Hugh and Butler, nothing else from that relationship holds any sentimental value for me. They are a constant reminder of the heart I broke without much warning or explanation.

My mother is not the only person to question the decision I made to break it off with Matt. We were the perfect couple in everyone's eyes, even my own. He's from a good family, has likeable friends, is good-looking and is on his way to becoming a master electrician. He also loved me with all his heart and always treated me with kindness and respect. Actually, it was painfully apparent that he loved me way more than I ever loved him. He was always so much more nurturing and sentimental than I was, which was sweet at first, but grew annoying with time. There was no question we were headed toward an engagement, which only made me feel more trapped. I've tried to figure out what was missing a million times, but all I know for certain is there just wasn't any spark between us.

Matt and I had been introduced by Evan, Shelly's ex. After Shelly and Evan parted ways, Matt and I continued dating. In no time, Shelly grew unhappy about him hanging around our apartment all the time. She once confessed to me that she felt like he was reporting everything she did back to Evan. But I know she also yearned for a partner in crime to be back on the dating scene with her. She would ask me to go out, I would tell her I already had plans with Matt, and immediately her eyes would roll. It became a pattern, one that had never been an issue when she was also paired up. At any rate, it ended with Shelly moving out and the temporary cessation of our friendship. Shelly and I didn't speak for a little over a year after that. It wasn't until last fall, when we surprisingly ended up in a graduate class together, that we reconnected. It saddened me that the addition of Matt into my life seemed to be followed so promptly by the exit of Shelly. I spent most of our relationship missing my friend. Maybe that had something to do with my unexplained dissatisfaction with him.

My answering machine continues to beep with irritating precision as I change into PJs—a ragged old high school gym T-shirt and shorts. I want nothing more than to wash my face, brush my teeth, and crawl into bed, but the incessant beeping will keep me up all night.

A monotone voice drones, *"You have, three, new, messages. Friday, eight, forty, two, p.m."*

"Hey, Chloe. It's Shelly. I know you're on your date so I don't want to call your cell. Call me when you get in if it's not too late. I can't wait to hear all about it! If I don't hear from you tonight, I'll assume it went well. Oh yeah, I was also wondering if you still want to work out together tomorrow. Talk to ya later."

"Friday, nine, twenty, three, p.m."

"Chlooo-eee. Just checking to see how your date went. I was thinking I could stop by later so you can tell me about it." It's Cliff, aka the loser.

"Friday, eleven, fifty, four, p.m."

"Chloe, just me again. Are you still out or in bed already? Pick up if you're there. Chloooeee."

I don't believe in love at first sight, but the first time I met Cliff, I became a believer in lust at first sight. It was a little over a year ago, during summer school. I was teaching, and he worked with the kids during afternoon recreation, after they were finished with their morning curricular activities. It had only been a few weeks since Matt and I stopped talking to each other and I think I was just looking for something easy. I'll never forget the instant attraction I felt toward him that first time we were introduced. With rich, dark skin and curly, black hair, Cliff was the antithesis of Matt. His hazel eyes, ranging from green to bluish-green to bluish-gray, depending on what he wears, still take my breath away. He looks like he belongs on the cover of an island romance novel. Too bad lasting relationships aren't based on looks and lust.

As much as I want to call him back, I shrug off Cliff's final message and crawl into bed, shivering when the cold sheets envelop me. Exhaustion has set in, but my brain won't relax. As usual. Behind closed eyes, I replay the scenes from my disastrous date. Then Drew's face, as I picture it, comes into view. Yes, I slip into the fantasy. He has light brown hair, blue eyes, and a dimple on his left cheek. His physique is . . . *Ring*. My eyes flutter open.

I stumble out of bed and shuffle a short distance into the kitchen. "Hello?"

"Were you sleeping? When did you get in?" Cliff sounds paranoid. And potentially drunk.

I roll my eyes. "It's two thirty in the morning, Cliff."

"I'm only a few minutes away. Can you unlock the door?"

"Can I just call you tomorrow? I was asleep."

"Please, Chloe. Just let me in when I get there. I don't want to drive all the way home."

Showing up late at night and begging his way in has been Cliff's MO for the past few months. We've been walking a fine line between intimacy and friendship. I really should just stop answering the phone.

"Fine, but I'm not telling you anything about my date, and you have to sleep on the couch."

"I'll see you in a minute," he says as if he never actually considered turning around to head home.

I tiptoe downstairs past my landlords' door, careful not to disturb them. Cliff is already peering through the window. I unlock the door and immediately turn to head back upstairs. My bed is still cold, but my tired body doesn't care. After an indeterminate amount of time, Cliff rouses me with a dusting of kisses on my neck, and I respond more out of habit than lust.

chapter four

"Chloe, you've really got to stop sleeping with Cliff. It's one thing to be friends, but how do you expect to move on if you're still physically involved with him?" Shelly says as she glances at me from her elliptical machine.

She's always been full of advice, solicited or not. Even now, what she's saying is true, but I can't stand the judgment in her tone. I consider bringing up the fact that she was sleeping with an ex-boyfriend off and on while she was with Evan, Matt's friend. But I guess that's like comparing apples to oranges. After all, she wasn't looking for a relationship; she was already in one and was simply cheating. "I know, but I haven't met anyone I'm too serious about yet."

"That's not the point. You know what you really need to do?" She doesn't even take a breath. "You need to just be single for a while. All you ever do is get into one relationship after another. You've had four boyfriends since we met, and I'm not even counting that guy you were pretty much just sleeping with."

At first, I think she's being a huge bitch, but then I realize she's right. I've had a steady stream of boyfriends since I was fifteen. Here's my golden opportunity to really get to know someone before making a commitment. I actually have a chance to do things differently this time, and I don't want to screw it up.

"You know what? You're right. But what's so wrong with me taking advantage of my friendship with Cliff?"

"Are you kidding me? Cliff doesn't really think you're going to find someone online. He may be young and carefree, but guys are all the same. He's going to freak out if you meet someone you like, even if he *is* screwing around in the meantime with anything that has a pulse."

The mention of Cliff "screwing around" turns my stomach, so I work to push the thought out of my mind. Given the circumstances, I don't have a right to care.

"Maybe you're right. For now, I'll just go with the flow and try to enjoy myself. No expectations and no stressing out if a date goes bad. My life is complicated enough with work and school to juggle."

"And Cliff," Shelly adds, the judgment still hanging in the air. "So, are you still going to The Forum tonight?"

"Supposed to. I'm really tired after last night, though. I need a nap before I can say for sure. Why? You wanna go?"

"Maybe. Do you think Jess would mind?"

Jess and Shelly are cordial and have hung out with each other many times, but the truth is, they don't have much in common. It's actually funny how my two closest friends are almost polar opposites. Jess is easy-going and tries to give everyone the benefit of the doubt. I know she would have been a hippie if she'd grown up in the Sixties. On the other hand, Shelly is a bit uptight and typically questions the motives of others. I suppose I'm kind of a mixture of the two.

"Of course not," I lie.

∽

I drive Shelly home and use her computer to check my messages.

Chloe,

Great to meet you and so glad that you responded. Hopefully you don't mind me saying so, but you are smokin' hot! I'd love to see you in person. Tell you what, I'm working this weekend so I've got a lot of free time on my hands unless there's an alarm. Why don't you give me a call so we can get to know each other better. My

number is 367-1456. Call me any time tonight or tomorrow if you're not busy.
Hope to hear from you!

Todd

Smokin' hot? No one has ever called me that before. I can't decide whether I'm flattered or annoyed.

Shelly peeks over my shoulder. "Wow. Nice. Are you sure that's not his senior picture though?"

"You're a hoot," I reply as I scribble Todd's number down and log off.

"He gave you his number already? Do you even know anything about him?" Shelly always raises her eyebrows when her judgment meter kicks in.

Suppressing a sigh, I say, "Shelly, after the date I went on last night, I think it might be smarter to just talk to someone over the phone right away to see if there's any chemistry. Emailing back and forth is pretty time consuming, and talking to someone is more revealing, don't you think?"

"I guess that makes sense. But be sure to call him from your cell phone so he won't see your last name on caller ID." She continues to hold the screen door open after I exit and yells, "And don't agree to meet him anywhere without letting someone know about it first!"

"Got it, mom," I say.

~

The sound of the answering machine kicking in stirs me. Diminishing rays of sunlight hint that it's close to dinnertime.

"*...and I'll get back to you as soon as I can. Thanks!*"

"Hellooo! Time to wake up! We have to figure out who's driving." It's Jess's voice.

I took a shower after my workout but desperately need another one to feel fully awake. Part of me wants to cancel going out tonight, but Jess and I made the plans weeks ago. The phone rings again.

"Hello?" I say, stifling a yawn.

"Hey, how was your nap?" Shelly has a mouthful.

"Hey. Good. What's for dinner?" She's always had a bad habit of eating while talking on the phone.

She laughs. "So, are we going out or what?"

Free time is scarce for me these days. Life is easier when I can get together with both Jess and Shelly at the same time, but I know Jess will be upset if Shelly joins us tonight. I should never have asked if she wanted to go. When I was younger and wanted to play with one friend but not another, I would simply tell the one I didn't want to play with that I was grounded. Mean but effective. And no one's feelings ever got hurt. Too bad I'm not a kid anymore.

"Yep, I just have to get ready. I'll pick you up in about an hour?" If I drive, then Jess might be less perturbed. Plus, Shelly and Jess only live a few blocks from each other.

"So, I'll see you in about an hour and a half then?" My friends and family know that I'm punctually challenged.

"Just be ready," I say with a chuckle. Then I hang up the phone and head toward the shower.

chapter five

It's a five-minute drive to Jess's from my place. We both live in small, one-bedroom apartments, but hers is only a few blocks from Lake Michigan.

The running joke about Jess is that she's like a gypsy. We were kids when she had her first move from a house seven blocks away from my childhood home—where my parents still live—to a newly built home in a developing rural area, about thirty miles away. She may as well have moved to another country as far as our twelve-year-old minds were concerned. It was long before email, so we kept our mailmen busy. We also ran up our parents' phone bills. I can still hear my mom's complaints. *"Chloe! You're on the phone again? Get off the phone. You girls don't need to talk every day. Two calls a day. That's all we get. Or we get charged extra. It's already highway robbery without you calling your friend every day."* We had a phone with a long, kinked cord. Sometimes I had to ask Jess to hang on so I could allow the receiver to dangle and spin from three feet of cord, until the mangled mess was straightened out. Much of our correspondence involved imagining the day when Jess could escape from solitude.

When she finally made her way back to civilization, she started making up for being sequestered in the country for the majority of her teenage years by living in every corner of the city. At least that has always been my theory. Her apartment by the lake is the sixth residence she's had in four years.

The beige, stucco, multifamily four-plex that houses her apartment is the second of three in a row. I park on the street and notice Ned's car in the back lot. Either he's here for a quickie, or he's crashing girls' night. Normally, a tagalong boyfriend would be taboo, but I welcome Ned's presence tonight in light of the fact that I invited Shelly.

I let myself in and go up to Jess's apartment. Her door is adorned with a wooden, black cat welcome sign. My hand hovers over the doorknob for a few seconds, the habit of simply entering built up over the years. But I decide to knock instead, not wanting to walk in on anything X-rated.

The door opens. Ned's bearded face and balding head appear. He's dressed like the car salesman that he is. "Hey there, Chloe. Great to see you. Come on in." His politeness makes me cringe. A nice guy dating your best friend is great, but it sucks when you know it's a facade.

"Hey, Ned. How's it going?" I smile.

"Not too bad. I hear you landed yourself a real catch from that online dating site." He smirks, making me want to punch him.

"Yep. Almost as big a catch as you." I turn and head toward Jess's bedroom without even waiting for a response.

"Hey," Jess says. She gives me a quick hug and then takes a seat at her makeup table. My suspicion about Ned joining us is confirmed when I realize she's not in jeans. Her ensemble consists of black, satin trousers and a gray, cashmere turtleneck sweater with shimmery pinstripes. My boot-cut jeans and red, V-neck sweater pale in comparison.

"Wow. What's the occasion? I thought we were going bowling."

"What do you mean? We *are* going bowling." She finishes applying her mascara. "So, I hope you don't mind if Ned joins us."

She knows I mind. "No, of course not. You don't mind if Shelly comes along too then, do you?"

She stops—gloss applicator two centimeters from her lips—and turns to face me. "Chloe."

"What?"

"The last few times we've gone out, she's been there. I was looking forward to just hanging out with *you*. The only reason Ned wants to go is because a couple of his buddies will be there."

"Why didn't you say anything when I called to let you know I'd pick you up?"

"Because he just showed up a little while ago. Besides, he won't even be near us for the most part. And he said he'd drive. Why didn't you say anything about Shelly?"

"Honestly? Because I know you can't stand her. But hey, I can't stand Ned, so we're even, right?"

She smirks and rolls her eyes. "Hey, Ned! Let's get going. We have to drop Chloe's car off at her place, and then we have to pick up Shelly," Jess concedes.

chapter six

The Forum illustrates why you should never judge a book by its cover. From the outside, the building is majestic with intricate copper fixtures. Even though the fixtures are green from oxidation, the architectural details are evidence that it was once the pride and joy of the neighborhood. The entryway is equally impressive, with tall granite pillars that lead to an elegant banister-lined stairway. At the bottom, visitors must turn left to enter another stairway that leads to the lower level. Instead of the beautiful, handcrafted wooden banisters you might expect, it's lined with cheap, silver handrails, which are chipped, rusted, and loose in several places. What you find upon entering the entertainment area is quite breathtaking—literally. The air is so thick with smoke that people don't even need to bring their own cigarettes, and nonsmokers can forget about avoiding people who indulge in nicotine. The average nonsmoker's body likely requires at least one week to cleanse itself from a single hour in this place. Yet despite the dank atmosphere, The Forum is a smorgasbord of activity, filled with people who are seeking more than a night of booze and darts at a typical corner bar. In addition to the multiple bars that line the perimeter, there's a concession area, an arcade, pool tables, dartboards, foosball and bowling. Scattered throughout are lounge areas with sofas, tables, and comfy chairs.

Our main objective tonight is to bowl, but our table tells a different story as a result of all the empty cocktail glasses.

"Str-r-r-ike!" Ned pumps his fist a few times as a fat cartoon turkey struts across the screen overhead.

I roll my eyes and say to Jess, "Thought he was meeting up with friends."

"Not 'til eleven. And knock it off. How many times have I had to hang out with your boyfriends?" I flip her off, and she returns the gesture.

Ned smacks Jess hard on the butt. "Your turn, babe."

"Anyone up for round three?" Shelly carefully maneuvers her hips sideways and makes her way between ball racks. She sets down a tray that holds four vodka cranberries, two vodka tonics, and two Mandarin seltzers. All of them are tall.

"What the?" I say.

"What? The drink special ends in a few minutes, so I got everyone two."

Jess misses her spare and gets a gutter ball. "Shit!" She returns to our table and grabs a fresh cocktail, not even flinching at the assortment.

"Someone's gettin' laid tonight!" Ned says as he swipes a drink for himself and then staggers off to the jukebox. Jess laughs.

I sneak a wide-eyed look at Shelly, who simply shakes her head and says, "What a pig." She makes her way to the lane.

"What did you say?" Jess asks, a challenge in her voice.

"Oh, nothing." Shelly poses, ball up. "Watch how it's done," she taunts.

Jess rolls her eyes and plops down next to me. "Have you noticed that those guys keep looking over here?" I follow her gaze to a table near the bar. "The one in the red is kinda cute."

"Woo-hoo!" Shelly jumps and spins to face us after her ball makes contact and each pin slowly topples over in succession.

Jess shakes her head. "Unbelievable."

"Way to go Shell!" I yell.

I sneak another peek at the three guys Jess mentioned as I walk to the lane. Sure enough, they are staring in our direction. Before I grab my ball, I give Shelly an obligatory high five and pretend to be completely oblivious to the eyes still on us.

As soon as we finish our hour of unlimited bowling—which amounts to roughly a game and a half because of all the drink breaks—we head into the poolroom. The atmosphere is more laid-back than in the arcade, and we don't have to listen to people hooting and high-fiving over a strike or moaning a collective "awwwww" over a missed spare.

One good thing about Ned joining us this evening is that he's already at the bar ordering another round. I don't expect him to buy me drinks, but he usually makes more money in one month than I make in six. The man was born to sell cars. Actually, he was born to sell just about anything. I guess that's why Jess can't seem to shake him. He has mastered the art of selling himself to her.

"So, when's your big bowling date with Scott?" Jess asks. She seriously doesn't know when to quit.

I'm about to let her have it when Shelly chimes in. "Hey, why don't you call him right now? After all, Ned's not supposed to be here. You might as well invite *another* guy to ladies night." I can tell she's only teasing, but I know already that it won't be taken well. That may be Shelly's biggest social flaw—after a few drinks, she doesn't always know how to deliver a joke that won't offend.

Jess stares daggers. I imagine the words on her lips and mentally implore her not to blurt out, *"Well, neither were you!"*

"Okay, okay. Very funny. I'm done with the Scott jokes. Give it a rest . . . both of you!" I do my best to sound like a super bitch. But Jess knows I'm only trying to diffuse the situation, and Shelly rarely reacts when someone is irritated. Her lack of empathy frequently puzzles me.

"Did you tell Jess about the firefighter?" Shelly asks.

Jess snaps out of attack mode. "You already have another one lined up?"

"First of all, I'm not lining them up. Second of all, we've only exchanged a couple of emails. We haven't even spoken yet. Third of all . . ."

"Wait. I don't think that's right," Shelly says.

Jess and I look at each other. "You don't think what's right?" I ask.

"I don't think second of all makes sense. Neither does third of all."

"Thirdly, then! Or third. Whatever!" I say, exacerbated. Jess is dying. "*Third*, I plan on getting to know as many people as I can. Hopefully, I'll meet a few guys with potential in the long run."

"And how is that any different from chatting with multiple people here, tonight? For example, what about *those* guys?" Jess motions toward the pool table where the three guys from earlier are hanging out now. She's too buzzed to focus on my online dating game plan.

Shelly and I follow her gaze. The guy in red is staring in our direction as he chalks up the tip of his pool stick.

"Cute," Shelly says. Then she refocuses her attention on me. "I think it's great that you're online dating. It's about time you date around instead of habitually searching for a boyfriend to hole up with every night. But I don't see any harm in continuing to have a look around when you're out." She cocks her head toward the bar. "Where are *our* drinks?"

Why can't my friends just leave me the hell alone when it comes to dating? One minute, they are making me feel like a relationship junkie who always needs a guy around, and then the next, I'm supposed to flirt with any guy who looks my way. I don't even think they realize how bipolar they're being.

"Ned probably ran into his buddies, so it could be a while. Don't get your undies in a bunch," Jess says. Suddenly, she sits upright. "Red hoodie guy, nine o'clock!"

To my left, three guys are making their way toward our table. Jess is purposefully watching them approach, as if to draw them in. I sense them passing behind me and wonder for a second if maybe they weren't looking at us after all. Shelly gives up looking for Ned and turns back to face us. Her gaze fixes on something behind me.

"Well, hi there." It's impossible for her to sound any cheesier. "Who's our new friend?" she asks.

I spin sideways and find myself staring at a red sleeve. A handsome young man with deep blue eyes, a dark goatee, and a dimple in his left cheek is grinning at me. His sandy blonde hair is short in the back but thick and wavy on top. He continues to smile and extends a hand to Shelly.

"Sam." He proceeds to shake Jess's hand and finally mine. "My friends and I are wondering if you ladies are up for some Cricket."

"I suck at darts," Shelly says. "It would be better for everyone involved if you counted me out."

"What about you two?" He looks to Jess and then turns to me.

"That depends on who you'd like to pair me up with," Jess says.

"Oh, gawd," Shelly mumbles and begins scanning the bar for Ned again.

Sam laughs. His friends arrive with freshly filled pint glasses. The really tall one hands a glass to Sam. "That's Tim." He gestures to the shorter one. "And this is Chad."

Chad's height mesmerizes me. I can't help but stare.

Jess elbows me. "This is Chloe. That's Shelly. And I'm Jess." She stands and heads straight for Chad.

Chad asks, "Y'all need drinks?" He's wearing a long-sleeved, collared shirt. The top button is open, revealing a section of smooth, muscular flesh. He isn't as good looking as Sam, but his physique is quite a draw.

"Actually, we . . ." I begin to tell him that we have drinks on the way, but Jess pipes in.

"I'd love a vodka press," she says.

Shelly rolls her eyes.

"And for you ladies?"

We take Jess's lead and allow Chad to order us another set of drinks. It occurs to me that she might be drunk because it seems like she's forgotten about Ned.

Ten minutes later, Shelly and I are playing Cricket against Sam and Tim while Jess and Chad are off in a corner becoming better acquainted. It happened so fast. Shelly barely had a chance to object before she found herself with three darts in her hand after Jess turned her back on the game and her attention toward the tall new stranger who had so quickly captivated her.

"So, you're a teacher. Bless your heart." Sam raises his glass, and we both take a drink. "You look like a teacher." His remark catches me by surprise, but he immediately goes into damage control. "Wait a sec. I didn't mean it like that. What I meant is that you look like a really nice person." He sucks in a breath and releases it slowly. "Okay, I'm really bombing here, aren't I?"

His squirming makes me smile. "No. You're fine. You should probably stop talking, though." We both laugh. "What do you do?"

"I'm in my final year at MSOE. Engineering."

"Wow, that's awesome," I say.

He takes a dollar out of his pocket and moves a few steps from our table to the jukebox. "What kind of music do you like?" I finally have a chance to check out his backside. Not bad.

"I like everything, but I love . . ."

"Your turn!" Shelly is holding the darts six inches from Sam's face, waiting for him to grab them.

He laughs and takes them from her. "All right. One sec. I'm picking a song for Chloe." Shelly sneaks a wide-eyed grin my way. Sam finishes making his selection and heads to the dartboard where Tim is smoking a cigarette.

Shelly briefly looks after Sam with what appears to be admiration. Then she rushes to my side. "I hate to ruin your night, but we have a problem." I follow her gaze and see Jess dancing with Chad. Her body is moving provocatively against his. *Shit.* "She always pulls this kinda junk, Chloe."

"I just closed out our twenties. You've got your work cut out for you now," Sam says with a wink. He hands me the darts and nods toward Jess and Chad. "Looks like they're hitting it off."

"Are we gonna wrap up this bloodbath or what?" Tim asks.

"Yep. On my way for our last stand," I say.

Poised to shoot my third dart, a loud commotion erupts behind me. Tim tosses his cigarette into an ashtray and takes off. I spin around and see Ned shoving Chad into a table, causing it to fall to the ground.

Sam and Tim form a barricade, preventing Chad from retaliating. Jess frantically tugs on Ned's arm, begging him to stop.

"Fucking asshole!" Chad yells.

Ned's friends are already escorting him away from the scene, and Jess is rushing after them.

Shelly and I stand with our mouths agape. It occurs to me that we should disappear into the crowd, but our new friends are already making their way toward us.

"Who *was* that guy?" Sam asks.

My mind searches for a response.

"It's her boyfriend," Shelly says, not even trying to hide her irritation. She looks at me and says, "We need to find them before we get stuck here without a ride home!"

"Screw these chicks. Let's go," Chad says. It's fair. He has a right to be upset.

"Chloe, we have to go." Shelly starts to walk away.

"Hey, guys, we're really sorry about all of this." Part of me hopes that Sam might still ask for my number, but he turns to follow his friends.

"Chloe, let's go!" Shelly tugs on my wrist, nearly pulling my shoulder out of its socket. I follow her, glancing over my shoulder as I watch one more potential walk away.

chapter seven

There aren't any messages on my answering machine when I get home. I wonder why Cliff has not called, but I fight the urge to dial him up myself. Maybe my sister Sarah was right—maybe I am codependent. That was the expert diagnosis she made when I started dating Cliff in the first place.

"Chloe, are you sure Cliff isn't just a rebound to help you get over Matt?"

"Uh, yeah. I don't need any help getting over Matt. I broke up with him, remember?"

"Can you remind me why? Because we still don't understand. What happened?" By "we", my sister was, of course, alluding to the joint opinion she and my mother held.

"Nothing happened. It just didn't feel right. What happened when you decided to break off your engagement to Dale? And what about Shane? What happened the two times you decided he wasn't good enough to marry?"

"That's not fair, Chloe. I was too young to be engaged to Dale, and Shane . . . well, my relationship with Shane was just way different than your relationship with Matt. Matt was a keeper. Come to think of it, so was James."

"James? Oh, my God! That was four years ago! You and mom and everyone else just need to lay off. Why can't I break up with someone without getting the third degree?"

"I'm not giving you the third degree. We just think it's time for you to start taking things more seriously. Every time you find a nice guy, he isn't good enough. Why is that? And why is it that you never go more than a few weeks without meeting someone new? I think you might be codependent, Chloe."

After that conversation, I started receiving articles about loving yourself via e-mail and self-help books in the mail. She also clipped everything she could find about codependency for me. And now Shelly thinks I'm obsessed with having a boyfriend. Maybe there *is* something wrong with me.

It's close to eleven, but I'm not tired. I plop myself down in front of the TV with a spoon and a jar of peanut butter. Ten minutes of channel surfing leads me to a Dateline-type show about a retired firefighter's bestselling book based on his 9/11 experiences. I glance over at the corkboard hanging above the phone in the kitchen. Firefighter66's number hangs there on a purple Post-It. I grab the phone and his number, begin dialing, and then press end. *It's too late to call.* Perhaps I'm a bit more buzzed than I realize, because the next thing I know, the phone is to my ear again. The call goes to voicemail. "Hi, Todd, this is . . ." The call-waiting indicator sounds, so I quickly finish leaving a message. "It's Chloe, from Yahoo! Personals. I know it's late, so I'll try you some other time. Bye."

I click over to the incoming call. "Hello?"

"Hi, this is Todd. I just missed your call."

"Oh, hi. I actually just left you a message. Sorry I'm calling so late. I . . ."

"No, no. It's not late. I was just reading. Who am I speaking with though?"

"Oh, sorry, it's Chloe. You emailed me your number today." I feel silly for assuming he would know who I am.

"No, don't be sorry. I'm glad you called. What's a *sexy woman* like you doing home alone on a Saturday night anyway?" There's a hint of seduction in his voice when he says "sexy woman."

Pretending not to notice, I reply, "Actually, I was out with some friends earlier tonight." I assume he'll ask what we did or where we went.

"Your friends, are they as *hot* as you?" Again, he stresses the word "hot" with an almost creepy intensity.

"Are you serious? Why are you talking like that?" I laugh, trying to hide my growing nervousness.

"Oh, hey," he says, "I'm really sorry if I made you feel uncomfortable. I was just joking around."

"Mm-kay." I'm not sure if I believe him, but I'm willing to see where the conversation goes. "So, tell me about yourself. How long have you been a firefighter?"

"Hmm, let's see, about five years now. How about you, how long have you been teaching?"

Well, at least he remembers something about me. "This is my fourth year teaching first grade."

He laughs and says, "My daughter is in first grade! Where do you teach?"

I know none of the first graders at my school have fathers who are firefighters, so I figure there's no harm in telling him. "I work for Milwaukee Public Schools."

"Yikes." He takes a breath through his teeth. "Pretty rough, huh? I mean, my ex-wife is an ER doctor in Milwaukee. She says there are a lot of people who don't speak English and don't have any insurance, not to mention the gang banger injuries."

"Uh, my school is located in a nice neighborhood. I work with a lot of great kids with wonderful families. It must be hard on your ex, though." *Ex talk already?*

"Yeah, she's always working, too, so I usually have to take care of everything around the house. Her hours are crazy, and then there's my schedule, of course, so we have a nanny who stays with the kids two or three days a week."

Either I heard him wrong or I'm confused. "So, do you and your ex-wife still live together?"

"Oh, it's not like that! We've been divorced for three years now, but yeah, we still live together. It's just easier on the kids that way. We're great friends. People think it's weird when they first find out our living situation, but we rarely even see each other."

Yep, sounds pretty weird. "Well, if it works for you guys, then I give you credit for doing what's best for your kids." I'm trying to keep an open mind. "So, tell me about your kids. You said you have a girl in first grade?"

"Yeah, she's a doll! Her name is Chelsea. We also have a one-year-old son. Connor. You don't have any kids, do you? I've found that sometimes women say they don't on their profiles, but they actually do."

"Nope, no kids. Just like my profile says." There's a moment of silence.

"So, Chloe," his voice is low, almost a whisper, "do you like dick pics?"

Surely, I misunderstood him. "Excuse me?"

"You know, *dick* pics."

"No. What are you talking about?"

"I bet I have the *biggest* cock you've ever seen."

"Look, *Todd*, I don't know what your problem is, but you're really creeping me out . . . I should get to bed."

"*Bed*? That's more like it. How would you like to . . ."

I hang up on Firefighter66. Then, still buzzed, I contemplate our conversation, unsure whether I'm remembering everything correctly. That's when panic sets in, and I start pacing my apartment. *Shit. I called him from my home number. What if he isn't just some pervert? What if he's a rapist, too? No, he's a firefighter. Firefighters aren't rapists. Right?*

I get into bed and pull the covers over my head. Worst-case scenarios plague my mind until I eventually drift off. So much for my brilliant plan to go straight to phone conversations in order to weed out the duds.

Even in my sleep, I feel like I need a shower.

chapter eight

"He tried to have phone sex with you?" Shelly is clearly horrified.

"Not exactly. I don't really know what he was trying to do. He mentioned something about dick pics."

"Like, pictures of dicks?"

"I guess so. Not sure what else he could possibly have been referring to. Oh, and get this. Apparently he has a one-year-old son with the woman he divorced three years ago. I'm no math genius, but those numbers don't quite add up."

"Wait. Can we get back to the dick pics? Was he talking about pictures of his own dick or pictures of other guys' dicks? And how many pictures was he talking about? Like, was there some kind of dick picture of the day club you could sign up for? Was he offering up free dick pics for life? And what was he expecting from you in return? Did he want pictures of your ... you know ..."

"I don't know, Shelly! I hung up on him before getting all the details."

"Well, at least this conversation didn't happen in person. Can you imagine *that one* going down at the Applebee's? He probably would have tried to cop a feel, too. Yuck." I can hear her shuddering on the other end of the phone. "So, you'll find out what this Drew character looks like in a day or two. Any other new prospects since you checked yesterday?"

As judgmental and opinionated as Shelly can be, she has this way of switching gears to open-minded and supportive pretty quickly. And she has clearly continued to be my number one cheerleader when it comes to dating as many people as possible—regardless of where or how I meet them—so long as I'm safe about it. I'm starting to think that may at least partially be because she likes the stories.

"Well, Sam would have been a nice prospect."

"Yeah, he seemed like a really nice guy. Sorry Jess had to go and screw that one up for you, along with her own relationship. Have you talked to her yet?"

"No, but I'm sure she'll call later. As far as new online prospects, I don't know. I'm trying to get all of my work done before I check. How are your studies going?"

"Okay, but I'm about to throw in the towel here because Craig and I are going over to my parents' house to watch the Packers game."

"Aww, Craig. What's going on with you tw . . ."

"Stop right there! Craig and I are just friends. Remember? And even if I *was* interested, we would end up with red-haired, freckle-faced kids."

"What's that supposed to mean? Red-haired, freckle-faced kids are cute."

She sighs.

Shelly met Craig two summers ago when they were both bartenders at Summerfest, an annual music festival that takes place along Milwaukee's lakefront. Tending bar during the ten-day event can be a pretty lucrative summer gig for teachers. Craig isn't a teacher, but he made so much money working the festival in college that he now takes vacation from his day job every year to return. After Shelly's first year, they became fast friends and kept in touch by email once the festival ended. When they worked together again this past summer, Craig finally made a move. He had apparently been head-over-heels for Shelly since they met, but was too afraid to jeopardize their friendship to admit it. They dated for a few weeks but then Shelly ended up asking him if they could go back to being just friends. Craig was the kind of amazing guy who graciously agreed and never gave her any grief about leading him on.

"C'mon, Shell. Look at the two of you. You're always together.

And when you're not together, you're talking on the phone to each other. Maybe you should consider giving it another try."

"Chloe, I really don't want to date anyone right now. Okay?"

"Maybe you subconsciously don't want to date anyone because you actually do have feelings for Craig. Ever think of that?"

"No . . . Never."

"All right, if you say so," I reply. "Have fun watching the game."

~

For the last several hours, I've had my head down working on my latest project for school. It's now nearly two o'clock on a Sunday, well past lunchtime. An overdue break for food is necessary. It will give my mother the opportunity to grill me about how I expect to find a husband and start a family if I continue to waste my time dating losers like Cliff and men from online. She'll likely suggest that I give Matt a call, just to see what he's up to. I can hardly wait.

I enter the kitchen where my mom is stir-frying vegetables: broccoli, carrots, bok choy, celery, red and yellow peppers, onions, and garlic. My parents' house always smells like a Chinese restaurant. Based on the light billow of steam rising from the rice cooker, I can tell that the rice will be ready to eat shortly. I fill a glass with water and take a seat at the table.

"Smells good, mom," I say. "I'm starving."

"Well, you should have eaten lunch," she uses the chopsticks to pop a piece of broccoli into her mouth. "I hope you're working and not writing love letters to men you don't even know."

Controlling the urge to roll my eyes, I say, "I only have a couple more hours of work to finish up. I'm saving my love letters until then."

"Hmph," is all she can muster as she adds a touch of oyster sauce to the stir-fry.

I fill a bowl with rice and veggies and sit down to eat. My mother leans against the counter, arms folded across her chest.

"Where were you all day yesterday? I thought you were going to do your work then."

"I went to the gym with Shelly, and then I needed a nap because Jess and I had plans to go bowling."

"Why did you need a nap? You left here at a reasonable time on Friday. Didn't you go to bed when you got home?"

My mother is an expert when it comes to giving someone the third degree. If she had been born in this country and received a formal education, she would have made a great interrogator. Instead, she's been practicing her skills on my stepfather, siblings, and me for the past twenty-plus years.

"Look, Mom, I saw Cliff. Okay?" I don't want to disappoint her, but I want the badgering to stop.

In an instant, her gaze darts toward the stove. My stepfather is picking veggies out of the pan.

"Glen, get a bowl if you want some," she snaps. "Do you want to contaminate all the food so no one else can eat any?"

"Okay, okay. Pipe down. I only had a taste."

"Put some in a bowl, and use a fork if you want a taste!"

To an outside observer, this exchange might seem harsh and dysfunctional. To me, it's as commonplace as seeing a squirrel collecting nuts in the fall. My stepfather sits down across from me with a bowlful. Now that he's in the room, I can mention Drew's pictures. If my mom has a problem with it, my stepdad will soon do something to send her off on another tirade, distracting her.

"By the way, I'm expecting some mail to arrive for me here either tomorrow or Tuesday."

"What kind of mail?" my mother asks.

"Someone is sending me some pictures."

"Who?"

"That guy I've been talking to. Drew."

"What do you mean he's sending you pictures?" Her voice has gone up three octaves.

"Well, he can't email them to me because his scanner is broken. So he's sending them here."

"Why would you tell him to send them here? And why do you need to see a picture of him? Does it really matter what he looks like? Matt is such a handsome man, and you still dumped him." The tone of her voice would convince most outsiders that this was my mother's version of yelling, but instead, it's her usual manner of speech.

"Actually, dear, it's probably safer if Chloe doesn't share her own . . ."

"Glen! Stop talking with a full mouth. You're spitting food all over the place." My mother frantically begins wiping the table. And just like that, the conversation is dropped.

You've got to love my stepdad.

chapter nine

Normally, I don't make the fifteen-minute drive over to my parents' house during the workweek, but my mom left me two voicemails in the middle of the day today. Her first message was in regard to my stepfather "screwing up" their TV remote, asking whether or not I might have time to look at it. I sometimes envy the fact that my brother lives in California and my sister lives in Las Vegas—not because they live where the weather is much nicer, but because I'm so much more accessible to our mother from a geographic standpoint. Her second message was to inform me that the pictures from Drew had arrived. *"You want me to open them? Let me know. I'll tell you if he's handsome or not. I won't sugar coat it either ... Well, should I open it or not? Let me know."* She has no concept of the fact that people can't hear her when she leaves a message on a cell phone. Most of the time, her messages begin with, "Hello, Chloe, are you there? Hello?"

Emotions flood me as I sit, holding the envelope. *Anticipation.* I'm finally going to be able to attach a face to Drew. I no longer need to use my imagination. *Excitement.* If I do find him attractive, Drew just might be a complete package. I can allow myself to grow closer to him, with the possibility of a physical relationship at some point. *Fear.* What if I don't find him attractive? What if he's bald? Overweight? And finally, *shame.* Am I really this shallow?

I insert my finger under one edge of the flap on the envelope and break the sticky seal apart, inch by inch.

"Well, what does he look like?" My mother is perched over my shoulder.

"I don't know, Mom. I haven't even opened it yet. Just give me a second."

"Fine. I don't see what the big deal is. If he's ugly, just throw 'em away." She turns back to her sewing machine.

Her comment about throwing the pictures away makes me feel guilty, because I know that's what I'll end up doing if I don't find Drew attractive. Not only will I throw the pictures away, but I will likely throw the entire relationship away as well.

Feeling what I presume to be a piece of paper wrapped around a couple of pictures, I pull the contents out of the envelope. My eyes are closed as I unfold the paper. When I open them, there's a male face staring back at me. I breathe a sigh of relief.

"Ugly, huh?" My mother doesn't even look up from her stitching.

Cute is the first descriptor that pops into my head. Drew has short, light brown hair, spiked a tad just above his forehead. He has medium-length side burns and is wearing stylish glasses with tortoiseshell frames. His smile reveals a set of perfectly straight, pearly whites, right out of an orthodontist's dream. He wears a navy blue polo shirt with a white T-shirt underneath. Honestly, he looks exactly like the type of guy that I've always pictured myself with: clean-cut and attractive. The second photo is of him at a Brewers game. He's sans glasses and decked out in fan gear. Again, he looks very cute. And this one was taken only a couple of months ago. Smiling from ear to ear, I dive into his note.

Dear Chloe,

I hope these photos are okay. I'm so nervous that you might not be interested after seeing how unattractive I am. (Smiley face inserted.) I cannot wait to meet you in person—if you're willing. Please give me a call as soon as you've finished reading this—but only if you're up to it. I know you don't have much time during the week. My home number is 877-3717.

Talk to you soon I hope,
Drew

"Hey there, beautiful." Drew always sounds genuinely pleased when I call.

"Hi. I just wanted to let you know that . . ." I exhale loudly. "Well, I got the pictures today, and . . ." I do my best to feign disappointment.

"And?" He sounds concerned.

"Well, I have to be honest with you . . ."

"Wait. Let me just say that I probably needed a haircut in that photo of me at the game."

I smile and continue. "It's just that . . . I've decided the pictures definitely aren't fakes."

His voice perks up a little. "Yeah, what brings you to that conclusion?"

"Well, because I could tell from your voice that you had to be pretty cute."

"Geez, Chloe! Thanks for giving me an arrhythmia."

We both laugh and move on to discussing our days, as usual.

"So, now what?" Drew asks expectantly.

Despite promising myself, and my friends, that I was not going to get too serious about anyone, I have butterflies in my stomach. For once, butterflies are bad.

"Well, I don't know. I guess we just keep on doing what we've been doing. Only now, I can picture your face whenever you've got me cracking up about something."

"So, you don't want to get together then?" He sounds shocked.

"Oh, that's not what I mean. We should totally get together. I just meant that we should continue being friends and see what happens. I mean, we're both still so new to online dating. We should keep meeting other people, right?"

There's an unexpected silence. In fact, it's the longest silence we've ever shared. "You're totally right. I didn't mean to sound like such a pouty child. I have just one request, though."

"Shoot."

"Let me cook dinner for you. Do you like corned beef and cabbage?"

"I've never had it, but I'd love to give it a try." The fact that he's offering to cook for me is sweet, but I'm slightly concerned, because it sounds like he's inviting me over to his place.

"You've never had corned beef and cabbage? Then, I *must* make some for you. So, my place then. Tomorrow, say sixish?"

The suspicion that he could be a serial rapist lingers in the back of my mind. I can hear my mother's voice. *"The most dangerous ones are the good-looking ones. You know? They trick you with their handsome faces. Just look at Ted Bundy."* It was the kind of sentiment I had heard from her a million times before, but she shared it again immediately after I had shown her Drew's photos. I shake away her voice and reply. "Sounds good! Email me your address. Can I bring something?"

I have to trust my gut, and my gut says Drew could have potential.

But I may pack some mace away in my purse, just in case.

chapter ten

"So, he lives in the Bluff View Apartments. 5507 Pine Way. Apartment fifteen." Jess repeats Drew's address to make sure she wrote it down correctly.

"Right, and could . . ."

"Wait a sec. I just want to confirm a few more things. His name is Drew Barrington. He grew up in Sun Prairie. He's twenty-five. And he's an accountant for Xerox?"

"Right. Anything else?" I ask.

"No, I think we're good. If I don't hear from you by nine, expect a call. And you better answer, or I'm calling the cops."

"Actually, I was hoping you could give me a call around seven, just in case."

"What do you mean? Just in case he turns out to be a serial rapist?" Jess and my mom think way too much alike.

"No. Well, maybe. But not really. I'm more thinking in case things aren't going well."

"Seriously? You're perfectly fine with meeting a guy at Applebee's all by yourself after seeing only his senior picture and talking to him once on the phone, but you're worried that things won't go well with a guy you've been sharing virtually every detail of your life with for nearly two months? Just relax and have fun! Barring any well-masked psychotic tendencies, I'm pretty sure everything will be fine. Like I said, if I don't hear from you by nine, I'll give you a call."

"Fine. I'm just nervous." I sit in my car and stare at building 5507. My palms are sweaty, and I'm starting to feel nauseous. A vision of Drew spying on me through a window enters my mind.

"Would you quit worrying? It's not like you've never been to a stranger's apartment before."

I think of the times that Jess could be referencing and realize she's right. I've been to plenty of after-bars, usually with friends, but alone as well. My nerves are probably just kicking into high gear tonight because I think I might like Drew, not because I think he could turn out to be cuckoo.

"Hello? . . . Are you still there?" Jess is clearly growing impatient with my introspection.

"Yeah, I'm here." I reply.

"Well, what's up? Are you at his apartment?"

"I'm here, but I don't know if this date is such a good idea." My nerves are starting to get the best of me.

"What are you talking about? What's wrong?"

"Jess, I really like him."

"My God, Chloe. So you like him. Is that a bad thing? You're allowed to like someone. That doesn't mean he has to be your boyfriend. Jeezus."

"Okay. Okay. Just don't forget to call me."

"I'll call you. Now, go!"

∼

I stand outside of Drew's apartment for what seems like an eternity. The only sound in the hallway is my own heavy breathing, and my armpits are sweating profusely. If he *did* see me sitting in my car, he must be wondering what kind of kook I am because that was at least ten minutes ago.

I'm standing on a Green Bay Packers doormat, and there's a matching welcome sign hanging on Drew's door. The items are homey and strike me as the sort of things a couple would display, not a single guy. The hallway is spotless and smells faintly of Lysol. These are good signs. I'm guessing the inside of his apartment is just as clean.

An older gentleman dressed in a sweater-vest and plaid derby arrives a few doors down. He has a briefcase and groceries in tow.

He nods hello before disappearing into his apartment. It dawns on me that I better knock before anyone else sees me standing in the hallway, staring at the door of apartment fifteen. I rap loudly four times, in quick succession. There's a muffled clanking of dishes followed by quick footsteps before the door opens. My apprehensions instantly vanish at the sight of Drew's wide grin.

"Chloe! I was starting to wonder if you were bailing on me. Come in!"

I return his smile. "No way. I've been looking forward to corned beef and cabbage all day long. Shelly says I'm in for a real treat."

Drew reaches out an arm, so I lean in slightly, thinking he wants a hug. Instead, he says, "Can I take your jacket and purse?"

My pulse quickens as I straighten my posture. Luckily, he didn't seem to notice my faux pas.

As he turns to hang my things over the arm of a chair, I take a quick peek at each of my armpits to check for sweat stains. To my horror, I catch Drew's gaze just as I finish inspecting the second pit. I close my eyes long enough to focus on Alex Trebek's voice coming from the living room. *"Daily Double!"* Now not only is my pulse racing, but my face is on fire too.

"How do they look?" Drew asks.

I open my eyes to find him smiling at me with those big, pearly whites, and we erupt into laughter.

"Oh, my gosh. I have no idea why I'm so nervous," I say.

"Don't worry about it. If it makes you feel any better, my pits are lined with three coats of deodorant." Drew's smile is contagious. He's an eye-smiler: The type of person who isn't capable of faking a smile. He also oozes emotion through his facial expressions.

Hands on hips, I scan the apartment. Drew's place is modern, built within the last three years. From where we stand in the living room/dining room combo, I can see a long hallway that begins just past a large eat-in kitchen to the right. The living room consists of a black leather sofa with a matching chair and ottoman, a glass-top coffee table with decorative, wrought iron legs, and two matching end tables. There's also a large framed black and white poster of Lambeau Field next to the cream vertical patio door blinds and a wall-mounted large screen TV. The adjacent dining room contains a traditional oak table with paisley, upholstered chairs. Place settings are already laid out for two.

"I like your apartment. It's so . . . clean."

"Thanks," he whispers, "I'm kind of a neat freak." He smiles sheepishly for a second before continuing. "Let me give you a quick tour before we eat." He extends a hand toward the hallway and places the other on the small of my back for a moment as I walk past him. The brief contact sends a wave of electricity through my unusually sweaty body.

As I walk down the hallway, I wonder if Drew is checking me out. Correction: I hope he's checking me out. I certainly looked him over within the first few seconds after I entered his apartment. His dating profile stated that he has a slim build, but his muscular arms beg to differ, making me wonder if he has a warped sense of his own appearance. Because his physique is definitely more athletic than slim.

"So, here's the bathroom," Drew says. Then he points to the room directly across the way. "Guest bedroom, but I also use it as an office . . . Wait a sec." He gently grabs my left hand and guides me into the room. "I want to show you something."

He leaves me standing just inside the doorway and hurries over to a desk. It contains a computer and a printer. A mangled mess of additional components and wires are resting on a large table next to the desk.

His hands wave about as he speaks, "I thought you might like to see that my scanner really isn't working. This whole setup is under construction. I just haven't had the time to fix it." He speaks briskly, like a child trying to explain his poor behavior.

Laughing, I say, "Drew, you don't think I believe you? I never doubted that you were telling the truth." *That's a big fat lie.*

He emits a sigh of relief and smiles his charming smile. More electricity. And just when I'm beginning to feel dangerously vulnerable, I notice a framed photo of Drew with three other people at a Packers game—two women and a man. He has his arm around a brunette and their cheeks are pressed together. I bend down to get a closer look. Drew chimes in, "Oh, that's from a Packers game I went to last season."

Well, no shit Sherlock. Thanks for clearing up where the photo was taken. How about clueing me in on who you're cozied up to? "Nice shot," I reply. The fact that he seems jittery concerns me.

We move on quickly through the master bedroom and end the tour in the kitchen where the aroma of corned beef and cabbage is most intense. I've never had a desire to try the dish, but I must admit that the smell is making my mouth water and my stomach growl.

Drew rattles off a variety of beverage choices but doesn't mention the one I'm really craving. Maybe it's for the best. After all, who knows what I might say or do with a little alcohol in my system? I carry two glasses of milk into the dining room, and Drew carries the pot of homemade Irish fare. Finally, we sit down and start eating.

"This is so delicious," I say between bites. Before I know it, my bowl is empty, and Drew is spooning in more. "Oh, my gosh. I totally scarfed that first bowl down."

"No worries. Eat up. There's plenty." Drew's perfect smile puts me at ease, so I go back to shamelessly shoveling food into my mouth. Although, I do make a concerted effort to eat a little slower.

When neither of us can stand to eat another bite, we move into the living room for a game of Scrabble, an activity that reminds me of my childhood.

After Jess moved, we would stay up late into the evenings during our sleepover weekends vying for triple word scores. We always joked that the day we found a worthy male Scrabble partner would be the day we found *the one*. It was a silly thing to think, but that childhood joke still crosses my mind whenever I'm in a new relationship. Neither Matt nor Cliff were fans of board games,

Scrabble especially. Whenever I talked either one of them into playing, it was so painful to watch them ponder for ridiculous amounts of time, only to decide on simple three-letter words. I'm not saying you need to be a genius to enjoy playing Scrabble, but it sure helps if you can think of words with more than three letters. It also helps if you can understand the concept of "double word score" in contrast to "double letter score." In all fairness, though, neither of them was too competitive about much of anything, which is in stark contrast to me.

A common love of Scrabble is something that Drew and I discovered the first time we "met" online.

"Suq? What does that mean?" I ask.

"No, not *suck*. It rhymes with *nuke*. S-U-Q." Drew smiles because he knows he'll win if he uses the Q.

"Well, I've never hear of a suq," I grin and narrow my eyes at him.

"Okay. So, you're challenging me?"

If I challenge him and I'm wrong, I lose. But if I don't challenge him, I lose anyway. The question is, do I think Drew is bluffing? He plays a good game of Scrabble, that's for sure. I've never played against a guy who's come close to beating me before.

"What does it mean?"

He shakes his head back and forth and wags an index finger at me. "Uh, uh, uh. You can only look it up if you're challenging. Are you challenging?" His smile becomes wider and more playful.

"All right then. Consider yourself challenged," I lunge for the Scrabble Player's Dictionary.

S-U-Q. Suq. Noun. Variant of souk. A marketplace in northern Africa or the Middle East; also: a stall in such a marketplace.

"Shit," I whisper under my breath. *He beat me.*

"What was that?" Drew cups his palm around his left ear. "Did you just congratulate me?"

"Where the heck did you learn the word *suq*?"

"It's sort of funny actually. It was the answer to a question on

Jeopardy about ten minutes before you got here," Drew says as he starts bagging the letter tiles.

"Hmph. Well, congratulations. You owe me a rematch."

"How about right now?" He looks up expectantly with a handful of tiles.

I look at the clock on the cable box. Eight forty-two. Jess will be calling soon.

"I wish I could, but I've got to get going. I have a meeting with a parent before school tomorrow."

"Well, at least now I know for sure there will be another date." That gorgeous smile of his gives me goose bumps. And the dimple on his left cheek . . . mmm. I feel warmth spread throughout my body, and an aching sensation settles between my legs.

"I should use the bathroom before I head out," I say, rising to my feet. The night has gone more perfectly than I could have imagined, but I have to leave—not because of my early-morning meeting, but because of the inappropriate urges I'm now feeling.

When I return, the Scrabble game is all packed up, and my glass of water has been refreshed. Drew is sitting on the sofa, waiting for me. He smiles and pats the cushion next to him. "I know you need to get going, but tonight has been so great that I was just hoping for a little more time with you. Ten minutes, tops."

This is when my bullshit meter would normally kick in, but Drew is so genuine. He's engaging, intelligent, educated, independent, good looking, and to top it all off, he can cook. There has to be a catch. Or, is there a chance he could be exactly what I've been looking for? I mean, he beat me at Scrabble on our first date. That has to mean something.

"I've had a great time too. This is actually one of the best first dates I've ever been on." I mean it too.

"So, what's next?" he asks.

"What are you up to on Friday night?"

"I've got something going on. How about Saturday?"

He has something going on? Okay, okay, Chloe. Don't get suspicious. He has no obligation to fill you in on his plans. Don't forget, you were the one who said you should both keep talking to other people. "Saturday works. How about I cook for you at my place this time?"

"That would be amazing."

After a few more random thoughts from both of us and another jab from Drew about his Scrabble victory, he walks me to the door and helps me put on my jacket. Then I turn to face him, anticipating a kiss. Instead, he pulls me in for a hug, his posture stiff.

"Thanks for a great evening, Chloe," he says in my ear.

"Absolutely. I had a great time," I say softly.

We part, and Drew opens the door for me. "I'll see you on Saturday then. Will you email me directions and what time you want me to be there?"

"Sure." I smile weakly. "Thanks again for dinner." I pause for a second to examine his demeanor. He doesn't seem the least bit nervous, which adds to my confusion about the awkward hug we just shared. "Bye."

He flashes me that winning grin one last time before I exit his apartment, causing me to imagine turning around and throwing myself at him. But the fantasy is disrupted by the sound of the door closing softly behind me.

chapter eleven

"I don't know what the hell happened!" I complain to Jess over the phone. After failing to call the night before, she rang in a panic this morning. Or maybe "panic" isn't the right word. I'm pretty sure she thought I had gotten laid, and she actually seemed to be excited about that possibility. When I told her the truth, I knew it was far less scandalous than what she had imagined.

"Are you sure you're not imagining a problem here? It sounds to me like you just expected a more intimate departure. Maybe he didn't want to make you feel uncomfortable, or maybe he's just not the type to kiss on a first date. It could even be that he thinks you're not the kind of girl who kisses on the first date. But if that's the case, you really aren't letting him get to know the real you." She snickers.

"Shut up! Uncalled for." I know she's only joking, but there's some truth to her jab. I tend to find myself in long-term relationships for a reason. After a first-date kiss, guilt usually causes me to continue seeing someone, regardless of any red flags. I get in too deep, too fast, often because of that physical intimacy. But still . . . I don't know how to handle not getting that kiss.

"Hey, I'm gonna have to call you back. We're getting ready to board the passengers."

Jess is a flight attendant for a small airline. She's had the job for nearly a year now. It's perfect for her, as far as Ned is concerned anyway. She's away overnight three to four days a week, allowing him plenty of free time. He loves his space and seems to enjoy having a girlfriend who's there when he wants her but unavailable just enough for him to still enjoy the freedom of bachelorhood. He isn't a cheat—which is his one redeeming quality—but he spends the majority of his free time playing golf and watching sports. He's also the quintessential momma's boy, so his daily visits with his mother drive Jess nuts.

"Okay. But give me a call tomorrow when you're back in town. I'm going out with Shelly tonight for this big ass burrito night she's been harping about."

"Big what?"

"Every Wednesday night, some bar offers these huge burritos for three dollars. I guess it's also ladies night from seven until eleven."

Jess takes a deep breath and moans as she exhales. "God, Chloe. Why do you let her talk you into going to these places?"

"You're kidding, right? Who introduced me to The Monkey Bar?" She laughs.

"That's what I thought. Talk to you tomorrow," I say.

"Yep. Have fun!"

Shelly is picking me up at my place in forty-five minutes, but I'm compelled to check my Personals account before I leave work. Drew has not emailed me at all today, which makes the hug even more troubling. On one hand, I'm hopeful that he may have left a message in my Personals inbox, but on the other, I hope he didn't because it would mean he checked his account the day after our seemingly perfect date. My account indicates two new messages and one poke. A poke is essentially a less aggressive icebreaker—a way to say, "Maybe I'm interested. Maybe I'm not." This particular poke is from a "social smoker." I don't understand this category. If you smoke socially, then you are a smoker. I get that it's supposed to create the illusion that you really aren't a smoker per se, but that you may sneak a few cigarettes if alcohol is in your system. I don't have time at the moment to look much closer at the poker's ad, so I move on to the messages. Neither one is from Drew, but I click on an old message from him, which leads me to his profile. It says that he signed into his account within the last twenty-four hours. *So, he was online today, yet he didn't bother to contact me?* I feel a combination of anger and sadness. My chest becomes tight, and I begin to contemplate my emotions.

The plan was to keep things casual and avoid becoming overly sensitive whenever a prospect didn't pan out. But thinking of Drew, I'm wondering if I'm even capable of that kind of casual.

∽

"Alright, alright. I'm coming!" I say, as I hurry down the stairs. Shelly lays on the horn of her silver Jetta as I race out the door. I open the passenger side, and my eardrums are immediately jolted by MC Hammer's "U Can't Touch This." Shelly's upper body gyrates to the beat as she lip-synchs every word perfectly. She loves Nineties hip-hop and rap. The irony of this goody two-shoes teacher getting down to groups like 2 Live Crew and The Fugees cracks me up.

"You're nuts!" I yell as I hop in.

Minutes later, we arrive at the Home Bar. When we enter, a middle-aged bartender yells, "Welcome home!" Shelly and I look at each other and giggle.

The bar area is narrow, but the rest of the interior spills into a wider section with dartboards, video poker machines, and more tables. There are plenty of open tables along the long wall to our right, but we decide to sit at the bar.

The bartender sidles up to us shortly after we slide onto our stools. "Ladies! What can I do ya for?"

Shelly replies, "We're here for some BABs."

"Well, you came to the right place. Whadda ya want in 'em? We've got yer typical Mexican fixins."

"I'll take cheese, lettuce, and tomato with just a little sour cream," Shelly says.

"Do you have chicken?" I ask.

"No chicken, hon. And just so ya know, it ain't gonna be low fat."

I smile. "That's fine. I'll take one with the works." I have no idea what my burrito will be loaded with, and I don't care. What I really want is a drink.

"Okay, little lady. A BAB with the works! I'll be damned if you finish half of it." He gives me a wink and moves to the far end of the bar near the entrance to make our burritos.

"Are they really that big?" I whisper to Shelly.

"Well, they're not called big ass burritos for nothing."

Moments later, the bartender plops down two burritos the size of dumbbells. "Holy shit," I say. They must be at least ten inches long and three inches wide. The term "big ass" doesn't do these burritos justice. Before tackling them, we order a couple of vodka tonics.

About three quarters of the way into reliving my date with Drew for Shelly, her friend Kalissa arrives. Kalissa is a dance teacher at the middle school of the arts. You wouldn't guess it just by looking at her, because she doesn't have a typical dancer's body. She has the height at five-eight, but her build is thick. Like Jess and me, Kalissa and Shelly have been best friends since grade school, but that's where the similarity ends. They grew up in an upper-middle class suburb of Milwaukee, while Jess and I grew up in a more blue-collar area. They come from divorce-free households, while Jess and I both grew up with stepparents. They had college funds, while Jess and I each worked to pay our own ways through school. Like Shelly, Kalissa is extremely outspoken. But Kalissa rarely says things without thinking them through. When she shares her opinion about someone or something, you know exactly where she stands—which is usually where her ultra-conservative moral compass points her. Unlike with Shelly, the possibility of changing Kalissa's mind is nil. I like that Kalissa has a heart of gold and is always as honest with herself as she is with others, but I can't shake the feeling that I need to be on my best behavior whenever she's around. There are even things Shelly wouldn't dare talk about in front of her for fear of being judged.

As soon as we're finished with all of the standard hellos and niceties, Shelly turns her attention back to me. "So finish telling us about your date." She shifts her focus to Kalissa for just a moment. "I told you about how Chloe has been online dating, didn't I? She had her second date last night."

"Yes, you mentioned that." There's an edge to Kalissa's voice. She takes a sip of water and leans back in her chair. I suspect she's allowing her thoughts on the matter to simmer a bit before revealing what she thinks about my new endeavor.

Shelly shrugs and turns back to me. "Okay, so, you were getting ready to leave."

"Well, he helped me put my jacket on, we hugged, and then I left. But it was sort of like a stiff bear hug, which was weird. I invited him over for dinner on Friday night, but he was busy, so he's coming over on Saturday instead." I want to explain how confused I was when Drew didn't try to kiss me, but with Kalissa there and the look of disapproval already forming on her face, I leave that tidbit out. Yearning for a first date kiss is probably one of those things she would look down on.

"Aww." Shelly clasps her hands together and hugs them close to her chest. "He sounds wonderful. I can't believe you met a good guy online!"

"You're having him over to your apartment for your *second* date?" Kalissa asks.

"Big deal. Their first date was at his place." Shelly smiles and looks from Kalissa to me. Kalissa raises her eyebrows at me.

"We're just having dinner, Kalissa. It's really not that big of a deal. I've been talking with him for almost six weeks now."

Kalissa's face softens a little. "Just be careful. Not just with him either—with any guy you meet online. It's not like you really have a chance to get a true feel for a person through email or even over the phone. You know how you just get a feeling about someone when you meet him in person? Sometimes you can just tell something's not right with a person, and other times things just click when you meet someone. That's harder to decipher online."

"That's true," Shelly chimes in. "I guess when you meet someone in a bar, you at least have the advantage of getting a face-to-face first impression. Even when you talk to someone over the phone, there are so many mannerisms and facial expressions that go unnoticed."

I know they aren't judging me, but I feel defensive for some reason. Maybe it's because Kalissa's advice makes me think of my date with Scott. I don't think *he's* trying to deceive anyone with his profile picture, but I suppose there are people who intentionally create fake personas.

"Chloe, are you listening to us?" Shelly waves her hand in front of my face.

"Yeah. Of course. You guys are right. I'll make sure my landlords are going to be home on Saturday night."

"What up, bitches?" Cally, another teacher friend of Shelly's, appears with her new girlfriend.

Shelly hops off of her stool and gives Cally a hug. I follow suit, but Kalissa stays put.

Cally hugs her girlfriend from behind. "Ladies, this is Lisa. Lisa, this is Shelly, Chloe, and Kalissa."

Shelly and I both shake Lisa's hand. "Do you guys want to move to a table?" Cally asks.

"Sounds good," Shelly says. She looks at Kalissa. "You coming?"

"I said I'd come out tonight, didn't I?" I suspect her disapproval of Cally's "lifestyle" is to blame for her rude behavior. I start to wonder why Shelly would even invite these two women out together.

"Awesome." Shelly ignores Kalissa's bitchiness. "It's seven o'clock! Let's get this ladies' night started!"

~

Smack! I hit the snooze button and knock my clock radio off of the nightstand in the process. I roll over onto my back and realize that I'm still fully clothed. Butler and Clover are cuddled together at the foot of my bed, and Hugh is sitting on my pillow. He stares as if he's wondering what the hell is wrong with me. It occurs to me that the radio was most likely blaring for quite a while before I came to. Either that or I had hit snooze several times. Panic sets in as I realize that I might be late for work. Sitting up quickly, I swing my legs over the edge of the bed and try to stand. The room spins as if I've just ridden a Tilt-a-Whirl, causing me to drop to my knees and place my head on the nightstand.

I do my best to piece together events from the previous evening, but I have a hard time getting past the point when Cally talked all of us into doing a shot. I vaguely remember Shelly complaining that Kalissa didn't know how to have fun and needed to learn to be more accepting of people's sexual orientations. Kalissa must have been gone by then, which means I was out until at least ten. Shit. There must have been more shots because I'm going to puke. I stumble to the bathroom and take the unrelenting dry heaves as a sign that I won't be making it to work today. I can't have my kids smelling the booze seeping out of my pores.

After calling in sick, I listen to two new voicemail messages on my cell. The first is from Drew. *"Hey, Chloe. Just calling to say hi and checking to see if you want to chat. I thought you'd be settling in for some TV before bed by now. I'll give your home phone a try."* The second is from Drew, as well. *"Hey you. I was really hoping we could talk tonight. I assume you're out, though, since you didn't answer your home phone just now. I don't remember you mentioning a date . . . well, give me a call when you get in. We've got to talk about Saturday. Talk to you soon."*

He sounded weird. I've never heard him sound anything less than enthusiastic, but now he sounded . . . depressed? I'll have to call him much later, after he's done with work and certainly after I finish paying for my stupidity from the night before. Hopefully everything is fine, but I can't even ponder that fully at the moment.

I just need to sleep the hangover away.

chapter twelve

The next few hours involve a vicious cycle of small sips of water, retching, moaning, self-loathing, regret, and unquenchable bouts of sleep. It isn't until around three, after two solid hours of catatonic sleep, that I feel well enough to sit down to a bowl of oatmeal with brown sugar and strawberries. I can feel each bite slowly working its way down my esophagus and into my exhausted and barren stomach.

I'm still mad at myself for drinking like that. And on a weeknight no less. What was I thinking?

The phone rings, and I curse the fact that it's hanging all the way across the room. It also sounds about ten decibels louder than normal.

"Hello?" I croak.

"*That's* why your phone is off! I didn't think you were going to make it to work today." Shelly's voice rattles my brain. She's chewing on something crunchy.

"What the hell happened? The last thing I can clearly remember is getting roped into doing a shot." The thought makes me gag.

"You don't remember all the shots after that with Chris?"

"Who's Chris?"

"The bartender! After we sang and danced with him to "Baby Got Back," he kept on offering us free shots. You didn't turn *any* of them down, of course. You seriously don't remember?"

"God, no. Tell me Kalissa was gone already."

"Are you kidding? She left as soon as Cally and Lisa started fondling each other, which was pretty much as soon as they sat down. I can't believe you called in sick."

"Shelly. I could barely stand up this morning. The only thing that got me to my feet was the fact that I had to barf. I still feel like I might die. You know I never would have called in if I thought I could actually make it. I hate that my kids had a sub today, and all because I got too out of control last night. Trust me, I feel shitty enough about it without you giving me a hard time."

It's quiet for a moment, except for Shelly's chomping. "Why did you drink so much last night anyway?" she asks.

"I don't know. I guess I'm just stressed about work and school, and I'm waiting for my thesis proposal to be accepted. It's all a little anxiety-inducing. I don't even really remember making the decision to drink that much though. I don't know how it happened." I'm not sure if Shelly believes me or not, but if she does, she shouldn't. I worked full time and took full-time classes in order to get my teaching degree. Ever since I was fourteen and had my first job as a cashier at Hardee's, I've never had a problem balancing work and school. Trouble with men is really the only thing that stresses me out —well, that and dealing with my mother. The truth is that I'm worried about things not working out with Drew. Already, I can't admit the truth to anyone though, especially not Shelly. She would give me the business about being so serious and would scold me for not just having fun with Drew.

When Shelly and I first met, she commented that my boyfriend at the time, James, and I reminded her of an old married couple. She also kept asking me if I was sure that I was only twenty-one, stating that I seemed more like an old biddy to her. It's a wonder we even became friends at all.

It only took a couple of months for her words to completely hijack my brain before I began living up what remained of my college days. That's how *that* relationship fell apart. I didn't just break his heart either. According to him, I "shattered" it and "ruined" him for anyone else. At the time, I was grateful to Shelly for encouraging me to act my age, but now I sometimes wish that I had just kept things the way they were. I would probably be happily married with children by now if I had.

"I guess I didn't eat enough before we started drinking either." *You know, just that Big Ass Burrito. Who am I kidding?*

"Mm-hm. Well, I just wanted to make sure you were alive. I don't suppose you wanna go work out."

"Seriously?"

Shelly laughs. "I'll talk to you later, lush."

∼

It's close to seven before I finally have enough energy to call Drew.

"Drew? Hi, it's Chloe."

"Hey you, I was getting worried. I thought maybe my food made you sick or something." He sounds much more like himself now compared to how he sounded on those voicemails.

I laugh. "No, your food was excellent. It was actually a bit too much alcohol last night that put me out of commission today."

"Oh?"

"Yeah, Shelly took me out to this place for their burrito-slash-ladies' night. What a mistake."

"The burrito or the ladies' night?"

"Both," I grin. "You wouldn't believe the size of these burritos. They're so big that people call them BABs, as in Big Ass Burritos."

"That's awesome! Maybe you'll have to brave another one sometime so I can indulge on one myself."

"It'll have to wait until I'm fully recovered. Probably sometime next year."

It surprises me that he doesn't ask any questions about my evening or whether I made it to work or not. It's nice, but different. Most guys I've ever dated in the past would have been playing twenty questions by now. I would have had plenty of questions, too, if the roles were reversed.

"So, what's up? You sounded like you really needed to talk in your message. I'm sorry I'm just now getting back to you."

"Oh, no, that's fine. I just, uh, wanted to find out if we're still on for Saturday."

"Of course we are! You like Italian food, right? I thought I'd make Italian chicken with linguine. What do you think?"

"Mmm. I think I wish today was already Saturday. Not just for the linguine either."

I give him my address and directions to my place, and then we continue talking for another hour or so. Phone conversations exactly like the one we have tonight are what make me wonder against common sense about the theory of soul mates. I don't even know if I believe in the term simply because I've had unique connections with so many people. But it does seem different with Drew. When an intimate conversation gets going between us, there aren't any barriers. I don't hold back, and neither does he. It feels like we've known each other for years instead of months. The only problem is that I'm trying not to treat what I have with Drew like a relationship. At least not a serious one. I have to remain open to other possibilities, which I haven't been doing a very good job of lately. But going against my natural inclinations has me feeling a bit off. Even so, Drew has to stay just a friend for now. Even though I'm already longing for more.

chapter thirteen

After a wasted Thursday, followed by a day of catch-up at work on Friday, it feels good to have a relaxing evening to myself. Drew and I exchanged emails throughout the day, but I never did find out what his plans for the evening were. Instead of worrying about it, I decide to respond to two new online suitors.

Fridays tend to be when I'm most likely to get a middle-of-the-night wakeup call from Cliff, formulating excuses to come over and arguing his way past my protests. But I'm pleasantly surprised to wake up on Saturday morning to the realization that neither phone rang at all during the night.

I get myself ready for the day and pick up Shelly on my way to the athletic club for an early morning workout. Then we do our grocery shopping together. When I return home, I carry out my weekly cleaning regimen. This routine is usually reserved for Sundays, but I have to get things tidied up for my date with Drew. My one-bedroom flat isn't spacious by any means, but being a bit of a neat freak—borderline obsessive-compulsive, actually—it usually takes me at least double the time it would take for a "normal" person to clean. Making dinner will also require at least an hour.

Come five forty-five, I look around with satisfaction. Everything is ready for Drew's six o'clock arrival. The kitchen table is set, I made a simple salad and a bruschetta appetizer, and the main entree is keeping warm in the oven. Two bottles of wine are ready to go as well. The red sits on the table while the white chills in the fridge. I decided to cover my bases, since I have no idea which Drew prefers. Come to think of it, I don't know if he drinks wine at all. John Mayer is playing in the background, and Scrabble is out on the coffee table, ready for my rematch. All I have left to do is dry my hair. I'm about to turn on the hairdryer when my cell phone rings. It's Cliff. If I don't answer, he'll call my house, so I quickly unplug my home phone. Maybe that's a bad idea. If he calls my home phone and can't get through, he might stop over. Ugh! Why now? Since our breakup, he has never once called before bar close on a weekend. I look at the clock: five fifty-one. Either I dry my hair or I call him back.

"What's up, Cliff?" I say, hastily and without interest.

"Whoa. Wait a second. Why are you so bent out of shape? You're always asking why I never call at a reasonable hour. Isn't this reasonable?" His voice is calm and soothing. If you didn't know what a sweetheart he truly is, you'd think he was being sarcastic.

"I have something going on tonight, and I need to finish getting ready. So, what's up?" I'm staring at my stringy, wet hair in the mirror.

"Do you have a date or something?"

I take a deep breath as I quickly check the clock. Five fifty-five.

"Yes, Cliff. I have a date, and he's going to be here any minute. So, can I please give you a call tomorrow?"

"How about if you give me a call as soon you get in?"

"Actually, we're staying in and I . . . I don't know when he'll leave. It could be late." I hear a car door.

"You mean you guys are hanging out at your place? How many times have you seen this—"

"Fine! I'll call you when he leaves. Okay?"

He hesitates. "All right. I'll talk to you later then. Just call me as soon as he's gone."

"Fine. Goodbye." As I snap my phone closed, the doorbell rings, my damp hair still clinging to my face.

∽

Drew stands before me with a colorful bunch of gerbera daisies.

"Thank you so much," I say. "They're beautiful."

As we climb the stairs and round the corner to my apartment door, the nervous tension caused by Cliff's call dissipates. The only things on my mind now are Drew and the daisies. I don't think I ever mentioned to him that they are my favorite. Could it be a sign of good things to come?

Hugh sits just outside the door, curious to see who's ascending the stairs behind me.

"Hey, kitty," Drew kneels down and extends his hand to scratch the large gray cat's head.

"This is Hugh. He's most likely the only one you'll see tonight."

My friends and family almost unanimously agree that having three cats is a deal breaker for most men. The crazy cat lady cliché has been put to good use in my circles. It's so irritating. I don't understand why having three cats would deter someone from wanting to get to know me. They're cats, not children. The only person in my life who doesn't give me a hard time is Jess—but that's only because she has three cats of her own.

Drew stands and enters my apartment. Hugh follows close behind and rubs against his legs.

"Would you like something to drink? I have wine, Miller Lite, water, iced tea," I say, opening the fridge and waiting for his response.

Drew is staring at me with a cockeyed grin. I'm about to ask what his deal is, but then I realize he's looking at my hair. "Oh, man. I'm so embarrassed," I say as I close the fridge and raise both hands to my head.

"What do you mean? I was just thinking about how gorgeous you look with wet hair." He reaches out and runs his fingers through my hair. It's enough to send chills down my spine, in a good way.

"Well, thanks. That's sweet of you," I say with a nervous laugh. "I meant to dry it but ran out of time." I step around him and take a few steps toward the kitchen table to retrieve the bottle of red. "Do you want some wine?" I ask, holding the bottle up as I turn to face him again.

"I'm actually not a wine drinker. But I'll take a beer." He smiles that charming smile of his, and I want to jump his bones.

I return to the fridge for a beer and twist the cap off as hand it to Drew. "Make yourself at home. I'm going to put these in some water," I say, grabbing the flowers from the counter.

"Thanks." Drew takes a small swig of beer. Then I catch a glimpse of his tongue moving across his lips. My cheeks become hot as I imagine what it would be like to kiss him.

"So, this must be your sister."

"What?" I look over my shoulder to find Drew pointing to a photo of my sister and me on the shelf above the kitchen table. "Uh, yeah. That's us on her wedding day."

As I finish with the flowers, Drew continues to check out the rest of the photos on the shelf, which are of my one-year-old nephew, my cats, and my friends. It suddenly occurs to me that displaying framed photos of my cats might be considered strange. People typically hang photos of their children, not their pets. I wish I thought to hide the proof that I might be a crazy cat lady after all. I join him in looking at the photos, hoping that a short explanation of each one might ease any heebie-jeebies he may be feeling about the weird cat pics. I cringe at the ones of me posing with all three felines. Cliff had taken those.

After I finish walking Drew through the photos, he says, "This one is my favorite." It's the one of me holding Hugh and Butler under my chin. I had just woken up and was sitting on my bed.

"You look so natural. I just love that you don't wear much makeup."

"Thank you. You're so sweet. I love your natural look too."

He winks and gently elbows me in the side.

"Well, what do you think? Ready to eat?" I try to sound normal, but I'm anxious to move away from the photos.

"Absolutely. I'm starving," he replies.

Our conversation flows effortlessly throughout dinner. Drew talks about growing up in a small town northwest of Madison. It was a bit of a culture shock when he began attending the University of Wisconsin-Madison, but he adapted quickly and was enjoying college life thoroughly come sophomore year. Yet his extremely religious parents were enough to prevent him from partying too much. I get the impression that disappointing his parents would have been more devastating to Drew than it would have been to them though.

At some point, between the bruschetta and the salad, it occurs to me that Drew might be too good for me. I even consider for a moment that Kalissa might be a better match for him.

"You just might be the nicest guy I've ever met," I say with a smile.

Apparently, that's the wrong thing to say because his salad fork pauses midair. He returns it to his plate without taking the bite. He looks at me, face sullen, then shakes his head emphatically. "No, I highly doubt that." He has the demeanor of a criminal who's about to confess his sins.

"What do you mean? Why?" I can't even begin to imagine why he's suddenly so bent out of shape. All I said was that he was nice.

"Chloe, I have to tell you something," he says.

He stares at me solemnly, and I stare back the way I might look at a first grader struggling to read a two-letter word. He still doesn't say anything though. We sit in silence. *Well, let's hear it. Spit it out!* He closes his eyes.

I can't wait any longer. "*Drew*. What is it?" I'm now terrified he's going to tell me he's married or something even more asinine.

"I've been seeing someone else," he says quickly.

"Ohh-kay." I don't see a problem here. He feels guilty for doing what he paid good money to do? "Well, that's the point of dating, right? Especially online dating. You're supposed to *see* a variety of people."

"No, Chloe. You don't understand." He places his forehead into his open palms, elbows propped up on the table.

"What do you mean?"

He looks as though he might cry. "Her name is Jessica, and I've been dating her for almost six months."

I narrow my eyes at him. "Are you telling me that you have a *girlfriend?*" Now he really has my attention.

He doesn't answer. Instead, he buries his face in his hands.

"Drew. Can you please just tell me what's going on?" I feel betrayed but can't get over the fact that he's so bent out of shape over this. He didn't even have to tell me about this girl.

He looks up. "You're not mad?"

"I haven't decided whether or not I'm mad at you yet. That depends on what else you have to say." This is getting old. I need the facts and need them quickly before I do blow my top. His hesitance is *really* irritating.

"I never meant to mislead you. I've really been online dating for almost a year now, but for the past six months I've only dated one other person. Then I met you." He glances up at me, and then quickly looks back down at his salad bowl.

"So, if you started dating this . . . what's her name? Jessica? If you started dating her six months ago, then what made you even respond to my ad? Is she dating other people too?" Questions flood my brain, but I try to keep from firing them all at him at once.

"No. She wanted to get serious with me only a few weeks after we met online. We hadn't even met in person yet, and she was already questioning me about whether I was looking for something exclusive or not. It kind of freaked me out, but I still decided to meet her. Things went well, and we started seeing a lot of each other."

"So, why did you even decide to respond to my ad if things were going so well with the two of you?"

"She freaked me out. Ended up canceling her account and then pressuring me to do the same. But I didn't know if I was ready to settle down with her, so I told her I needed a few days to think. And that's when I found your profile. I hadn't been in my Personals account for weeks."

Then it dawns on me why Drew is so distraught over telling me about this other woman. "She doesn't know that you're still online dating, does she?" I stare at him intently, daring him to break eye contact.

My stomach drops because I know the answer even before the words form on his lips. I knew Drew was too good to be true.

"No, she doesn't," he says. "Look, Chloe . . ." Suddenly, he's on his feet. He slides his chair next to mine and sits facing me. He's so close that I can feel warmth emanating from his body and his breath on my face when he speaks. "The time we spent getting to know each other online was more intimate than the last six months I've spent getting to know Jessica in person. I know your intent is to date more casually and get to know a lot of people, which is why I had to tell you about her."

"I don't get it. Why even tell me about her at all when you know that I intend to date other people too?"

He grabs my hands and holds them gently. "I guess I'm just hoping that you feel the same way about me that I feel about you. It seems like we have a special connection that could become something really great."

Now I'm really confused. Is he insinuating that we should be exclusive with each other? Part of me might be tempted, but his little revelation is enough to pull me back and remind me what I set out to do in the first place. It's time for me to start following my head instead of my heart. I've always fallen straight into relationships with people who I should have just dated casually. I need to follow through with the commitment I've made to myself to stay single and carefree for a while.

"I really like you, Drew, and I'd like for us to continue getting to know each other, but I still want to meet other people too. I'm also . . ."

"You're also what?" He leans in a little closer.

"I'm also not sure how I feel about Jessica."

"What do you mean? You just said you want to keep seeing other . . ."

"*Meeting*, I said meeting other people. Not *seeing* other people. There's a difference. And it even sounds like you and Jessica are doing more than just *seeing* each other."

He removes his hands from mine and leans back. He looks both shocked and hurt. There's even a hint of anger, which sort of makes me glad about the way I responded. So much for keeping things casual.

"Chloe, it's not as serious as you think. Trust me."

Oh, right, I'm supposed to trust him now?

He gets up and shoves the chair he had been sitting on back into its place. Then he sits down in front of his food. I feel like I'm watching a child have a temper tantrum. We eat in silence for a few minutes until I can't stand it any longer. I pour myself a glass of red wine and grab another beer out of the fridge for Drew. I'm about to twist the cap off when he stops me.

"Chloe, I don't need another beer. I'm good." He flashes me one of his to-die-for grins. I wonder if Drew is reverting to his calm, laid-back, easy-to-talk-to self. But then he says, "I can barely deal with how I'm feeling about us right now as it is. If I drink any more alcohol, I'm afraid I'll ruin everything with the things I'd say."

I put the beer back in the fridge and attempt to ignore his last few comments. Now things feel awkward beyond repair, at least as far as this evening is concerned.

"Chloe?"

"What's up?" My voice sounds far more pleasant than I feel.

"I didn't mean that I'd say anything bad. I meant the opposite. I'd probably tell you how much I . . ."

"Drew, can we just finish dinner and have fun tonight? We really don't need to talk about this kind of stuff right now, do we? I'm fine with the whole Jessica situation for now. What I really want to talk about is how I'm going to whoop you at Scrabble tonight."

He thinks for a long moment. "You know what? You're right. No more serious stuff. Unless you need to be consoled after I beat you again." He smiles for real this time.

To my surprise, things between Drew and I return to normal fairly quickly. We both act as though the whole dinnertime conversation, or whatever it was, never happened. By the end of our meal, strange, dramatic, brooding Drew is gone and the good old Drew I've grown to really like is back. He eventually beats me at Scrabble again and sticks around to gloat for another hour or so before heading out.

The night isn't a total bust, but I feel differently about him now, more hesitant. It has nothing to do with his confession about dating someone else though. It's more about his strange behavior. Even though I've been getting to know Drew for a while, I'm reminded that it takes a very long time before you can truly know someone.

Unfortunately, the only way I've ever truly gotten to know someone is through being in a serious relationship. It took living with Matt for almost a year to figure out that I could not stand how sensitive he was. There were times when he would toss and turn at night because I didn't want to cuddle after sex. It always seemed like our roles were reversed, like I was the guy and he was the girl. In prior relationships, I had always been the more needy one, so Matt's incessant need for affection started to irritate me and was the catalyst behind our breakup. I can't help but wonder now if Drew might have some of the same needy tendencies as Matt.

∼

When I walk Drew downstairs, he pulls me in for a hug. It's a gentler, more intimate hug than the one he had given me the other night. I'm caught off guard when he turns his head in to give me a kiss. I panic and turn away, causing his lips to brush against my cheek instead. He sighs and pulls me in even tighter. I'm still attracted to him and curious about what it would feel like to kiss him, but it seems like we need to take a few steps back before things progress any further. After I close the door, it occurs to me that he might call Jessica. Maybe he'll even see her. These thoughts turn my stomach, so I need to remind myself that his relationship with Jessica doesn't matter because I'm dating other people too.

There's a soft knock on the door as I turn to head back upstairs. I go to open it, thinking Drew must have forgotten something. Instead, Cliff is standing on my doorstep.

chapter fourteen

"What are you doing here?" I hold the door open just enough to stick my head out to see if Drew's car is still out front. Luckily, it's gone. "My date *just* left. What if he saw you?" I hiss.

"Don't worry. I waited until he drove off before I came to the door. Can I come in?"

"What? You watched him get into his car? How long have you been here?"

"Look, I was driving by, and I saw the guy walking to his car. So I parked down the street and waited for him leave. He didn't see me. Can I please come in?"

"You know what? I don't even care if he saw you. What I care about is that you're invading my privacy! What the hell, Cliff? Why would you drive by? I told you that I'd call after he left."

"Chloe, can we please just go upstairs?"

Knowing that he's not going to give up, I let the storm door slam in his face and stomp up to my apartment. This is a scene that has played out dozens of times: I leave him standing outside, he lets himself in, closes the door, and follows me upstairs.

There was a time when I didn't care if Cliff dropped by unannounced. In fact, I used to welcome his late-night visits when we first "broke up." But lately, it's just starting to seem more and more frustrating.

I knew from the beginning that our relationship wasn't going to amount to anything, but my feelings for him were so strong. They still are, if I'm being completely honest. After over a year of being a couple, I know I'll always care about him on some level. Even so, his unpredictable phone calls and visits have become a nuisance over the last few months. I'm frustrated at myself when I give in and irritated with him for not respecting my wishes. What's worse, it seems like his random visits have only increased since I started online dating. How can I move on with him constantly checking in on me? And at what point is he going to respect me enough to stay away when I ask him to?

Cliff immediately heads to the fridge and grabs himself a beer. "Please. Make yourself at home," I say, hoping my sarcasm is palpable. I begin to clean up the kitchen as he swigs half the beer in under thirty seconds.

"So . . . you like this guy?" He isn't even looking at me when he asks.

"Yes, I do. He's really nice."

"He looks like an uppity nerd if you ask me."

"Well, no one asked you. Nerd or not, at least he has a career and a steady job." I feel bad immediately. Cliff's employment status and job aspirations were huge issues in our relationship. When I first met him, he worked the summer recreation program at my school. That should have been enough to deter me from acting on my physical attraction to him. He was so young and inexperienced when it came to working a full time job. With some encouragement, I convinced him to apply for a third-shift position at Target. It was a good job for a college student, except Cliff never followed through on his plans to enroll. So, he worked at Target for a few months and then thought he was improving his career path by landing a warehouse job with Frito Lay. It was actually a pretty decent paying job with opportunities for advancement. But when he turned twenty-one, he started going out drinking with his friends a lot, and got himself fired instead. That was months ago, and he still hasn't found himself a new job. Doesn't really matter though, because he still lives with his mom. And that's just one of the many reasons why we were never going to work.

Cliff sits at my kitchen table in silence for the next few minutes as he finishes his beer. I rinse and stack the dishes with my back to him, guilt flooding over me. I'm guessing that what I said about

Drew having a steady job really hurt his feelings. I turn toward him. "So, what did you do tonight?" I ask, hoping to change the mood.

"I went to this chick's house," he says.

A chick's house. Now I'm certain he took offense to my comment. Cliff never talks about any of his dates, flings, or whatever they are. Not with me, at least.

"So, you had a date?" I really don't care to hear about his night but desperately want him to stop brooding so we can wrap things up, and I can go to sleep. Part of me doubts that this "chick" is even real anyway.

"Yeah, I've been seeing her for a couple of weeks now." He gets up, grabs another beer, and walks past me into the living room. Cliff isn't a very skilled manipulator, so I consider the fact that this "chick" might actually be real for a moment. A small spark of jealousy ignites in my gut.

The remaining mess is the only thing that compels me to resist the urge to follow Cliff and give him the third degree. Dirty dishes, clothes lying around or clutter of any kind drives me nuts. As I finish cleaning up, I reason with myself that I'm dating other people, so why shouldn't he? Plus, he's the one who started dating other people first. I'm the dumbass who continues to sleep with him.

Cliff sits in his usual spot on the futon, and Clover has found her way onto his lap as usual. I sit down next to him and rub Clover's head for a few minutes before speaking.

"So, tell me about your new friend."

"Her name is Rachel. We met at that party I went to a few weeks ago. She's a friend of Jarrett's cousin."

I cringe at the thought of Cliff dating anyone associated with his friend Jarrett's cousin.

"She's nothing like Jeanie, Chloe. I know what you're thinking. She owns a house and has a good job."

Stripping isn't what I consider a good job. "Really? What does she do?" I know that I should let this go, but the jealous spark I felt earlier has become a flame, and there's no waiting for it to go out on its own now. I want details.

"She's an accountant."

Accountant my ass. "An accountant? How old is she?"

"Twenty-seven. What's with the twenty questions? What does your guy do? How old is he?" Cliff laughs. Apparently, he's in a better mood now.

"Whatever, Cliff. I'm just curious." I'm actually pretty miffed at this point, and with our history, I'm not hiding it very well.

Cliff leans over and puts his arms around me. I try to wiggle away, but he holds tight.

"Someone is jeaaaalous." He continues to playfully squeeze me.

The second I crack a smile, he leans in and begins kissing my face repeatedly. Before I know it, he's lying on top of me, still pecking. Only the pecking has become a lot less playful, and his movements are now much slower and full of tenderness. I run my fingers through his thick, wavy hair and evaluate my internal struggle for about twenty seconds before I kiss him back. I allow myself to indulge in the moment, and our movements intensify. Cliff's warm kisses are like my favorite, ratty old high school gym T-shirt and shorts—I love the familiarity and comfort they provide, but I know they need to be thrown out. He picks me up, and I wrap my legs tightly around his waist. We continue kissing as he carries me to the bedroom and plops me down on the bed. He only presses against me for a few seconds before we frantically disrobe each other. In one hard thrust, he enters me, and I climax almost instantly.

As Cliff continues working toward his own orgasm, the cloud of lust that envelops my brain begins to clear. It's slowly replaced with a haze of guilt. Why do I keep doing this?

Cliff pauses his feverish pounding. Or maybe he's done. I'm lost in my thoughts, so I have no idea. "Chloe, what's wrong? Are you okay?"

I gently push him off of me and sigh heavily. He props himself up onto an elbow and reaches over to stroke my hair.

"I don't know why that just happened, or why it keeps happening, but we can't do it anymore," I say it without even looking at him. And for the first time, I know I really mean it.

He doesn't respond. Instead, he lays his head next to mine, wraps his arm around me, and closes his eyes.

chapter fifteen

I pull up to my parents' house just after nine. I'm determined to get in a full day of schoolwork so that I'm ready for the night classes I have coming up on Tuesday and Thursday. My arrival is strategically scheduled so there's just enough time for me to say hello before my parents leave for church, which begins at ten. Even though it's only a ten-minute drive away, but my mom always insists on leaving twenty minutes early because my stepdad is "the slowest driver in the world."

"Hello!" I call out as I enter the house.

Country music blares in the kitchen, and the TV in the living room is on, so I have to repeat my greeting.

"Hellooo!" This time I yell.

It makes no difference what my parents are doing. One of them could be napping, watering the garden, exercising, or talking on the phone, and there would still be electronic devices on in at least two different rooms. Yet my mom refuses to set her thermostat any higher than sixty-five degrees in the winter or any lower than eighty degrees in the summer because she wants to keep her energy bills manageable.

"Hello? Chloe, is that you?" My mom calls from the bathroom.

I make my way through the kitchen, past the living room where no one is watching the TV, and down the hallway to the bathroom.

"Getting ready for church?" I ask.

"Yeah, why? Are you going with us?"

"Not today. I have a lot of work to get done."

"You know, that's why things didn't work out with you and Matt. And that's why you're never happy. Because you don't have a relationship with God."

"I have a relationship with God, Mom."

"Yeah? How? You never go to church. How do you expect to get to know God if you don't go to church?"

I sigh. We've been having this conversation since I was a child. One time, my biological father had to carry me out the door and throw me into the car as I kicked and screamed because I didn't want to go to church. I think I was three when that happened. My mom swears that was the day Jesus decided I would have to work extra-hard to win back his affections.

"Well, suit yourself. If you want to continue to be a lost soul, that's up to you. You don't have to take my word for it."

There's no need for me to respond. She'll continue the conversation on her own, regardless of what I say.

"I'll just keep on praying for you. You and your sister. Your brother, too."

"Okay, mom."

I move myself into the kitchen where my stepdad always has coffee brewing. In five minutes they have to be out the door. My mom will enter the kitchen, put on her shoes, and then yell to my stepdad at the top of her lungs that it's time to go. Then, while she waits for him, she'll complain about how he's never ready to go on time.

I'm sitting at the kitchen table—drinking a cup of coffee and reading the entertainment section of the Sunday paper—when my mom enters. She rambles as she puts on her shoes.

"You know, Chloe, maybe if you started going to church and trusted in God to guide your love life, you wouldn't have to waste your time meeting men on our computer. Or maybe if you'd stuck with Matt..."

"Mom! Enough about Matt!" My tolerance for her rants about my relationship with God is pretty high, but the topic of Matt is wearing on me.

"Fine. You don't want to listen to me? Don't then. You never have. You or your sister. Your brother never listens to me either. I don't know why I even bother. Glen! It's time to go!"

"What?" My stepdad yells from the basement.

"Time to go!" My mother shakes her head. "He's *never* ready to go to church on time. All he cares about is those *stupid* computer games. You know, he gets up at five in the morning to play those games?"

Of course I know this. I hear about it on a regular basis. My parents continue to bicker as they head out the door for church. My mom's parting words to me are, "Don't forget to lock the door if you leave before we get back. We don't want someone to break in and steal everything."

∼

Before getting to work, I check my Personals account. The first message is from Drew. He thanks me for dinner and apologizes for the awkward conversation we had. He also mentions that he and his friends have plans to hang out next weekend and is wondering if I'm interested in meeting them. The next message is from Engineer92.

> Hi there,
>
> My name is Frank. I really enjoyed reading your profile. It seems like we have a lot in common. Check out my profile, and if you like what you see, maybe we can hang out some time. I'm fairly new to this online dating scene, so hopefully you'll let me down easy if you're not interested.
>
> Best,
> Frank

He seems nice, but they all seem nice at first. I click on his profile link. *My my.* Frank is attractive. He has dark brown hair styled in a classic tapered cut and gorgeous blue eyes.

∼

Engineer92 – 28
Location: Cudahy
Seeking Soulmate

Relationship Status: Never Married
Kids: Yes
Want Kids: Maybe
Ethnicity: White / Caucasian
Body type: Athletic
Height: 5' 10"
Religion: None
Politics: Conservative
Smoke: Yes
Drink: Social Drinker
Pets: No
Education: Master's
Employment: Professional
Income: 60,000-70,000

∼

I'm really starting to question the effectiveness of specifying what I'm looking for in a mate, because people don't pay attention anyway. This guy has kids, doesn't follow any particular religion, and smokes. I could never live with a smoker and can't see myself dating someone with a kid. Maybe it's harsh, but the thought of being with someone who has ties to another woman in the form of offspring irks me.

Then I realize that the only men from my list of "matches" who have shown an interest in me are Scott and Drew. Does that mean *my* stats are unattractive to the type of person *I'm* looking for? Or are most of the people who match my criteria too shallow to give someone without a profile picture a shot?

I enlarge Frank's profile picture. He really is gorgeous. Trendy sideburns creep halfway down his face, and a masculine hand rests under his chin. Despite his smoking habit, he has beautiful, white teeth. After examining all of his photos, I decide to respond because he's way too good-looking to pass up.

Hey Frank,

I wasn't going to respond to your message at first because I'm not a smoker. Not passing judgment on you—just making sure you're okay with the fact that I'm not too keen on cigarettes. Maybe we could chat by email a bit to figure out if it would be worthwhile to meet each other. So, tell me a little bit more about yourself?

Chloe

I attach a photo and click *send* without rereading my message, something I rarely do. I often overthink things, especially email and voicemail messages. Sometimes I worry so much about how people are going to react to what I say that I end up not saying the things I really want to say at all. Frank's handsome face continues to stare at me from the computer screen. I wonder if his clothes, skin, and breath reek of cigarette smoke. I wonder if he whitens his teeth. How else could a smoker have such a glowing smile? Then it occurs to me that my stipulation about dating only non-smokers might make me look like a snob. Maybe that's why I'm not getting that many responses from my matches. I click on "settings" and change my profile preferences to "doesn't matter" for smoking. Then I peruse my new matches and send out a few icebreakers. I also delete a message from a guy whose profile matches what I'm looking for to a T, solely because I don't find him attractive. I feel bad for letting Packer Fan's appearance be the deciding factor, but there's no point in responding to someone who I don't find attractive.

The reality of just how shallow I may be starts to sink in, but I shake the thought away and focus on my schoolwork instead.

chapter sixteen

"Well?"

"I don't know. I have to wait until Ned tells me what his plans are. Why don't you ask Shelly? Then, if Ned and I aren't doing anything, Shelly and I will both be there to check Drew out."

"Jess, this is dumb. Why are you planning your life around Ned? He never considers you when he makes plans."

"Who are *you* to talk? I hardly ever saw you when you were dating Matt." I almost hang up on her, but then she says, "Look, I'm sorry. I just want to patch things up with him. He's finally starting to act normal again. We're going to dinner with his mom tomorrow night."

"Jess, you don't even like being around his mother. Why would you agree to dinner with her? Making yourself miserable is not going to make your relationship with Ned better."

"No offense, Chloe, but I don't think you're qualified to be doling out relationship advice."

A lump forms in my throat, and I want to scream at her. Instead, I don't say anything.

"Chloe?"

"What."

"Look. I don't want to argue with you. Just let me find out what Ned is up to this weekend, and I'll let you know if I can make it on Saturday or not. OK?"

"Fine. But it's really not a big deal if you can't. I'm going to meet up with them whether you can be there or not. I just thought it would be nice for you to meet Drew and tell me what you think." Except right now, I don't really care what she thinks.

"Okay. I'm pretty sure I'll be able to make it but just let me give

Ned the courtesy of checking with him first. Are you still going out with that engineer guy tonight?"

"I think so. Probably just for a beer or two."

"Well, have fun and be safe."

"Thanks. Have fun at dinner tomorrow night." After we hang up, I continue to stew over Jess's comment about me not being qualified to give relationship advice. Just because I haven't found the right person yet doesn't make me unqualified. Besides, I wasn't really giving her advice. I was simply sharing my opinion. If I wanted to give Jess relationship advice, I would tell her that flirting with another guy isn't a very effective way to show your commitment to someone. What do I know though?

After I finish typing a permission slip for my class's upcoming field trip to the museum, I decide to check my messages to make sure Frank hasn't called off our date tonight. There isn't anything from him, but there's another message from Packer Fan. This is the third message he's sent in four days.

Hi again Chloe,

You're probably starting to think I'm a real nut job! Let me explain. I just signed up for an account, so the first message I sent was sort of a test run. Since I didn't hear from you, I thought maybe it didn't go through, so I sent the second message. Now that I know how to tell when messages go through, I'm sending this one to apologize for the two identical ones! (I'm really not crazy.) Anyway, let me know if you're interested in getting together for a little chitchat. I'm not big on email—you learn so much more about a person face to face. Would LOVE to know more about you.

Take care,
Patrick (Packer Fan)

I didn't even read his first two messages before deleting them. I click to look more closely at his profile picture—again, I still don't find him very attractive. He has a shaved head and roundish face. I can't tell if he has a receding hairline or not. His teeth aren't perfectly straight like Drew's or Frank's, but he has a very nice smile. Two additional photos are posted with his profile: one is of him decked out in Packers gear and the other is a close-up of his face. In the close-up, his face is painted half green and half yellow, and his face is contorted into an expression that screams manic football fan. I burst into laughter.

~

Frank and I are meeting at a pub and grill near General Mitchell airport in Milwaukee. It's a good midway point between my place in Bay View and his place in Cudahy. After a couple of emails each, he included his number and asked me to call if I felt comfortable. Despite the issues I initially had with his profile stats, I actually felt pretty comfortable about moving forward with calling and meeting him. I even considered offering up my number before he sent me his, but I didn't want to come across as too forward.

It became clear in our emails that his smoking habit and religion—or reported lack thereof—weren't so cut and dried. Frank responded to my first email with a friendly explanation of his ongoing struggle to quit smoking. He joked about owning stock in GlaxoSmithKline, the makers of Nicorette gum. Apparently, he hasn't had a cigarette for nearly three months but reports being a "smoker" on his profile because of his continued craving for nicotine. Since he was such a good sport about me questioning the smoking thing, I decided to address his religion in my second email. He explained that while he believes in God, he values *all* religions and doesn't want to commit to just one. His explanation actually got me thinking. I'm not that knowledgeable about the various religions, and it seems like Frank might be more spiritual than I am. I might even need to reconsider specifying a religious preference for my matches.

On traditional face-to-face dates, I probably wouldn't have had the courage to address my issues with Frank's profile. But hiding behind a computer gave me the gumption to just get things out in the open right away—another benefit to online dating. I just couldn't bring myself to mention his daughter, though. I'll wait and see how things go tonight before broaching that topic.

I'm really looking forward to our date tonight, but I'm also nervous. Frank is an engineer with his master's degree, so there's no question that he's intelligent, and something about intellectual guys makes me nervous. I guess they intimidate me because I wonder if they think I might not be worth their time. This insecurity usually causes me to overlook really smart guys. But given my unwarranted hesitance over Frank's smoking and religious classifications, he's an excellent example of why I need to be more open-minded and confident. It's definitely time for me to adjust my online-dating radar.

Upon entering the Landmark, I'm surprised by how crowded the bar area is for a Wednesday night. Most of the tables are empty, though, with the exception of two. A group of three is sitting at one and Frank is at the other. He stands and greets me with a wide grin.

"Hi, Chloe," he says as he extends a hand. "How are you?"

"Hi. It's so nice to finally meet you in person." I smile and revel in the discovery that he's even more gorgeous in the flesh. So gorgeous that even the feel of his hand in mine causes me to perspire.

It seems like an eternity before he speaks again, and he's so good looking that I have a hard time concentrating on what he's saying. "Would you like to *blah, blah, blah, blah, blah* . . ."

"I'm sorry. What?" *Oh, my God. He's going to think I'm an idiot.*

He smiles. "Would you like to sit at a table or at the bar?"

"A table is fine. I hope I didn't keep you waiting long." We make our way over to the table where Frank was sitting before, and he pulls a chair out for me.

"No worries. I wasn't here long before you arrived. Can I get you a drink, Chloe?"

I gesture toward his beer. "A Blue Moon sounds good. Thanks."

"Great. I'll be right back."

With perfect posture, Frank glides toward the bar in his cerulean blue sweater and khaki cargo pants. While he's waiting for our drinks, a woman sitting at the bar says something that makes him laugh. Seconds later, the same woman speaks to him again. This time, he shakes her hand and her friend's hand. Then, he points in my direction. The first woman swivels her stool around to look at me. *Holy crap. Cassie Thurman.* Cassie squeals. "Oh, my, gosh! I know her!" She waves emphatically and then motions for me to join them at the bar. Frank looks amused.

Cassie throws her arms around my neck. "Chloe! What a surprise! How are you darlin'?" She releases me but grabs ahold of my hands.

I glance out of the corner of my eye at Frank who's still grinning politely. "I'm good. How are you?"

"Oh, you know . . . I'm hanging in there." She releases my hands and starts wringing hers. "I'm sure you heard about Ted." I glance down and realize that her ring finger is bare.

That's when Cassie's friend pipes in. "Cassie? Aren't you going to introduce me to your friend?" The tall blonde smiles at me politely.

Cassie snaps out of the trance she's in. "Yes, of course! Where are my manners? Chloe, I'd like you to meet my good friend Deidre. Deidre, this is Chloe. I worked with her for a while over at Park School." Then she nudges Frank. "And how did *you* land yourself this fine specimen?"

I know she means no harm, but her comment makes my blood boil. "Well, Cassie, thanks to you, I met Frank online."

She gasps. "Oh, Chloe. You didn't." She stares at me wide-eyed. "Can you two excuse us for a moment?" She asks Frank and Deidre.

"Of course," Frank says. He gives me a wink and takes a seat next to Deidre at the bar.

Cassie links her arm around mine and pulls me back to the table where Frank and I should be sitting, enjoying our date. "Chloe, you have to be careful about who you meet online."

"Cassie, you're the one who convinced me to give it a try. I thought you and Ted were a perfect fit. What happened?"

"Chloe, Ted was . . . Ted was not right in the head. He pulled the thickest wool there is over my eyes. He looked so good on paper—or should I say online? He looked so good that I missed so many warning signs."

"Look, I don't know what happened with you and Ted, Cassie, but I . . ."

"He's a pedophile, Chloe! A pedophile!" She whispers.

I can't believe my ears or my eyes. Cassie's always-perfect mascara has begun running down her cheeks. "Oh, Cassie, I am *so* sorry." I hug her close and pat her back. Frank and Deidre are deep in conversation.

"Chloe," Cassie pulls away from me and adjusts her posture, "do you have a tissue?" I hand her a napkin from the table. She dabs her face clean, and to my surprise, she smiles. "I'm so sorry. My wounds are still fresh. This is the first time I've been out in public since I found out. Well, besides going to work."

"No, no. Don't be sorry." I'm dying to know all of the details but refrain from asking any questions. Why put her through the pain? Instead, I change the subject and we catch up on other things.

"Cassie?" Deidre says. I didn't even notice her heading toward us. She puts her hands on Cassie's shoulders. "Are you ready to get going?"

Frank looks on from the bar.

Cassie looks up at Deidre. "I think that might be a good idea." Then she turns back to me and looks me in the eyes. "Be careful."

Cassie and Deidre return to the bar for their coats, and Frank joins me at our table. He has a fresh beer in each hand. "Everything okay?" he asks as he hands me one of the beers.

"Yeah, everything's fine. Sorry about that. I haven't seen her for a while." I'm still a bit shaken by Cassie's news about Ted.

He raises his beer. "To our first date."

I feign a smile and raise my beer, as well. "To our first date."

∼

Frank watches as I drive away. I peer at him in my rearview mirror and see him wave one last time before getting into his car. After Cassie left, there was just enough time for us to finish our beers before he had to leave. Despite the whole Cassie situation, I really enjoyed myself. Not only does Frank have movie-star good looks, he's also polite, classy, and well spoken. He also has a good sense of humor and seems to have a pretty down-to-earth attitude about life. I imagine he's the kind of guy I could use to persuade my mother to let go of Matt once and for all. But despite all of his glowing characteristics, my initial attraction to Frank has tapered off significantly. This bothers me because he's a total package—he's everything a woman could want. So why am I not more excited about seeing him again?

My apartment is roughly ten minutes from the Landmark, but I choose to drive the additional fifteen minutes to my parents' place because I need to know more about Ted. Even though it's after nine, there's a good chance my mom will still be up watching TV.

As soon as I pull into the driveway behind my stepdad's station wagon, I'm blinded by a motion light. As I walk up the driveway, another motion light illuminates. Then, as if it isn't already light as day, a third motion light goes on the moment I set foot on the porch. My key isn't even fully inserted into the lock when the curtain over the window in the door is lifted, and my mom's face appears.

"Chloe? What are you doing here?" she yells.

I try to turn my key, but she's holding the doorknob from the other side, so it won't budge. "I need to use your computer, mom. Can you let me in?"

"It's so late. Why do you need to use the computer now?"

"Mom, the door. Can you open the door?" Finally, she lets me in.

"Don't you have to work tomorrow?"

Maybe I should have just gone home. "Yes, but I just have to check something."

"Your sister's coming next Wednesday. You can pick them up from the airport, right?"

"Yeah, I think so. Can we talk about this later? I just need to check something quick and then I need to get home."

"Hmph. You know, it would be nice if you came over to visit sometimes—instead of just using the computer all the time."

"I know. I'm sorry. I'll come over this weekend. Maybe we can rent a movie. Okay?"

"Yeah, I'll believe that when I see it."

When I Google Ted's name, nothing comes up. I can't believe he's a pedophile. I wonder what Cassie meant by that. I mean, I know what a pedophile is, but I find it hard to believe that he actually is one, partly because Cassie is a bit of a drama queen. I feel bad for thinking this about her, given what she's been through, but it's true. The next phrase I Google is 'Ted Taylor court case'. Nothing comes up. The clock on the computer reads nine forty-five. I really need to get going, but for some reason I'm desperate to find out what happened. Then I navigate to the Wisconsin circuit court website, a site I've used in the past to look up information about relatives of students. I type in Ted's name. Bingo. He was convicted of *Sexual Intercourse with a Child Age 16 or Older* nearly two weeks ago. Poor Cassie. I feel terrible for doubting her. While this conviction doesn't exactly make Ted a pedophile, it's still a serious offense. Chills run down my spine as I think about how smitten she was with Ted. He was *perfect*.

chapter seventeen

"Starbucks? You're kidding, right?" Shelly says.

"Yeah, so? I want to meet him somewhere crowded—and neutral."

"Neutral? What do you mean?"

"A place where you might meet your brother or a colleague you don't know very well. Starbucks doesn't exactly scream *date*, you know?"

Shelly laughs. "Why are you even getting together with him if you don't want to call it a date? Why don't you see what Frank is up to tonight?"

"I told you. This Packer guy seems really nice. And Frank has his daughter this weekend. But I might see him on Sunday.

"So, you're meeting the Packer guy tonight, going out with Drew tomorrow, and maybe getting together with Frank on Sunday? Wow, you're really getting your money's worth!"

I laugh. "Yeah, I guess I am. But this thing tonight is really no big deal. I just think he might be fun to hang out with. I doubt I'll find him attractive—he's bald, you know.

"Well, that's mean."

"What's mean?"

"The fact that you're stringing him along. If you don't think you're going to find him attractive, why waste his time? How would you feel if someone went on a pity date with you? You'd be pissed about having your time wasted. And, by the way, plenty of women love guys with bald heads. Look at Jess."

Maybe she has a point. "Well, it's too late now. I'm on my way there."

"Maybe you should cancel and come to my sister's house for cards tonight."

"Nah. I want to get home early. I'm thinking it'll be a late one tomorrow. Who's going to be there anyway?"

"The usual. Kasey, Bob, Tom, Kalissa, Craig, my mom and dad . . ."

"Whoa, whoa, whoa. Back up. Did you say Craig?"

"Yeah, so?"

"Nothing. I'm just surprised you're introducing him to the whole family. Sounds like progress."

"We're just friends!"

"Whatever you say. Hey, I just pulled into the parking lot, so I have to let you go."

"Okay. I know you don't plan on staying long, but text me anyway when you leave. Just so I know."

"I will. Have fun tonight!"

∾

There's not much of a crowd at Starbucks. I suppose coffee isn't the drink of choice for most people on a Friday night. I decide to hold off on placing my order and wait for Packer Fan. Even though I know his name is Patrick, I can't stop thinking of him as Packer Fan, or Packer Fan Patrick. Maybe it has something to do with the close-up of him with a green and yellow face. I'm willing to bet that his body was probably painted as well. It's kind of crazy that we're meeting in person without even talking on the phone first, but Packer Fan Patrick kind of reminds me of an old high school friend who was always the life of the party and always had people rolling with laughter. In my response to the three messages he had sent, I asked about his profile pictures, which all appeared to have been taken at Packers games. He responded by detailing his lifelong history as a Packer fan. It all started when he was three . . . Three paragraphs later, he explained that his recently deceased grandfather left him and his brother season tickets. I couldn't help but laugh at the way he used ten exclamation points at the end of a sentence that mentioned his dead grandfather.

I take a seat at a table near the window so I can watch for Packer Fan Patrick. Just as I'm getting comfortable, my chair begins to shake.

"Boo!" Someone continues to jiggle my chair back and forth.

Startled, I grip my seat, one hand on each side, and look over my shoulder to see Patrick grinning maniacally. "Okay, okay. Where did you come from?" I grin, trying to hide my unease.

Before I'm able to turn back around, he scurries to the other side of the table. Instead of sitting across from me, he picks a chair up with one hand, plops it down next to me, and takes a seat.

He laughs boisterously and extends a hand. "Chloe! Good to meet you!"

"Nice to meet you, too. I didn't think you were here yet," I say. I'm genuinely smiling now—partly because his friendly demeanor is contagious but also because of his outfit. Patrick is wearing a Packers sweatshirt with green and gold Zubaz pants. As if that isn't enough to show his fan spirit, he's also wearing yellow sneakers with green Nike emblems. I wonder if he dressed this way to be funny or if he wears Packers apparel all the time.

"Ha!" He slaps his knee and points toward the back, near the bathrooms. "I was sitting at that table over there. I thought it would be funny to sneak up on you." He laughs hysterically and slaps his knee again.

People are starting to stare. Maybe Patrick is a bit too energetic for Starbucks.

"Good one. You really got me," I say, smiling politely. "Do you want coffee?"

"Nah. I don't drink coffee. Makes me jittery." He holds his hands out in front of him and makes them shake as he speaks. At this point, I wonder if he might be on something.

"Okay. Well, I'm going to get a coffee. Do you want . . ."

He jumps out of his seat and says, "Come on. Coffee's on me."

By the time I grab my purse and get to the counter, Packer Fan Patrick is already talking to the barista. ". . . half skim, half whole, extra whip, with an extra shot of espresso."

"Did you say grande?" she asks.

Patrick bursts into laughter. "I'm just messin' with you! You're good though. Really good," he says as he shakes a finger at her.

She frowns. "Well, is there anything I *can* get for you?"

Patrick continues laughing, oblivious to the barista's irritation. "I'll take a hot chocolate. And whatever this little lady is having." He gestures toward me.

I give her a weak smile and hope that she doesn't spit in our drinks. "Hi. Can I please have a grande, non-fat Caramel Macchiato?"

She nods and looks at Patrick. "Six seventy-five."

"Whoa Nelly! For a coffee and a hot chocolate?" He shakes his head as he pulls a ten out of his wallet and hands it to her. Then he looks at me. "We can go over to the bar across the street and get two shots of Jack Daniels for six bucks." He gives me a wink.

I smile at him. Even though I'm a tad embarrassed by Packer Fan Patrick's behavior, at least he's amusing. More than a few chuckles came from other customers during his exchange with the barista, and a few of the other employees were even giggling.

The barista hands Patrick his change, and to my surprise, he quietly shoves the bills into her tip cup. She doesn't even notice.

We get our drinks and return to the same table near the entrance. Patrick talks about some of the most memorable Packers games he's been to and tells me a few stories about his job as a high school math teacher. I feel like I could listen to him talk for hours, but I also know that I could never date him. I just don't find him physically appealing. And Shelly was right; it would be unfair of me to string him along.

"So, Chloe, how do you feel about getting those shots of Jack?"

"Right now?"

"Yeah. Come on. My treat." He drums his fingers loudly on the table.

"Oh, I can't." I look at my watch. "I actually have to get going."

For the first time tonight, Packer Fan Patrick doesn't have a smile on his face. He doesn't say anything for a moment either. The drumming stops. "We're not going to have a second date, are we?"

He catches me off guard, so I sit speechless as he waits patiently for an answer. I consider lying, the way I lied to Scott, but decide I can't do that to him. Without making eye contact, I say, "Patrick, I think you're a *really* nice guy, and I'd actually love to get together again, but..."

"But you're not interested." At first, I assume he's angry, but then I look into is eyes and all I can see is sadness. "Hey, that's cool. I totally get it."

I feel terrible and begin reconsidering his offer to go out for a shot. "You know..."

That's when his phone rings. It's not a normal ring though. It's the song they play at Lambeau Field right before Packer fans yell, "GO PACK GO!" Except Packer Fan Patrick's ringtone is customized. After the ditty plays, it's Patrick's voice yelling, "GO PACK GO!" He grabs his phone to silence it. "Sorry about that. What were you saying?"

"I was just going to say that I would really like to hang out again, but as friends." I know this won't happen, but I want to leave on good terms.

He nods. Then he jumps out of his seat and says, "Let's blow this joint."

As I drive out of the Starbucks parking lot, I wonder if Packer Fan Patrick has ever been in a long-term relationship before. He seems like the type of guy who might always get his heart broken because he's just too nice. Then I feel sick to my stomach because it occurs to me that maybe I'm the type of girl who's always going to break the hearts of guys like Patrick.

chapter eighteen

It irritates me to find that all of the curb space within half a block of my apartment is gone. I'm forced to park ten houses down. As I draw closer, it becomes clear that my landlords are having a party. Cars are packed into the driveway, bumper to bumper, and "Crocodile Rock" blares into the otherwise silent atmosphere every time a smoker opens the side door.

"Hi, how's it going?" I say to three smoking partygoers.

Deena, one of my landlords, exits her apartment the second I enter the common area. "Chloe! I haven't seen you for a couple of weeks. How are you?"

Deena is a gorgeous, blonde flight attendant for Midwest Express. Her boyfriend Mike, my other landlord, also works for Midwest as an air traffic controller. He's just as attractive as she is. Not only are they two of the most beautiful people I've ever seen, they're also two of the nicest. Talk about a perfect couple.

"Hey, Deena. I'm good. How are you?"

"Doing great! Hope you don't mind the noise. We're having a birthday party for Mike. You should grab some food or at least some cake."

"Thanks, but I think I'm going to hit the sack."

"Really? So early? But it's Friday night. Are you feeling okay?"

To be perfectly honest, I'm feeling a bit down in the dumps. Packer Fan Patrick really has me thinking about my past relationships. I don't know what the hell I'm looking for anymore. It seems like all I ever do is sabotage my chances with the good ones and chase guys who are not good for me.

"Actually, I think I might be coming down with something. I appreciate the offer though. Tell Mike I said happy birthday."

The first thing I do when I enter my apartment is change into sweats and a T-shirt. Then I wash my face, brush my teeth, and crawl into bed. I close my eyes and hear Packer Fan Patrick's voice: *We're not going to have a second date, are we?* Then I picture Matt the night I told him I was moving out. I had just returned from visiting my sister and her family for two weeks in Las Vegas. Moving out hadn't even crossed my mind until our fickle reunion prompted the decision. He was happy to see me at first, but his true feelings began seeping out little by little as the night progressed. *Why hadn't I called? What were we so busy doing that I hadn't thought of him? Did I ever consider that he might worry when I didn't call for two weeks? Did I miss him at all?* I didn't have any good answers for him. It just hadn't occurred to me to call. I figured it was a nice break for us. I tried to ignore his insecurities, but then when I rolled away from him that night in bed—simply because he was making me too hot—he lost it. He jumped out of bed and nearly flipped the mattress over on top of me. *What the fuck, Chloe! Why can't you acknowledge that not calling was really shitty? How can you be so insensitive? You are such a cold, fucking bitch sometimes!"* As Matt screamed at me at the top of his lungs, I found myself wondering why I didn't feel bad for causing such a gentle, caring, mild-mannered man to lose his marbles. At that point, I realized I wasn't in love with him. Two weeks later, he helped me move into Mike and Deena's duplex. Packer Fan Patrick's words were almost identical to the last words Matt had ever spoken to me in person: *We're not going to get back together, are we?*

When the music downstairs stops playing, it's quiet in my apartment for a moment. Then my answering machine beeps. "Nooo!" I moan as I crawl out of bed.

"Friday, six, twenty-two, p.m."

"Chloe? Chloe, are you there? Well, where are you? Hello?" My mom thought she hung up, but must have pushed the wrong button, so the message continues. *"Why does she even have a phone anyway? She never answers either one of her phones. Glen? Did you see my glasses? I need you to come in here and read Chloe's cell number to me!*" I hear my stepfather's voice in the background, and my mother begins dialing. "*It's not ringing. Hello? Why isn't it ringing?*" Then the call disconnects.

"*Friday, eight, thirty-three, p.m.*"

"*Hey, Chloe. Just calling to let you know that I'll be there tomorrow, but not until around ten or eleven. I picked up a Chicago flight. If you decide to meet somewhere even less classy than the Home Bar, leave me a message. Oh, and Ned might show up too, if that's okay.*"

"*Friday, nine, fifteen, p.m.*"

"*Chlooooee. Where are you? And why is your cell phone off? I'm kickin' it with friends in your area tonight.*" There's loud music playing in the background, and I can hear women laughing. "*Just wondering if I should stop over later? Call me. Or maybe, I'll just swing by.*"

This is the first time I've heard from Cliff since our indiscretion last weekend. Determined not to make the same mistake, I unplug my home phone and check to make sure my cell phone is still off before checking to make sure the door is locked.

I'm done with Cliff.

chapter nineteen

"Welcome Home!" Bartender Chris points me toward the back of the bar.

I make my way to the back room where I find Shelly, her sister Kasey, her brother Tom, and Craig standing around a table. "Hey guys!" I wave to Kasey and Craig, who are deep in conversation.

"Hey, lady," Tom says. He slides his hand down toward my rear as we hug.

"Keep it clean, mister." Shelly says as she elbows him out of the way to give me a quick hug. "So, tell us about your *non-date*." She makes quotation marks in the air.

"It was fine. He was *really* nice."

"A date? Who's the lucky guy?" Tom says.

"Tom, I told you, there isn't a lucky *guy*. Chloe is dating lots of lucky *guys*."

"Oh, right. The online thing." He laughs. "I'll bet my entire salary for next month that it'll be down to one guy by the end of the year." He looks at me. "Chloe's a one-man kinda woman. I *could* be that man if my meddling sister would stay outta my love life."

"Would you *shut* up? You're not allowed to date my friends. And I'll take that bet. New Year's is only five weeks away. There's no way she's going to give up all of her newfound freedom that quickly. Right, Chloe?" Shelly says.

"I would hate for you to lose all your money, Shell, but I think that could be a safe bet. I'm kind of getting used to not being tied down." I have no idea why I say this. Tom's right. I *am* a one-man kind of woman. Even though I'm trying to stay positive about dating around and keeping things casual, a big part of me longs to be at home on my couch snuggling with someone special.

"Who needs a drink?" Craig says as he throws an arm over my shoulder and gives me a quick squeeze hello.

"I do!" Shelly and I say in unison.

As soon as Craig and Tom are out of earshot, Kasey begins talking a mile a minute. "Shelly, Craig is *absolutely* nuts about you." She briefly looks at me. "Chloe, I know you'll back me up on this." Then she takes Shelly's hands and leans in so that their faces are inches apart. "You're *crazy* if you don't give him a chance. He's the *nicest* guy on the planet." I nod in agreement. "Hell, if I wasn't already married with children, I would snatch him right up from under your nose."

Shelly pulls her hands from Kasey's grasp. "You guys are *really* getting on my last nerve. How many times do I have to tell you? WE ARE JUST FRIENDS. I tried dating him, remember? Didn't feel right."

"That was when you were still holding out for Jeff. Now that there's *no* chance that you two will ever be together again, it's time to move on sister." Kasey wags an emphatic finger at Shelly.

Jeff was Shelly's high school boyfriend. They were on and off all through college. Even while she was dating other people, she was always open to hopping back into the sack with him. She really thought they were going to end up together for good after they both graduated. But then Jeff revealed one drunken evening that he had to cut Shelly loose because he had found the love of his life—an artist named Ben.

"I *really* hate you sometimes, Kasey. Not everyone ends up as lucky as you with a husband who works his *ass* off so that you can just pop babies out one after the other and stay home eating bon-bons all day long." And just like that, Shelly storms off to the bathroom in a huff.

Kasey stands there frozen, mouth open. I stifle a laugh.

"You shouldn't have said anything about Jeff," I tell her. Kasey pouts as I continue. "Just let it go. She knows Craig would be good for her. Why do you think she hangs out with him all the time? We just need to keep our mouths shut and let her figure it out."

She rolls her eyes and takes a seat at the table. "I *do not* sit around eating bon-bons all day long."

I sit on the stool next to her. "I know you don't, Kasey."

With a sigh, she attempts to change the subject. "So, I hear we're going to meet an Internet guy tonight. Tell me about him."

"Well, his name is Drew, and he's the first guy I started talking to online."

"And how many guys have you met?"

"Well, I've *met* dozens, but so far I've only seen four of them face to face, including Drew."

"So, when you say *met*, that doesn't really mean you've actually met. You really just know their name and some generic stuff about them."

"I suppose that's true."

"I don't get it. How do you decide who you want to meet in person?"

"Well, if I seem to be getting along with someone through email, then we talk on the phone. If our phone conversations go well, then we meet in person."

"That still doesn't make sense. There's no way to tell if you're going to have chemistry with someone through email or over the phone. You need to look into someone's eyes. You need to see the way they walk—the way they carry themselves. You need to see their facial expressions when they talk to you for crying out loud."

Kasey's rant leaves me speechless, not because the things she's said are unreasonable but because these are the very things I've been starting to realize about online dating. Kasey didn't even need to spend several weeks meeting guys online to figure out that the system is flawed.

She sips her vodka tonic, waiting for me to respond. When I don't, she shrugs and says, "Well, at least you're meeting a ton of guys. You're bound to find a few keepers, right?"

Shelly returns from the bathroom. "What are you guys talking about?" she asks as if her tirade never happened.

"Shots anyone?" Craig comes up from behind. He's holding a tray full of snakebite shots, and Tom has a tray full of beer bottles and cocktails. Cally and her girlfriend Lisa are with them. Everyone grabs a shot from the tray.

Tom raises his and says, "To Chloe's online dating adventures." Everyone laughs and downs their shots.

Two hours later, I'm feeling buzzed enough to make a fool of myself on the dance floor—not that the Home Bar actually has a dance floor. Shelly, Cally, Tom and I are dancing in front of a dartboard to "Rock Your Body" by Justin Timberlake. Tom slips behind me and presses his body against mine. I stop moving for a second to watch for Shelly's reaction. She laughs and continues dancing, so I figure what the hell. I resume moving my hips to the music. Then Tom leans in and whispers in my ear. "I think your date might be here." My eyes dart toward the bar, and there's Drew. He's standing with his friends, watching me gyrate with Shelly's brother. I try to make it obvious that Tom and I are not getting fresh with each other by elbowing him in the gut. Tom buckles over, laughing.

"Drew!" For some reason, I feel guilty.

"Hey, Chloe." He leans in and gives me a stiff, one-armed hug. "These are my buddies, Tanner and Bill." His friends smile and nod. I can't help but think of the words Cliff used to describe Drew: *uppity nerd*. Drew's friends don't seem uppity, but they do have a nerdy air about them.

Tanner looks from Bill to Drew. "You guys want a beer?" Then he looks at me. "How about you, Chloe?"

"Sounds good," Drew says.

"Thanks. I'm good," I say.

Bill says, "Yeah, I'll go with you."

They turn to find an open spot at the bar and leave Drew and me standing there alone.

"I'm glad you guys made it! How was the basketball game?"

"Good. The Bucks won," he says. "How long have you guys been here?"

"Uh, two, maybe three hours." I smile and shrug.

"Are you going to introduce me to your friends?"

"Oh, gosh, I'm sorry. Of course! Come on." I grab his hand and lead him to our table. "Guys, this is Drew. Drew, this is Kasey, Craig, and Lisa." They all shake his hand. "And that's Shelly, her brother Tom, and Cally," I say as I point to the "dance floor."

"Hey, Drew!" Tanner calls from the bar. "They don't have Hacker-Pschorr. Mostly domestic beer." He shrugs and raises his hands, palms up.

"Can you all excuse me for a moment?" Drew says. He touches my back lightly and then walks off to the bar.

"He's kinda cute," Kasey says. "A little brainy looking, but cute."

Lisa is about to add her two cents, when the sweaty dancers join us. "What's with the nerd herd?" Tom asks.

"You're such a dick," I say, laughing.

"Now, now. Let's all treat each other the way we want to be treated," Shelly says in her best teacher voice.

Kasey's "brainy" comment and Tom's "nerd herd" comment make me feel self-conscious. I want to find out what some of my friends think of Drew, but he just got here and they're already cracking jokes about his appearance.

"Do you guys really think Drew looks nerdy?"

Tom is about to answer when Shelly stops him. With her hand over his mouth, she looks at me and says, "Does it matter? I thought I was here to tell you what I think about his personality, not give an assessment on his looks." She removes her hand from Tom's mouth and looks at him. "And Chloe isn't interested in your opinion, Tom. So keep it to yourself." She turns and gives me a wink.

∽

Our large group, which eventually grows to include Jess and Ned, monopolizes the back room of the bar as we take turns playing pool and darts. At the moment, the girls and I are dancing to "All My Loving" by the Beatles. I peek over at Drew, who's bonding with the guys over sports and beer. He catches me looking at him and smiles. Tom follows Drew's gaze. Then he dances over to us and joins in the fun. Drew looks on, sans smile.

"All My Loving" ends, and "Let It Be" starts playing. Everyone pairs off—Cally and Lisa, Jess and Kasey, Craig joins Shelly, and Tom grabs me. Drew's buddies are on their way to the bar and Drew is having a conversation with Ned. Tom turns me so that I can no longer see Drew and smirks. "Guess he doesn't want to dance with you."

"He just hasn't had as much to drink as we have," I say, grinning back.

Tom and I always share a few dances whenever we're out together, but I can't help but feel that this time it may not be such a good idea. Drew has to be wondering what's up between Tom and me, even though there's absolutely nothing there. Not that I haven't thought about it. He's attractive, and we definitely have chemistry. But if I know Shelly, she wouldn't like it one bit. They might only be a year apart in age, but he's still her baby brother.

"Hey. Looks like Ned needs you." Tom stops dancing and nods toward Ned and Drew.

I look, and Ned is holding out my phone. "What are you doing with my phone?" I ask, rushing over.

He puts his hands up. "Hey, I just heard it ringing, so I answered it. Sorry."

I snatch the phone from his hands and look down to see that it's Cliff. "Asshole," I mouth to Ned. He smirks and turns back to Drew.

I think about disconnecting the call, but I have no idea what Ned has said to Cliff. The jackass might have told him where we are. Heck, he might even have invited him.

"Hello?"

"Wild night tonight?"

I sigh. "What do you want, Cliff?" I make my way to the front of the bar as I talk.

"I want to know why you haven't been answering my calls. I also want to know what all of those people were doing at your place last night."

"Excuse me? Why is that any of your business?"

"Because it is."

"*No*, it's not."

"Look, I think I want to get back together."

"You're kidding, right? Because we're not getting back together. You're the one who wanted to date other people in the first place. So now I'm dating other people, and it's pretty nice not having to deal with your immature B.S. all the time."

"Chloe, come on. Can I come over tonight?"

"No way. Absolutely not."

"Chloe, listen, I . . ."

"No, you listen to me. I'm hanging up now, and I'm going to turn my phone off. Don't leave any messages because I won't listen to them. And don't call my house either because the first thing I'm going to do when I get there is unplug the phone. And if Ned told you where we are, don't even *think* about showing up here." I can hear him breathing, but he doesn't say anything. I can only assume he's either shocked or hurt; I've never really been this direct with him before. But it's necessary now. This has to stop. "Look, I don't want to hurt you, but I need you to understand that I'm moving on. Okay?" Still nothing, so I hang up. Hopefully he got the hint.

A chorus of clapping and whistling startles me. I turn to see Jess and Shelly high-fiving each other.

"How long have you guys been standing here?" I ask.

"Long enough," Jess says as she hands me a drink. "Ned told me about the dick move he pulled, so I figured we should check on you."

"What do you mean, *check on me*?"

"My *God*, Chloe, why are you getting so defensive?" Shelly says.

"I don't know. That depends on why you guys thought you should *check on me*."

Jess laughs. "Just never mind. You're drunk. Bad choice of words on my part, okay?"

I realize she's right. I am drunk. "Hey, Chris, can I please have some water?"

"Absotutely-lutely," he says. Seconds later, he delivers three tall glasses of ice water.

"So, what do you guys think of Drew?"

Neither Shelly nor Jess says anything. Jess reaches for a glass of water, and Shelly sips her vodka tonic. I wonder if maybe they had trouble hearing me over the music.

"What do you guys think of Drew?" I say, louder this time.

They look at each other, and then they look at me.

"What? You guys don't like him?"

Jess sighs. "I hate to fill your mind with doubt, but he was pretty pissed about Cliff's call. And he was asking Ned a bunch of questions."

"What kind of questions?" I ask.

"I don't know. I think he asked how long you dated Cliff and when the last time you saw him was. Ned got out of the conversation pretty fast. That's probably the only reason he came over to tell me that you were on the phone with Cliff—to get out of talking to Drew."

"Yeah, I don't like that he was asking questions about you and Cliff, especially since he technically has a girlfriend," Shelly says. "He also asked Craig some questions about you and Tom."

"So he's curious. You guys are making him sound crazy."

"Curious?" Shelly asks. "No, curious would be asking me how long I've known you. Curious would be asking how *we* met. Curious is *not* asking a guy he barely knows about your relationship with another guy. That's weird, not curious."

"I agree, Chloe. That's insecurity and might hint at possessiveness.

And Shelly is right about the fact that he has absolutely no right to care if you're dating other guys. I mean, he's been seeing that other girl for a long time. What's her name? Jessica? It almost seems like he doesn't want to cut her loose until he has you in the bag."

"Wow. I'm so glad you're finally getting some use out of your psychology degree," I say.

Jess frowns. "You know what? Forget it. Keep dating him. See what happens. I don't care anymore. You always want advice because you're too afraid—wait, no, afraid isn't the right word. You're too insecure to make relationship decisions on your own, yet you never listen to what anyone tells you."

I'm speechless.

Shelly puts her hands on Jess's shoulders and looks her in the eyes. "Jess, can you please tell us how you really feel now?"

"Shut up," Jess says. But she cracks a tiny smile.

"We're all insecure," Shelly says as she puts an arm around me. "Let's not start throwing stones at each other." I slump down under the weight of Shelly's arm and stew over what Jess said. "Chloe, I don't know what to tell you. I think he has issues. Do you care if I ask him about Jessica?"

"Not at all. But just so you know, I don't care that he's dating her. I'm dating other people too, remember?"

Jess groans. "*Chloe*. He's not just *dating* her. He's been with her for *six* months."

"I know. You have a point. Let's just go back. It's almost closing time."

As we make our way toward the back, we notice Drew and his friends standing at the other end of the bar. They are putting on their coats. "Shit. He's leaving," Shelly says. She hurries ahead of Jess and me, weaving her way through groups of people.

By the time Jess and I get there, Shelly is ordering a round of shots. Drew and his friends have their coats on, but they appear to be in no hurry.

Drew looks at me. "Hey, long time no see." He smiles. "I think we're gonna get going."

"Oh? We still have about an hour though," I say.

"Okay, okay. Let's do these," Shelly says. She hands shots to Drew, Jess, and me, but Drew's friends don't seem interested. They have now taken seats at the bar and are watching a poker tournament on ESPN. As soon as Drew slams his shot glass on the bar, Shelly takes him by the arm. "Come on, Drew. Let's chat." He gives me a curious look and follows her to a nearby table.

"I have to see what Ned is up to," Jess says as she heads to the back room.

I hop onto a barstool next to Drew's friends and pretend to watch the poker tournament, but I'm really trying to make out bits and pieces of Shelly's conversation with Drew. I distinctly hear Shelly say Jessica's name, and then the bar fills with Jimmy Buffett's "Margaritaville." I sigh, and Drew's friend Tanner looks at me.

"You okay?" he asks.

"Yeah, I'm fine," I say, but he has already turned his attention back to the TV. *How weird*. His friends seem nice enough, but that's the most either one of them has said to me since Drew introduced us. Is it because they're guys? Or are they reclusive Dungeons & Dragons weirdos who don't know how to talk to girls? And if they are D & D nerds, what does that make Drew? Of course, it's also possible they think I'm the weirdo. Either way, if his friends and I aren't comfortable with each other, is it even possible for Drew and me to continue dating?

I swivel on my stool so that I can at least keep an eye on Drew's and Shelly's body language. They both have very serious looks on their faces. *Did he just roll his eyes?* I'm about to hop off my stool to interrupt what appears to be an unpleasant conversation when Jess and Ned appear in a frenzy.

"Chloe, would you *please* tell Ned what we did last night?" Her eyes are pleading.

I have no clue what Jess is talking about, and there's no way I'm going to be able to come up with the right answer.

"I thought he knew what we were doing." I widen my eyes, hoping that she'll lead me in the right direction.

"I knew it! This is bullshit! Where were you?" Conversations around us stop, including the one between Shelly and Drew.

Jess turns to Ned and whispers, "Can we please . . ."

"You know what? I don't even care." Ned shoves past Jess and makes his way to the door. Jess is hot on his heels.

I hop off my stool and head over to where Drew and Shelly are standing. Bill and Tanner follow, clearly looking for an excuse to leave. They say some quick goodbyes and then head out.

"What's going on with Jess?" Drew asks.

Shelly rolls her eyes. "I think I'm ready to get out of here. Ready to go, Chloe?" I know she's irritated, but I don't know whether it's with Jess or Drew.

"Did you ride with Shelly?" Drew asks.

"Yeah, I did . . . I'm so sorry about all this."

"The only person who should be sorry is Jess," Shelly snaps. "C'mon, it's late. Let's get going." She gives me a look.

"Chloe, how about if I drive you home? I don't mind," Drew says.

"Uh-uh. You're not driving her home," Shelly suddenly sounds fierce.

Drew recoils. "Chloe's a big girl. Why don't you let her make her own decision?"

I can't believe they're arguing. What is going on?

"Chloe, I'm getting Craig and letting everyone else know that we're leaving. I'll be back in a sec."

"Well?" Drew says.

"Well, what?"

He smiles, moves in close and puts his hands on my waist. "*Well*, can I drive you home?"

All I can think about are his hands touching me and how close his face now is to mine, but somehow I hold strong. "Um, I . . . I think I should just ride home with Shelly and Craig." I'm afraid of what might happen if Drew drives me home. I also need to know why Shelly was so argumentative with him. He must have said something that didn't sit right with her, a thought that has me feeling less eager about him already.

"Okay," he says flatly. He backs away and his smile is gone. "So, when are we going to see each other again? No offense, but I feel like I didn't even get to hang out with you tonight."

"I know. I'm sorry. Let's talk tomorrow. Maybe we can make plans for next weekend."

"You're busy until next weekend?"

"Well, no, but I have to work and I have homework. And this has been a *long* weekend."

"Well, what about tomorrow? We could watch the Packers game together."

All of a sudden, I feel like I'm being badgered. "Drew, I'm busy tomorrow."

"Oh, okay. Well, call me whenever then, and we'll see if we can coordinate our schedules for next weekend." There's a hint of venom in his voice.

"Sounds great," I say, pretending I didn't notice his sarcasm.

We all walk out of the bar together. I initiate a lackluster hug from Drew before getting into Shelly's car. As soon as we pull out of the parking lot, Shelly is fuming.

chapter twenty

My ears are ringing and my brain feels like it's going to explode. Shelly has been going on and on about her conversation with Drew for what seems like an eternity. Craig is driving, and we're waiting for what must be the longest red light in the city of Milwaukee.

". . . and then he says to me, *not that there's anything wrong with being gay, we just don't agree with it*."

"Wait. What?" I'm not sure how the topic of being gay became part of their conversation.

"I asked him why his friends didn't talk much to any of us, and he said they felt uncomfortable around Cally and Lisa. Frickin' homophobes!"

Craig laughs. "Just because they're uncomfortable being around two girls making out with each other doesn't make them homophobes. I don't necessarily enjoy watching Cally make out with women either, but that doesn't mean I don't like her as a person."

"Craig, just drive. Okay?" Shelly turns in her seat to face me. "Chloe, I'm all for you continuing with online dating, but you need to cut Drew loose. He was *so* rude to me."

"Maybe he felt like he was being attacked. How did you go about bringing up Jessica?"

"I already told you. I flat-out asked him about her. Then he flat-out told me it's none of my business. He kept watching you out of the corner of his eye the whole time too—like he was afraid you were going to talk to his friends or something."

"Maybe he was watching the poker tournament on TV?" I know that I'm grasping at straws here, but I'm desperate to rescue Drew, if only so that I can have a chance to get to the bottom of who he is myself. Something isn't adding up but I don't know what. It's as if he's a completely different person when we're alone. I can't say this to Shelly, but I'm starting to wonder who the real Drew is. I still don't want her telling me who I can and can't date though.

"Whatever! He was keeping tabs on you. What irritates me most is that he was perfectly fine with everyone when you were around—he was laughing and talking no problem with the guys. But when it was just the two of us, he barely made eye contact. I'm telling you, something isn't right about that guy."

I lean my head back against the seat and look up at the sky through the rear window of the car.

"Look, I know you've invested a lot of time getting to know him, but I don't think he's the kind of guy who likes sharing a girl." She smacks Craig in the shoulder. "What do you think, Craig?"

Craig looks at me in the rearview mirror. "I hate to say it Chloe, but I think Shelly's right."

She starts up again. "If you continue dating him, I'm afraid you might end up with a psychotic mix of Matt and Cliff—a guy who can't stand the thought of you being with anyone else *and* who won't take no for an answer. Why can't you just meet someone *normal?*"

Well isn't that the million dollar question, I think to myself.

We drive in silence the rest of the way to my apartment.

∽

The first thing I do when I get in is call Jess, but it goes straight to voicemail. I consider driving over to her apartment to see if she's there, but I'm too tired and drunk to walk a straight line let alone drive a vehicle. I would have asked Craig to drive over there, but Shelly would have been pissed. She has no tolerance for what she refers to as 'Jess Drama' because she thinks Jess brings bad things upon herself. Of course, Shelly isn't completely off base. But to be fair, Jess has had a lot of unfair bullshit happen in her life. Jess's mom was only seventeen when she had her, and her dad wasn't really in the picture in the beginning. It wasn't until Jess was three that he started wanting to be a part of her life. Then, after they had developed a somewhat decent relationship, he died in a tragic accident involving faulty car brakes. Jess has always been suspicious that her stepmom had something to do with it. After all, the woman collected a hefty life insurance payout; Jess didn't see a penny.

Whenever I bring up Jess's childhood struggles, Shelly shrugs them off and says people eventually need to stop feeling sorry for themselves and move on when bad things happen. I wonder if she ever thinks that about me. Shelly had a perfect childhood though, so I'm not really sure she's entitled to that opinion.

After I leave a second message for Jess, I make good on my promise to Cliff and unplug the phone. My cell phone remains off and in my coat pocket.

Images of the evening replay in my mind like scenes from a movie as I lay in bed. I see the warning signs that Shelly was talking about: Drew's blank stare as he watched me dance with Tom, the look of anger that crossed his face when he was talking to Shelly, the way he squeezed in between Craig and me at the table, and the desperation in his eyes as he gripped my waist at the end of the night.

I groan and curl up into the fetal position. I don't know if it's because I'm saddened by the realization that Drew is no longer a prospect or simply because I'm already frustrated with online dating, but tears begin to roll down my cheeks.

Why does it have to be this hard?

chapter twenty-one

A light dusting of snow falls on my windshield as I drive over to my parents' house. It's around noon, so they are likely back from church and getting ready to eat lunch. I need to put the finishing touches on an assignment, but I also plan on spending some quality time with my mom, which means listening to her talk.

I turn onto my parents' street and pass the duplex where I used to live with James. The car parked in the driveway tells me that he still lives there. Sometimes, I get the urge to stop in and see how he's doing. Other times, I wish I would stop recalling random moments from our relationship every time I drive by. The sight of James's house reminds me of a time when I *thought* I knew exactly what I wanted in a relationship. It also reminds me of the second time I duped myself, when I repeated the same mistakes with Matt. When I lived with James, my sister got into the habit of honking every time she drove by. I think she still honks when she's in town, obviously not because I live there, but because she still wants to pay tribute to James. Don't get me wrong, she shares my mom's adoration for Matt, but I think she loved James even more.

Actually, James and Matt are a lot alike. Both work with their hands—Matt as an electrician and James as a wood repair specialist at a local furniture store. Both were very friendly but rather non-social and somewhat reclusive. Neither cared much about what he wore—or what I wore, for that matter. And neither had any objections to settling down with me for the rest of their lives. The interesting thing was that Shelly bashed the idea of quiet movie nights at home when I was with James, but after she and Evan set me up with Matt, intimate nights at home were no longer highly criticized. Her acceptance of my return to a less social calendar didn't last long, though. As soon as her relationship with Evan imploded, she went back to calling me an "old biddy."

Of course, she never seemed to recognize the irony.

My parents have a large kitchen window facing their driveway, so it's impossible for anyone to approach the back door without being seen. I can see my mom standing at the stove cooking as I walk to the door, the sounds of country music—Kenny Rogers—playing around her.

"Hi, mom!" I say, cheerily.

"You here for lunch?" Even on the phone, she rarely offers a greeting.

"I'll probably have something, but I didn't come here just to eat lunch."

"Hmph. You and your sister only come here when you want something. Your brother too."

"That's not true, mom."

I can tell she's in a bad mood, not because of her combativeness—she's always a little combative—but because she has prepared a smorgasbord of food. When my mom first came to the United States, she barely spoke any English, so she was not able to communicate very well with my dad's family and friends. One thing she could do, though, was cook. Over the years, she started cooking as a way to calm her nerves whenever she felt anything less than content.

"So, who's coming for Thanksgiving dinner?" I ask, hoping to steer her away from whatever is bothering her.

"The usual. Oh, and maybe your brother."

"*What*? I thought he was going to Carol's mom's house." Carol is my brother's second wife. I've only met her a few times, but from what I've gathered, she isn't exactly a girl's girl. She once said my sister seemed like "a corner bar kind of woman" based on Sarah's request for a bottle of beer at a bar. And that was to Sarah's face and in front of my dad and my stepmom.

"Hmph. He's not *with* Carol anymore," she says.

"What? When did that happen?"

"It happened as soon as he found out *Carol* is *still* married."

"What do you mean? How the heck did they even get married if she's still married?"

"Who knows? That kind of stuff happens in California."

"Okay, mom." I roll my eyes. "How did he find out?"

"Her ex-husband called your brother and told him."

"What? Did he threaten Jim?"

"No. Why would he threaten your brother?"

"Because Jim is married to the guy's wife."

"No. He's not interested in Carol. He's interested in her money. He just wanted to tell your brother that he still has full rights to Carol's money."

"Oh, my God. Jim must be pissed."

"Anyway, you might have to pick your brother up from the airport too. You know what? I knew there was something wrong with Carol. And that daughter of hers. *My God.* Do you know she was caught giving a stranger a hand job on the plane when they flew to Hawaii?"

"Yeah, I heard. I feel bad for that girl. She obviously doesn't have the best role model, and I don't think she's ever met her father." I feel bad gossiping like this, but I also know there will be no way derailing my mother from this topic anytime soon.

"Well, *your* father's not around, and you don't go around giving hand jobs to strangers." For the first time since I arrived, she stops cooking and looks at me. "*Right?*"

"Seriously? Of course not. Why are you looking at me like that?"

"Well, how do I know? You're out there dating all these guys you know practically nothing about. I suppose you could be giving hand jobs."

"All right, that's enough." Time to cut this conversation off, even though she's right. Not about the hand jobs, but about me going out with guys I hardly know.

"Speaking of your father, have you talked to him lately?"

"Not lately, no." I actually spoke to my father last week, but I have no desire to listen to my mom talk about him for the next thirty minutes, so I don't dare tell her.

"I hope he's still happy with *that woman*. You know, he's stuck with her whether he likes it or not."

Here we go again. The *woman* she's referring to is my stepmother. My mom swears that my father's alleged affair with my stepmother was what caused their divorce. She has zero proof though, so it's always been her word against his. I don't really know what to believe. Even though my dad and stepmom moved to Texas together two years after he divorced my mom and got married a year later, I don't feel like it's fair to believe everything my mom says about him. After all, there *are* two sides to every story.

"Do you know that they had sex in this house?" My mom continues, her voice becoming louder with every word. I've heard this same story dozens of times, so I concentrate on the pattern of the tile floor instead of her tirade. "Right in *that* bathroom." She waves a large chef's knife in the general direction of the first-floor bathroom. "I kept knocking on the door and asking them what they were doing in there. You know what he told me? He said they were just talking. Yeah, right. Talking my ass." Her voice is just below a scream, and she has completely forgotten about the fish balls that are more than likely overcooked by now.

"Mom, you don't know for sure that they were having sex."

"Yeah, what did *he* tell you?"

"Dad didn't tell me anything. We've never talked about it." Of course, that's not totally true. I have talked to my father about it—but only once. And it's not anything worth getting into with her. What good does it do to rehash things from the past anyway?

"Well, you should ask him about it. I'd like to hear what he has to say. He'll probably lie to you just like he always lied to me. Hmph." She extinguishes the flame under the boiling fish balls and turns off the beeping timer. "You better not end up with a man like your father. Otherwise you'll end up . . ." My mother notices that my stepdad is using his fingers to help himself to a piece of steamed eggplant. "Glen! Get a fork! *And* a bowl! Why are you always contaminating the food?"

Following her suggestion, or rather her order, my stepdad gets a bowl and starts filling it. But my mom takes the serving spoon from his hand and finishes the job for him. Then he takes a dry spoon from the dish rack. "Why are you getting a spoon?" my mom asks. "Use a fork, Glen!"

Sometimes it saddens me to hear the way she talks to him. I wish he wouldn't put up with her nagging, but I've only seen him stick up for himself a handful of times. I don't understand it. Most men would snap on her on a regular basis, even the most patient ones. But my stepdad is more than just patient. He's a saint. Or maybe he just really loves her.

"Why can't he use a spoon?" I ask.

"Because, this is the kind of food you eat with a fork."

"Mom, who cares what kind of utensil he eats his food with? You just don't want him to use his fingers, right?"

She scoffs. "Don't encourage him, Chloe."

"I'm not. I just don't get what the big deal is."

She huffs at me, but her tirade seems to end. At least momentarily. We all sit down together to eat lunch and talk some more about my brother's soon-to-be ex-wife—or whatever you call a person who you *thought* you were married to but really weren't—and her delinquent daughter. We also discuss plans for Thanksgiving. I even show her some of my new matches, and she selects a few for me to poke. My mom only mentions Matt one time and only because one of her motion lights is on the fritz. All in all, it's actually a pretty successful visit with my parents.

As I'm getting ready to leave, she says, "You know, your dad and I were happy in the beginning. Then he got that job at the hospital and started meeting new people and going out after his shift. That's when he started thinking the grass was greener on the other side."

"Yeah, I know," I say.

"Do you? Are you sure?"

"Yes, mom, you've told me these things about dad a million times before."

"I'm not talking about your dad. I'm talking about you. You're just like him. You always think the grass is greener somewhere else."

I sigh. "Thanks for lunch mom. I have to get going."

"Okay, but don't forget, you have to pick up your sister on Wednesday at five o'clock. I'll call you about your brother. Or maybe he'll call you himself." A call from my brother would be a shocker. And *such* a treat. My sister and I are only five years apart, but my brother is ten years older. He harbors some serious resentment that dates back to the summer he was forced to babysit for me. I highly doubt it was the *entire* summer, but that's what he claims, and my mom doesn't remember. Consequently, most of the infrequent conversations I have with my brother revolve around *that* summer. I wish he would just let it go, but I have a feeling he's always going to see me as the brat who ruined the summer of 1977 for him. He was only ten for God's sake. What kind of excitement could I possibly have kept him from?

"Yeah, okay. I'll see you Wednesday then. Bye, mom."

No response.

As I pull out of the driveway, I can see my mom's head in the kitchen window above the sink. She's standing there doing the dishes when my stepdad appears behind her and hugs her tightly.

For just a moment, my mom almost looks happy.

~

I try to call Jess on my way home but am forced to leave another message. It would be worrisome if I couldn't get ahold of Shelly, but unanswered calls are not unusual for Jess, especially since she started dating Ned. My guess is that they are trying to work things out. Otherwise, I know Jess would be seeking a shoulder to cry on:

preferably the shoulder of someone who would be up for getting drunk with her.

Shelly thinks Jess's tendency to always put Ned first makes her an untrustworthy friend, but this is coming from a woman whose friendship motto really is "chicks before dicks." She says it often enough just to be funny but I know she actually means it. Sometimes I wonder what made her decide to forgive me for not being a better friend when things with Evan went sour. I'm not sure I could have been so forgiving if our roles had been reversed. But I also know I would never put a guy before our friendship again.

Frank is scheduled to show up at my place at six o'clock, so I have about half an hour to straighten up before he arrives. The first thing I notice when I enter my apartment is a fur ball in the doorway of my bedroom. As soon as I finish cleaning it up, I move on to the litter boxes. Nothing is more embarrassing when guests are over than the scent of a dirty litter box wafting through the air. Oh, the joys of cat ownership.

By the time I'm done with all of the cat business, it's five forty-five. Just enough time for me to put the dishes away, light a few candles and freshen up. As I stare at my reflection in the bathroom mirror, it occurs to me that I'm not the least bit nervous. I allowed my hair to air dry today, so it looks a little unkempt. But for some reason, I don't even care. This sense of calm is a complete one-eighty compared to how I felt when Drew came over. Come to think of it, I was more nervous even when I was sitting across from Scott at Applebee's. I begin to wonder what's wrong with me, but my analysis is cut short when the doorbell rings.

I rush downstairs and open the door so fast that it grazes my left foot. Pain sears through a bloody pinky toe, as I hop up on one foot. In a flash, Frank is standing next to me. "Are you okay?" He's holding both of my shoulders, trying to provide support.

I look up at him. Man, he's gorgeous. "My toe hurts." *My toe hurts?*

He laughs. "Well, you *did* just slice it open with the door. Come on. Let's get you upstairs."

To my surprise, he bends down and lifts me up in a cradle hold. "Whoa! What..."

"It's okay. I don't mind." He glides smoothly up the stairs.

This man is in *really* good shape.

Somehow, he's able to continue holding me while he opens the door at the same time. I expect him to put me down as soon as we enter my apartment, but instead, he walks me into the living room and puts me down on the futon. "Where are your first aid supplies?"

"Oh, you don't need to get me anything. I can walk to the bathroom and take care of this in there."

"Are you sure?"

"Of course. Thank you so much for . . ." I position my arms as if I'm carrying something. *Why do I act like such a buffoon around him?* "You know . . . for carrying me up the stairs."

He grins. "No problem. I don't mind at all. I'm so sorry you hurt your toe." We both look down at my foot, but instead my eyes are drawn to a huge fur ball about two feet away. Anyone who has cats knows that fur balls are not very furry looking. They are wet, slimy clumps that resemble feces. I look up at Frank, who has also seen the nasty mess.

"I'm *so* embarrassed. I hope you know that's *not* a pile of poop."

To my relief, he laughs. "No, I know a fur ball when I see one. We have two cats. My daughter and I." *That's right. He has a daughter.* I'm amazed at how little I've thought about that fact since we first met in person. I guess it doesn't bother me as much as I thought it would.

"Tell you what," he shakes me out of my thoughts. "I'll clean that up while you take care of your toe."

"Are you serious?" This guy is too good to be true.

"Of course I am. Is your carpet spray under the kitchen sink?" How is he so incredibly pleasant?

"Um, yeah, but I can get it for you." I move into the kitchen and grab the cleaning solution and a rag.

He takes them from me and says, "Go ahead. Fix up your toe," and then he gets to work on the fur ball.

I sit on my toilet and smile as I apply Neosporin to my toe. Even though nothing has gone right in these first ten minutes of our date, I actually feel like everything is perfect. Frank came across as being a really nice guy when we hung out a few days ago, but part of me wondered if it was really him or if it was just a first impression act. There has not been any acting going on tonight though.

I'm applying a Band-Aid when I hear the sound of the door closing. *Did he just leave?*

I limp through the kitchen into the living room to find that Frank is gone. I guess the cat vomit was too much for him. I plop myself down on the futon with a sigh. So much for perfect.

Then I hear the door again. "Frank?" I get up and walk toward the kitchen.

"I set this down in the hallway when I grabbed you." He holds up a bottle of Cabernet.

I laugh. "I thought you left."

"What? No way. I just cleaned up after your cat. I deserve a drink!" This guy might really be a good one.

I open the bottle of wine and pour two glasses while Frank sets up Scrabble. He suggested we play, and of course, I never pass up an offer to play Scrabble. We're only eight turns into the game when I realize that Frank is no slouch when it comes to this game either. He's already fourteen points ahead. "All right, that's enough of that. I'm done going easy on you." I tease, pushing my wine glass away, sitting up straight and cracking my knuckles.

"Bring it on," he says.

Forty intense minutes later, the score is 229 to 228. He's in the lead, and each of us has only one letter left. I have the Z and I know that he has the Q. Both letters are worth ten points. I place my Z on the board to create the word *zit*. Even if he finds an open spot to make *qi*, *zit* has just earned me twelve points. "Your turn." I grin proudly.

"Nice one." He rubs his chin and tilts his head as he examines the board.

Sure of my win, I say, "Wow, this was a *really* close game."

He smiles at me as he plays the Q. I look down to see that, sure enough, he has created the word *qi*—twice.

"Sixty-two," he says.

"What?" I look up at him, shocked.

"My Q is on a spot marked triple-letter score. That means I just got sixty-two points." He smiles with pride.

"You totally suck." At this point, I'm actually thinking about how much Frank doesn't suck.

He laughs and stands to stretch. Then he refills both wine glasses and hands me mine. "So, how long have you been online dating, Chloe?" Instead of sitting back down in the chair across from me, he sits next to me on the futon. Not too close, but close enough that I know he's interested. He's facing me and has an arm over the top of the cushion.

"Almost eight weeks. How about you?"

"Three."

The phone rings. Luckily, I turned off the answering machine. I really should have just unplugged the phone though.

"Do you want to get that?"

"No. I really don't need to. So how's online dating going for you? Have you met anyone interesting?"

"Well, I met you. Wait." He shakes his head. "That sounded cheesy. Yes, I've met a few women, but you're the first person I've had a second date with. I was getting ready to call it quits just before we met. I'm still not sure if I'm such a good fit for online dating."

The phone continues to ring.

Frank raises his eyebrows. "Are you sure you don't need to . . ." The ringing stops.

"I completely understand. I've thought about calling it quits several times. They really keep you hooked by sending new matches every day though." I laugh.

"I know. I don't even have time to sift through all of them." He takes a sip of wine. "So, how do you feel about having dinner with me on Wednesday? I'm dropping Kaitlyn off at her mother's around five thirty for the holiday weekend."

"I'd like that. But I have to pick up my sister and possibly my brother from the airport and take them to my parents' house. I might not be available 'til around seven. Can I get back to you?"

"Yeah, of course. Where do your sister and brother live?"

"My sister lives in Las Vegas and my brother lives in California."

The phone starts ringing again. I cringe at the thought of who it most likely is.

"Maybe you should get it. I really don't mind," Frank says.

"Sorry." I stand and head into the kitchen. Times like this make me wish I wasn't too cheap to pay for caller ID. I put my hand on the receiver and pray that the person on the other end is anyone but Cliff. "Hello?"

"What took you so long to pick up?" *Another unanswered prayer.*

"What do you want?" I say in a hushed voice.

"Why are you whispering? Is someone there?" I can tell Cliff has been drinking.

"None of your business. Either way, I can't talk right now. *Please* stop calling."

"Who's over? Is it the same guy as last time? Look, I just want to talk. I miss you. I need to see you."

"*No*. Not gonna happen. I'm hanging up now. *Do not* call back."

"I swear I'll come over if you hang up on me again."

I'm about to respond when I notice Frank standing in the doorway.

"Chloe? Are you there?"

Click. I unplug the phone. "I'm so sorry. That was . . ."

"Chloe, you don't need to tell me anything. Don't worry about it. Look, this has nothing to do with your phone call, but I have to get going."

I look at the clock. It's just after eight. "Oh, okay."

"I need to call my daughter before she goes to bed, and I forgot my phone."

"You can use my phone."

"That's really nice of you, but I don't think that would be a good idea. I would get the third degree from her mom wondering where I'm calling from. Trust me. This has nothing to do with the call you were on or anything else. Scouts honor." He holds up three fingers.

"I understand. Let me walk you downstairs." I remove his coat from a kitchen chair and hand it to him.

As we make our way down, I feel nervous for the first time tonight. *Does he really have to call his daughter? Did he really forget his phone? How much of my conversation with Cliff did he hear? What if Cliff does come over? What if he gets here when Frank is leaving?*

I open the door and lean against it, waiting for him to pass. "Thanks for coming over. It was fun."

"I had a good time too. Thank you for having me. So, you'll let me know about Wednesday?"

"Yeah, I'll call or email you by Tuesday."

"Sounds good."

Frank starts leaning in for a hug, so I follow his lead. But as soon as our faces are within an inch of each other, he tilts his head for a kiss. Startled, I jerk away. Within seconds, I realize what I've done and feel like a complete idiot. *Why didn't I just kiss him?*

He holds the pose for a split second and then straightens back up slowly. I expect things to be awkward, but instead, he laughs. "I'm sorry. It's been a while. I guess my ability to read signals is a bit rusty. Can I get that hug?"

"Absolutely." Now I really wish I had kissed him when I had the chance.

"Bye, Chloe. I'll talk to you soon." With one last wave, Frank is gone.

∽

Before I tidy up and get ready for bed, I check my cell phone to see if Cliff has called. I'm also curious to see if Jess and Drew tried to call.

Nothing. I consider plugging my home phone back in just in case Jess tries to call, but decide it's not worth risking being woken up in the middle of the night by Cliff.

I haven't heard from Drew at all since last night. I wonder if he has tried calling, but my attempts to avoid Cliff left him unable to reach me as well. Or maybe he's decided to just stick with Jessica and give up on me. It would probably be for the best, considering I've already made up my mind that it would not be wise for us to continue seeing each other. The more I think about Drew's relationship with Jessica, the less attracted to him I feel. In fact, I even feel kind of bitter about the fact that he led me to believe we were learning to navigate the world of online dating together. Plus, he would never be able to hang out with my friends again. Well, not Shelly anyway—she wouldn't spend time with him again if I paid her. I guess it's a good thing that he hasn't called. Maybe Drew and I are thinking the same thing: that we can just move on quietly and spare each other a final awkward goodbye.

chapter twenty-two

I open my eyes in a panic when I realize the sun is peeking through my blinds. Relief sets in when I see that it's only six forty-five. My alarm is not set to go off for another fifteen minutes.

I hop out of bed and raise the blinds completely, flooding my bedroom with light. I fall back onto the bed and lay with my arms spread snow-angel-style. Eyes closed, I mentally prepare for the day ahead. Even though it's Thanksgiving week, I still intend to make my kids work. Of course, that can be quite a challenge when their minds are daydreaming of turkey, pie and an extra two days off from school.

Just before the alarm sounds, it occurs to me that I'm in a great mood. Maybe it's the excessive amount of sunlight this morning, but I feel ready to forget about Cliff, Drew, and anything else that has been giving me a headache lately.

I'm ready to leave for work fifteen minutes earlier than normal, so I decide to turn on my cell phone to see if Jess has called yet. To my surprise, I have five new messages.

Sure enough, the first one is from Jess. "Hey, Chloe." I can tell that she's been crying. "I'm so sorry for not answering or returning your calls. I'm just so embarrassed. Ned and I are done. Like, for good this time. I already found people to cover my flights for the next two days, so call me whenever you can. I promise I'll answer. Bye."

The second message is from Drew. "Hi, Chloe. It's Drew. But I'm sure you already figured that out. Just calling to say hi and see how your day was. I did the usual. Way to go, Pack! Anyway, give me a call back tonight if you want. I'll be up for another hour or so. Talk to you soon."

The third message is no one. Well, it is someone, but whoever it was decided to breathe for a few seconds into a voicemail message and then hang up. I'm guessing it was Cliff.

The fourth message is from Drew. *Again.* "Hey, Chloe. I'm sorry to call again, but your home phone just keeps ringing for some reason. Just wanted to let you know in case something is wrong with your line. It's Drew, by the way." For some reason, I don't buy his reason for calling again.

As I move on to the fifth message, I have a sinking feeling that I know who it is. Normally, my money would be on Cliff, but not today. "Chloe, it's just me again. I can't sleep. I have to be honest with you. I'm so incredibly worried that I ruined things between us. You know, with this whole Jessica thing—which really isn't a *thing* at all—and with the way everything went last night. I hope we can still continue spending time together. I know we're not a couple or anything like that, but I can't help but feel like we're on the verge of breaking up or something. I won't call you again, promise. But please call me when you get a chance. I hope to hear from you soon. Bye."

Based on Drew's messages, I'm now thinking that Shelly's warnings about him may not have been that far off base. The word neurotic came to mind when listening to his final message. Goose bumps actually formed on my forearms when I heard it was him again. The last thing I want to do is call back, but I'm worried that he won't keep his promise to not call me again if I don't respond soon. I'm also worried that letting go of Drew might not be so simple if he has anything to say about it—which he clearly does.

As an added ray of sunshine, I find a note from Cliff on my windshield. It's written on a stained cardboard Jim Beam coaster.

Dear Chloe,

I'm not giving up on us. I love you too much.

Cliff

So much for peace of mind.

chapter twenty-three

I return Jess's call during my lunch break, but it goes straight to voicemail. "Hey, Jess. I hope everything is okay. Just returning your call. If you can call me back within the next fifteen minutes, I should have time to talk. Otherwise, I'll call you after work. And, hey, whatever caused your argument with Ned, please don't beat yourself up over it. He's just not worth it. I'll talk to you soon. Bye."

I use the rest of my lunch break to take care of other personal business. I email my sister to see what her plans are for Friday night. After the long flight with the kids, I suspect they will want to just get my niece and nephew to bed and relax. If that's the case, I can have dinner with Frank. It crosses my mind that maybe I should email my brother too, but I decide it doesn't really matter what his plans are. Plus, I'd rather use the time I have left to log into my Personals account. Since last night, I've received three emails notifying me of new messages.

When I see who *all* of those messages are from, my entire body tenses up. I feel myself losing my appetite. Every single one is from Drew. I stare at the screen, shocked. Not wanting to believe that Drew is going "Fatal Attraction" on me, I try to think of a reasonable explanation for these messages. *Maybe his computer froze up and he accidentally hit send three times. Maybe there's something wrong with the Yahoo! Personals site, causing old messages to pop up as new. Maybe Jessica hacked into Drew's account and is trying to make him look like a lunatic.* I hover over the first message, not yet mentally prepared to read it. I'm about to click, but then the bell rings. Looks like I'm going to have to wait until after school to find out just how fatal Drew's attraction to me really is.

As soon as I walk my students to their bus lines, I bolt back to the classroom. A mandatory staff meeting is starting in fifteen minutes, so I need to read Drew's messages fast. Message one was delivered shortly after the first voicemail he left me last night.

Dear Chloe,

I'm writing because I need to get some things off of my chest. I know I won't be able to sleep otherwise. It just kills me to think that this whole Jessica thing might ruin things between us. You need to know that I have never really been that serious about her. I just never wanted to hurt her feelings. I realize now though that she needs to know the truth even if it hurts her. I promise that I intend to let her know how I feel very soon. I don't want to drop it all on her at once though. Please understand. As far as we're concerned, I hope we can just pretend that Jessica doesn't exist and go back to the way our relationship was before I told you about her. I know there's something special between us, and I know you feel the same way.

Respectfully yours,
Drew

Message two was left ten minutes after message one.

Chloe,

I just left you a message on your cell but thought I better tell you here too that your home phone isn't working. It just keeps ringing and ringing. I hope everything is okay. I also hope you're not avoiding me. I noticed that you logged into your account today, so I know you could have messaged me if you wanted to. I don't want to sound paranoid but what's going on with us? Are you still upset about Jessica? Or does Shelly not approve of me? (She was pretty rude to me last night.) I'm sorry if I'm being too forward. I just want to figure out what's going on with us. Please call or email soon.

Drew

I'm beginning to wish that I never met Drew when I see that the third message was delivered close to one in the morning.

Hey Chloe,

Sure enough, I can't sleep. All I can do is think about how I screwed everything up between us. I've decided that I'm going to tell Jessica about us tomorrow. Or, actually, it would be today. That's how serious I am about patching things up between us. I'm willing to give up my relationship with Jessica even if there's a chance you and I might not even end up together. I hope you can see now how much I value our relationship. I'll call you tonight after I talk to her. Okay?

Drew

I can't believe this is happening. Shelly was right. There's definitely something wrong with Drew. Never in my wildest dreams would I have pegged him for a closet nut job though.

I'm barely able to concentrate during the staff meeting because I can't stop wondering who I should be more worried about, Cliff or Drew?

What have I gotten myself into?

chapter twenty-four

I'm just sitting down for some tuna casserole when my cell rings. After seeing who it is, I breathe a sigh of relief and answer. "Jess?"

"Hey. I tried to call your home phone, but it just kept ringing. Is your machine off?"

"Nope. The phone is unplugged."

"Why?"

"Long story. Can we talk about what's going on with you and Ned first?"

"I guess. But there's not much to talk about. We're done."

"Well, what happened? I'm sorry I didn't know what to say the other night. You kind of put me on the spot though. Why did you want me to tell him I was with you? Who were you really with?"

"Give me a break, would you? I had to suffer through hours of Ned interrogating me. Now you want to interrogate me too?"

I fight the urge to ask her what the fuck her problem is, deciding to take a different approach instead. I can only imagine the torture Ned put her through, but she doesn't get to take that out on me. "You give me a break, Jess. I'm not interrogating you. I just want to know what's going on. If you don't want to tell me, fine. But don't be a bitch just because you're upset about Ned."

The line is silent for a moment and then Jess sniffles. "Chloe . . ." She's sobbing now. "I really fucked up this time."

And now I feel guilty . . . "Jess, please don't cry. What happened?"

"Well, remember that night we went to The Hangar?"

"Yeah. The night I met all those work friends of yours, right?"

"Mmhm. Do you remember that pilot I introduced you to?"

"I think so. Brant, right?"

"Yeah. Well, I was with him."

"What were you doing with him?" I realize how stupid my question is the second I ask it. I already know what they were doing. "Wait. Isn't he married?" I could care less that she cheated on Ned. It's about time she did something to get rid of him. But if Brant is married, the rest of this conversation is not going to be pleasant. Jess's father cheated on her mother, and I've had to listen to my mother's suspicions about my father since I was seven. Messing around with a married man is *not* cool in my book. I always assumed Jess was on the same page.

"Jess. Isn't he married?" I ask louder this time.

"Yes."

"Well, that's really shitty."

Her crying intensifies. "I know."

I'm so incredibly angry with her, but the sound of her tears convinces me to back off. At least for now. She's too distraught for me to lay in on her for being a damn mistress just yet. "All right, so, that's why things are over with you and Ned? You told him about Brant?"

"Not exactly."

"What do you mean?"

"Well, we actually made up on Saturday night—somehow I got him to overlook the inconsistencies in my cover story for Friday. But he went right back to interrogating me on Sunday morning. We got into another huge fight. Like a screaming and swearing and name-calling kind of fight. One of my neighbors even knocked on the door to see if everything was okay."

"Nosy Nancy?"

"No. It wasn't even her. It was that guy who never says hi. The one who looks like Anderson Cooper."

"Oh, my God. It *must* have been bad. What happened?"

"So, anyway, after Ned told me his mother was right about me and called me a lying slut, he stormed out. I don't know why I did it, but I called Brant. Actually, you know what? I do know why I called him. Because he makes me feel good about myself. Anyway, Brant came over and we started to fool around. And wouldn't you know it, for the first time *ever*, Ned came back to apologize. Needless to say, he let himself in." I gasp. "And there you have it. We're done."

"He walked in on you guys?"

"Yeah."

"Shit." Even though I can't stand Ned, I still feel bad for him. The guy walked in on his girlfriend screwing another guy. He may be a dick, but it still had to hurt. "Then what happened?"

"Nothing. Brant jumped up out of bed and . . ."

"Was he completely naked?"

"Well, yeah. Anyway, I was expecting Ned to charge at him or something. But Ned just removed my key from his key chain, threw it at me and left."

"Did you try to call him?"

"Yes, but he didn't answer."

"And what about Brant? Was he pissed?"

"No. Why would he be pissed? He knew about Ned."

"Oh, right. Well, maybe this is for the best. I mean, you weren't exactly happy with Ned, right? Otherwise, none of this would have happened."

"It still feels pretty shitty."

"Yeah, I know." I want to ask if she plans to see Brant again, but decide it might be best to wait until everything with Ned blows over. "So you called in sick for tomorrow too?"

"Don't remind me. Now I'm probably going to just sit around feeling sorry for myself. Hey, do you feel like getting a drink?"

"Now?"

"Well, not now, but maybe a little later."

"I can't. I have to work tomorrow, and I have class."

"So, I guess you can't tomorrow night either?" I don't want Jess to feel lonely because I know that could drive her to call Ned, but going out would be a really bad idea.

"I'm sorry, Jess."

"Don't worry about it. Enough about me. Let's talk about you. Why is your phone unplugged?"

I fill Jess in on everything that Shelly and I talked about on the way home from the bar on Saturday night. She thinks Shelly is being dramatic, as usual, but then reconsiders her stance when I describe Drew's voicemail messages and emails.

"Well, that changes things. God, I thought he was just a little insecure, but now he sounds kind of crazy. So now what? You're just going to keep your phone unplugged and hope he goes away?"

"I don't know. Maybe."

"Well, don't answer your door either unless you know who it is. Actually, you know what? Maybe this is a good thing."

"What, that the first guy I sort of liked from online is acting like a stalker?"

"No. That this might help you get rid of Cliff too. Two birds, one stone."

"Very funny."

"I'm not trying to be funny. I'm serious."

I sigh. "You know, for two intelligent women, we sure have pretty messed up love lives."

"Chloe, it's not our fault. It's because of all these messed up guys." She laughs, and I do too, but deep down I know the guys are not the only ones to blame.

chapter twenty-five

"Happy Thanksgiving, Ms. Thompson!" Students wave from the bus. A few tiny hands are even braving the cold as they stick out of the windows to ensure being seen. I smile and wave back enthusiastically.

I've been looking forward to the next four days since the school year began. Finally, a break. I scurry out of the cold and into the warm building. I have a little over an hour before either of my siblings' flights are scheduled to land, so my plan is to finish prepping lesson materials for the following week and see if I have any new messages.

I made a pact with myself on Monday night to not check my email or Personals account until today. I assume that no calls on my cell from Drew for the last two days has to be a good sign. Nothing from Cliff either. But who knows what kind of ridiculous emails might await me.

As I switch books out at literacy stations, I think about Frank. When I called to let him know that my sister's flight wouldn't get in until five twenty and my brother's was closer to six, he offered to bring dinner to my place at seven. I started to feel kind of bad about ditching my family for a date, but then I remembered that I was going to be with them *all* day Thursday. Plus, my sister did say they would be too tired to do anything after flying with the kids anyway.

At five, I sit down at my desk and take one last overall inventory of the classroom. Then I log in to my Personals account. There's nothing from Drew, but I have two icebreakers and a poke. One of the icebreakers is from a 48-year-old guy who already poked me last week. I'm certain my mother would disown me if I showed up with someone old enough to be my father. The other icebreaker is from

DangerouslyHandsome01. I click to see his profile and find myself staring at an out-of-focus photo. *Wait a second.* I enlarge the photo but have to squint because it's still not very clear. Then I realize the face staring out from under the rim of a baseball cap looks familiar. *Scott. You have got to be kidding me.* Why on Earth would he send me an icebreaker? Does he think I'm not going to recognize him just because he changed his profile picture? What a weirdo!

I delete Scott's icebreaker and move on to the poke from NiceGuy26.

NiceGuy26 – 26
Location: Racine
Sincerely Seeking a Special Someone

Relationship Status: Single, Never Married
Kids: No
Want Kids: Yes
Ethnicity: White / Caucasian
Body type: Athletic
Height: 5' 8"
Religion: Catholic
Politics: Middle of the Road
Smoke: No
Drink: Social Drinker
Pets: No
Education: Bachelor's +
Employment: Student
Income: Less than 20,000

Two things stand out on NiceGuy's profile: his height and the fact that he's a student. My parameters for height are set at five-nine or taller, and my employment parameters are set to deliver matches with careers. I'm about to delete the profile, but then a little voice in my head says, *stop being so picky*! I click to enlarge NiceGuy's profile picture. He's wearing a baseball cap backwards and a light blue polo shirt. I can tell that the photo was taken at the Milwaukee County Zoo in front of the Humboldt penguin exhibit. Clearly, I've been on way too many field trips to the zoo. By the look of the stubble on his face, it appears that he may have been on day three or four without a shave, which I find kind of sexy. He has piercing blue eyes and is holding a stuffed tiger. I don't have time to type out a response, so I simply poke NiceGuy back.

As I enter the password to my email inbox, my sister calls.

"You made it!"

Sarah lets out a long, tired sigh. "A little early—thank God—but it'll probably take us about twenty minutes to get our luggage. Are you just going to drive through?"

"Actually, Jim's flight is supposed to arrive in like fifteen minutes, so I thought I'd just park and come in."

"Chloe, didn't you talk to mom? His flight was delayed. He's not getting in until seven twenty now."

"Oh, all right. Well, I'll just get you guys then and take you to mom and Glen's. Someone can pick up Jim later, right?"

"I'm not sure. We'll figure it out."

"Okay. How was my little buddy on the flight?"

"Dave was great. He took a nap and . . ."

"Not *Dave*. *Simon*. You're such a dork."

Sarah laughs, and my brother-in-law Dave yells in the background. "Hey, how's my favorite sister-in-law?"

"Tell him I said hi," I say.

"Chloe says hi," I hear Sarah say in the background. Then she says, "Simon was perfect. Sadie was great too. They're both tired though."

"Well, tell those two little monkeys I'm on my way."

"K. See you soon."

The airport is only about five minutes from my school, so I have a little time to finish checking my email. The contents of my inbox turn my stomach. The majority of the sixteen new messages are from Drew. Note to self: never give your personal email address to an online match again. I click on the first one, expecting to see at least a few sentences, but all it says is: *Chloe, why are you ignoring me?* I skip to Drew's next message. *Chloe, please call me.* Every single message contains just one sentence. Taken individually, the messages seem perfectly normal, but because there are ten of them, they are downright creepy. Instead of deleting them, I create a new folder and label it *Deranged Drew*.

～

My brother-in-law waves as I pull over outside door six of the baggage claim. I've known Dave since he and Sarah were middle school classmates. I was only six when I first met him, but I remember wishing he was my brother instead of Jim. Jim was always so mean to me, but Dave was always kind. Whenever he saw me, he would give me high fives and gum and pull quarters out of my ears. I swear, Dave still has the same chipper demeanor he had back when he was thirteen. I hop out and give him a hug before I start helping him load their suitcases into the trunk.

"Hey, Chloe. How's everything going?"

I shrug. "Work is great. My thesis proposal just got approved. Things are . . . good. Where are Sarah and . . ."

"Ahn Co-ee! Ahn Co-ee!" My two-year-old niece Sadie runs toward me.

I pick her up and swing her around. "Hi Sweetie! Aunt Chloe missed you!" Then I see my sister and my nephew.

Still holding Sadie, I bend down to pick up Simon too, but he says, "Aunt Chloe, I'm not a baby like Sadie."

"Oh, right. I almost forgot. You're a big four-year-old now, huh?" I put my hand up and he jumps to give me a high five.

"Chlo-eee!" My sister squeezes me tight.

Dave takes Sadie from me and scoops Simon up too. "C'mon ladies. It's frickin' freezing out here. Let's get going."

We all get into the car and begin the fifteen-minute drive to my parents' house.

"I'm glad you guys are here. The flight was good?"

"Yeah, it went pretty smooth," Sarah says from the passenger seat. "So, you said on the phone earlier that you have a date tonight. Someone new?"

"His name is Frank. He's . . ." I still have not told my sister that I'm online dating.

"Wait. Frank isn't code for Cliff, is it?" Sarah asks. Dave stifles a laugh. I glare at him in the rearview mirror.

"No. Why would you even say something like that? I told you, Cliff and I are done." Sarah gives me a look that says she doesn't believe me. "I'm serious. It's been like an entire month since I've spoken to him." As soon as the lie escapes my lips, I hope that my mother doesn't mention I recently admitted seeing him.

"All right, if you say so. Anyway, where did you meet this Frank guy?"

My chest tightens as I desperately try to come up with a plausible answer. Why didn't I think something up ahead of time? Sarah is about to speak again when Simon pipes in.

"Aunt Chloe?"

Thank God for Simon. "Yeah, buddy?"

"Is Frank a loser?"

"What?"

"You know, like Cliff. Mom and dad said that you only like . . ."

"Simon!" Sarah turns in her seat to face him. "What have daddy and I told you about our private conversations?"

"What mommy? I don't want Aunt Chloe to marry a loser."

"Hey, Simon, look, it's the State Fair! Remember the cows and pigs we saw there?" I glare at Dave in the rearview as he tries to distract my outspoken nephew.

Sarah looks at me. "Chloe. I'm sorry. He . . ."

I cut her off. "I need to concentrate on the road," I say.

I don't even go inside to say "hi" to my parents when I drop my sister and her family off. I help them carry their bags to the porch, kiss my niece and nephew, and leave without even asking who's going to pick up my brother. They can figure it out themselves.

～

Thanks to the unfortunate turn of events in the car, I have enough time to stop and pick up some wine before Frank is supposed to arrive. Unfortunately, a long line at the liquor store puts me behind schedule. I speed home, hoping Frank will be a little late too, but he's already parked out front when I get there.

Chinese food in hand, Frank is quick to hop out of his car to open the car door for me. "Hi." I say, smiling. "You're too sweet. Thank you."

"No problem." He returns my smile and looks even more attractive than the last time I saw him.

"Sorry I'm late." I hold up a bottle of wine in each hand.

"Well, you're forgiven. But only because you got two bottles of red." He puts his empty hand on the small of my back for a moment as we walk.

When we arrive at the door to my apartment, I see that there's a note taped to it and my heart begins to race. With one glance, I recognize Cliff's handwriting. I reach up quickly to pull it off the door but can't get a good grip with the bottle of wine in my hand, so the note slips between my fingers and stays put.

"Let me get that for you." Frank pulls the note from the door. He briefly looks at it and then meets my eyes. "Sorry. I shouldn't have . . ." He takes a bottle of wine and hands me the note in return. Whatever he saw has clearly made him uncomfortable.

I shove the note into a pocket and open the door. "I'm starving. What did you get?" I say, as if Cliff's note isn't even on my mind.

"General Tso's chicken—extra spicy—and steamed Chinese vegetables." He starts removing white cardboard containers from the carryout bag. "I remember you saying how much you like spicy food."

"Really? Good memory. And I love General Tso's chicken too."

I wash my hands and grab a couple of plates and forks. Frank gets wine glasses out of the built-in China cabinet in my kitchen as if he has done it a dozen times. It has only been a week since we met, yet his presence already feels natural.

Our conversation during dinner could not be better. We start by talking about the basics—family, friends and work—but then we move on to things like drunken college regrets and favorite Saturday morning cartoons from when we were kids. It almost feels like I'm talking to Shelly or Jess. Before we know it, it's close to nine.

"Do you want more?" Frank holds up the unopened bottle of wine.

"Sure. But only if you help me finish it." I smile one of the most sincere smiles I've smiled in a very long time. I genuinely like Frank. And it has more to do with his amazing personality than anything else. "I just have to use the bathroom first."

As I sit on the toilet, I remember Cliff's note. I take it out of my pocket and uncrumple it. Then I recrumple it and toss it into the garbage. I don't care anymore about anything Cliff has to say.

When I flush the toilet, I think I hear the muffled sound of a phone ringing but decide it's just the wine's doing. When I open the door though, I hear the sound of my own voice. It can't be. Shit. I scurry into the kitchen, but it's too late.

I frantically push buttons on my answering machine, but the recording won't stop. The cordless handset isn't there for me to answer either. *"Chloe, it's Drew. Jessica and I are done. You know I broke up with her for you, so what the hell . . ."* As I stand there, eyes closed, picturing myself yanking that piece of electronic crap right off the wall and throwing it on the floor, someone knocks. I open the door and find myself face to face with my landlord, who's chipper as ever. "Hey, Chloe! I hope you don't mind. Your friend plugged in your phone because I asked to borrow it. Something is wrong with our line and I had to find my cell." Deena hands me my phone. "Someone called you by the way." She tilts her head, looking concerned. "Are you okay? You look kind of pale."

No, I'm not okay. Do you have any idea what you have done? I suppose you're the one who let Cliff tape a fucking note to my door too. "Yeah, I'm fine. Did you find your phone?"

She laughs. "It was in the fridge. Can you believe that? I have no idea what I was thinking. Well, have a good night. Tell your friend thanks."

"Yep, I will. You have a good night too."

Frank looks up at me when I enter the living room. His expression is hard to read. He doesn't look mad, but I'm certain that he isn't happy either.

"Sorry it took me so long," I say.

"Oh, don't worry about it." He takes a sip of wine and then returns to looking at the floor.

"That call. That was embarrassing. I'm sorry."

"No. I'm sorry. I shouldn't have plugged your phone in. I should have assumed there was a good reason why you had it unplugged."

"Frank. *You* are not the one who should be sorry."

"But I am. I'm sorry because I really like you. And I'm sorry because I can't do this."

"What do you mean?" My heart feels like it's going to explode.

"I think you have *a lot* of unfinished business that needs to be worked out." He nods toward the phone. "I have a daughter. I can't . . ." He puts his wine on the table and leans his head back against the futon. Both hands rest on his forehead.

I'm afraid to say anything because there's a good chance I might burst into tears if I do. I want to put my arms around him and kiss him before I never get the chance to. But I fear he would reject me, so I stay put.

"Frank, you don't understand."

"You're right. I don't understand what's going on with you and these guys, and to be honest, I wish it didn't matter to me. But the reason why Kaitlyn's mom and I couldn't make it work is because she had an ex who wouldn't stay away. It was just too hard to deal with. I can't get involved with another situation like that."

The temptation to tell him everything that has happened with Drew and about how hard I've been trying to get rid of Cliff is strong. I want to tell him because I want to vent my frustrations to someone, but most of all I don't want him to leave. I don't want him to walk out of my apartment, and I certainly don't want him to walk out of my life for good. But the fear I have of making a fool of myself is too strong, so I swallow the words that are on the tip of my tongue.

Frank stands. "I should go."

I'm about to follow him downstairs, but he looks at me and says, "Chloe, I'll let myself out. Okay?" Then he turns and disappears down the stairs.

I stand there in the hallway outside of my apartment and listen as the downstairs door closes. Then there's nothing but silence.

Before I crawl into bed, I dig Cliff's note out of the bathroom garbage.

Dear Chloe,

I'm ready to be everything you need me to be.
I won't give up on us. Please call.

Love Always,
Cliff

There was a time when my heart would have melted over these

words from Cliff, but seeing them now really pisses me off. Why all of a sudden does he want to work on our relationship? And why did he have to tape a note to my door today of all days? Who the hell even gave him the tape? I rip the note into tiny pieces and toss them into the garbage.

What the hell is wrong with me? Why am I so drawn to these men who fill my life with chaos?

As I drift off to sleep, a thought occurs to me. With Matt and James, there was comfort. Peace. Sure, I never felt much passion for them, but at least life was easy. Now, I seem to be chasing that head-over-heels passion that just blows up in the end.

Will there ever be a happy medium? Or am I forever going to be forced to choose between passion and security?

chapter twenty-six

After a fitful night of sleep, I crawl out of bed on Thanksgiving morning feeling groggy and unmotivated. It's close to ten, but the sky is dreary—just like my mood—so it seems much earlier. I stand next to my bed, wishing that I could just crawl right back under the covers and sleep the day away. But I said I would arrive at my parents' house before noon, which means I've actually got to pull it together.

After dragging myself into the bathroom, I stare at my reflection in the mirror instead of hopping right into the shower. My eyes are puffy from crying. It's an image that reminds me I'm back to square one with online dating. I know now that this process is not as easy as I was led to believe.

I glance down at the garbage and see Cliff's shredded note. I pick the can up and walk it into the kitchen, feeling a spark of . . . *something* forming in my chest.

Resolution? Strength?

Whatever it is, I stomp my foot down to open the lid of the kitchen garbage bin and add the trash from the bathroom.

That's it, I'm done. Quit feeling sorry for yourself, Chloe. Time to move on.

I swear, if I have to move to get away from these guys, I will. But they won't keep me from finding someone better.

My brother is pacing outside my parents' house and smoking a cigarette when I arrive. He has been a smoker for twenty-plus years but is constantly going through the process of "quitting." Coming for a visit usually screws up any success he may be experiencing at the time.

When he sees me pull into the driveway, he stops pacing. I wave, but he just stares and continues taking short, frequent puffs of his cigarette. That's my brother in a nutshell: serious and aloof. My sister, on the other hand, would be waving and possibly jumping up and down simply at the sight of me. You've got to love the differences between siblings.

"Hey, Jim. Happy Thanksgiving!" I say as I close my car door.

"Happy Thanksgiving." He continues to puff on his cigarette.

I approach, arms open for a hug, but my brother makes no motion to hug me until my arms are already around him. Then, without warning, he picks me up and nearly squeezes the life out of me. "Ow! Okay, okay. Enough." He puts me down, grinning deviously. "Can't you ever just give me a *normal* hug the way a *normal* brother would?"

"No." He's back to puffing the cigarette.

"So what time did you finally get in?"

"Eight."

"That sucks. Who picked you up?"

"Glen. Even though *you* were supposed to pick me up. *Spazz*." He has been calling me Spazz for as long as I can remember.

"Well, I had plans. And why am I always expected to pick you and Sarah up? Just because I live close to the airport? I still have to drive all the way over here and back." The way he just stares at me as he continues to smoke would make most people uncomfortable, but I'm used to it. "Whatever. I'll see you inside."

"Okay," he says in a somewhat pleasant voice, likely because he's glad I'm done talking to him.

I'm greeted by the aroma of turkey upon entering the house. No one is in the kitchen, but it's clear that some serious cooking has been going on.

"Happy Thanksgiving!" I say as I enter the living room.

"Aunt Chloe!" Simon runs to me, followed by Sadie.

Everyone, except for my mother, delivers a Thanksgiving Day greeting in return. Instead, she says, "It's about time you got here. Why are you so late? You didn't let that guy sleep over, did you?"

"Mom," I snap, eyes wide. Simon and Sadie didn't hear her though, as they have turned their attention back to the Macy's Thanksgiving Day Parade.

"Anyway," Sarah says. "How was your night? Did you like him?"

"It was fine." I move over to the snack table and load up a plate with summer sausage, cheese and crackers.

"*Just* fine? Are you going to see him again?" Sarah presses on. My mom, Glen and Dave appear to be watching the parade with the kids, but I suspect they all have one ear on our conversation, especially my mom.

"I'm not sure." I figure that being vague eliminates the need for me to go into great detail about Frank. If I say yes, then she's sure to grill me on every last detail about him. If I tell the truth, then she will want to know why I'm not going to see him again. I just don't feel like getting into any of it. It's all still a little too raw.

"Oh, okay." Sarah pops a black olive into her mouth. I know her well enough to know that she's not quite ready to move on to a new subject. Otherwise, she would be jabbering about something else already.

"So, where did you say you met this guy?"

"Frank," I say. "His name is Frank."

"Oh. Sorry. Where did you meet *Frank*?" Sarah has a sly grin on her face, and my mom is sitting down at the dining room table next to where we're standing. Dave, too, has decided to join us at the snack table.

I look from Sarah to my mom and sense that they have already discussed how Frank and I met. "Well, I'm guessing you already know how I met him, right?"

"What do you mean? You haven't been telling me a whole lot about what's going on in your life lately, so how would I know?" she says.

"Okay. Enough dancing around the subject." Dave's mouth is full of food. "Chloe, I think it's great that you're online dating. What better way is there to line 'em up and sift through 'em until you find one that's perfect for your mom and sister?" He shakes his head at Sarah. Then he heads over to the liquor cabinet.

"Thanks a lot, mom." I sit down across from her knowing that I'm in for a *long* discussion.

"What? You thought your sister wasn't going to find out anyway?"

"Uh, no. How would she? Besides, that's not the point. I wanted to tell her myself. That's why I asked you not to say anything."

"Well, now she knows." My mom looks at Sarah. "Now, tell your sister she's never going to meet anyone as nice as Matt online."

I groan. "Hey, Dave, can you please make me one of those?"

"See, Sarah. I told you. She's been drinking a lot more and going out with so many different Yahoo! guys. Don't you think it's a little early for vodka, Chloe?" My mother's accusatory tone is like nails on a chalkboard.

"Are you kidding me? Dave is having a drink. And I bet all of you had mimosas with breakfast."

Finally, Sarah decides to rejoin the conversation. "Actually, mom, I think online dating is a good option for Chloe."

My mom and I nearly snap our necks as we turn our heads to look at Sarah. "What?" we say in unison.

Sarah looks at my mom. "Clearly, Chloe is *not* getting back together with Matt," she looks at me for a second as she says, "or James." Then she looks back at my mom. "I've heard good things from some of the girls at the gym about online dating. There are *a lot* of guys to choose from, so maybe all of the options will help Chloe figure out what she's looking for."

"Hmph. Even if she does find someone as good as Matt, she'll probably dump him too. So, on top of it being unsafe, it's a waste of money in my opinion."

"Hello? You guys are talking about me like I'm not even here! And I never asked for your opinion, mom."

My brother appears, beer in hand. "What are we talking about—Chloe's virtual love life?"

I want to scream, but instead, I put my head down on the table.

"What do you mean, *love*?" My mom says. "She isn't going to find *love* online. She had somebody who loved her, but she threw that away."

That's it. I've had it. I stand up to give my mother a piece of my mind. "*Love*? You want to talk about *love*? You have a man right over there who loves you, and you treat *him* like crap!" Then I turn to face my brother. "And you. Your *wife* is married to someone else! Don't make fun of me for using a dating system that's going to help me avoid the married ones. Maybe *you* should give it a try." Then I look at Sarah, but before I can say anything to her, she's trying to diffuse the situation.

"Calm down, Chloe! Why are you so upset? We just care about you and want you to find someone who's good for you."

"Well, what do you think I'm trying to do? Don't you think I want to find the same thing?" As I speak, she shakes her head. "What? Why are you shaking your head?"

"Because you had a good guy. In fact, you had two of them."

"You guys think I don't know that Matt and James were good guys? There are a lot of good guys out there. I'm not just looking for a good guy though. Just because someone is a *good* guy doesn't mean I'm going to fall in love with him. Maybe this won't make sense to you or mom, but I want to be in love with the person I spend the rest of my life with."

"Ouch," Jim says. And for once, my mom says nothing.

Sarah stares at me, knowing I'm insinuating she's not in love with Dave. I deeply regret the words as soon as I say them, but I know there's some truth there as well. They don't get it. My mom once told me that the key to a good marriage was marrying someone who loves me more than I love him. She also said it was okay to not love the person you marry as long as you know he's going to be faithful and a good provider. Sometimes I wonder if my sister took my mother's words to heart when she married Dave. He had a crush on her from the moment they met, but for years Sarah seemed disinterested in him. Dave just kept on being the best friend he could be to her though. But when she became engaged to her high school boyfriend, Dave disappeared for a while. It wasn't until years after college and after she had been through a long stretch of failed relationships that they reconnected. She was feeling defeated when she ran into him in a bar. The comfort and familiarity of being around him led them straight into bed, and she ended up pregnant with Simon shortly after.

I honestly think it's the best thing that ever happened to Sarah, but somehow she's forgotten how she ended up with the "perfect" husband and family.

I glance over at Dave to make sure he hasn't been listening in on our argument. To my relief, he has Simon on his back and is crawling around like a horse. Glen is sitting in the La-Z-Boy and is bopping Sadie up and down on his knee. They are oblivious to how heated things have become around the table where we will enjoy Thanksgiving dinner in just a few hours.

I expect the argument to continue, but to my surprise, Mom gets up and says, "Well, I better peel the potatoes. Come on, Jim, why don't you help me?"

Before Jim disappears after my mother into the kitchen, he turns and says, "And for the record, Chloe, I couldn't care less *who* you date. You could be a lesbian for all I care, as long as you're happy. *Spazz*."

Sarah is watching Dave play with Simon. She looks dismayed, but then she smiles and turns to face me. "So, how about you show me how this online dating thing works?"

"Really?"

She takes my hand and pulls me up out of my seat. "Yeah, come on. Let's go."

And with that, everything is back to "normal." One thing I can say for our family is that we have always been good about bouncing back quickly after a disagreement. I do love my sister, and it means a lot to me that she's at least trying to be open-minded.

As Sarah and I head downstairs so I can show her all of the *good* guys who are waiting for me to find them online, I secretly pray there won't be any new messages from Drew.

chapter twenty-seven

Jess calls as I'm headed home from dropping my siblings off at the airport the following Sunday. "Hey, Jess! How was your Thanksgiving?

"It was good, except I ended up leaving my parents' house early for work."

"Why? I thought you were off."

"I was, but I volunteered for extra hours since I didn't work on Monday or Tuesday. I got holiday pay though, so it was worth it."

"That's great!" I know Jess really needs the money, but I can't help but wonder if these extra hours have anything to do with a certain married pilot. I want to ask but don't want to be wrong—especially since she's probably still upset about Ned.

"So, how was your Thanksgiving? Are you still sane after spending so much time with your family? And did you tell your sister about your new dating adventures?"

I laugh. "Thanksgiving was good. A little rocky at first, but everything ended up okay. And no, *I* didn't tell Sarah that I've been online dating. My *mom* did."

"She *didn't*. I told you not to tell your mom about it. I knew she would tell your sister."

"The good news is it turns out Sarah actually thinks it's a good idea."

"No way. She couldn't even handle you dating Cliff just because he's five years younger. I can't believe she's okay with you online dating."

"I know. And you aren't going to believe what I let Sarah, Dave and Jim do."

"What?"

"I let them pick some guys for me to send icebreakers to."

Jess laughs hysterically. "Did your brother actually take it seriously? I can see Dave and Sarah picking someone normal, but your brother?"

"I know. I thought he was going to be a pain in the ass about it, but he actually pointed out a guy who I have a lunch date with on Saturday. I haven't heard back from any of the guys my sister picked though."

"Wait? Did you say you have a lunch date with someone on Saturday?"

"Yep. And I have a dinner date on Wednesday."

"How did that happen so fast? Have you already talked to these guys on the phone?"

"Nope. I hung out with my family all weekend. I didn't even go home—Deena and Mike fed the cats. I just emailed the guys to see if they wanted to get together. I don't feel like wasting any more time. Either I'm going to feel a spark when I meet someone or I'm not. Simple as that."

"So you're just gonna start meeting people right away?"

"Well, yeah. Emails don't reveal anything. And when I think about all those hours I spent on the phone with Drew, well, I just don't want to waste any more time."

"Oh, my God, Chloe. Do you really think that's safe?"

"Why wouldn't it be? I'm meeting them in crowded public places."

"Yeah, but, what if someone tries to follow you home?"

I sigh. "I doubt that will happen. Besides, someone could still try to follow me home after a first date, even if I did talk to him on the phone first. Look at Drew. I spent nearly two months getting to know him by email, on the phone *and* in person, and he's nuts."

"Hey, what's going on with him anyway? Has he called you? And what about that engineer guy?"

I tell Jess about my botched date with Frank. She laughs hysterically when I tell her about Cliff's note *and* Drew's message. I do too. I don't know if it's because the actions of these guys are so over-the-top unbelievable or if it's simply because if I don't laugh I might end up in tears again. But there I am, laughing with her over the one that got away.

"Have you heard from any of them since?"

"Nope. I don't expect to hear from Frank, but I was sure Cliff and Drew would try to call. I'm actually hoping they both might have finally given up."

"Drew's no dummy. He probably went crawling back to Jessica—if he was even being honest about breaking things off with her to begin with. But Cliff, well, you have to admit, Cliff isn't the sharpest tool in the shed. He probably just took the weekend off. He'll be back. Have you told Shelly about all of this yet?"

"No. Her family spent the four-day weekend in the Dells."

"You know she's gonna pull the I-told-you-so card on you about Drew, right?"

"I know. I don't care. I'm just glad it's over. Hey, I gotta go. I've been sitting in my car for like ten minutes. I'll call you Wednesday after my dinner date. Maybe we can get together for a quick drink."

"I can't. I have to work. But call me for sure to tell me about your date."

"I will. Why are you working? You never overnight on Wednesdays."

"I know, but one of the girls who covered for me last week needs me to cover for her."

Again, I wonder if she's still seeing the pilot. "Jess, is there something you're not telling me?"

"No. Why?"

"I don't know. It's just that you haven't mentioned Ned at all, and it seems like you're working a lot of extra hours."

"I didn't mention Ned because I don't want to make myself sad by talking about him, and I've been picking up more hours because Christmas is right around the corner. You want a gift, right?"

"I'm sorry. I shouldn't have brought him up. You just let me know if and when you do want to talk about him. Okay?"

"Okay."

Before I head inside, I grab a stack of mail from my mailbox. It seems like a lot for two days' worth. I realize why when I start sifting through the pile. There are at least four notes from Cliff. This time they are in envelopes, and they appear to be much longer. Instead of reading them, I rip them up and toss them into the trash.

chapter twenty-eight

The Chili's parking lot is surprisingly full for a Wednesday night. NiceGuy26 is meeting me here for dinner. Afterwards, I have plans to catch up with Shelly at the Home Bar. Maybe NiceGuy can join me if things go well.

Aside from the couple of emails we exchanged to set up this dinner date, I know nothing about NiceGuy beyond what is in his profile. He says he's a student, so I really want to know what he's studying. When I first set up my profile, I made up my mind to only date people who were done with college and had an established career. But lately I've been pondering all those parameters I originally set. Maybe all that matters is the big picture, which I've always had a hard time envisioning—things like whether or not the person is driven, regardless of what stage of his schooling or career he happens to be working on. I still don't feel like I'm "established," and I know a lot of people who have degrees and full-time jobs but they still have no idea where they are headed. Jess is a perfect example. So I guess it really might not be all about what I can see on paper.

That's what I'm telling myself anyway.

As I approach the entrance, I have a flashback from my date with Scott, causing me to experience a wave of nausea. Chili's is pretty darn similar to Applebee's. I stop walking for a moment and stare at the pavement as I think about how badly I don't want this date to suck.

When I look up, I see NiceGuy standing at the door waiting for me. I know it's him because he's wearing the same red baseball cap he had on in one of his profile pictures. He even has it on backwards, just like in the photo.

As I approach, he opens the door for me and then rushes to grab the inner door as well. "Here, let me get that one for you, too."

"Why, thank you," I say as we come face-to-face with each other just inside the foyer.

"Hi, Chloe. I'm Sean," he says as we shake hands.

"Hi. Great to meet you." I look over at the hostess, who's smiling at us. I smile back. "Should we put in our names?"

Sean holds up a pager and grins to reveal a dimple on his left cheek. "Already did. Shouldn't be much longer."

I look at my watch. "I'm sorry. Am I late? I thought we planned on six."

"No, no. You're right on time. I just wanted to get here early so we wouldn't have to wait too long." He motions to the bar, exposing a nicely toned forearm. "Do you want to wait at the bar?"

"Sure. Sounds good." As we make our way over to the bar, I take a quick inventory. Sean is on the shorter side. His profile says five foot eight, but he's not much more than a head taller than I am, so he might actually be closer to five foot seven. For a second, I wonder if he lied. I chase the thought away though, reminding myself he's far from unattractive.

There isn't any hair peeking out from under his hat, so I can't tell for sure what color it is, but his facial hair, which appears to be the result of at least five days without a shave, is sandy blonde. I can't help but smile a little because stubble happens to be a real turn on for me. As for his attire, he's wearing jeans and a Cornhuskers T-shirt, but his appearance is clean and athletic. There's a good chance he would catch my eye if we weren't already here together.

The pager goes off as soon as we finish ordering our drinks, so I offer to wait for them and meet Sean at the table. Instead, he hands me the pager and says that he will wait. I take it and smile as I head back to the entrance.

"First date?" The hostess asks as she escorts me to an empty table.

"Yeah. Is it that obvious?"

"No, not just by looking at you two together, but your date was telling us how nervous he was when he first arrived. It was *so* adorable. Do you wanna know what I heard him say to himself when he saw you coming?"

For a second, I wonder if I do or not. "Sure." I finally give in.

"He said, '*Oh my gosh. She's so pretty.*'"

I look at her, surprised. "Really?"

"Yep. He sure did. He seems like a real sweetheart." She gives me a wink and turns to leave just as Sean arrives at our table. Before disappearing for good, she puts a hand on his shoulder and says, "Enjoy your dinner."

"Thanks, Lisa. I appreciate it. You have a good night." Sean slides into the booth and hands me my drink. "Here you go, Chloe." He smiles at me before taking a sip of beer.

"Thanks. Can I give you some money?"

"Absolutely not. Tonight's on me, and so are any future dates we might have—you know, if things go well here tonight. By the way, I hope this doesn't make you feel uncomfortable, but I have to tell you how pretty you look tonight. I mean, I knew you were pretty when I saw your pictures, but they really don't do you justice."

For a moment, I'm speechless because my overly suspicious mind thinks he's being sarcastic or trying to win brownie points in an attempt to get into my pants. But my silence doesn't seem to affect him in the least. He takes another sip of beer and begins scanning the menu.

"Thank you," I say. A little late, but I have to say something in response to his compliment.

He glances up from the menu for a second and laughs but doesn't say anything, so I blabber on. "Took me a while, I know. I'm just not used to receiving compliments like that." *Shut up and just decide what you want to eat, Chloe.*

He closes his menu and looks at me with intense blue eyes. The smile on his face appears to be permanent. It's a subtle, sweet smile though—not the slightest hint of crazy. "Well, you're welcome."

The conversation flows freely at our table throughout dinner.

There are no awkward silences and, so far, Sean has not exhibited any strange behaviors. I find out that he has a bachelor's degree in social work and is pursuing another bachelor's degree in history from the University of Wisconsin-Parkside. He spent less than a year working as a social worker before he realized the job was too emotionally draining for him, so now he wants to be a history teacher. After we finish discussing my job and my graduate studies, we move on to online dating stories. I share just enough to let him know that things have not been a piece of cake, but not enough to make him wonder if Drew might be spying on us as we dine. I'm shocked and relieved to find out that he has been out with a few loons himself.

When the waitress delivers the check, I don't get a chance to peek at it because Sean hands her a credit card without even looking at the bill himself.

"Can I at least pay the tip?" I dig around in my purse for my wallet.

"Don't even think about it," he replies.

After Sean signs the receipt, he stands and holds out a hand. He helps me out of the booth and continues to hold my hand as we walk toward the exit. I concentrate on remaining calm so that my palm—and the rest of my body—stays dry, but my heart is racing so fast that odds are not in my favor.

"Chloe, do you mind if I use the restroom real quick? I'll just be a minute."

"No, not at all. How about if I wait for you by the hostess station?"

"Sounds great. See you in a bit." He slowly lets go of my hand so that our fingertips linger together for a second.

Still thinking about the way his fingers felt laced through mine, I watch as Sean walks to the bathroom. Then I begin to wonder what to expect next. *Will we talk more in the foyer before saying goodbye to each other? Is he going to try to give me a hug or maybe even a kiss? Should I invite him to the Home Bar?*

"Chloe? Is that you?" My thoughts are interrupted by a vaguely familiar voice. I look to my left and see a former student teacher of one of my colleagues. Apparently, she's only here for happy hour because she's holding a drink in her hand.

"Renee! How are you?"

"Wonderful! How are you? I heard from Stacey that you're getting ready to work on your thesis. How awesome! What is your research going to be about?"

"I'm doing a comparative analysis of direct instruction versus balanced literacy."

"Oh, cool." Her response is not very convincing.

"What about you? You're teaching high school geography now, right?" I already know the answer to this question because Stacey—the cooperative teacher Renee worked with at my school—already told me. She also filled me in on the fact that Renee has been messing around with her very own student teacher and that her marriage is on the rocks because of it.

"Yeah, I *love* teaching at the high school level. Little ones just aren't up my alley, I guess." She shrugs.

Finally, Sean returns, but he doesn't seem to realize I'm talking to Renee. "Ready to go?"

Renee clears her throat to get Sean's attention. Then she raises her eyebrows at me. "Are you going to introduce me to your friend?"

"Of course. Renee, this is Sam. Sam, Renee. She did some of her student teaching at my school last year."

My face becomes hot. *Did I just call him Sam?*

My fear is confirmed when Sean extends his hand to Renee and introduces himself. "Hi. I'm *Sean*."

Renee shakes his hand. "Nice to meet you." Then she gives me a confused sideways glance.

I want to die right then and there, but I have no such luck. Instead, I'm forced to wrap up my conversation with Renee and endure an awkward trip out to the parking lot with Sean at my side. As we walk, I prepare myself for an uncomfortable goodbye and wonder if he might even keep walking straight to his car without ever making eye contact with me again. But when I muster enough nerve to look at him, he's smiling at me.

I try to apologize. "I am so . . ." But Sean interrupts.

He extends a hand and says, "Hi. It's nice to meet you. My name is *Sean*. What's yours?"

I let out a huge sigh as I shake his hand. His grip is tight for a second but then he releases my hand and pulls me in for a hug. Then he whispers in my ear. "You do know you're going to have to learn my name in order for us to go on another date, right?"

The warmth of his breath and the sound of his voice give me butterflies.

Finally. Online dating might *finally* be paying off.

chapter twenty-nine

"Welcome Home!" Bartender Chris yells. He immediately begins making me a vodka seltzer with lime.

"For me?" I ask.

He winks. "Nice to see you again, sweetheart. First one's on the house." He plops the drink down in front of me and then moves on to the large group that walked in behind me.

I leave him a dollar, grab my cocktail and move toward the back room.

"Chloe!" Shelly abandons her turn at the dartboard to greet me, causing Craig to throw his hands up in exasperation. I laugh to myself because I know exactly how he feels. Shelly has the attention span of a three-year-old, so a game of darts with her usually takes hours.

"Hey guys. What's new?" I give them both quick hugs.

"Not much. Did you have a nice Thanksgiving?" Craig asks.

"I did. How about you? Were there a lot of people in the Dells?"

Shelly responds this time. "Not really. We were actually surprised by how dead it was at first, but I get it now. Thanksgiving just isn't the same when you don't celebrate it at home. Don't you think, Craig?"

"I totally agree with you. But at least your whole family was at the resort."

My smile widens as I realize Shelly and Craig are behaving like a couple, despite Shelly's insistence over the past few months that they could never be more than friends. But people of the opposite sex who are "just friends" don't usually spend the majority of their free time together. And they certainly don't spend the holidays with one another's family.

"Why are you smiling like that? Do I have popcorn in my teeth?" Shelly licks her top teeth and then starts making sucking noises as she tries to remove kernels that are not even there.

"No. You guys are just really cute. That's all."

Shelly scrunches her eyebrows together as her tongue continues moving back and forth across her top teeth. I sense her debating whether or not to ask what I'm talking about in an attempt to carry on the façade that they are still nothing more than friends. But then she smiles slightly and says, "Oh, please. Don't make me gag."

Craig grins and leans down, putting his arms around her neck from behind. She elbows him and whispers, "No PDA."

Shelly's actions don't surprise me in the least, but Craig's response sure does. Instead of releasing her, he puts her in a headlock and gives her a noogie. "What are you doing, Craig? Ow! Knock it off!"

"Oh my gosh, Shell, it's like you're dating your brother."

"Shut up, Chloe. Get him off of me!"

Finally, Craig releases her. "I need another beer. Do you girls want anything?"

Shelly is too busy straightening her clothes and her hair to answer, and I'm too busy cracking up as a result of the scene I just had the pleasure of witnessing.

"I'll go ahead and grab you guys a couple of refills." Craig sneaks me a fist bump as he heads off to the bar.

"Seriously, Shell, you and Craig are so perfect for each other."

"Did you see what he just did to me?"

"Yeah, it was great."

"Very funny. That's *totally* something my brother would do to me. Wait a second. Eww. It *is* like I'm dating my brother."

And there it was: a dating admission. "But look at it this way: you and your brother have an awesome relationship."

Shelly rolls her eyes and lets out a huge sigh. "So? Tell me what's been going on with you. I'm dying to hear about Drew. And how was your date? Did it suck? Is that why you didn't bring him?"

"No, not at all. He was wonderful. He just has an early class tomorrow morning. And I think he had about a twenty-five-minute drive home. He lives in Racine."

"Racine? Yuck."

"What's wrong with Racine?"

"I don't know. Isn't that where Cliff's new skanky girlfriend lives?"

"Yeah, but I don't think she's representative of the entire population down there. And I don't think she's his girlfriend."

Shelly shrugs. "What do you mean he has a class? What does he teach?"

"He's not a teacher—yet. He has a few more semesters at UW-Parkside."

"How old is he?"

"I don't know. Twenty-six, I think. Why? Does it matter?"

"I just thought you wanted to date people who are done with college and kind of settled. You know?"

"I know. But his situation is different. He worked as a social worker for a while but didn't like it. So he wants to try teaching."

"Oh, okay. Well, does he have a job?"

"Yes! What's with the barrage of questions? He's a really good guy."

"Hey, I'm just curious. I know how attracted you are to needy, younger guys." She coughs a little and says "Cliff" as she does it.

"He's not needy and he's not younger. He's also not *at all* like Cliff. Jeez. What is with you?"

"I'm sorry. I've been with Craig for four straight days without a break. I have to figure out how to tell him that I want to sleep alone tonight."

"Well, in my opinion, he deserves a medal. After four days with you, a noogie wouldn't be enough to express my frustration."

"Shut up!" She laughs.

"Just tell him. You know he'll be cool with it. You both have to go back to work tomorrow anyway. Use that as an excuse. You need a good night's rest."

"Yeah, I know he'll be fine. I'm just worried about why I feel this way."

"Shelly, don't sweat it. You're just not used to having someone around all the time, not someone who you're romantically involved with anyway." I find it amusing the way my friends and I tend to give each other sound relationship advice, yet we manage to make such a mess of our own personal lives.

"You're right. Let's get back to your date. What's this new guy's name anyway?

"Sean. He really was very sweet."

Craig returns just in time to hear all about my date. I tell them about every last detail leading all the way up to when I got into my car and Sean closed the door for me.

"Wait a sec. So, you called him Sam, and he still wants to see you again?" Shelly asks. Before I can respond, she looks at Craig. "Would you go on a second date with someone if she messed up your name?"

"I don't know. It depends on what she looked like."

Shelly groans. "Whatever, Craig. You're such a . . . guy."

I laugh. "*Anyway.* Yes, he wants to see me again. We're going to a movie on Friday night."

"A movie? How do you get to know someone while you're watching a movie?"

"I don't know. You don't. I don't care though. It'll just be nice to hang out with him, and I haven't been on a movie date for so long. Come to think of it, I haven't *seen* a movie in a really long time."

"Hey, Craig. Maybe we should go with them." Shelly says.

Craig looks from me to Shelly. "Don't you think we should ask them first?"

"Oh, yeah." Shelly looks at me. "Can we tag along?"

"I don't mind. But let me check with Sean first, okay?"

"Okay, sounds good. It'll be a good test to see if he might be the possessive type. Speaking of possessive, what's going on with Drew? And how was your date with Frank?"

I take a nice long sip of my drink before giving Shelly and Craig a recap of my disastrous date with Frank. They don't think Cliff's note was that big of a deal, but they are appalled when I tell them about Drew's message.

"What did I tell you?" Shelly says. "He's deranged. You seriously never noticed anything weird about him the entire time you guys were emailing each other and talking on the phone?" She gives me a look that insinuates I must be an idiot. In retrospect, that's exactly what I feel like. All the time I spent on Drew also makes me feel like a failure when it comes to online dating.

"No, I didn't." I look down at my drink and begin poking at the wedge of lime with my straw.

Craig puts his hand on my shoulder. "Don't beat yourself up over it. Get back on the horse, and go for another ride."

I look at Shelly and can tell she's suppressing the urge to laugh. "Get back on the horse?" she says to Craig.

"Hey, I'm trying," he says.

"Thank you for your support, Craig. I appreciate the effort," I say. "So, maybe I need to start introducing new prospects to you guys or Jess within the first two dates. Just to get an earlier opinion. What do you think?"

"Yeah, why not?" Shelly says. Craig nods in agreement. "In fact, let's start with meeting Sean on Friday night."

"All right. I'm sure he'll be fine with a double date, and if he's not, then maybe I shouldn't be going on a second date with him anyway. I really think you guys are going to like him though."

At least, I hope they will.

chapter thirty

Since Sean lives south of the movie theater and Shelly, Craig and I live about fifteen minutes north, we decide to just meet there. When I mentioned that Shelly and Craig were interested in joining us, he jumped at the opportunity to meet my friends. To top off his willingness to share our date with others, he also offered to pick us up. I told him there was no need for that, but these gestures made me even more excited about the prospect of getting to know him.

"So, what are we seeing?" Craig asks.

"*Love Actually*." Shelly and I respond at the same time.

Craig looks at me in the rearview mirror. "Does your guy know we're seeing a chick flick?"

"Yeah, he's the one who suggested we see it. His sister saw it and she told him it's the perfect date movie."

"Aw. That's so sweet that he talked to his sister about your date."

"Why is that sweet?" Craig asks.

"Because I think any guy who talks to his sister about his love life is probably pretty sensitive and thoughtful."

Craig laughs. "That's a load of crap. Your brother talks to you about his love life *all* the time."

"Yeah, I guess you're right. Anyway, are you nervous, Chloe?"

"No. Not really. I'm actually a little excited to see him."

We pull into the parking lot right when I told Sean we would arrive. He's already waiting out front.

"There he is," I say as we drive past.

"Ooh. He's cute," Shelly whispers.

I notice that Sean is wearing a different baseball cap this time. The hat is dark blue, and it's forward facing. I wonder if collecting hats is a hobby or if he just likes to accessorize. But most of all, I wonder if he ever goes anywhere without wearing a hat.

"I thought you liked tall guys," Craig says. "What is he? Five-six, five-seven?"

"No, five-eight." I know this is probably not true, even though it's the height he listed on his profile, but the fact that Craig is pointing out a height deficiency bothers me.

"Uh uh. He is *not* five-eight. Trust me." Craig shakes his head.

"Who really cares?" Shelly pipes in. "If Chloe doesn't care how short he is, why should you?"

How short he is? So, Shelly thinks he's short too? I almost ask Shelly how tall she thinks he is, but the car is parked and my friends are already getting out.

As soon as Sean sees us, he rushes over and gives me a hug.

"Hey. It's so nice to see you again," he says.

When our torsos part and we're face-to-face, I'm reminded of how good this guy makes me feel. "Yeah, it's nice to see you too." I turn to face my friends. "Sean, this is Shelly and Craig." They all exchange greetings before we enter the theater. Sean pays for my ticket and his own and then leads me to the snack bar where he orders a small popcorn, a Sprite and a pack of Twizzlers. It all feels so natural, and I'm reminded of what it feels like to have a boyfriend. There's just something about going on a movie date that screams *couple*.

During the movie, Sean and I can't keep our hands off each other. There's hand-holding, snuggling and leg rubbing. I recognize some of the same feelings I had the first time I ever went on a movie date with a guy. I was thirteen and we saw *Pretty Woman*. I remember being so focused on my date's every move that I barely watched any of the movie. It was the first time I ever touched a boner, and it was the first time a guy ever put his hand up my shirt. Granted, I didn't touch Sean's boner—not that he even had one—nor did he feel me up. But still, the same feelings of excitement, anticipation and desire were present.

After the movie, we decided to go to a nearby bar that none of us had ever been to before. We placed our drink orders with the bartender and then Shelly dragged me off to the bathroom. As soon as the door closed behind us, she said, "My God. You guys were so porno during the movie!"

"What?"

"Don't *what* me. Craig wanted me to tell you guys to get a room. What's up with all the fondling?"

"Give me a break. We were *not* fondling each other. What's wrong with a little hand holding?"

"Are you kidding me? You guys were all over each other, and you just met."

Without responding, I enter a stall. Shelly walks into the stall next to me and continues talking. "Seriously Chloe, I think you need to take a step back before things get out of hand. Don't get me wrong. Sean seems really nice, but you guys are already acting like a couple."

"Uh, Shelly, can we talk about this *after* I'm done wiping my ass?"

I hear her toilet flush. After I finish taking care of my business, I open the stall door to find her standing there, arms folded across her chest. "Well?" she says.

I brush past her, moving to the sink to wash my hands. She follows with her arms still folded.

"Well what?" I ask.

"Well, don't you agree that you're moving a little fast?"

"No. Well, maybe. I don't know. I'm just really attracted to him for some reason."

"Chloe, you found Drew and that Frank guy physically attractive too, but you weren't getting all freaky with them. What gives?"

I give her my best are-you-fucking-kidding-me look and say, "Freaky? What is that supposed to mean? Shelly, I'm a grown woman. If I feel like messing around with someone, I'm entitled to do so. You're acting like we had sex, but technically, we haven't even made it to first base."

Her face softens and she finally unfolds her arms. "I'm sorry. Bad word choice. I guess I just want to help you follow through with your plan to date around a bit and get to know people before inadvertently diving into exclusivity."

"Okay, Shell. I get it. But trust me, I'm not interested in anything serious right now. I still want to just live in the moment and have a little fun. But I also want to allow myself to feel good without worrying about things so much. Any chance you can just let me do that without judging me?"

We look at each other in the mirror, and then both of our eyes shift to an older woman who has just exited a stall. She smiles at us and says, "Hey, I know this is none of my business, but you only live once girls. Nothing wrong with a little fun!" Based on the way she's swaying, we can tell that she's drunk. It doesn't matter, though. Shelly and I both burst into laughter and the tension is immediately gone.

"Come on," she says, putting an arm around my shoulder. "Let's go get you a little fun."

∽

Three hours later, I'm sitting in the passenger seat of Sean's car. His hand is resting on my knee.

I stare out the window at the streetlights as we zoom by and debate whether or not to invite Sean in when we get to my place. I know he will be perfectly fine if I don't, so there's no pressure, but Shelly's apprehension about how fast she thinks we're moving is heavy on my mind.

"What are you thinking about?" he asks.

"Oh, nothing. Just looking at stuff. This is one of my favorite things, being a passenger in a car, a plane, a train—whatever. I like watching everything along the way." I have no idea why I'm rambling. A simple *nothing* would have been sufficient.

"Perfect. I like driving." He rubs my knee.

When we pull up to my place, Sean turns off the car, but he doesn't move to get out. Instead, he turns toward me and leans his cheek against his headrest. I do the same.

"I had a really good time tonight. Your friends are cool."

"Thanks. About my friends, I mean. They are cool. I had fun too."

We sit and stare at each other. I imagine climbing onto his lap and passionately kissing him. At the same time, I think about just giving him a quick peck and then hopping out of the car. As I struggle with deciding on the best way to end our date, Sean makes the decision for me. He leans over and plants a sensual, lingering kiss on my lips. I close my eyes and allow a warm feeling to spread throughout my body. Then a yearning sensation develops in between my legs. *Oh man.* Our lips part, but our faces remain close. I reach up and run my hand down the side of his face, and I'm about to kiss him again when he speaks. "Can I call you tomorrow?"

Instantly, my delirium is gone. *Thank God.* "Of course." I sit up straight and lean forward to pick up my purse. He runs his hand down my back. "I better go inside."

"Okay. I'll talk to you tomorrow."

As I reach for the door handle, Sean pulls me in for one last kiss. Again, I feel aroused and want more than just a kiss, but somehow I muster the strength to get out of the car. He doesn't pull away until I unlock the door and wave.

A huge smile is plastered to my face as I walk upstairs to my apartment.

Lying in bed, I wonder if Shelly was right about things moving too fast with Sean. I understand if she's concerned that I might become too comfortable with dating just him, but if it's the idea of making out with him too soon that bothers her, I don't really care. The whole point is to be dating, having fun and figuring out what I want.

And right now, I want more of Sean's kisses.

chapter thirty-one

The sound of a gagging cat wakes me the next morning. As soon as I realize what is going on, I leap out of bed in an attempt to remove the perpetrator from my carpeted bedroom and into the hallway before a mess is made. After all, linoleum is much easier to clean than carpet. "No, no, no, no, no," I say as I relocate the overweight cat. Luckily, we make it to the hallway in time.

As I head into the kitchen to retrieve cleaning supplies, portions of a dream I had hit me. I see clothes strewn about and flashes of flesh on flesh. I have no idea who the naked man is supposed to be, but the face I summon belongs to Sean. The same smile I had on my face before drifting off to sleep replaces the fading memories of my dream.

The clock on the microwave reads six fifty. *So much for sleeping in.* I pick up the phone to call Shelly, but then I realize how pissed she would be if I woke her up this early on a Saturday just to see if she wants to go to the gym. Instead, I get started on my weekly cleaning routine.

Since I'm up a lot earlier than expected, I take the opportunity to bag up the last of Cliff's things. Part of me wants to toss it all in the trash, but I can't justify doing something so mean—even though he has become a huge pain in the ass. Upon examination of the items he left behind, it hits me just how different we are. The trash bag on my bed is filled with a few articles of clothing, two rap CDs, a pair of overpriced sneakers (the kind that no one would actually wear to do anything active), pomade, a hair clipper set and a diamond stud earring. I suddenly feel like I've been dating a teenager who has nothing better to worry about than keeping up with all the latest fads and looking cool in front of his friends. What was I thinking staying with him for so long? I tie a knot in the bag and put it in the hallway outside of my apartment. I figure I will just drop the bag off on his mother's doorstep late one night.

Now that Cliff's things are gone, it doesn't feel so wrong imagining what it would be like to bring Sean into my bedroom. Not necessarily for a make-out session, but even just to cuddle.

By the time I finish cleaning and putting in a final load of laundry, it's nearly nine. I hate working out on an empty stomach, so I sit down to a bowl of cereal. As I eat, I stare at the pink Post-it that has been tacked to my corkboard since last Friday. On it is a reminder of the lunch date I have scheduled for today.

∼

Computer Pro – 36
Location: Milwaukee
Let's Meet

Relationship Status: Never Married
Kids: No
Want Kids: Yes
Ethnicity: White / Caucasian
Body type: Fit
Height: 5' 9"
Religion: Christian
Politics: Middle of the Road
Smoke: No
Drink: Social Drinker
Pets: No
Education: Bachelor's
Employment: Professional
Income: 100,000+

∼

Computer Pro happens to be the guy my brother picked out. He *would* be on my list of matches, except he's much older and makes more money than what my parameters are set for. Of course, these are the two stats that stood out most to my brother. Thinking back to the conversation my brother and I had the day he sent the icebreaker to Computer Pro, I'm convinced this date is probably a bad idea.

That's why you're not having any luck, Spazz. You need to date someone older . . . No, just because someone is in his mid-thirties does not mean there's something wrong with him. There's nothing wrong with me . . . On your salary, you should be looking for someone who makes at least eighty K. Why would you even consider dating someone who might expect you to scrape up enough money to pay for your own dinner? You're broke, remember?

I think I'm okay with the eleven-year age difference between Computer Pro and me, but I feel weird about his salary. He makes at least triple what I make in a year, which is really intimidating. Sure, it would be convenient to date someone who could afford to pay for everything, but why should a guy be expected to pay all the time just because he makes more money? I see two problems with a huge salary gap. One, I never want to be viewed as a gold digger and, two, I never want a man to think he has to take care of me. I'm more than capable of taking care of myself, even if I *am* broke.

I consider calling Computer Pro to cancel, but decide to think it over a little more while I'm working out.

At the gym, I choose a treadmill overlooking the basketball court. On Saturday mornings, a large group of men—likely in their thirties, maybe forties—is always there, huffing and puffing as they chase the ball up and down the court. Most of the guys are a little overweight, but there are a few who are pretty fit. I have no idea if any of them are married or if any of them have kids, but I would guess that this routine game of basketball is something each of them looks forward to all week long. As I watch them play, I imagine what it would be like to date someone who has his shit so together that waking up early on a Saturday morning to play basketball with his buddies is top priority. Would it make me feel more secure? Would I be more sure of myself and care less about what my friends think? I want to find the right person so badly because I want to start a family and just *feel* settled. But it does have to be the right person. I want someone who is sure about what he wants and confident about who he is. Maybe the right person for me *is* someone older.

∼

I rush out the door ten minutes before I'm supposed to meet Computer Pro. Arriving late is not the kind of first impression I want to make, but it's going to happen today. By the time I get to the restaurant and park, I'll be lucky if I'm just five minutes late.

We're meeting at a bar called The Palomino, which usually draws a large lunch crowd on weekends, so we will be far from alone. It's not the classiest place to meet for lunch, but it does have some excellent Southern food. As unhealthy as they may be, I'm a huge fan of the hush puppies and fried okra.

A wave of nostalgia hits me when I enter The Palomino. Shelly and I used to frequent this bar before Evan and Matt came along. I came here once with Matt when we first started dating. My eyes are drawn to the table where we sat for six hours getting to know each other. It was the night of our first kiss. Suddenly, I regret choosing this place for my first date with Computer Pro. Before I have a chance to regroup, I see a man waving from the far end of the bar. I smile politely at Computer Pro as I approach him, but the fact that he hasn't even bothered to stand annoys me, even though he is kind of handsome. When I'm finally standing next to him, he reaches over and removes a coat from the stool next to him and gets to work wrapping it around the back of his own stool. He doesn't even bother to say hello.

"Hi, I'm Chloe." I wait for him to finish with his coat before extending a hand.

But instead of a handshake, he envelops my hand in his and holds the awkward position long enough to say, "Well, of course you are." Then he smiles and calls out, "Bartender!"

I flinch and quickly look around to see if anyone else is put off by Computer Pro's obnoxious tone. Luckily, it appears that I'm the only one.

The bartender arrives with an irritated look on his face. "Ready for another?"

Computer Pro holds up a nearly full bottle of Heineken. "No. Does it look like I'm ready for another? My date is finally here." He nods in my direction.

I contemplate hightailing it out of The Palomino but decide to give this guy the benefit of the doubt. After all, I *was* late.

The bartender simply stares at me as he waits for my drink order. Great, now I'm on his annoying-customer list just because Computer Pro is being a royal jackass. "May I please have an Absolut greyhound?" The bartender nods and disappears to make my drink.

"A greyhound, huh? I wouldn't expect a dainty young thing like you to order such a drink."

"Oh? What would you expect me to order?"

"Hm. Let me see." Eyes to the ceiling, he rubs his chin. Then he smiles. "Got it." He points at me and says, "A kiddie cocktail." The asshole laughs as though his attempt at humor is actually funny.

I nod slowly and imagine pouring the Absolut greyhound that the bartender has just delivered over Computer Pro's egotistical head. Not being one to waste alcohol though, I decide to drink it before ditching him when he says, "Put it on my tab." Heck, I might even have lunch too. After all, my profession requires the ability to ignore poor behavior.

When his prolonged laughter finally dies down, I say, "So, do you want to sit at a table or are you okay with eating at the bar?"

He takes a drink. "What do you want to do, Chloe?"

The way he has his head cocked gives me chills for some reason. *Am I on a date with another psycho?*

"I really don't care. I'm fine at the bar."

"Well, good, because I already ordered us some food."

I should probably be annoyed that he ordered for me, but the date is already a disaster, so I just go with it. "Oh, awesome."

While we wait for the food to arrive, Computer Pro talks my ear off about his job as—you guessed it—a computer pro. Now, I happen to be useless when it comes to discussing computers, so most of what he says goes way over my head. It's not so bad though—at least the thoughts inside my head are more engaging than anything he has to say. At one point, I realize that I don't even know Computer Pro's name. I'm about to interrupt to ask, but then he says, ". . . and that's when I said to myself, *David*, you are smarter than anyone in this room . . ." *David. His name is David.*

Our food finally arrives. It appears he has ordered every side item on the menu, including hush puppies and fried okra. I dig in, and he continues telling me about the bonus he expects to receive at the end of the year. As I eat and pretend to be interested in everything David says, it occurs to me that maybe the date isn't going as badly as I thought it would. I'm enjoying a free lunch, my second free greyhound and the freedom to just sit back and relax while my date does all the talking. I feel no pressure to say or do the right things because I don't care what this guy thinks of me. Actually, I might agree to go out with him again if he asks.

"Hey, Chloe, do you want to see something?"

"What?" I was not expecting him to ask me a question.

"I said do you want to see something?"

"Sure. What is it?"

He pulls a paper rectangle out of his pocket and begins unfolding it. When it's completely unfolded, he's holding a sheet of computer paper that's covered with a picture I recognize. The picture is from a recent *Milwaukee Journal Sentinel* article about the summer reading program that took place at my school. It's a picture of me reading with students.

My heart begins to race. "Where did you get that?"

"I printed it."

"I can see that. How did you find it?"

"Well, you told me your name and that you teach in Milwaukee, so I did some research and found this picture. I also figured out where you live." He smiles proudly. "Isn't Google amazing?"

I'm speechless.

"Anyway," he refolds the picture and shoves it into his back pocket, "back to my story."

David goes back to talking about himself, but I can't concentrate on a word he says because I'm consumed by paranoia. *He did some research? He knows where I live?*

"Chloe? You really have to listen to this part or you won't understand the rest of my story."

I look up at David. "I'm sorry. I don't feel so good. I think I need to get going."

"Oh, okay. Well, do you want to hear the rest of the story real quick?"

"David, I really don't think I can."

"Oh, all right." He looks at the bartender who's standing no more than three feet away from us. "Bartender!"

This time, the abruptness in his voice causes me to see stars for a second. *What am I doing with this guy? He's rude and arrogant. AND he printed a picture of me from the Internet. Who does that? I have to get out of here.*

I'm in the process of taking money out of my wallet because I decide it would be wrong to let him pay when I have no intention of seeing him again, but David stops me. "Oh, I got this. You're a teacher. I know how much you make."

Under different circumstances—say, if this was Ned talking to me—I would have confronted him about the reference to my salary. The last thing I want to do is prolong this date though, so I do my best to ignore the rude remark. "Okay. Thanks."

As David is busy putting on his coat and hat, I glance down at the credit card slip. On the tip line, it says: *Go to college. You're not a very good bartender.* While I agree with him that the bartender didn't provide the best service, his *tip* is beyond rude.

"You ready?" he asks.

"One sec." I pull a five-dollar bill from my wallet and plop it down on top of our bill. "Okay. Now I'm ready."

"Why did you do that?"

I roll my eyes and start walking. I hear David mutter something to himself as he follows me out of the bar.

I reach out a hand. "Well, it was nice meeting you. Thanks for lunch."

Instead of shaking my hand, he says, "Can you wait here for a moment?"

I slowly return my hand to my side. "Sure. I guess so."

He trots halfway down the block to a black BMW. I panic when he opens the passenger door and leans inside, thinking he's about to pull a gun on me. (I can't help it—my mother's influence I guess.) I'm ready to bolt back inside, but he emerges with a bouquet of pink carnations. *Oh great, even worse.* He walks briskly back to where I'm standing and hands me the flowers.

"Wow. Thanks." I'm not sure what he expects to happen now, but I'm still dying to leave.

He puts his hands in his pockets and smiles at me. Again, he looks very proud of himself. "I wasn't sure how things would go, so I left those in my BMW."

Well, for your information things didn't go very well, so if you don't mind, I'm ready to take off now in my Chrysler. "Thank you. They're very pretty."

"I know they're not the most expensive flowers. Maybe I'll spend more next time." He winks.

Next time? I contemplate letting him down easy by saying I'll call or email soon, but instead I decide it's time to act like an adult. Plus, this guy is kind of a jerk, so what do I care if his feelings get hurt? "David, I'm sorry, but I'm not really interested in going out with you again."

His smile quickly turns into a frown. "Really?"

"Really. I just don't think we have a lot in common."

"Oh, okay. Well, apparently we have enough in common that you felt just fine letting me buy you lunch *and* two drinks. You're not even sick, are you?"

I laugh because I remember that the only reason I'm on this date is because of my brother Jim: matchmaker extraordinaire.

"You think this is funny? I even got you flowers."

"You know what? I don't want your flowers." I shove the carnations into his chest and say, "Thanks for lunch," as I turn to leave. Before rounding the corner, I look back just in time to see Computer Pro throw the carnations on the ground and flip me off. Then he heads back into The Palomino.

chapter thirty-two

It's after three when I get home. I try to call both Jess and Shelly to see what their plans are for the evening. I'm also dying to tell them about my date with Computer Pro, but neither one answers. For a fleeting moment, I think about giving my brother a call too but decide I don't feel like arguing about his lack of matchmaking abilities.

Since I have no plans, I mull over going to my parents' house to complete some final grad school projects for the semester. I unload everything from my backpack onto the kitchen table. A quick review of my to-do list reveals there's plenty of work that I can do at home without a computer, so I make myself a cup of tea and get comfortable on the futon with an adolescent novel called *Monster*. My task is to create a literature circle guide to accompany the book.

Four hours later, my ringing cell phone rouses me from an unexpected nap. I guess the alcohol during lunch had more of an effect on me than I thought. A heap of items falls off my lap when I stand. The sun has set, and I stumble in the dark to answer before the call is lost. My first thought is of Sean. He asked if he could call me today. Maybe it's him.

By the time I get to the phone, the call has gone to voicemail. It was Jess. I flip on the kitchen light, take a seat and lay my head down on the table. I think about just going to bed and returning Jess's call tomorrow, but then I realize I haven't eaten anything since lunch. I need to get some food, and I don't really feel like talking about my date anymore. While the whole situation was humorously annoying at first, I just want to forget about it now. *Ah, Computer Pro. What am I supposed to take away from meeting you? And Sean, why haven't you called yet?*

Instead of wallowing over my disastrous date and the fact that Sean could be out with another online match, I turn on the TV for some background noise and fix myself something to eat: leftover lasagna and a salad. I'll call Jess back later. As I eat, my cats gather around. Luckily, prospective matches don't have the option to view random snippets from my life, because this moment would surely scare away anyone with potential: A twenty-five-year-old woman surrounded by three cats, eating leftovers on a Saturday night.

My home phone rings while I'm in the shower. I know it can't be Sean because the whole Drew debacle has taught me to refrain from giving guys my home number, among other things. It's probably just Jess again. I finish washing up and then stand under the steaming water with my eyes closed. My peaceful shower only ends when the water turns lukewarm, warning of the impending cold.

I'm surprised to find a flashing red '3' on my answering machine, because I only heard the phone ring once. I must have been too zoned out in the shower.

The familiar electronic voice drones, *"You have, three, new, messages. Saturday, nine, twenty, p.m."*

"Chloe, it's Cliff. Where are you tonight? If it's okay, I'm gonna stop by."

Shit. The only thing I've heard from Cliff lately has been in the form of a letter, but he has not called for weeks. I thought we were done playing phone games.

"Saturday, nine, thirty, four, p.m."

"Chloe, it's Cliff again. Where are you? Pick up, pick up, pick up."

Crap. Mike and Deena know that Cliff and I are done, but they're out of town this weekend. What if he's on his way over? No one is here to scare him away if he's full of liquid persistence.

"Saturday, nine, forty, five, p.m."

"Chlooo-eee, where are you? I'm on your side of town and want to stop over. Are you there? Look, I need to talk to you. I need to see you. If you're there, please pick up. I'm just going to stop . . ."

The phone rings, interrupting the message. I know it has to be Cliff again, so I let the machine kick in. *"Hi, you've reached two nine five, one five nine five. I can't take your call right now, so please leave a message."*

"Chloe, I'm on my way over so . . ." I frantically grab the handset.

"Cliff, I'm not interested in . . ."

"I knew you were there. I'm on my way ov . . ." Clearly, he has been drinking.

"Cliff, you can't come over. I told you, I'm done with this. I don't want any more letters, and I don't want any more phone calls. No amount of talking is going to change my mind."

"Chloe," he hiccups, "I just need to see you one last time. I'm outside your place right now. I'm walking up to the door. Please let me in." The doorbell rings.

I used to feel like my heart was going to burst out of my chest when Cliff would call and beg to see me. Now, I just feel angry. As annoying as online dating has been, it has still provided me with the opportunity to meet some good guys. And Cassie was right, I really don't know my "type" the way I thought I did. Online dating has been proof of that. Even though Drew ended up having a screw or two loose—well, maybe even three—I still felt something for him. Then there was Packer Fan Patrick. What a great guy. And Frank. And now Sean.

The doorbell rings again. "Chloe, please come to the door."

Knowing it would take a phone call to the police to get Cliff out of here, I finally say, "Fine, but you can't stay long." Unlike past surprise visits from Cliff, this one is truly not welcome. I don't even want to look at him.

I make my way downstairs and open the outside door. Then I turn to head back upstairs without uttering a word. I know that he will close the door and follow me up just like old times.

When Cliff enters my apartment, he stumbles over and tries to hug me. He smells like a dirty distillery. The nasty odor reminds me of all the late nights I used to spend haggling with him over his excessive partying. I pull away. "Can you just back off and tell me why you need to see me so badly?" He gives me a forlorn look, so I refuse to make eye contact in an attempt to avoid feeling bad for him.

"Chloe, can we sit down first?"

"No. Absolutely not." I don't intend to have our impromptu meeting anyplace other than the hallway. "And make it quick. I want to go to bed."

He looks down at Clover, who's rubbing against his leg. "Hey, Clover. How's my little kitty?" He bends down to scratch behind her ears and she begins to purr.

Cliff got Clover for me for my twenty-fifth birthday. As much as I enjoy the companionship of my cats, it really sucks that all three are a constant reminder of failed relationships.

"Okay, Cliff. Enough delay. If you want to talk, start talking. You have five minutes." I don't even try to hide my irritation.

He scratches Clover's head once more. Then he stands and reaches for my hands, but I quickly fold my arms across my chest. "I miss you, Chloe, and I was hoping that you might change your mind about not dating each other anymore. I can't stand being without you."

"So, I assume it didn't work out with Rachel?" The jealous woman in me really wants to say, *So, I assume it didn't work out with that slut you were seeing*, but I know it's not her fault. She probably never even knew I existed. And it really makes no difference whether he's still dating her or not. I'm dating other people and I'm done with Cliff.

"Chloe, you don't understand. There was no *it* with Rachel. We were just messing around."

His reference to "messing around" with someone else tempts me to open the door and kick his ass out. Instead, I take a deep breath and look at the clock. Only two minutes left.

"I told you, I just wanted some time to sow my oats."

"Sow your oats? Why don't you just call it what it is? You wanted to screw as many women as possible! Time's up. Now get out."

He stares at me, shocked. Then he staggers toward the door, but instead of leaving, he leans against the wall.

"Cliff? Can you just leave?"

"I think I'm gonna puke."

I watch in horror as he stumbles down the hall toward the bathroom. Then I rush after him when it occurs to me that he might be too drunk to aim for the toilet. The second I enter the bathroom, it happens. He throws up all over the closed lid of the toilet. Vomit splatters everywhere.

"No! Dammit, Cliff. Look what you did!" I scream at him in a way I've never screamed at anyone before. But now he's too busy dry heaving into my sink to care.

The stench is unbearable, so I back out of the bathroom and slide down the wall in the hallway until I'm sitting on the floor. I hug my bent knees and wait for Cliff to be done making a mess of my bathroom. As I sit there listening to his moans and groans, I wonder if God might be punishing me. From Drew and Frank to the asshole I met this afternoon and this very moment, it's clear that I'm being punished for something. Maybe this is what I deserve for hurting James and Matt. If I didn't always overanalyze everything so much, maybe I would be happily married to one of them and online dating would just be some strange new concept advertised on TV.

After a few minutes of silence, I return to the bathroom. Cliff's shirt is covered in vomit, and his tall, curled-up body is taking up most of the floor. I straddle him, careful not to step in anything, and touch his chest to make sure he's still breathing. After all, who knows if alcohol is the only thing in his system. I'm about to stand when I notice a discolored spot on his neck. I assume it's a smudge of puke, so I wet a washcloth and get to work wiping him clean. The specks around his mouth and on his chin are easy to remove, but the spot on his neck stays put. When I scrub a little harder and it still doesn't budge, I lean in for a closer look. *What the hell?* Turns out, the mark on Cliff's neck is not vomit. It's a hickey.

"Cliff!" I stand and kick his thigh. "Hey, asshole, wake up!" I kick him again.

"Wha . . ." He lifts his head slightly and squints at me.

"I said, GET UP! It's time for you to go."

But Cliff has passed out again. And despite my best efforts to wake him, he's utterly unconscious.

I stand in the bathroom examining the mess he has made. My eyes fill with tears, and I want to scream. Then I see something that distracts me from feeling sorry for myself. Cliff's phone is sticking out of his pocket.

At first, my plan is to call his mother and ask her to pick him up, but then I start scrolling through the list of contacts. The list is filled with dozens of women's names. It makes me wish I was strong enough to carry him downstairs so that I could simply throw him out on the lawn. *Betsy. Colleen. Daisy (probably a stripper). Faith. Gretchen.* I continue to scroll through the names. Then I see one that really grabs my attention: *Rachel.* Now the plan has changed.

I start at the top of the list with a woman named Amy. She doesn't answer, so I leave a message. "Hi, you don't know me, but my name is Chloe. I'm Cliff Crayson's ex-girlfriend. Just in case you're dating him, it's important for you to know that he has been begging for me to get back together with him for weeks. Hopefully, you don't think I'm crazy or anything. I just don't want anyone to get duped by him. That's all. Have a good night."

I proceed to call every single woman in Cliff's list of contacts. Most, even the ones who claim they don't know him, thank me for calling. But a few are hostile, calling me a bitch or telling me to mind my own business—these are the ones who sound excited when they answer before realizing it's not Cliff who's calling. I save Rachel for last.

"Hey babe. Are you on your way?" The pleasant sound of her voice takes me by surprise.

"Um. Sorry, but this isn't Cliff."

Silence.

"Is this Rachel?"

"Yes. Who is this?" She asks with trepidation.

"My name is Chloe. I'm . . ."

"I know who you are," she says with indifference. Then she mutters, "*Asshole.*"

"Excuse me?"

"Oh, I'm not calling you an asshole. I'm talking about Cliff. I was afraid you guys might get back together."

"Oh, no, you don't understand. We are *not* back together."

"You're not?" I don't understand why, but now her voice sounds hopeful.

"No, but he has been trying to contact me for the last few weeks, telling me how much he misses me and wants to get back together. I just thought you should know."

Again, the line is silent for a moment, but then I hear her sniffle.

"Rachel? Are you okay?"

"Yeah, it's just that . . . well, things have been going so well with us, and he promised me he would stay away from you. And now he's at your house?" She blows her nose.

Based on Rachel's reaction, I realize that Cliff already has her duped. And suddenly, I feel bad for her.

"Hey, it's not what you think. He's wasted and passed out on my bathroom floor." Part of me wants to tell her about the mess he made, but I refrain. For some reason, this call has become less about exposing Cliff and more about helping this poor woman. "I don't want anything to do with him."

"Do you need me to come and get him? There's no traffic. I could be there in fifteen minutes."

"Wait a second. Do you know where I live?"

Silence. Sniffle.

"Do you?"

"Well, how do you think I've kept him away from you this long? I told him that I would drive by your place at random times to make sure his car wasn't parked outside. I guess I should have been monitoring his phone too."

Oh, my God. She's been driving by my apartment? I'm beginning to think Cliff and Rachel might be perfect for each other.

"So? Do you want me to come and get him?"

"I don't understand. Why would you want to come and get him? You do realize that he's probably involved with other girls too, right?"

"Unlike you, I want my relationship with Cliff to work. I'm not going to give up on him just because he's made a few mistakes."

"Okay. Whatever. Look, I'm just . . ."

"I'm coming to get him."

"Uh, no you're not. I'm going to call his mother."

Rachel laughs. "Patty already thinks you're ridiculous. And now you're going to ask her to drive forty-five minutes to pick up her son because he's a little drunk? *You* are a real piece of work."

She's already on a first-name basis with Cliff's mom? And what did she just call me?

"You know what? Just forget I called. I'll let Cliff sleep it off here, and I'm sure he'll come crawling back to you tomorrow. But if you know what's good for you, you won't let him."

"No offense, but I don't need your advice. You should probably just focus on your own . . ."

I hang up on Rachel and immediately turn off the phone.

∼

I open my eyes the next morning to find Cliff sitting on the corner of my bed. He's slumped over, elbows on his knees, with his head in his hands. My first reaction is to yell at him for coming into my room with vomit on his clothes, but then I notice that his hair is wet and he has on different clothes. He must have found his bag of things in the hallway.

I sit up but don't say anything. I went to bed expecting to be just as angry with him this morning as I was last night, but for some reason, I'm not. Maybe it's because of the defeated look on his face. Maybe it's because I feel bad for calling all of those women last night or because I found out what a crazy bitch Rachel really is. Or maybe it's because I have a sense this might really be the end of the road for us.

"Cliff?"

He removes his head from his hands and looks over at me, but he doesn't answer.

"Why are you just sitting there?" I ask.

He reaches down and produces his phone. He holds it a few feet from my face so that I can see all of the new messages he has. "Because of this."

The calls seemed like a good idea at the time, but now I realize I was acting like a spiteful teenager. I'm actually ashamed.

"I'm sorry. I probably shouldn't have called all of those girls. You have to admit I had a right to be pissed about all of those numbers in your phone though."

"No, I don't. I don't have to admit that at all. Why do you have a right to be pissed? You don't even know who any of those girls are. Hell, I don't even know who most of them are. I collected a bunch of numbers after we first broke up. And I never lied to you about my intentions. I told you that I was going to date other people. I'm the one who should be pissed."

"What? Why do you have a right to be pissed?"

"Chloe, you looked through my phone. I've never once looked through your phone or anything of yours. What you did was really rude, not just to me, but also to all those girls who probably have no idea who I am. I've already listened to a bunch of messages from some really confused people. Oh, and from Rachel."

Hearing her name makes me queasy.

"I don't get it Cliff. Why have you continued trying to contact me for all these weeks? Especially when Rachel made it sound like you two are a couple?"

"You want to know the truth?"

"Yeah. Of course."

I know he intends to cut right to the chase because he looks at me in a way that he has never looked at me before, and tears are forming in his eyes.

"The truth is that Rachel and I started dating seriously after you had that guy over, but I just can't imagine feeling for her the way I feel about you. I love you. I told her that, so she's been trying to help me forget about you, but I can't. I want to, but I can't. I fucked up. I never should have dated other people in the first place. We were fine." A tear trails down his cheek.

His long-overdue sincerity is like a punch in the chest. I'm overwhelmed with a desire to hug and kiss him. But I don't because I know it would only lead him on.

"Cliff. I'm sorry. Not just for calling all those girls either. I'm sorry that you feel this way. I love you too. Always will. But we just aren't right for each other."

"I know," he says, to my surprise. Then he stands and picks up the garbage bag with his things in it. "Sorry about your bathroom. I cleaned everything up the best I could." He throws the bag over his shoulder and moves toward the door. Before he exits the bedroom, he says, "Goodbye, Chloe."

And that's it. Just like that, Cliff is out of my life.

chapter thirty-three

I'm huddling under the covers and crying when Jess calls. I muster a nasally "Hello?" only because I'm afraid that if I don't answer, I will succumb to this pit in my heart and never crawl out of isolation again.

"Chloe, are you crying? What's wrong?"

I sigh. "Long story."

"Well, are you okay? No one died, right?"

I laugh through my nose, despite myself. "I'm fine. And no one died."

"Okay. Well, maybe you can tell me what's going on while you drive me to pick up my car."

"Where's your car?"

"I left it downtown."

"Oh?"

"Yeah, why didn't you call me back last night? Or does it have something to do with why you're crying?"

"Um, yeah . . . that."

∼

When Jess hops into the car, I can tell right away from her scent that she must have really boozed it up last night. She reeks of smoke and liquor, and her long black hair is matted with a greasy sheen.

"Whoa. Rough night?"

She lifts her sunglasses just enough to reveal dark circles and bloodshot eyes. "What gave you that impression?" She drops her sunglasses into place and then runs her fingers through her thick hair. It doesn't help much.

I pull into a Starbucks drive-through. "You want something?"

Jess moans. "Yeah, for you to cool it on the quick turns. My head is killing me."

"So, is that a no?"

"Do you want me to puke in your car?"

"Please don't." The mention of puke triggers thoughts about the previous night, and I can't help but feel sad again.

"Chloe. I was just joking. I'm not going to puke. But I wasn't kidding about the turns. What's wrong?"

It isn't until we're headed toward downtown Milwaukee, where Jess left her car parked outside a bar, that I begin filling her in on what was most likely my final Cliff encounter.

"Chloe, I know you feel bad about invading Cliff's privacy, but you did all of those women a favor—even the ones who claimed to not know him. Maybe one of those women will feel empowered enough to stand up to another sneaky bastard someday themselves."

Obviously Jess doesn't understand the source of my sadness. Sure, I feel kind of bad for snooping through Cliff's phone, but I don't regret calling those women. What I'm really heartbroken over is the fact that Cliff and I will probably never see each other again. I know that's what I've been wanting all along, but it just felt so . . . final. I don't expect her to understand though. After all, I don't even totally understand why I feel the way I do. I just . . . do.

Instead of trying to dissect those feelings, I simply say, "Yeah, maybe you're right. So, tell me about your night."

"Well, I met a guy . . ."

Before Jess started dating Ned, this was how many of our conversations began, so I already know what to expect from her story. *She didn't feel like being cooped up on a Saturday night. She tried to call me, or someone else who didn't want to go out or wasn't around, so she decided to go out by herself. At some point during the evening, a guy offered to buy her a drink (or she asked someone if he would like to buy her a drink). They hung out all night long—dancing, shooting dice, talking—and stayed until bar close. They were having such a great time together that he ended up taking her home, and one thing led to another until they ended up sleeping with each other.* I've heard versions of this story dozens of times. The thing that's different about Jess compared to other girls in this type of situation is that she never expects anything afterward. She's able to call it what it usually is: a one-night stand. Sometimes I envy her for her ability to avoid becoming consumed with worry over what other people might think about her.

". . . So anyway, I hope you don't mind, but I asked him if he wants to hang out at the Home Bar on Wednesday night. You guys will be there, right?"

"I think so. You and Ned are really done then?"

"Well, I haven't heard from him."

"Hm."

"What do you mean 'hm'? You just sounded like your mother."

"Whatever. No, I didn't."

"Okay." Jess shrugs. "Tell me then. What does 'hm' mean?"

"Nothing. I just hope you're sure that you and Ned are done before you start something with someone else."

"Why? Just in case he decides to come crawling back to me and scares away whatever guy I happen to be with at the time?" She laughs. "Don't worry. That's not Ned's style."

"Jess, I couldn't care less about how Ned feels. I'm talking about you. Are you done? Are you ready to move on?"

"Yes, I am." We pull into the spot next to Jess's car. "Shit. I got a ticket."

"Hopefully the sex was worth it," I say.

Jess laughs as she gets out of the car. She leans down a little before closing the door and says, "Hey, how's online dating going? Any new guys?"

"Actually, yes. I have a couple of interesting stories for you. Do you have time for breakfast?"

"Sure. But let's go to a place that serves Bloody Marys.

"Sounds good. You lead the way."

After breakfast, I head straight to my parents' house. They should be at church, so I can expect at least an hour of uninterrupted time to work. Well, and to see if Sean has sent a message. At the end of our date on Friday, he said he would call, but I still haven't heard from him. Normally I would be wracking my brain wondering why a guy hadn't called when he said he would, but something about Sean makes me feel like I can trust him. Plus, I'm feeling a renewed sense of optimism about my love life now that the Cliff era has come to a definitive end.

My Personals account indicates three new icebreakers and two messages. I go straight to the messages and let out a sigh of relief when I see that one is from Sean. The other is from someone with the screen name *Paul*. I click on Sean's first.

Chloe,

First off, I'm so sorry for not calling today. I ended up working a double shift. (With Christmas right around the corner, I'll be taking a lot of those.) You would not believe the number of packages I loaded today. Sometimes I miss wearing nice clothes to work, but I do love the physical aspect of my job. Crazy, I know, but I'm actually going to miss UPS when I graduate. Anyway, back to my apology. I'm just beat right now, so I honestly don't feel much like talking, but I had to let you know why I didn't call—hence, this email.

Moving on...I was hoping we could sneak in a quick drink or something before our date on Wednesday, but my schedule is pretty crazy. (I'm sure yours is too.) Maybe we can chat one night before then though? Give me a call if you have time, even if it is just to say goodnight. 262-505-2314. Just in case you lost it.

Talk to you soon!
Sean

The voices of my mother and my friends echo in my head as I read through Sean's email. *Hmph, sounds like he was busy with someone else! . . . Oh, please, he didn't have time to make one phone call? . . . He doesn't know yet that you're too cheap to pay for text messaging. I wonder if he tried to text you?* But I shoo away these thoughts because I don't want to allow any suspicious ideas to take root. Instead, I smile as I think about his perfect apology. I tap out a quick reply letting him know that I intend to give him a call sometime before Wednesday and that I accept his apology, of course.

Next, I move on to the message from *Paul*.

Hi there Chloe,

I'm pretty new at this, so I'll just keep it short to reduce the risk of making a fool of myself! My name really is Paul. I know a lot of people use aliases, but I feel better about sharing my real name right off the bat.
What attracted me to your profile is the fact that you're a teacher. I'd love to see a photo and for you to take a peek at my profile and let me know what you think. No pressure.

Sincerely,
Paul

Paul's profile picture shows him standing on a sailboat. He's wearing a khaki fishing hat and a casual oxford shirt with the top three buttons open to expose his chest. His look is clean and preppy—a huge turn on for me. His face is hidden in the shadows of the hat, so I can't really make out his features, but his overall look is enough for me to take an interest. I also like the fact that we both used our real names. I almost skip his stats because this section has not proven to be very much use to me so far. But I look at it anyway, just out of curiosity.

~

Paul – 28
Location: St. Francis
Searching for a Sailmate

Relationship Status: Never Married
Kids: No
Want Kids: Maybe
Ethnicity: White / Caucasian
Hair: Sandy Blonde
Eyes: Blue
Body type: Athletic
Height: 5' 10"
Religion: Christian
Politics: Conservative
Smoke: No
Drink: Social Drinker
Pets: No
Education: Master's
Employment: Professional
Income: 60,000-80,000

~

Sailmate. Cute. Paul's stats seem perfect. I wonder how conservative he is though because I've been known to butt heads with ultra-conservative types. I've also never been sailing. But there's only one way to find out if we might be a good fit for each other, so I compose a quick response to his message that includes a photo and my number.

Finally, I sift through the icebreakers. I have zero interest in two of the senders, but one intrigues me a bit. He says he's a mapmaker and loves to bike, hike and play disc golf. *Interesting.* Another thing that stands out is his height: six foot six. I stand and tilt my head back, imagining how much he would tower over my five foot two frame if we ever went on a date.

"What the hell are you looking at?"

I stumble backward at the sound of my mother's voice. "Uh. Nothing. I was just . . . stretching."

She shakes her head and moves into the laundry room. "I'm so tired of having to straighten out your stepfather's clothes before washing them. You know what he does? He pulls his socks off and leaves each one all balled up and inside out! Do you know how annoying that is? And he *always* leaves T-shirts inside his sweatshirts. So *lazy*. If you ever stop being so picky and decide to live with a man again, make sure you look through his laundry first!"

My mother's last statement makes no sense. In the same breath, she has accused me of being too picky *and* encouraged me to scrutinize someone's laundry before deeming him worthy to live with. Sometimes (well, most of the time) I just don't get her.

As my mother continues complaining about Glen, I quickly sit back down and delete all three icebreakers. Then I open a few books, a notebook and a new Word document to make it look like I've been hard at work.

"Cat got your tongue?" My mother is now peering over my shoulder.

"What? No." I do my best to create the illusion of concentration. Hopefully, my mother won't question the blank screen. "I'm just trying to finish an assignment."

"Hmph. Maybe if you didn't spend all of your free time with those Yahoo! guys you'd be able to have a conversation with your mother once in a while."

"*Mom.* Seriously? I was here all last weekend. We'll have plenty of time to talk in a few weeks when I'm on winter break and the semester is over. And just how much free time do you think I have? I work all week long, I have class on Tuesday and Thursday nights, and I'm here doing homework every weekend. That doesn't leave a lot of time for socializing. *And* I'll have even less time after break once I start my thesis, so please don't start complaining now."

She stares at me blankly, as if she's contemplating whether or not to fire back or let it go. To my surprise, she chooses the latter. "Yeah, I guess. We're going to lunch. Are you hungry? I can bring you something back."

"That would be great. Thanks, mom."

Instead of saying "you're welcome," she goes back to complaining about Glen as she heads for the stairs. "Hmph. Your stepfather wants to go to that Chinese restaurant with the lunch buffet. I'll tell you what. Of all people, he certainly doesn't need a buffet." From the top of the stairs she yells, "We'll be back in about an hour!"

I sigh, and even though I'm tempted to log back into my Personals account, I resist. There's too much work that needs to be done. I really do have to concentrate.

chapter thirty-four

When I enter the Home Bar, I'm not greeted with the usual "Welcome Home" that I've become so accustomed to. Quickly, I see why. Chris is at the far end of the bar laughing with Shelly and Craig. Finally, they spot me and I'm greeted with a simultaneous "Welcome Home!"

"A little late, but thanks anyway, guys," I tease.

I climb onto the stool next to Shelly, and Chris gets to work making my usual Wednesday night drink. Shelly and Craig are already feasting on BABs.

"So?" Shelly says with a mouthful.

"So what?" I say. "Hey, Craig."

Craig smiles and nods as he takes a bite of his burrito. Then he goes back to watching the local news.

Shelly speeds up her chewing and swallows before continuing. "So? When is he coming?"

"He said he'd be here by seven."

"You haven't seen him since Friday, have you?"

"No. But I did see Cliff."

"What?"

Craig looks over, suddenly interested in our conversation.

"Yeah. He came over on Saturday night."

"Chloe! You let him in?"

"Trust me. It's not what you think. You're going to be so proud of me."

I relive the whole Cliff saga for them. Shelly cringes when I get to the puking part, but Craig laughs. Shelly then laughs when I describe calling the women, and Craig cringes. Neither says a word when I tell them about my final conversation with Cliff. They just look at me with sad faces.

"So, *now* it's over," Shelly finally says.

Shrugging, I say, "Now it's over." I finally take a sip of my drink.

"Are you sad?" Craig asks.

"I was at first, just because I really don't think I'll ever see him again. But I'm fine now, and I'm really excited to move on."

Shelly leans over, puts an arm around me and gives me a little squeeze. Before I can even relax into her embrace though, she quickly sits upright. "Hey, Chris, shots please."

"Shelly, no, I can't. I need to take it easy tonight."

"Aw. Come on. Just one. To celebrate."

"Fine. Just one."

By the time Sean arrives, I'm on my third. As I slam an empty shot glass down on the bar, Sean announces his arrival by saying, "The next round is on me guys." Leaning over and giving me a hug from behind, he whispers "hi" into my ear. I turn my head to look at him, and he surprises me with a soft kiss on the lips. Before I know it, he's upright, saying "hi" to Shelly and shaking Craig's hand. My thoughts linger on the kiss. It was so perfect and I want another, but Sean is now busy discussing something football-related with Craig.

My secret longing is interrupted by an elbow to the ribs. "Whatcha thinking about?"

I wonder if Shelly is grinning because she can sense the indecent thoughts running through my mind. "Nothing. I'm just surprised by how glad I am to see Sean."

She laughs. "Oh, I thought you might be wondering why he's *always* wearing a hat."

"Why would I be wondering that?"

"Well, you *are* kind of particular about a man's hair. And teeth. And feet. And . . ."

"All right, that's enough out of you." I put my palm up inches from her face.

"Are you telling me it hasn't crossed your mind?"

"What? His hats? No." *Not until now anyway.*

Shelly is right. When I first set up my profile, I wanted to include a sentence in the 'About Me' section to specify my preference for men with full heads of hair and straight white teeth. Jess was appalled by my snobbery, but Shelly didn't see a problem with detailing out exactly what I was looking for. Ultimately, I decided against sharing the information because I figured it would look pretty arrogant and I would never get a date.

"Well, now that you guys are on your third date, I'm sure you'll see him without it very soon. Maybe even tonight." She winks.

I laugh. "Are you serious? Miss shame on you for getting freaky in a movie theater?"

"Yeah, well, I overreacted a bit. Besides, a third date means it's okay for you to round second base now."

"What does that even mean?" I ask.

But Shelly doesn't have a chance to explain because Jess arrives. She's accompanied by a bearded man.

"Hello ladies," Jess says cheerily. "This is Jake." She touches his chest.

"Hi, I'm Chloe." I shake his hand.

"And I'm Shelly." She waves.

"Hi there," he says with a nod. "It's nice to meet you both."

Jess puts both hands on Jake's chest and looks up at him. "Jake, can you please get us some drinks? I'd love a vodka cranberry."

"Sure. No problem." He kisses her forehead and squeezes into an empty spot at the bar.

Shelly and I raise eyebrows at each other right before Jess turns to face us. "So, who's the hottie?" She nods toward Sean and Craig. "And I'm *not* talking about Craig."

Shelly sneers and reaches for her drink.

"That's Sean," I say.

"Nice. A tad short maybe, but still really cute."

"Well, thanks for the assessment. Jake seems nice. A tad hairy, but nice." I smile at Jess, and Shelly chokes on her drink as she laughs a little. "Come on. I want to introduce you to Sean."

I hop off my stool and lead her over to where he's standing on the other side of Craig. Shelly goes back to eating her BAB.

"Sorry to interrupt, guys," I say. "Sean, this is my friend Jess. Jess, Sean."

Jess gives Craig a little wave. Then she says, "Nice to meet you, Sean."

Jake returns with drinks. "And this is Jake, Jess's . . . friend."

"Hey, man. Nice to meet you." Sean and Jake shake hands.

After all of the introductions have been made, Sean purchases a round of shots. Then the guys excuse themselves to play the dart game 301. Before Sean takes off to the back room with Craig and Jake, he buys a beer for himself and another drink for me, kissing me on the cheek as he passes it off. I nervously look around to see if anyone noticed the peck, but no one is watching. It's not that I mind his kiss, but it just seems more like something a 'boyfriend' would do.

While I wait for Shelly to finish with a call from Cally and for Jess to return from the bathroom, I watch the guys playing darts. Sean and Craig are laughing at something that Jake is saying. They really seem to be enjoying each other's company, and for some reason it makes me wonder if this is how things are supposed to turn out—Shelly with Craig, Jess with Jake, and me with Sean. I know the idea is stupid, but it still seems appealing. The entire time that Cliff and I were together, we only hung out with my friends a handful of times. We never spent time with his friends either. Maybe it had something to do with the fact that I was always complaining about what losers they were. But who knows? He could have been thinking that my friends were stuck-up bitches.

"Well, Cally's on her way," Shelly says.

"Lisa too?"

"Uh-uh. They're done. That's why she's coming. She needs to blow off some steam."

"What happened?"

"Lisa was becoming way too possessive. I guess even lesbian relationships can be complicated."

I'm about to respond to her last comment when Jess returns.

"Aw. The guys are bonding." She giggles. "Isn't it cute?"

"I wouldn't call it cute, but I was just thinking about how nice it is."

"Speaking of nice, Sean seems like a catch. Look, he isn't even keeping tabs on you. And that sweet kiss he planted on your cheek before. What haven't you told me?"

I don't even bother answering her right away because I know Shelly is about to dive into the conversation.

"You didn't tell her about your make-out session with Sean at the movie theater? Oh my God, Jess. They were all over each other. If I was just some stranger, I would have pegged them as a couple of horny teenagers."

"*Chloe*? Making out at the movies? Sounds like fun."

Shelly rolls her eyes. "You would think that."

"Oh, Shelly, give me a break. Like you've never made out in public before."

"Actually, no, I haven't. I don't like PDA."

"Whatever," I say, sick of listening to the banter between Jess and Shelly. "Can we just have fun? How about a game of Ship, Captain, Crew?"

Two games and two shots later, I can barely see straight. I've reached the point of no return, where even a gallon of water could not prevent the hangover I'm going to be experiencing tomorrow. Shelly, Jess, Cally and I are in the back hanging out while the guys play another game of darts. Cally is in a reckless mood due to her recent breakup, so she's downing drinks like water. Shelly is busy consoling her and telling her to slow down. I wish she had discouraged me from doing shots on a school night while she was at it.

We're listening to Cally describe waking up and finding Lisa snooping through her phone when Sean puts his arms around me from behind and nuzzles my neck. I can't get over how natural things feel with him. It's like we have known each other for months.

"Do you want another drink?" he asks.

"No. I don't think so. I need to sober up. What time is it?"

He looks at his watch. "Almost eleven."

"I should really get going soon. What about you? How long can you stay?"

He smiles and pulls me down from my stool. We begin swaying slowly to "One Last Breath" by Creed. "I was hoping I could stay at your place," he whispers. His hands are moving slowly up and down my back.

"Yeah, I guess that would be okay. You *have* had a few drinks. It's probably safer if you don't drive all the way home."

The next thing I know, I'm sitting on a toilet with my head in my hands. I feel like I'm moving in slow motion as I finish up and stumble out of the stall. Jess is washing her hands, and Cally is leaning against the wall next to her. They're talking about something but I'm not in the right frame of mind to figure out what exactly.

"You guys, how long was I in there?"

Jess looks at me. "I'm not sure." Then she looks at Cally who shrugs. "Three minutes maybe. Why?"

"Because I think I passed out for a second."

"You what?" Jess asks.

"I think I passed out."

"Really? All you've had for the past hour is water. How many drinks did you have before I got here?"

"Five. Maybe six? I'm not sure."

"Well, I've only seen you drink three shots and you never even finished your second drink. Are you sure you passed out? You didn't drink any more than you're used to. Maybe you're just tired."

"You're probably right. I should get going." I start toward the door, but Jess and Cally don't follow. "You guys coming?"

"Yeah. In a sec. Can you tell Jake I'll be right out," Jess says.

"Sure."

I'm curious about why they can't finish their conversation in the bar area, but decide it's probably just too loud. Maybe they are bonding over the fact that they are both going through a breakup.

No one from my group is in the back room, so I turn and head toward the bar. I check my phone, expecting it to be around eleven, but I'm shocked to see that it's after midnight. I close my eyes and lean against the wall outside the bathroom when the floor starts to spin.

"Chloe?" I open my eyes to discover Shelly's face inches from mine. "What are you doing?"

"I need to go home."

"I know. The guys are waiting up front. I just need to use the bathroom. Are Jess and Cally still in there?"

"Yeah."

"Okay, well, I'll meet you up front." She enters the bathroom without noticing how out of it I am.

As soon as the door closes behind her, I hear a commotion coming from the ladies' room. I rush inside, and the scene before me is enough to sober me up—for a few minutes anyway. Jess's shirt is unbuttoned and she's in the process of buttoning her pants. There's plum-colored lipstick smudged on her chest and bra. Cally, whose plum lipstick is now smeared onto her cheeks and chin, has her hands on Shelly's shoulders.

"Calm down," Cally says.

"I'm calm! Geez. Excuse me for being freaked out for a second." She removes Cally's hands and glances at Jess as she enters a stall. "So now you're a lesbian?"

"Wait, were you guys . . ." I start, but Jess cuts me off.

"No, I am *not* a lesbian. Give me a break." She storms out of the bathroom.

I brace myself with one hand on the wall. "I need to go home."

Cally links her arm around mine. "Come on. Let's wait for Shelly up front."

When we get to where the guys have been waiting, Jess and Jake are already gone.

"Where's Jess?" Cally asks.

"She said they had to go." Craig shrugs.

I'm too disoriented to care, but Cally looks perturbed. "I'm outta here too, guys. Craig, tell Shelly I'll see her tomorrow."

"Are you ready?" Sean asks as he slips his arms around my waist.

"Yeah, but we should wait for Shelly to come back first."

But Craig says, "No, you guys go. It's late. She won't mind."

I start to protest, but Sean is already pulling me toward the door.

~

I open my eyes, and it takes me a few moments to realize I'm on the futon in my living room. Sean is on top of me, and he's exploring my left breast with his tongue. I lie still, enjoying a perfect state of ecstasy. He pauses at the center, swirling slowly around my nipple, just long enough to make me feel like I'm going to explode. Then he moves on to my right breast. When I realize he's fumbling with my belt, I plant my hands firmly on his chest, putting us face-to-face. I can tell he's no longer wearing a hat, but I can't make out how much hair—if any—he has, because the room is so dark.

"Are you okay?" he whispers.

I nod into the darkness, ignoring the voice inside my head that's whispering *are you sure you're ready for this?*

"We don't have to do anything you're not comfortable with," he continues. Then he kisses my forehead, my cheeks, and finally my lips. I graciously accept his tongue as he slips it into my mouth. My body quivers. It wants more—so much more—but then I hear the voice again. So I end the kiss, wrap my arms around him, and take a few deep breaths as I contemplate giving my body what it wants. After a few seconds, Sean slides onto the futon, leaving an arm and a leg wrapped around me. The warmth of his quick breaths against my neck feels so good, so enticing…

Sunlight shines through the large picture window in my living room. The goldenrod walls only add to the brightness that blinds me when I open my eyes. A cat is sitting on the coffee table three feet from my face, and next to him is an unopened condom. *A condom?* That's when the events from the previous night hit me. *Bar. Shots. Passed out on the toilet. Jess and Cally. Sean.* I close my eyes and see flashes of Sean and I making out, but that's all I can muster—flashes. In fact, everything after the awkward moment with Jess and Cally in the bathroom is fuzzy.

When I glance down and find our bodies naked and entangled, my breath hitches because, clearly, more went on than I can remember. This scene is similar to something I might daydream about—hot and heavy sex followed by a can't-get-enough-of-you cuddling session that lasts throughout the night. It reminds me of the morning after the first time Matt and I slept together—except *we* had been dating for months, not two weeks, and I had been sober. Instead of the sense of satisfaction I felt after taking my relationship with Matt to the next level, all I feel now is guilt.

I glance over at the clock and realize I need to leave for work in thirty minutes. Careful not to wake Sean, I wiggle myself off of the futon. I'm tempted to look back at him, but in addition to guilt, I'm also feeling extremely embarrassed, so I sneak away.

A flurry of thoughts race through my mind as I shower. *Is this what he does? Does he meet women online just to see if he can get them into bed? Does he think this is normal behavior for me? Will we continue to date? Should we continue to date? Why did I have to drink so much?*

Two muscular arms envelope me as I stare into my closet. I start to turn around, but Sean hugs me tightly and whispers, "Good morning." Then he kisses my neck. I close my eyes and tilt my head to the side, inviting him to continue.

Wait, I need to get going.

I turn to face him. He's fully clothed, hat included. I try to recall whether he had any hair or not, but that turns out to be one of the many details I can't remember. "I have to get ready," I say.

Without hesitation, he leans down and kisses me. Again, I lose focus because he's such a good kisser, and seconds later, he has me on the bed. That's when a fuzzy memory of me contemplating whether we should have sex flashes through my mind, catapulting me into a state of confusion and disappointment. *Did we, or didn't we? And if we did, how am I going to break it to him that I don't remember?*

"Sean?"

He continues kissing me.

"Sean, I have to get going. Or I'll be late for work."

He gives me a quick peck before pulling me up off the bed.

"I'll let you finish getting ready in peace then. Call me later?"

"Of course."

He pulls me in close and kisses me one last time. My initial annoyance quickly turns into arousal when I feel him hard against my abdomen. Then he leaves.

I rush into the living room to look for my belt, but the sight of the condom on the table stops me in my tracks. I search the futon and the floor for a used one. Nothing. *Is it possible we didn't have sex? No, probably not.* People don't wake up buck naked next to each other after a night of cuddling. If there is a used one, he must have thrown it away.

Belt in hand, I grab my bag and rush out the door.

chapter thirty-five

I'm on my way to my final graduate class of the semester when Jess calls.

"Hey, Jess."

"So? Did you guys get it on?" she asks.

"Well," I ponder her question for a moment, "I think so, but I'm not sure."

"How can you not be sure? Either you did or you didn't."

"Jess, I had a lot to drink, so last night is kind of fuzzy."

"Well, were you wearing clothes when you woke up this morning?"

"No. Neither of us were." She doesn't say anything. "I know, I know. But I didn't see a condom this morning. Actually, that's not true. I saw one, but it wasn't open."

"Uh-oh. Do you think he didn't use one?"

"I don't know. I couldn't stop wondering about it all day. You know what though? I vaguely remember contemplating whether we should have sex or not. So, maybe we didn't."

"Chloe, I hate to break it to you, but drunk and naked usually equals sex. Why don't you just ask him? *He* barely had anything to drink, so I'm sure *he* knows what happened."

"Yeah, I'm really looking forward to *that* conversation. I'm sure he'll be thrilled when I tell him I don't remember what happened."

"Don't beat yourself up over this. He seems like a really nice guy, and you two seem to have great chemistry, so I'm sure things will be fine whether you had sex or not. Wait, you're still on the pill, right?"

I want to ask her about the chemistry between her and Cally, but I decide that topic warrants a completely different conversation. "Yeah, but what about an STD?"

"Sean *does not* have an STD. But if I know you, you're going to obsess about it whether you had sex or not, so go to the doctor and get tested. I'm sure you're fine though."

"Yeah, you're right. I mean about me obsessing over it. I'll make an appointment tomorrow. I also have to make sure I *never* get that drunk again when I'm on a date."

"You probably just didn't have enough to eat."

I sigh heavily. "I'm so embarrassed."

"*Chloe*, trust me. You have nothing to be embarrassed about. But maybe it will make you feel better to talk to Sean about how you feel."

"Yeah, I think that might help."

"Okay. Well, I'll be back in town on Saturday. Jake is having people over. You guys should come."

"Us guys?"

"You and Sean. And Jake told me to see if Craig wants to go."

"Just Craig? What about Shelly?"

"Fine. I guess she can come too."

I laugh. "You're such a brat."

"You too. I'll talk to you later."

∼

It's a struggle for me to not fall asleep during class, but the trek to my car results in a second wind. The air is bitter cold, and there's a light dusting of snow on the ground. It feels so good for the semester to be over, but I'm already dreading the next. Four weeks off doesn't seem long enough.

I hop into my car and crank up the heat. Then I check my phone. No calls. Because he has not called, part of me worries that whatever happened between us didn't mean anything to him. It also adds to my paranoia about the condom. But then again, I said *I* was going to call. And I still want to be careful not to let things with him get too serious anyway. Suddenly, I'm annoyed with my own thoughts, so I crank up the radio. But even Bob Marley fails to take my mind off of Sean.

For the rest of the drive home, I rehearse what I intend to say when I talk to Sean. And I prepare for the worst by imagining all of the different things he might say: *Yeah, we had sex. Thanks for a great night . . . Sorry, but I'm not really interested in seeing you again. I just wanted to get laid . . . What do you mean you don't remember? Well I have news for you. It wasn't all that memorable for me either.*

Ten minutes from home and convinced that I'm ready to make the call, I pull over and dial Sean's number. Then I stare at the screen until it goes dark. *This is so stupid. Just call him.* Eventually, I flip the phone shut and start driving again.

It's nearly nine thirty when I enter my apartment. Sean's shift ended at nine, so I know he's probably home by now. But since I still can't muster the courage to call, I get ready for bed and make my lunch for the next day.

Twenty minutes later, I sit in bed and stare at his number on my phone screen with my thumb resting on send. I can't figure out what scares me more—the idea of embarrassing myself by telling him that I don't remember much of what happened or finding out that he got what he wanted so now he's no longer interested. I know these are not the only possible scenarios, but I have a habit of expecting the worst. The second I press the button, the doorbell rings, so I immediately press end.

Out of habit, my first thought is of Cliff. I rush to the living room to look out the window. A car is parked out front, but it's not Cliff's. The doorbell rings again.

I open the door, and a red baseball cap stands out in the darkness. Crap—now the holes in my memory are going to have to be addressed face-to-face. I flick on the outside light, opening the storm door just a crack.

"Hi. What are you doing here?"

"I don't know." He shrugs. "I couldn't stop thinking about you. So, I came here instead of going home after work." A barrage of emotions hits me as I process his explanation. The look on his face is so sincere. "Wait. Are you freaked out? I'm sorry. I should have called first. I can just—"

"No, no. It's fine. Actually, I was just about to call you. Come in." I open the door wide.

"Are you sure? I really should have called first."

"Yes, I'm sure. Hurry, get in here. It's cold."

When we enter my apartment, he removes a backpack that I hadn't noticed. I'm about to ask what's in it, but then he sets it on my kitchen table and says, "I have something for you." From the backpack he removes a half-gallon of vanilla ice cream and a pint of fresh raspberries.

My heart skips a beat. "You brought my favorite dessert?"

He smiles. "To celebrate the end of the semester. Where are your bowls?"

"Sean, that's so nice of you."

As I grab bowls and spoons, Sean hangs up his coat and places his shoes on the shoe mat by the door.

"I can't believe you remembered. It was like a twenty-second conversation. How much . . ."

But before I can finish asking how much ice cream he wants, I feel his arms around me, and the warmth of his midsection is pressed against my back. A familiar throbbing begins in between my legs, but I do my best to ignore it. *Nothing* can happen until we discuss last night.

"Hey, Sean? Can we talk about something real quick?"

"Sure. What is it?" He backs away, and I turn to face him.

"I was just . . . I was wondering . . ." *Just spit it out!* "Did we have sex last night?"

He cocks his head. "You mean, you don't remember?" I can hear the disappointment in his voice.

"No, I do. I just . . ." *Stop lying!* I sigh heavily. "Things are just kind of fuzzy. And when I saw that unopened condom on the table this morning . . . well, it freaked me out."

He leans against the stove and rubs a furrowed brow. Then he looks up at me, his expression earnest. "I asked you, Chloe."

"You asked me what?"

"I asked if you were on the pill, and you said yes."

"Oh." Out of shame, I break eye contact.

He laces his fingers on top of his baseball cap and looks to the ceiling. "If I knew how drunk you were, I never would have taken things so far." Then with a long sigh, he drops his arms to his sides, his chest and shoulders simultaneously falling into a slump. His remorseful eyes meet mine. "I'm sorry. I feel like a total asshole."

"Wait. *You* feel like an asshole? No. Trust me. *You have nothing to feel sorry for.* I mean, you must think I'm a total lush. I'm really not though. It was just a bad case of me overdoing it."

He looks at me and shakes his head. "No. I don't think that at all. I think you're great."

Relief washes over me, but I still want to clear the air about how fast things have been moving between us. "Sean? Can we talk about one more thing that has been on my mind all day long?"

"Please."

"What happened last night isn't something I do. I don't . . ."

"Chloe, I know. You don't have to explain anything to me. I don't either, but there's just something about you—about us." He reaches out and pulls me in until our faces are only inches apart. "I'm just *really* drawn to you."

I also mean to tell him that I'm not looking for anything too serious at the moment, but his closeness makes my body tingle and renders me speechless.

We kiss, and all the drama fades away. Then Sean lifts me and carries me to my bed. Even though I can barely remember anything from the night before, his body and every move he makes seems so familiar. It feels like we're moving in fast forward and slow motion at the same time. After a long day of worrying and overanalyzing, my brain rests and carnal desire takes over.

Over an hour later, I lie in Sean's arms with my head against his chest, lulled by his slow, steady breaths. As he slumbers, I admire his strong jawline and get my first good look at his high and tight hairstyle. *See, Shelly, he just likes to wear hats.*

chapter thirty-six

I sit at my desk, peanut butter and jelly sandwich in hand, with the Yahoo! Personals login screen up on my computer. Normally, I spend Friday lunch breaks checking email and sifting through matches. But today I just don't feel like looking at any new faces. I know it has everything to do with spending two nights in a row with Sean. I can still feel his hands on my body, and I hate to admit it, but I'm dying to see him again.

The last time I logged in was Monday. At my request, Paul, the 'Sailmate' guy, had given me his number. He also mentioned that maybe we could get together this weekend. I wish I wanted to, but I don't. I need to go out with someone besides Sean though, otherwise I risk developing the forbidden I'm-in-a-relationship mentality.

I log in to find dozens of new matches, five icebreakers and four messages. This is one benefit of online dating—there's never a shortage of prospects to choose from. But the overabundance of potential dates can be overwhelming. I never have enough time to sift through everything, so I end up deleting icebreakers and messages based on snap judgments made within seconds of viewing a profile. Sometimes I wonder if I could be passing up the love of my life.

I go straight to Paul's message and copy down his phone number. Sean and I are going to Jake's party tomorrow night, but I don't have any plans for tonight. So maybe I will give Paul a call—just to talk though. I don't feel ready to go on a date just yet. I'm still trying to figure out how to acclimate myself to sleeping with Sean and dating others at the same time.

The bell is about to ring, so I log out of my Personals account without looking at any of the other messages. I'm on my way out the door to pick up my class from the lunchroom when the phone rings.

"Hello. This is Ms. Thompson," I say.

"Hi, Chloe. It's Mary. Can you please stop in the office on your way up from the lunchroom?"

"Sure. No Problem. I'll be there in a few minutes."

"Okay. Thanks, hon."

Mary is one of the school secretaries. She once tried to set me up with her son, but things didn't go so well. He picked me up twenty minutes late and asked if I still had to change even though I already had. The second question he asked was about my ethnicity. When I told him I was half Taiwanese, he let out a sigh of relief and said, "I'm so glad you're not Mexican." I was tempted to tell him the date was off then and there, but I decided to give him a chance for Mary's sake. Needless to say, that was an early night for me. Before the setup, Mary always talked my ear off about how handsome and charming her son was. She could not figure out why he never had a girlfriend. I didn't have the heart, or the nerve, to tell her that her son was a jerk and a bigot.

I park a line of students outside the office and put an index finger to my lips, signaling for them to wait quietly. Then I step just far enough into the office so that I can see Mary and keep an eye on my class.

"Hi, Ms. Mary."

She smiles and stands, but instead of responding, she bends down behind the counter. When she appears again, she's holding a vase of red roses. "Someone thinks you're pretty special, Ms. Chloe."

"Oh, my gosh. They're beautiful," I say.

"Well, come on sweetie. Open the card. Let's see who they're from. Or do you already know?" She grins.

I peek back at my students. They are still waiting patiently but a few are starting to talk. "Children, I need to go into the office for one second. You are waiting so patiently. Keep up the great work."

I scurry over to the counter where Mary is holding a tiny

envelope out for me. I remove the card from the envelope and read the scrawled message to myself.

Dear Chloe,

Just wanted you to know how much I've enjoyed our time together.

Sean

"Well? Who are they from? Not Cliff, I hope."

I smile at her. "No, they're not from Cliff. They're from a new guy I've been seeing. Sean."

She raises an eyebrow at me. "You have made quite an impression on Sean, haven't you?"

"Well, he has made quite an impression on me too," I say as I grab the vase off of the counter and head for the door. "Thanks, Ms. Mary."

"I want to hear more about this Sean character," she calls after me.

～

After work, I head straight to a doctor's appointment. When I made the appointment, I said I needed a checkup instead of revealing that I really wanted to be checked for STDs. I figure while I'm there I can just mention it. I mean, surely the doctor will think it's a good idea anyway since I've never been tested before. While sitting in the waiting room, I give Sean a call to thank him for the flowers. In my head, I know this might be a strange time to call him—while I'm waiting at a doctor's office to find out if he gave me the clap (or some other depressing disease). But it's the first opportunity I've had all day to pick up the phone, and I just really want to hear his voice. I know he's at work, but I figure I can just leave a message if he doesn't answer. After the fourth ring, I prepare to leave a message but am surprised when a woman answers.

"Hellooo. Sean's phone."

"Um, hi. Is Sean there?"

"Not right now. Can I take a message?"

I want to ask who she is, but my nerves have gotten the best of me. "No. That's okay." Shaken, I hang up.

Before I can even begin to speculate about who she was, a nurse calls my name.

As soon as we're seated in an examination room, she takes my blood pressure and pulse, and we go over the basics like allergies and medications.

"So, you're here today for a standard physical?"

"Right. But I was also wondering . . . well, I'd also like to be tested for a few things."

"Okay . . . what do you think you need to be tested for?"

I pause for a long moment. "Well, it's just that I've never been tested for STDs. So . . ."

The nurse gives me a curious look. I don't sense any judgment on her part and I'm sure people are tested regularly at this clinic, but I still feel uncomfortable.

"That shouldn't be a problem, hon. You just sit tight and Dr. Skinner will be in soon."

"Thanks."

While I'm waiting for the doctor, I browse the pamphlets that are hanging on the wall. I remove one of several about STDs and take a seat. Chlamydia, gonorrhea, syphilis, HIV—suddenly, I feel sick. I'm about to grab a pamphlet about herpes, but there's a knock at the door.

"Hello, Chloe. How are you today?"

"Hi. I'm fine, thank you."

I glance down at my hands and realize that the STD pamphlet is still on my lap, so I get up and put it back in its place.

"So, you're here for an annual exam?" he says as he reads my chart.

"Yes, that's right."

"All right. Why don't you hop up on the table, and I'll check you out? Do you have any specific concerns?"

"No, not really. I've been tired lately, but I probably just need more sleep."

He finishes listening to my lungs and looks down at my chart. "Your weight looks good. You don't smoke. Casual alcohol consumption. Exercise three to five days per week." He looks up and smiles. "Your blood pressure looks good too. You're the healthiest person I've seen today. Before I send you down for some routine blood work, can you think of anything else that might be bothering you?"

I can't be sure, but I feel like he might be alluding to the pamphlets. Or maybe the nurse noted my inquiry about STD testing? Suddenly I feel like a teenager who's hiding something.

"Well, there's nothing bothering me physically. But it might be good for my mental health if I could be tested for STDs." There, I said it.

I'm expecting a barrage of questions, but all he says is, "Not a problem." He opens a drawer and pulls out a paper gown. "I'll step out of the room for a moment while you undress from the waist down and cover yourself with this." He hands me the gown. "When I return, I'll examine your pelvic area and take a swab." He removes examination tools as he continues talking. "Then you can head down to the lab to have your blood drawn for an HIV test and some routine blood work." He smiles at me as he opens the door to leave. "I'll be back in a bit."

Nurse Jenna is with Dr. Skinner when he returns. As soon as he finishes examining me, she has me sign a consent form for the HIV test. Then she leaves.

"We should have results for you by Monday or Tuesday, when

either Jenna or I will give you a call." He smiles and pats my shoulder. "Good to see you."

I return his smile. "Thanks. You too."

⁓

The first thing on my mind when I walk out of the examination room is the mystery woman who answered Sean's phone. He's supposedly at work, so maybe it's just a co-worker. But what kind of person answers her co-worker's phone? I certainly would not answer any of my co-workers' phones. And why hasn't he tried to call me back yet? Surely this woman has already told him that I called—unless she didn't want him to know and erased the call.

I sit in my car and hold onto my cell phone, willing it to ring. To my surprise, it does, but it's not Sean.

"Hey, Shell. What's up?"

"Hi. Whatcha doin'?" She's chewing on something crunchy.

"I'm just leaving a doctor's appointment."

"What's wrong with you?"

"Oh, nothing. Just a routine physical. What are you up to?"

"Not much. I think we're just staying in tonight and renting a movie. You can come over if you want. Craig won't mind."

"That's okay. I'm just going to stay home tonight I think. I want to get rested up for Jake's party tomorrow night."

"Have you talked to Sean?"

Shelly has no idea what happened between Sean and me. As far as she knows, he drove me home on Wednesday night but left right away—and no one knows about last night. I don't want to deceive her, but I also don't feel like being judged. "Yeah, we talked last night for quite a while actually. He's great, isn't he?"

"He is. But don't start losing yourself, okay? Remember your purpose for online dating. Just keep it casual. He could still wig out on you, you know."

A knot forms in my stomach. "Shelly, you're making it sound like I shouldn't even be excited about meeting this great guy."

"I am not. I'm just reminding you what *you* said you wanted out of online dating." The knot grows even more because *I'm* not the one who came up with the idea to just date people casually. She did. But I seem to be allowing my friends to influence me a lot lately. "Hey, if you want to get serious with Sean, go ahead, but I have a feeling you'll regret it."

I know she has the best intentions here, but due to the hypersensitive state I'm in, I'm desperate to have her see reason here. I need her to understand why it might not be the end of the world to treat my relationship with Sean like something special.

"Well, maybe putting restrictions on what I do regardless of what my heart feels is a dumb idea."

"*What* are you talking about? What exactly does your heart feel, Chloe? I mean, I know you're physically attracted to him, but you've only been out with him three times. How could your heart feel anything yet? You barely know him."

That's where you're wrong, Shelly. I know him much better than you think I do. "I know, but I just feel like there's something there."

"You felt that way about Drew, too."

"It was not the same. I was not as physically attracted to Drew."

"Look Chloe, I don't know what you want me to say. I just think you need to focus on taking things more slowly when you start dating someone. When I said it might be okay for you to round second base, I meant make out. Heck, take your shirt off. But I really don't think much more would be appropriate yet. Otherwise you might never really get to know him."

Her last few statements really piss me off, mostly because I know she's right. "Fine. You're right."

"I can't tell if you're being serious or sarcastic."

"I'm serious. You're right." I may have already ruined my chances of really getting to know Sean. It might not matter though when I find out who answered his phone.

"I don't want to be right. I just want you to be happy."

"I know. Look, I'm home so I'm gonna get going. See you tomorrow?"

"Yep, we'll be there. Do you want to drive together? Or is Sean picking you up?"

"He's picking me up, but we could pick you guys up on our way."

"That sounds perfect. Then Craig and I can both drink."

"We'll be there at eight then."

"Okey doke. See you tomorrow."

∽

Four hours later, Sean still hasn't called, so I'm on my hands and knees scrubbing the kitchen floor because that's what I do when something really bothers me—I clean.

"This is ridiculous," I say out loud. "Why the hell am I stressing over this?"

I stand, hands on hips, and stare at the roses on the kitchen table. *He would not have sent roses if he was seeing someone else. Or is that why he sent the roses? Does he feel guilty? Stop thinking like a crazy woman!*

In an attempt to squash the obsessive thoughts that plague my brain, I pour myself a glass of wine and turn on *Braveheart*. But I've seen this movie dozens of times, so my mind wanders anyway. It has been three and a half months since I started online dating. That's a lot longer than it took Cassie to meet Ted. Of course, things didn't end up working out with them, so maybe I should forget what started me on this whole online-dating journey in the first place. Despite all of the pitfalls I've experienced, at least seeing other people gave me the strength to get rid of Cliff once and for all. But all of the thinking that goes into whether or not someone could be right for me is starting to feel like a second job. And then there's the whole "don't get too serious" aspect of it all. Is it really for my own good, or could it ultimately prevent me from finding the one?

The wine is starting to hit me now, so watching the movie has become impossible. I stand and head to the kitchen to pour myself another glass. Before I head back into the living room, I grab my cell and Paul's number out of my purse. Sean has not called yet, so what the hell? I dial the number.

"Hello?"

"Hi. Is this Paul?"

"It is. I'm guessing this is Chloe?"

"Good guess," I say with a smile on my face.

"Well, not really. You're the only person from online who has my number."

Hm. That's interesting. Am I really the only woman he has encountered who's hell bent on expediting the process of online dating? Or is he just really new to this?

"Really? I hope it wasn't too forward of me to ask for your number."

"No. I'm glad you did. I'm tired of wasting so much time emailing people back and forth only to find out that they aren't what I expected when we meet. It's exhausting."

"I hear you."

"Say, I'm kind of busy at the moment. Are you free to talk tomorrow night? Or maybe we could even get together."

"Actually, I have plans tomorrow. What about Wednesday night? Are you busy then?"

"Nope. No plans. What do you have in mind?"

"Well, my friends and I usually go to this place called the Home Bar for ladies night on Wednesdays. It's also Mexican night. Are you interested?"

"Hm. How about if we get together just the two of us? We could meet at . . . How about The Social?"

I've heard good things about this bar but have never been there. "Sure. What time do you want to meet?"

"Why don't you give me a call before then? I mean, it would be nice to talk a bit before we meet in person. You know?"

"Yeah, I agree. Should I give you a call on Tuesday night?"

"It's a date."

"Okay, then. I'll talk to you Tuesday."

My conversation with Paul was short, but I already like the fact that he has the same mentality as me when it comes to not wanting to waste time. His seemingly straightforward, no-nonsense personality also appeals to me.

Despite my best efforts to keep thoughts of Sean at bay, I check the list of incoming calls on my phone to make sure I haven't missed any. Shelly's number is still the most recent.

Even though I know I won't fall asleep for a few hours, I decide it's time to hit the sack, mostly because I'm less likely to continue drinking if I'm lying in bed. I down my second glass of wine and watch as William Wallace secretly marries the love of his life. *Do people ever find love like that in real life?* As I'm turning everything off in the living room, the doorbell rings.

Out of habit, my first thought is of Cliff, but then I realize it's more than likely someone else. I jump up and look out the window to see Sean's car parked outside.

My heart feels like it's going to beat out of my chest as I open the door and stick my head outside. "You're here again," I say calmly, trying to hide the fact that I'm excited to see him.

"I am. Did you get the flowers?"

"I did. They're beautiful. Thank you."

He chuckles a little. "Well, are you going to invite me in?"

"I tried to call you earlier. You know, to thank you for the flowers."

"I know." He smiles.

"Well, why didn't you call me back?" I startle myself by sounding a bit too much like a pouty girlfriend.

He laughs again. "Chloe, that's why I'm here. My sister brought me dinner and answered when you called. I was in the bathroom. Then she proceeded to use my phone to call her deadbeat boyfriend. Twenty minutes into their arguing, my phone died. I was so mad at her because I knew you would be wondering who she was and why I didn't return your call. So I thought it would be best to apologize in person. Honestly, though, it was all my annoying little sister's fault."

He smiles, and my heart goes pitter-patter. I open the door wide, but he doesn't walk right past me the way Cliff usually did. Instead, he envelops me in his arms and holds me tight. It feels so right that I'm already thinking of how to cancel my date with Paul.

chapter thirty-seven

I open my eyes to find Sean staring at me—not in a creepy way though. It's an affectionate stare, one that makes me smile.

"How long have you been awake?" I ask.

"Twenty minutes or so."

"You were staring at me for twenty minutes?"

"No. For twenty minutes, I've been wondering how someone as tiny as you can produce such loud snores."

"Shut up. I don't snore."

He laughs as he puts his arms around me. "Yes, you do." He kisses my cheek, and then he moves in to kiss me on the lips, but I turn away.

"Uh-uh. I'm not kissing you until I brush my teeth."

"Well, go brush then, because I desperately need a kiss."

As I brush my teeth in front of the bathroom mirror, I see the reflection of a very happy woman staring back at me. Life is good. I have a job that I love. I'm almost done with my master's degree. I have wonderful family and friends. And I'm on my way to finding the last piece of the puzzle. Whether that last piece is Sean or not, I'm not sure. But what I do know is that I *really* enjoy spending time with him.

Before I leave the bathroom, I spritz myself with some body spray and throw on a robe. When I return to the bedroom, Sean's eyes are closed. Assuming he has fallen asleep, I crawl over him slowly. When I'm just about to lie down on my side of the bed, he throws his arms around me and pulls me on top of him.

"Where do you think you're going?" he asks playfully.

I laugh. "I thought you fell back to sleep."

Suddenly his face is serious, and he's opening my robe. He looks intently at my body as he slowly moves his hands from my ribcage down to my hips. I feel his hardness grow beneath me, making my body tingle with anticipation.

∽

"So, can you be back by eight?" I ask Sean as we stand in the hallway outside my apartment.

"I can be back by noon if you stay in that robe."

"Really?" I whisper.

He laughs softly. "No, but I wish I could. I should be able to get out of work at six, so eight works." He gives me one last squeeze and then releases me. "I'll see you soon."

"Okay. Bye."

I watch as he disappears down the stairs and then stand there for a moment wishing he would return.

∽

Cars line the street, so Sean insists on dropping Shelly and me off in front of Jake's house. Craig tries to join us until Shelly gives him a look that says he better hop back into the car with Sean.

Sean drives a few feet but then backs up and rolls down the window. "Go inside. Don't wait for us out here," he says. Craig nods from the passenger seat.

"Are you sure?" I ask.

"Yeah, it's too cold."

"Okay. We'll see you inside."

When Shelly and I enter, a wave of smoke hits us. She coughs obnoxiously. "Gross."

"Sorry. I had no idea it was a party-party. I thought it was just a small get together. Let's try to find Jess."

"I don't know, Chloe, maybe we should wait here for the guys. It's so packed."

"Yeah, maybe you're . . ."

"Ladies! Can I take your coats?" Jake helps me remove my coat as Shelly removes hers. "Follow me. I'll show you where to find the booze."

"Where's Jess?" I ask.

"She's where the booze is!"

When I look at Shelly, I can tell she too is wondering what the hell we're doing at a party like this. We were used to this type of atmosphere when we were in college. Heck, we even used to have parties like this when we lived together. But that was a few years ago, so we feel kind of like a couple of fish out of water now.

Jake hangs our coats and then leads us through the crowd into the basement where there are two kegs and a bar full of hard liquor. I know for certain that we won't be staying long when I spot a couple of beer bongs.

"What can I get for you ladies?"

"Vodka cranberry," Shelly says.

Jake nods and looks at me.

"You have Absolut Mandarin?"

"We have everything."

"Okay. Then I'll take a Mandarin and seltzer. But can you show us where Jess is first?"

Jake points and then leaves to make our drinks. We spot Jess across the room playing beer pong.

"Oh, my, God," Shelly says.

"Come on. Let's go over there."

Jess is poised to take a shot when she sees us approaching. "Chloe! Shelly!" She looks around at the group of guys surrounding her. "Hey, guys, these are my friends Chloe and Shelly."

One by one, they all come over to say hi, and before we know it, we're surrounded by men. I take a quick inventory of the crowd and realize that there are very few women at the party.

"So, what do you think?" Jess asks as she pulls me aside.

"About what?" I glance over at Shelly, who's talking to a big teddy-bear type with gelled hair.

"About all of these guys. You don't need to spend money to find guys anymore. Jake has all sorts of friends for you to choose from."

"Jess, Sean and Craig are here with us."

"Yeah, so? That doesn't mean you can't mingle."

I sigh. "Look, I don't know how long we're going to stay."

"Why not?"

"I don't know. Because I didn't know this was a kegger."

We both look around and laugh.

"At least the drinks are free," she says.

"True." I take the drink that Jake is holding out in front of me.

He hands me another. "Can you give this to Shelly?"

"Sure."

Then he grabs Jess's hand. "I need your help with something in the other room."

She smiles at him and gives me a wink before they disappear into what I assume is a bedroom. I haven't really had a chance to talk to Jess about her love life lately, so I wonder if she's still hurting over Ned and if she's still seeing the married pilot. I also wonder if she might be using Jake as a rebound.

When I get back to Shelly, she's no longer talking to the same guy. Now she's standing with three new guys who are actually kind of cute. I hand her the vodka cranberry. "Here you go."

She smiles and introduces me. "This is Chloe."

"Hi guys."

One is about to say something to me, but then his gaze migrates to something behind me. I turn to see Sean and Craig. Shelly kisses Craig, clearly trying to make a point to all of the unfamiliar men at the party—little miss no-PDA. Then she says to the guys standing in front of us, "This is my boyfriend, Craig." She looks at Sean and then at me.

"Um . . . this is . . ." I stammer.

Sean extends his hand to the guy in front of me. "Sean."

"Jay."

As conversation resumes around us, my face becomes hot. I feel stupid for hesitating when introducing Sean, but I'm not even sure why. Surely, he didn't expect me to introduce him as my boyfriend because he isn't, but it was still awkward. I glance at him as I quietly sip my drink. He's already conversing with the three guys as if they are old friends. His demeanor exudes confidence and he's so darn friendly. Why wouldn't I want this guy to be my boyfriend?

"Hey, Chloe? Do you want to help me find a bathroom?" Shelly asks.

"Sure." I put a finger up to let her know that I will be a minute, and then I give Sean's back a little rub to get his attention. He smiles at me. "Shelly and I are going to find a bathroom. Do you want me to bring you another drink?"

"No, I'm good. Thank you though."

∽

After our trip to the bathroom, Shelly and I get sidetracked by a group of girls hanging out in the kitchen. In addition to girl talk, we get roped into downing beer through a bong—something I haven't done since my freshman year in college. Shelly is taking her second turn when Jess arrives.

The sight of Shelly drinking from the bong makes Jess choke on her drink. She laughs and says, "Well, I was coming to make sure you guys weren't getting ready to ditch out on me, but I guess I don't have to worry about that anymore."

"Okay, so I have to admit, this is kind of fun," I say. It could be the alcohol talking though.

"Did *you* do one?" she asks.

I grin.

"Are you nuts? You're mixing liquor with beer? You are so going to have a hangover."

"No I'm not. Beer before liquor makes you sicker, but liquor before beer and you're in the clear. Remember?"

She rolls her eyes. "Yeah, I'm sure that rhyme has never failed you before. So, has anyone caught your eye?"

"Considering I'm not looking, no."

"Oh, come on. Just because you're here with Sean doesn't mean you can't look. It's not like you guys are an item. Or has one night of passion got you head-over-heels already?

"A night of passion?" Shelly asks.

"Yeah, you know, between Chloe and Sean."

Shelly gives me a shocked look. "*Chloe*, you and Sean slept together?"

I glare at Jess as she sips her drink and looks away. Then I look at Shelly and sigh. "We did. Wednesday night after the bar. I was totally out of it and I barely remember any details. I'm sorry I didn't tell you. It's just that . . . I feel so embarrassed."

I expect an immediate response, but Shelly has an uncomfortable look on her face. Then I realize that someone is standing behind me. I turn and lock eyes with Sean. Craig is standing next to him. *Dammit.*

"Oh, hey. Sorry we're taking so long. We got sidetracked." I do my best to pretend that Sean didn't just hear what I said to Shelly, but I know he did.

I expect him to be a little upset, but he doesn't seem like it. "That's okay. Just making sure you guys didn't get lost." He smiles and touches my back. "I'm going to use the bathroom."

Shelly and Craig are huddled together talking, so I take the opportunity to lay into Jess. "Thanks a lot."

"Sorry. I figured she knew. Nice recovery with Sean, though."

"I wouldn't call that a recovery. God, I wonder what he thinks of me now."

"Come on. You didn't say anything that bad. And you already talked to him about not remembering much right? So, what's the big deal really?"

Jess has no idea what has been going on between Sean and me, so she couldn't possibly understand that he might be hurt by the fact that I haven't told my closest friends what is going on with us. I want to tell her now, but I don't want to risk Shelly and Craig overhearing anything.

"I don't know. I just don't want him to think I take what happened lightly."

"You know, I saw him downstairs talking to one of Jake's female friends."

"You did?" I know it probably isn't a big deal, but I still feel a small spark of jealousy.

"Yeah. One of his co-workers. And she's single. Hey, why do you have that look on your face?"

"What look?"

"I don't know. You look like you . . . care. Wait. You like him, don't you?"

Sean and Jake appear before I have a chance to answer.

Maybe it's just my imagination, but as the night progresses, I would swear Sean is acting distant. I know it's likely just paranoia about some of the earlier awkwardness, but it still makes me feel bad. It also has me considering the possibility of ditching online dating and concentrating on just getting to know Sean. One good thing about my paranoia is that it has prevented me from doing a whole lot of drinking. I should at least be able to talk things over with him at the end of the night.

～

At nearly two in the morning, Sean and I watch as Shelly and Craig stagger up the walkway to her door. When she stumbles a little, Craig hoists her over his shoulder and waves goodbye to us.

We're silent all the way to my apartment. It's only a five-minute drive, but unlike other quiet moments we've shared, it feels awkward. When we pull up in front of my place, Sean doesn't turn off the car.

"Are you coming in?" I ask.

He turns in his seat and looks at me, but doesn't say anything.

"Sean?"

"Chloe, why are you online dating?"

"What do you mean?"

"Well, I can tell you why I'm online dating. I'm tired of searching. I know what I'm looking for, and I'm ready to make a commitment to someone."

"I know what I'm looking for too."

"I'm sure you do. But do you know what you want? Are you ready to give it a go when you find what you're looking for? There's a big difference between knowing what you're looking for and being ready to grab it and hold it tight when you find it. Some people just aren't ready. And some aren't willing. Do you know what I mean?"

I know exactly what he means, but I don't admit it to him. Somehow, he has me totally pegged.

"Is this about me getting tongue-tied in front of those guys or about what you overheard me saying to Shelly?"

"No. Well, not directly, but I suppose it's indirectly related to those things. I don't care what other people know or think about us. But I do care about what you think, and I get the feeling that you are confused about what you want."

I don't respond, simply because I don't know what to say. This guy is amazing, and the chemistry between us is mind-boggling. But he's right, I'm afraid to pull the trigger. I'm afraid I'll end up doing to him what I did to Matt and James. Or maybe I'll get what I have coming to me, and he'll be the one to break *my* heart.

"Sean, I'm sorry. I can't think right now. It's late. I don't know what to say."

"It's okay. The fact that you don't know what to say actually speaks volumes."

I'm not really sure how to respond to his last statement, so I say, "Can we just go inside?"

He sighs. "Chloe, as much as I want to go inside with you, I can't. Tell you what, why don't you think about what you really want for the next few days, and give me a call when you figure it out—regardless of what you decide. I'm not saying that I'm going to sit by the phone waiting for your call, but know that I'm willing and able to see where this could go if you're truly interested as well."

"Sean."

I grab his hand, and for a moment he looks at me as though he's going to change his mind about coming inside. Instead, he says, "It's late. I have to get going."

I want to tell him that I'm willing to give things between us a try, but the words get stuck in my throat. "Okay."

Sean watches as I walk to the door. He waves when I look back, and then he's gone.

chapter thirty-eight

I spend all day Sunday cooped up in my apartment. I eat crappy food, watch sappy movies and clean. I also spend a lot of time looking through old photos. Some are from past relationships but most are from when I was a little girl, before my father left. The photos don't reveal anything was amiss. My mom and dad have smiling faces, and my siblings and me look innocent and carefree, completely unaware that life was going to throw us a curveball. It would be a curveball that would influence the way we would look at and behave in relationships for the rest of our lives. But the variation in our ages caused us to remember the drama surrounding the divorce differently. I think this is why we all have our own unhealthy relationship habits. My brother always thinks he can change people, my sister lets people walk all over her and I'm the saboteur. There are not many pictures from after my father left. I guess my mom decided she didn't want too many reminders from the most difficult stage of her life.

Everyone I talk to on a regular basis—my mom, Jess, Shelly and even my sister—call, but I don't feel like answering. There's no point in driving others crazy with my confusion, because deep down, I know what I have to do. I have to let Sean go. Yes, he's amazing. But that's the point. Someone as amazing as him doesn't deserve to be strung along. Not that that's *exactly* what I would be doing if I decided to date him exclusively, but there's a good chance the passion would fade and I'd end up feeling the same way I did about James and Matt. I had the same kind of passion with them at first too. It faded in both cases though, and then I was too much of a wuss to be honest with myself right away about the fact that I couldn't stay in the relationships. The only way I can protect Sean from my lunacy is by letting him go. I clearly don't know what I want and I'm terrified of hurting him the way I did them.

Protecting him from me just feels like the right thing to do. Maybe my mom's onto something about me always thinking the grass is greener. Maybe that's why there's this little voice in the back of my mind telling me to let this one go. And maybe I have totally unrealistic expectations about what a long-term relationship should look like. Either way, I think I really need to stick with my plan of keeping things casual, at least until I can figure out what it is I really want. I don't know that I'm good for anyone right now.

Before bed, I think about calling Sean to apologize for my indecisiveness and for wasting his time. But for some reason, I feel like calling would just waste more of his time. Instead, I crawl into bed and try to shove away my own guilt for how things turned out. My final thoughts before falling asleep have to do with what I learned this time around. I can't change any of it now. The timing just wasn't right, and you know what they say . . .

Timing is everything.

chapter thirty-nine

On Monday, I go straight for my phone at the end of the school day. Dr. Skinner told me my test results might be available today. Sure enough, the clinic number appears in the call log and there's a message.

"Hi, Chloe. This is Jenna, Dr. Skinner's nurse. Just calling to let you know we have your test results. Dr. Skinner would like you to schedule an appointment for tomorrow to discuss the findings from your blood work. Thank you!"

Jenna's message puts me immediately on edge. I can only assume that I need to make an appointment because something is wrong. Otherwise, she would have revealed the results in her message. Right? My overactive imagination goes into high gear. I picture Dr. Skinner holding my hand and telling me that I have a bad case of asymptomatic syphilis. I shake my head, forcing away the ridiculous thought, and call to schedule the appointment. To my surprise, the receptionist says there's an open slot in ten minutes. I shut down my computer and leave immediately.

～

"Drug-induced lupus," I repeat.

"What?" My mother yells.

More slowly, I say for a third time, "Drug...induced...lupus."

"I don't know what you're saying. What does that mean?"

"The medicine I've been taking for acne has put me at risk for developing lupus." I don't even bother telling her about my reduced liver function.

"What? Why would you put your health at risk to get rid of a few pimples?" *Oh, mother. If only you knew the kind of risks I had been taking, and the reason I had that blood work done in the first place. Trust me, this wasn't what I expected either.*

I sigh. "Well, if I had known there was a chance the stuff might affect my health, I never would have taken it."

"Why the hell didn't your stupid doctor mention this could happen?"

"Because he didn't know my body would react to the medication this way. It's sort of like an allergy."

"So, now what?"

"I just have to stop taking the medication. He said everything will eventually go back to normal."

"Is he sure about that? Maybe you should get a second opinion."

"Mom, for now, I'm just going to stop taking the medication and have my blood tested again in a few weeks. If there are still red flags, then I'll get a second opinion. Okay?"

"I guess so. If that's what you want to do."

"Look, I have to return a call from Sarah. I'll give you a call later this week. Okay?"

"Hmph. Okay. Bye."

∼

Sarah doesn't answer, so I leave a message. Then I change clothes and do Tae Bo. Normally I would go to the gym, but I know Shelly might be there, and I don't feel like talking about Sean. I wish I could tell her everything that happened with him, but she already knows that I lied to her once. If she finds out I still wasn't being completely honest with her, she will judge me until her head explodes—not just for withholding information, but also for moving so fast with him. So it seems best to just tell her that he was upset about me not remembering the night we spent together. She will never know how upset I am that things didn't work out, but it's probably for the best. Of course, my hesitance to be completely honest with her makes me wonder which one of us is the questionable friend.

I'm twenty minutes into my workout when the phone rings. Billy Blanks is telling me to get some water, so I take a break and answer it.

"Chloe?" my sister says with concern. "You have lupus? How is it treated? Are you going to be okay?"

"What?"

"I just got off the phone with mom and she said . . ."

I hear my message playing in the background.

I sigh. "Sarah, I'm fine. The lupus is drug induced and I haven't even noticed any symptoms yet. My liver and everything else will go back to normal as soon as the minocycline is out of my system."

"Oh. I guess I should know better than to listen to mom. Wait, your liver?"

"Yeah, that was one of the biggest red flags. I guess I have slight liver dysfunction."

"Chloe," she says with a hint of excitement in her voice. It feels a little inappropriate, given what we're discussing. "Didn't the Angel Lady say something would happen to your kidneys or your liver?"

I think for a moment. "You know what? I think she did."

The Angel Lady is a clairvoyant in Las Vegas who is known to help people make life decisions based on things she's able to "see." She's called the Angel Lady because she claims to talk to the "angels" that surround her clients. Over a year ago, Sarah, Dave and I met with her.

"You're not going to believe this, but that isn't the only thing she was right about."

"What do you mean?"

"Well, I have some exciting news."

"What?"

"We're moving back to Milwaukee!"

"Oh my gosh! You are? When?"

"In April. Do you remember how she said Dave and I weren't

settled? Remember how we thought she was crazy because we had just bought our house?"

"Yeah, but she also said Dave was going to go back to work for the same company he worked for before you guys moved."

"Chloe, she was right about that too."

"What? He's going back to Sloan?"

"Yep."

"Oh, my gosh."

"I know. And that's not all. There's something else she was right about."

"What?"

"Do you remember when she said she could see another soul in our lives?"

"Are you telling me you're pregnant?"

"Yes!"

"Oh, my God! I don't know what's more exciting—that you're moving back or that you're having another baby!"

"I know. But what about this whole Angel Lady thing? Isn't it crazy?"

"It is kind of strange. I should take another look at that sheet she filled out for me."

"You definitely should. These things with Dave and I can't be coincidences. I bet she was right about other stuff too."

We continue discussing the early stages of Sarah's pregnancy and their plans for the move, but my mind isn't fully present. I'm busy trying to remember everything the Angel Lady told us. I picture the way she started our group reading. She went around the circle and said one thing to each of us to prove her ability. She told Dave he wasn't sure what career path to take. She said to Sarah, "You're a doormat. Stop letting people walk all over you." Even after she said these things—which were true—I was still skeptical. But when she got to me and said, "You have serious mother issues," I knew she was the real deal. I was amazed by everything that she said that night, but then when I got back to Milwaukee, I forgot all about her.

"So, anyway, get well, and I'll talk to you this weekend," Sarah says.

"Sounds good. Love you."

"Love you, too."

As soon as I hang up, I retrieve the stationery box from my nightstand. This is where I store small keepsakes and memorabilia, such as the Angel Lady's notes. I plop myself down on the bed and unfold the paper. It's divided into four sections: relationships, career, money and health. Under the health section it says: *"Watch for issues with your liver or kidneys,"* and *"Watch where you step—injury of the foot, ankle, or leg?"* She's one for two in this section. The liver thing does seem peculiar, but my legs, ankles and feet are fine. My eyes drift over to the section about relationships. It says, *"He's younger, but not a bad guy. It's NOT OVER yet."* Hmm. At the time of the reading, Cliff and I had just split. Moving on. *"The one you'll be with is from a place that begins with a V—Virginia, Vermont? Older than you by two years. Background in education. Two souls—boys."* While some of the details in the relationship section could have been about Cliff, the rest means nothing to me. And I'm uncertain about what the *"two souls"* part means—maybe it has something to do with future children. The next section is careers. I have to admit, a few goose bumps form when I read what it says. *"You are meant to work with children. The fruits of your labor will pay off—more money and more respect very soon."* None of us told the Angel Lady what we did for a living. In fact, the only thing each of us said to her before the reading was our own names. Then, at the end, we were allowed to ask one question each. How could she have known I work with children? And how could she have known about graduate school? And the pay raise I will get when I receive my master's degree? As for the money section, all it says is: *"See career section. You will always have enough."*

I lay back and hold the piece of paper to my chest. Is it possible that this woman really knows what the future holds? If so, why doesn't everyone go to her when faced with difficult decisions or when they just don't have enough patience to wait for life's mysteries to be revealed? And why isn't she rich and famous? Even if the Angel Lady can see what is in store for people, what if every little move we make alters our paths? Maybe the outcomes she saw for me changed the second I walked out of her apartment.

The information from the reading is compelling, but life is full of coincidences. I refold the paper and bury it at the bottom of the floral stationery box, the skeptic in me fully prepared to forget about it. But the believer in me wonders whether or not I know any guys from Vermont or Virginia.

chapter forty

I'm supposed to meet Paul in five minutes, but I'm lost. Turns out, I have no clue where The Social is located. I pull over and dial Jess. She knows where everything is.

"Hey," she whispers. "What's up? We're getting ready to take off, so I can't talk long."

"I just need to know how to get to The Social."

"Really? Why?"

"I'm meeting a new guy there."

"Oh. What's going on with Sean?"

"I thought you had to go."

"Right. I do. Where are you?"

"I'm near the Monkey Bar."

"Hey, we haven't been there for a while. We should . . ."

"Jess, I'm gonna be late, and you have to go, remember?"

"Oh, right. You just have to take First Street until it turns into Water Street. Then take a right on Barclay—I think. You'll see it."

"Great. Thanks."

When I finally find the place, I'm forced to park three blocks away. And for some strange reason, it has begun to rain, even though it's the middle of December. I open the trunk, hoping to find an umbrella, but the only means of coverage I find is a Six Flags Great America rain poncho. I grab it and hold it over my head as I jog the three blocks to the bar. When I enter, Paul is standing just inside the entrance, checking his watch.

He gives me an amused look. "What is that thing?"

Normally, I would feel self-conscious about showing up for a first date dripping with rain and sweat and holding a cheap, plastic poncho over my head, but not today. Ever since I looked at the Angel

Lady's notes, I can't stop wondering if the person I'm meant to be with has already been determined by fate. If so, then I've been spending way too much time trying to figure out who's good for me and who isn't. I've also been wasting time contemplating what to say and what to do when I meet new people.

I shake my head and start folding up my bright blue poncho. "Do you believe it's raining in the middle of December?"

"Well, if you had been on time, you would be nice and dry like me. Stylish poncho, by the way."

One thing I learned about Paul after talking to him for nearly twenty minutes on the phone last night is that he's a smart ass. He's giving me a hard time to be funny, not to be a jerk. I can live with that.

Grinning, I say, "Well, maybe if you had picked a place with a parking lot, I wouldn't have had to jog three blocks."

"Fine. I forgive you for being late. Let's get some drinks."

He grabs my hand and leads me to the bar.

While Paul talks about his job as an engineer for a small construction company, I try to decide whether or not I find him attractive. He's about five foot ten and has a lean, athletic build. He's dressed in casual business attire—probably what he wore to work. His sandy blonde hair is short and thick, and a subtle dusting of freckles covers his fair skin. I do find him relatively attractive, but it has more to do with his confident demeanor than his physical features.

"My friend's dad owns a construction business in Bay View." I say, trying to show I know at least a little about what he does.

"Really? That's where my company is located."

"What's the name of your company?"

"O'Neill, Inc."

"You're kidding."

"Nope. Who's your friend? Kasey or Shelly?"

"Shelly. I can't believe you work for her dad. So, you know her brother too then."

He laughs. "Yeah, Tom is a real character. I know him pretty well actually. But I really don't know Kasey or Shelly that well. I've only met each of them a few times."

"Wow. Small world."

"It sure is. Now it's your turn. Tell me about your job."

As I talk about my job, Paul listens intently. He makes me feel like every word I say is of the utmost importance. I don't feel a sliver of the physical attraction for him that I felt for Sean, or even for Drew, but I feel very comfortable around him. We discuss all sorts of new things with each other.

During our second round of drinks, we talk about family. When Paul tells me that his family is full of teachers, I think about the Angel Lady. She said the person I would end up with would have a background in education. Did she mean he would be an educator himself or that he studied education? Or could the background apply to his family? She also provided information about where he would be from. It doesn't hurt to ask.

"So, is your family from the Milwaukee area?"

"No, a small town near Madison."

"Oh? What town?"

"Verona."

"Verona?"

"Yeah, why?"

"Oh, nothing." But I'm sweating, because it really is something. "I've heard of Verona. That's all."

He looks at his watch. "I have to get going soon, but do you want one more drink?"

I glance down at the nearly empty cocktail in my hand. Then I think back to that drunk night with Sean. "No. I'm good."

Paul and I finish our drinks and make dinner plans for Friday night. He helps me with my coat. Then he grabs my blue poncho and my hand in a single, fluid motion. The way he holds my hand doesn't seem like a romantic gesture though. It seems more like he's just trying to be a gentlemanly.

From inside, we can see that the rain has turned into sleet. Paul lets go of my hand and shakes the blue poncho out. "Good thing you brought this." He opens the door and holds the poncho up high so that we can walk under it together.

I'm too busy smiling at Paul to notice a patch of ice that has formed on the step just outside the door. The moment my right foot makes contact, it starts to slide. But instead of grabbing onto something to break my fall, I lean forward with all of my weight in an attempt to prevent the fall altogether. It works. I don't fall. Instead, my ankle emits a crackling sound. Then I'm crouched down on the ground, gripping my ankle and writhing in pain.

"Oh no! Chloe, are you okay?" Paul is still holding the door open and crouched down beside me.

"I don't know. I don't think so. Did you hear that?"

"I did. Let's go back in and take a look."

He helps me up and provides support as I hop back inside on one foot. Paul sits me down and disappears. I hear him talking sternly to the bartender about the slippery step. Then he returns with a bag of ice and a shot of whiskey.

"Here." He hands me the shot, which I down immediately. Then he crouches down and gently lifts my leg up onto a chair. He removes my boot, lifts my pant leg and shimmies my sock down to reveal an ankle that has already swollen to the size of a grapefruit. "Shit. You need to go to an emergency room."

Paul looks at me with sympathy as I close my eyes and breathe deeply due to the pain. "Okay. I better call my . . ."

"No, you don't need to call anyone. I'll be happy to take you."

"Really?"

"Yes, of course. Come on."

Three hours later, we're still sitting in the emergency waiting area at Saint Luke's Hospital. Thanks to Paul, it doesn't seem nearly that long though. Every once in a while, I remind him that I can call my mom or Shelly, but he insists on staying, at least until my name is called. He hardly has to twist my arm because I'm thoroughly enjoying his company. I hear all about his childhood pets, how he got into sailing, his plans to go to graduate school, the bands he has seen in concert, a part he had in a play when he was in third grade—the wide variety of topics goes on and on.

When my name is finally called just after midnight, he tells me what a great time he has had and makes me promise to email or call the next day to let him know how I'm doing. As a nurse helps me into a wheelchair, I smile at the thought of Paul and my injured ankle. Maybe the Angel Lady really does know what she's talking about.

chapter forty-one

"Chloe, are you trying to say that you think the psychic reading you had in Vegas predicted Paul?"

"It's possible."

Jess chuckles, and I have flashbacks from months ago when she first started giving me crap about online dating.

"Wait. You're serious, aren't you?"

"How do you explain all the stuff she said about Sarah and Dave? How do you explain the stuff about my liver and my ankle? And Cliff?"

"Maybe she's an expert at sizing people up. Dave and Sarah are a young married couple. It wasn't that far out of the realm of possibility for her to guess that they might move. And a baby? That's what young couples do—they breed. And the stuff about Cliff? I just don't see what's so amazing about her mentioning a good guy that you had unfinished business with. Everyone I know has gone through a breakup with someone nice. I think you're reading way too much into everything this psychic said."

"Angel Lady."

"What?"

"She's known as the Angel Lady."

Jess begins laughing hysterically. "Chloe, she lives in Vegas for crying out loud. It's all for show."

Jess isn't trying to upset me, but the mounting frustration I feel toward her makes me want to scream. "Jess, what about my ankle and my liver? There's no way she could have guessed *both* of those things were going to happen."

"Okay, well, that *is* kind of weird. But I still don't buy it. Have you talked to anyone else about this?"

"About Paul? No."

"Do me a favor, okay? Don't tell anyone else about this Angel Lady, and try not to think about the things she told you. Otherwise, it will affect the decisions you make. You want to know what I think?" She's going to tell me either way, so I remain silent. "I think you're still frazzled about what happened with Sean. And I'm not belittling what happened with him—by the way—but I think you might be feeling vulnerable. I mean, c'mon, you really think Paul is *the one* based on a psychic reading? I'm sorry to be such a naysayer, but he most likely isn't."

"How do you know? You haven't even met him."

"And how many times have you met him?"

I hesitate before answering. "Once."

"Well, okay then. Let's keep things rational here. Go forth, and date."

"Whatever. How's Jake?"

"We're not seeing each other anymore."

"What? Why?"

"How do you think I know you're probably just feeling vulnerable after the whole Sean thing? I felt the same way when I met Jake."

"But I like Jake. He's a nice guy. Why aren't you seeing him anymore?"

She's quiet for a second. "Please don't freak out."

"Why? What's going on?"

"Ned and I are back together."

Don't freak out. Don't freak out. Don't freak out. "Oh? How did that happen?"

"Chloe, you know how these things go."

Jess is right. I do know how these things go. So who am I to judge? "Well, I hope things work out this time."

"Yeah, me too. Hey, we're going out on Friday night. Do you want to come? We're going to that dive bar on the East side. The one with shuffleboard." She knows how much I love shuffleboard.

265

"As enticing as that sounds, I'm going to dinner with Paul."

"Bring him with you."

"Nah. I have this annoying boot cast. It'll be a pain to hobble through the crowd. You guys have fun though."

The truth is I don't want to introduce Paul to Jess and Ned—not just yet anyway.

"Okay. Hey, Chloe?"

"Yeah."

"Thanks for not giving me a hard time about Ned."

Guilt washes over me because I wanted to scream at her for being so stupid when she told me they were back together. "Hey, we have to support each other, right?"

chapter forty-two

The doorbell rings at six on the dot, but I'm not ready. When I told Paul he could pick me up any time after five, he insisted that I be more specific. Promptness is just something the two of us do not have in common. He even calls exactly when he says he will. Some people would call this polite, but I think it's being just a bit anal-retentive.

I unplug my unused curling iron and throw my hair up into a sleek ponytail. The doorbell rings again. Hobbling around my apartment, I turn off lights as fast as I can. The doorbell rings again. Finally, purse in hand, I hobble down the stairs.

Paul's face is inches from mine when I open the door. He smiles and whispers, "Hi."

It amuses me the way he appears to be so calm and collected, even though he's obviously a freak when it comes to punctuality.

"Hi. Sorry you had to wait." I look down at my boot cast. "This darn thing . . ."

Suddenly a bouquet of lavender roses appears. I stare at them and think about how I've gotten more flowers while online dating than over the course of ten years of regular dating.

"Chloe?" Paul shakes the bouquet a little. "Here."

I take the flowers and bury my nose in them. "Thank you so much. They're my favorite color."

"The color symbolizes how I feel about you."

"Really? What does purple symbolize?"

"Enchantment."

The way he's looking at me makes my cheeks warm, causing me to look away. "I have to put them in water."

"Give me your keys. I'll do it," he says, holding out an upturned palm.

I hand him the flowers and my keys. "This is all so sweet of you. There's a vase in the china cabinet in the kitchen."

He returns holding a single rose, which he hands to me. Then he helps me through the doorway.

Enchantment, indeed.

∽

We had dinner at Blue Jasmine, a restaurant specializing in contemporary American cuisine. I've wanted to eat there since the place opened last summer but it's a bit pricey. I just don't have the money to spend on fine dining! When Paul told me where we were going I couldn't help but gasp—due to the cost, yes, but also because I couldn't believe he was taking me there for our second date. When he asked if I was okay, I told him I was just really excited about his restaurant choice. But on my publicly disclosed teacher's salary, I'm sure he also knew this wasn't the kind of place where I was normally able to eat.

To my surprise, we were seated within minutes of checking in with the hostess. I had heard that even diners with reservations typically waited a good twenty minutes before being seated at Blue Jasmine. But the surprises didn't stop there. When we arrived at our table, it contained a short vase of fresh lavender rosebuds and a bottle of wine. Then as Paul pulled my chair out for me, he whispered, "I thought you could use some more roses." And the magical date progressed flawlessly from there with engaging conversation, delicious food, long but comfortable glances and a little bit of footsy under the table.

∽

"Are you sure you want to go?" I ask Paul as we're leaving the restaurant.

"Yeah. It's fine."

"Because I can call Shelly back and tell her we changed our minds. Actually, I don't even have to call. They won't miss us if we don't show up."

"Chloe. I told her we would go, so we have to go."

"Okay. But we won't stay long—unless you want to."

Instead of the movie we had decided on earlier, we're off to Shelly's brother's house. He's hosting a game night. Shelly called during dinner to invite us. When I told her we were going to a movie, she asked to talk to Paul. The next thing I knew, we were ditching the movie.

"Chloe, just so you know. Tom and me, we get along, but we've never really hung out."

"Okay."

"One more thing. I once dated an ex of his. He was kind of short with me at work until I stopped seeing her, but we never got into it or anything."

I shrug. "Oh. Okay."

Unlike Shelly, Tom skipped college and started working for their father right out of high school. He finally saved enough money to purchase a duplex and move out of his parents' house a few months ago. Shelly told me her parents were willing to put up a down payment years ago, just to get Tom out of their house, but he wanted to do it on his own. Shelly sometimes gives her little brother crap for living the life of a thirty-something because he spends most of his free time fixing up his house. I think his dedication is admirable though. I mean, he's only twenty-four and already has his life lined up pretty well.

The front door swings open as we're walking up the front steps. "You guys made it!" Shelly calls out.

"Hey, Shell. Are you sure Tom is okay with us showing up?" I ask.

She shrugs. "Why wouldn't he be?" Then she looks at Paul. "How have you been? It's been a while."

"I know. I haven't seen you since . . ." He rubs his chin.

"Since the Christmas party last year," Shelly says.

"That's right. Your brother knows I'm with Chloe, right?"

"No. But he's going to be surprised as hell when he finds out."

Paul raises his eyebrows at her and then gives me a sheepish grin. I have a feeling there's more to his history with Tom than he let on earlier.

Shelly leads us into the living room where there are about a dozen people playing Taboo. The guys are in the middle of their turn, and Kasey is the buzzer. As soon as the timer runs out, Shelly says, "Hey everyone, this is Chloe and Paul."

Everyone greets us, and Kasey announces that she needs to refill her drink and use the bathroom. The group disperses.

Tom stays put on the couch and stares, wide-eyed, at us. "Are you two here together?"

"Well, hello to you too, Tom," I say with a laugh.

Paul gives a nod. "Hey, Tom."

"*Yes*, they're here together. Do you believe they met online? Small world, huh?"

"Yep. Sure is." Tom stands and stretches. "You guys want drinks?"

"Sure. Probably just one or two though. We aren't staying long," I say.

Shelly grabs Paul by the elbow. "Come on. I'll get you a beer and introduce you to my boyfriend."

I watch as they walk toward the kitchen and ponder my feelings for Paul. My thoughts are interrupted by Tom's voice in my ear.

"You're dating *Paul*?"

"Yeah, so?"

"The guy's a player, Chloe."

"What are you talking about? Wait. Does this have anything to do with that girl you both dated?"

"He told you about that?"

"Yes. Well, sort of."

"Did he tell you how he pursued her even though he knew I had been dating her for three months?"

"No."

"Did he tell you that after he got what he wanted from her, he simply stopped returning her phone calls?"

"Tom, no offense, but I don't really care. It's in the past. Time for you to get over it."

He grips my shoulders. "Chloe, I'm only telling you because I care about you. I don't want you to get hurt."

I've never seen Tom so serious before, so I can't help but laugh.

"I'm not trying to be funny, Chloe. I really don't think you should get involved with this guy. He's not what you're looking for."

"How would you know what I'm looking for?"

"Look, if you can go out with *that* guy, then I definitely think it's time you went on a date with me."

My smile instantly fades. "That's not funny, Tom."

"Again, I'm not trying to be funny here. I'm serious."

"No. You're not. Shelly would . . ."

"Wait. You're worried about Shelly? Trust me. She won't care. So what do you say? Can I take you to dinner tomorrow night?"

"Hey, Tom, get in here!" a voice calls from the kitchen.

Tom stares at me with pleading eyes.

"Tommy," Kasey enters the living room. "Everyone is doing a shot. Come on. You too, Chloe."

Relieved, I walk past Tom toward Kasey.

"So, you and Paul, huh? My dad says he's a really smart guy," Kasey is chatting as we walk into the kitchen together, clearly oblivious to the tension she just interrupted.

After everyone does a shot, Taboo play resumes. I join the women's team, but Paul decides to watch. When the game ends, Tom's roommate suggests we move into the dining room to play cards. All of the guys, including Paul, gather around the table, but only two girls join them.

Shelly grabs my arm just as they are dealing another round, "Hey, Tom, do you mind if I show Chloe what you're doing to the basement?"

"I don't care. Just watch your step. There could be nails on the floor."

Shelly leads me to the basement and through a maze of wall studs.

"So, this is going to be an extra bedroom, and he's going to put a bar in over there. Nice, hey?"

"Yeah, it's going to be great. He's really talented."

"It is great, but I don't know when he'll ever find time to go on another date again if he keeps up with all these renovations."

"Um, speaking of going on a date, I should tell you something."

"What?"

"Your brother kind of just asked me out."

She smiles. "He always asks you out."

"No, he *really* asked me out this time."

"What do you mean?" She's no longer smiling. "Why would he do that?"

"What do you mean why would he do that? He said he didn't think I should date Paul anymore, and then he asked if I would have dinner with him tomorrow night."

"You didn't agree to go out with him, did you?"

"Why? Would you really care?"

"Uh, *yeah*."

"Why is that?"

"Chloe, let's just not get into it. Okay?"

"No, it's not okay. Why would you disapprove of me going out with Tom?"

"Chloe, my brother might joke around a lot, but he's ready to settle down with someone—someone stable. And he's getting too old for casual sexual encounters."

"So, you don't think I'm stable, Shelly? And why do you assume we would do anything sexual?"

"No, I didn't mean it like that. I just don't want my brother getting his heart broken. Okay?"

"Oh, and *I'm* the kind of person who would do that?" I honestly don't even know if I want to go out with Tom, but having Shelly so against it suddenly has me feeling defiant.

"I'm not saying you're any kind of person. But you have to admit, you have been going on a lot of dates lately."

"Seriously, Shelly? You once encouraged me to ditch a *stable* relationship so that I could go out with you more often and *act my age*. And you're the one who has been encouraging me to date as many people as possible."

"Exactly, *date*. I didn't say sleep around."

My heart sinks. "You know what? I think we're just gonna get going."

"Why? Are you mad?"

"No. I'm not mad. I just want to leave."

"Look, the bottom line is I'm afraid you would break my brother's heart. And then our friendship would be ruined."

Tears begin forming in my eyes, as I think to myself that it might already be ruined. So I head upstairs without saying another word to Shelly.

∼

I stare out the window at bright Christmas lights as Paul drives me home.

"Are you okay?" he asks. "This is the quietest you've been all night."

"Yeah, I'm fine. I'm just tired. And my ankle is throbbing."

"No offense, but I'm glad you wanted to leave. I was getting a weird vibe from Tom. I don't think he was too happy about me being there. Did he say anything to you?"

I consider telling Paul about Tom's warning, but decide his past is really none of my business. Plus, Tom might still be trying to get over a crushed male ego. "No. He just asked how long we've been dating."

"Do you want to get another drink somewhere?"

"No. I think I'm ready for bed."

"Sounds good to me." Paul laughs when I nearly snap my neck to look at him. "Chloe, I'm just kidding."

Shelly's words are still fresh in my mind. The judgment and venom about the one guy I had sex with in all of this. Even though she didn't say it, I feel like Shelly doesn't think I'm good enough for her brother. I also can't help but feel as though she was calling me a slut. I know I shouldn't care what she thinks, but it stung. So the last thing on my mind is doing anything intimate with Paul.

"Yeah, I figured you were just joking." I try to recover.

We pull up in front of my place, and I'm dying to hop out. All I want to do is feel bad for myself in the privacy of my own home, but Paul turns the car off.

I unbuckle my seatbelt, and grip my purse in one hand and the door handle in the other. "Thanks for dinner. Sorry I'm not up for another drink."

"That's okay. You're welcome." He has a subtle grin on his face. "I can help you upstairs if you'd like."

"Oh, no, that's okay. I'm getting used to having this thing on," I say as I lift my leg slightly. "It's just a little sore. It'll feel much better as soon as I lie down and prop it up."

"I could rub it for you. Would that help?"

"Seriously, it's fine."

"Well, I'm going to at least walk you to the door. Okay?"

I smile. "Sure."

When we get there, Paul hands me the single rose that had been left on the dashboard during our date. "Just so you know, I'm even more enchanted by you than I was earlier."

"Well, thank you. You're not so bad yourself."

We stare at each other for a moment and then he steps in closer. We have reached the point at the end of the date when a prospective kiss hangs in the air. I expect him to make a move, but he surprises me by saying, "Is it okay if I kiss you, Chloe?"

I want to kiss him to see if I will feel anything, but part of me is still struggling with the conversation I had earlier with Shelly. Without answering, I throw my arms around his neck for a hug. He pulls me in close, and I think about how different it feels to hug him compared to Sean. It's nice to feel wanted, but the passion on my end is lacking.

He strokes my back and whispers in my ear. "Are you sure you don't feel like hanging out a little longer?"

"Actually, no, I'm not sure. But I think it might be best if we get to know each other better before we spend time alone at my place or yours. You know?"

He squeezes me a little tighter and lets out a vocal sigh—making it clear that wasn't the answer he was hoping for. Then he gives me a peck on the forehead and starts walking backward down the driveway. "I'm leaving for my parents' house on Wednesday, and I won't be back until Sunday. I can call you while I'm there though."

"I'd like that. Thanks again for dinner. I had fun tonight."

"Me too." He waves before turning and heading to his car.

chapter forty-three

Today, I'm doing something that I haven't done since Easter. I'm going to church with my parents.

"What are you doing here, Chloe? You don't have schoolwork to do, do you? Why are you dressed like that?"

"I'm going to church with you guys."

"What?" My mother says loudly. "Why? Wait, are you feeling guilty about something?"

"*No.* My gosh. You complain when I don't go to church, and now you're complaining because I want to go. I can't win either way." She's right though. I do feel guilty. But that's not the only reason I want to go to church. I also feel conflicted about whether or not I should have started online dating in the first place. After all, the last thing the world of online dating needs is another person who has absolutely no idea what she wants. I feel like a bad person for hurting James and Matt. I feel guilty for not being more understanding when Cliff wanted to date other people. I feel like a hussy for getting drunk and having unprotected sex with someone I barely knew. And I feel torn about continuing to date Paul even though he seems like a wonderful guy so far—aside from the things Tom told me, but who knows if there was any truth to his claims. Plus, I was raised to believe that only God knows what is in store for us, so I'm also leery about everything the Angel Lady seems to have been right about.

"Well, maybe going to church today will help cure you."

"Cure me?"

"Your sickness. I've been praying for God to heal you, but it helps if the person I'm praying for goes to church."

"Mom, I'll be fine. I already stopped taking the medication."

"Well, I'm sure my praying will help."

~

My parents still go to the same church we went to when I was a little girl. My mom and stepfather are loyal to this church beyond reason. The congregation consists of less than fifty people, most of whom are not regular attendees. Whenever my mom complains about a sermon or about my stepfather having to serve as an usher every week, I remind her that they can always try a different church. But to her, that's like suggesting they ditch their old VCR for a DVD player. No matter how dissatisfied she is with something familiar, the idea of trying anything new is preposterous.

Greetings abound as soon as we enter the foyer. Kathy Dumas, who has been the organist ever since I can remember, hugs me. "Chloe, welcome. It's so nice to see you, dear." The smell of her hyacinth perfume takes me back to my days in Sunday school. Her perfume would always waft out of the choir area, filling the entire upper level of the church with its heavenly scent.

"It's nice to see you too, Mrs. Dumas."

After distributing bulletins, my stepfather finds a seat near the back with the other usher and I follow my mom up the center aisle. I nearly collide with her when she stops abruptly, just short of the second set of pews. "Hmph."

"Mom, what are you doing?"

"Someone is sitting in my seat."

Sure enough, directly in front of the podium in the first row is a family of four: a young couple with small children. "So what. Either squeeze in next to them, or sit behind them."

"I always sit there though."

Kathy Dumas has begun to play the organ, signifying that the service will begin shortly.

"Who cares, mom?" I squeeze past her and pull her along after me into the second row.

Less than five minutes into the service it's time to greet our neighbors. I turn around and say good morning to the four people sitting behind us. Then I turn back to find my mom shaking hands with the people in front of us. I make eye contact with the young mother and nearly choke when I realize I know her. It's Sadie Blanchard, a girl Shelly and I went to college with. My shock has nothing to do with the fact that she's standing in front of me. Rather, it's because I recognize the guy standing beside her, and each of them is holding a small child.

"Sadie?"

"Oh, my gosh. Chloe?"

The wave of memories flooding my brain is interrupted. "Okay. Okay. Talk after church. Not now. Time to focus on God," my mother says.

But instead of focusing on God, my mind wanders back to my sophomore year in college when I met Shelly and Sadie. The three of us had Introduction to Children's Literature together. Just like Shelly, Sadie thought I acted too old for my age. Out of the three of us, Sadie lived up her college years the most. It never occurred to me until now that Sadie might be the reason Shelly gave up her miss-goodie-two-shoes image for a while to enjoy college life. Not because she pressured her the way Shelly had pressured me, because Sadie never pressured anyone to dump a boyfriend or join her at a party in lieu of the library. She had no problem doing those things on a regular basis herself though. Sitting beside Sadie in the pew is the guy who was her on-again-off-again college boyfriend, Lane. Lane once showed up at a party just to carry a passed out Sadie back to her dorm room—they were off at the time. Too much partying caused her to drop out right before we were all supposed to start student teaching. Shelly and I were certain she would end up an alcoholic single mother. But from the looks of it, we were way off.

After the service, I linger near the bathroom hallway and look on as people drink coffee and eat donut holes. Sadie is helping her toddler-aged son eat a donut, and Lane is holding their infant. Sadie looks around as she holds the last bit of donut out for her son to finish and we make eye contact. She smiles, says something to Lane and then they are heading my way.

"Hi, Chloe. How are you?"

Lane smiles but he's too busy with the children to say anything.

"I'm good. Wow, look at you guys. How old are your kids?"

"Two and six weeks."

I look her up and down. "You look amazing for having a baby only six weeks ago."

"Thanks. You look great too. Is that your mom and your stepdad over there?"

"Yeah. This is their church. I actually went here when I was a kid but don't attend regularly now."

"Oh. Well, we're just visiting Lane's grandparents, Mark and Mary." She points to a small group.

I shrug. "I don't know too many people here anymore."

"So, what's going on in your life?" She leans sideways and peeks at my left hand. "No husband yet, I see. Do you have a boyfriend? Any kids?"

"Uh, no. Neither."

"Really? I never would have guessed you would still be single. Good for you though. Enjoy it." She laughs.

"Hey, watch it. You love being married to me." Lane interjects right before he scurries after their little boy.

"What about Shelly? Do you still talk to her?"

"I do. She's good. We're both teaching, and she's dating a really nice guy."

"Well, that's wonderful."

"So, where do you guys live?"

"We're in Minnesota for now, but Lane's company might be relocating us back to the area."

"Is that what you're hoping for?"

"It sure is. Do you remember my sister? She went out with us a few times. Well, she has four-month-old twins. It would be great if our kids could be closer growing up." I see her eyes wander back to her little boy. "Hey, I'm sorry, I have to go. But it was great catching up with you. Tell Shelly I said hi."

"I will. Let me know if you do move back into town. We could get together." Even as I say it, I know I will probably never see Sadie again.

I watch as she joins her husband and children at the coat racks. They look so happy. No one would ever believe Sadie and Lane used to smoke marijuana on a daily basis. How in the world did Sadie Blanchard end up marrying her college boyfriend and becoming a mother of two? It makes me feel like such a failure.

"How do you know Mark and Mary's daughter-in-law?" As usual, my mother has appeared out of nowhere.

"We had some college classes together."

"College? Really? Then I guess it isn't so unrealistic for me to think it's about time for you to settle down and start a family. Just think, if you had stayed with Matt, that could be you." She looks over at their perfect little family. "Hmph."

"Yeah, well, I took a different path."

"Yeah, well, the path she took led to a husband and two beautiful children. You have three cats and a bunch of boyfriends."

"I don't have a bunch of boyfriends, mom. I don't even have one."

"I thought you were supposed to meet the perfect guy online," she whispers.

"Mom, why are you whispering?"

"Because. I don't want anyone to know you've been meeting men on our *computer*." I can barely hear her when she says the word *computer*.

I sigh. "Well, let's not talk about it then. And can we get going soon? I need to finish my Christmas shopping."

But checking my Personals account and giving Paul a call are suddenly on my mind as well.

chapter forty-four

I wave as several buses loaded with antsy children drive off. Then I hightail it back inside out of the cold. Christmas is three days away and I won't see my students until the New Year. My plan is to work late and get everything ready for our first two weeks back.

Tonight is Ladies' Night at the Home Bar. I know Shelly, Craig and a lot of other people will be there, but I don't plan on going. It has been four days since I spoke with Shelly, but I refuse to be the first one to call after the hurtful things she said. I haven't spoken with Jess either since she spilled the beans about her reconciliation with Ned. Who knows? Maybe Shelly and Jess will end up at the Home Bar together tonight. That would be perfect. Then they can discuss what I should and shouldn't do with my life without me there to interrupt.

It's close to six when I finish prepping my classroom. Since I don't have plans for the evening, I call to place an order for Chinese food. Then I log into my Personals account to see if any of the icebreakers I sent out on Sunday at my parent's house panned out. Turns out, none of them have. Plus, I still haven't heard from Paul since our date on Saturday night and there's no message from him either. No word from Paul is even more annoying than not receiving any responses from the icebreakers because I left a voicemail when I called him on Sunday after church. I try to soothe my bruised ego by telling myself he may just be busy with Christmas right around the corner. But then I realize that this reasoning is seriously flawed. How hard is it to return a phone call?

Who knows? Maybe there was some truth to the things Tom said about Paul. Then I do what any suspicious online-dating woman would do: I check his account to see if he has logged in lately. When

I see that he has not logged in for over a week, I realize how crazy my behavior is. I really need to bone up on my casual-dating skills.

~

I'm spooning steamed chicken and veggies onto a plate when the doorbell rings. For the first time in a long time, Cliff is not my first thought. I have no clue who the unannounced visitor could be, but since I'm still wearing the boot cast, I bypass hobbling into the living room to look out the window and just head straight to the door instead. I'm halfway down the stairs when I hear keys jingling and the downstairs door opening. I figure Deena or Scott must have rung my doorbell for some reason, so I turn to head back up to my apartment. But then I hear Deena's voice.

"What did you say your name was?"

"Paul."

"Okay. Wait here. I'll see if she's home."

Paul? What on earth would he be doing here?

Deena rounds the corner. "Chloe! Oh, my gosh. You startled me!"

I laugh. "I'm sorry. I was heading down to get the door."

In a low voice, she says, "There's some guy here looking for you. Do you know a Paul?"

"I do." *But I have no idea what he's doing here, and I'm having Cliff flashbacks at this very moment.*

She leans in close and whispers, "He's pretty *cute*."

"He is, isn't he?" I say to myself as much as to Deena.

"Well, have a good night." She peeks her head around the corner. "Hey, come on up." She turns back to smile at me and then leaves.

Paul sticks his head around the corner. "Hey, Chloe."

"Hi. What are you doing here? I thought you were leaving for your parents' house tonight."

"I am. I was on my way, but something drew me here."

I stare at him, thinking about how I told him we should get to know each other better before hanging out alone in my apartment.

"I brought something." He climbs three stairs until he's right in front of me. I notice he's wearing jeans, a worn-in Badgers sweatshirt and a baseball cap—a look that makes me realize I'm physically attracted to him. He pulls a DVD out from behind his back. *Harold and Maude.* "Are you up for a movie?"

"So, you didn't really decide to pull off the freeway and stop over on the fly, did you?" I'm taken aback by the suspicious tone of my voice.

He laughs. "I always bring a few movies when I visit my parents. My family is full of movie buffs. Nice sleuth work though. If you don't want me to stay, that's fine. I understand. But keep this in case you get bored waiting for me to take you on another date." He hands the DVD to me.

It's just a movie, Chloe. No big deal. "All right. Let's watch it."

~

Ten minutes into the movie, I notice out of the corner of my eye that Paul is staring at me. I look at him sideways and say, "Are you going to watch me or the movie?"

"Sorry. I can't help it." He reaches down and grabs my injured leg. Then he slowly lifts it and turns my body so that my leg rests across his lap. "You should elevate your ankle."

Now I have to turn my head to watch the movie, and my attention is drawn away from the movie when he begins taking my boot cast off. "What are you doing?"

"I'm taking this thing off so I can rub your leg. Is that okay?"

Even though I feel a bit uncomfortable, my numb leg could use a rub. "I guess so. Thanks."

Paul rubs my foot for a while and then, bypassing my black and blue ankle, he begins rubbing my calf. I do my best to pay attention to Harold and Maude's bizarre love story, but nothing makes sense because Paul's hands are inching up to my thigh. The word *stop* is on the tip of my tongue, but my rapidly beating heart has hijacked my brain once again. So, I pretend to watch the movie and enjoy Paul's touch. *A leg rub is not sexual*, I reason, but the warmth between my legs tells a different story.

When Paul reaches my hip, he stops rubbing and shimmies behind me into a laying position. Then he drapes his arm around my waist. My body freezes, but my brain becomes a hive of activity as I contemplate what to do if he kisses my neck or tries to make an even bolder move. But three minutes later—yes, my eyes have been on the clock the whole time—Paul still has not tried a thing. I turn my head a sliver and peek at him out of the corner of my eye. He's not looking at me though, he's watching the movie.

At the end of the movie, Paul stands and pulls me up with him. He stretches and yawns. "Did you like it?" he asks.

"It was interesting. Sad at the end though."

"At least he found his soul mate." He pats the pockets of his jeans to make sure he has his keys. Then he retrieves the movie from the DVD player and places it back in the case. "I have to get going. My mom won't go to bed until I get there. She's a worry wart."

"That's so cute. Thanks for stopping by." The fact that he didn't attempt anything more than an innocent leg rub and snuggling has me intrigued.

We walk to the door hand in hand. When we get there, he bends down for a hug and then opens the door. I stare at him, wondering if he's going to turn around and kiss me, but he simply looks back over his shoulder and says, "Bye, Chloe. I'll call you soon."

"Okay. Drive safe."

chapter forty-five

I wake up Christmas morning feeling better after being sick for two days. The morning after Paul's surprise visit, I woke up with body aches and a sore throat. I guess it was a good thing he didn't kiss me after all.

Anxious to leave my apartment, I get ready in record time and make it to my parents' house as they are sitting down for breakfast.

"Merry Christmas!" I say.

Glen says, "Merry Christmas, Chloe."

My mom says, "What are you doing here? I was sure you wouldn't be here until lunchtime!"

"I just wanted to get here early. What are you guys having for breakfast?"

"Hmph. So that's why you're here early."

"Jan, would you just get Chloe a plate of food? It's Christmas for Christ's sake." He looks at me. "There's a fresh pot of coffee. Almond mocha."

"Thanks, Glen."

He winks and goes back to eating his pancakes and bacon.

"Where have you been?" my mom asks as she plops a plate of food onto the table.

"I was sick. I spent the last two days in bed."

"So, your doctor was wrong. You stopped taking that medicine and you're still sick. And why are you still wearing that thing on your leg? It's been two weeks. All you had was a bad sprain. Your ankle should be healed by now."

"Mom, my sickness had nothing to do with the medicine I was taking. I had a sore throat. I work with germy kids, remember? And the doctor said I can try going without the cast after today. Actually,

I don't see why I can't take it off now." I bend down and undo the Velcro straps of my boot cast.

"Well, if he said you can take it off *after* today, then you should leave it on."

I sigh and redo the straps. In an attempt to change the subject, I say, "It sucks that Sarah and Dave couldn't be here."

"They'll be here all the time soon enough," my mom says. "Did your sister tell you about all that Angel Lady nonsense?"

"Why do you say it's nonsense?"

"Because no one but God knows what is going to happen in the future. Your sister thinks that lady talks to angels? I say it's black magic."

"Well, whatever it is, she knew a lot of things about us, and the predictions she made about Sarah and Dave weren't the only ones that turned out to be accurate."

"Why? What did she tell you?"

"She said that I would hurt my foot or my ankle and that I would be getting a raise at work."

"So what? People get raises all the time."

"I know, but she also said I would be earning more respect at work."

"Hmph. That's useless information. Did she mention if you would be having kids before you turn thirty?"

"No. But she did say I would meet a man with a background in education and that he would be from some place that starts with V."

"Well, that narrows it down." Her tone is rife with sarcasm. "And that's just great, because now you're going to start bypassing men just because they aren't teachers. So much for you marrying anyone with money I guess."

"That's not true." Although, she isn't completely wrong. The last time I checked my Personals account, I made a point to search for matches that mentioned teaching experience or a background in education. I didn't just do this because of what the Angel Lady said though. I also did it because I figured I might have more in common with someone who has a similar career. I'm fully aware that basing life decisions on a psychic reading is ridiculous, but it makes sense that I would end up with someone in an education-related field.

"Are you dating anyone right now?"

"Yes. He's an engineer." *And I know it's a stretch, but his mom, uncle and sister are teachers. And he's from Verona.* I don't dare mention these things to my mother though. If I did, she would go back to badmouthing the Angel Lady.

"*Oh*. Engineers make a good salary. Probably not as much as a master electrician, like Matt, but enough."

"Mom, I couldn't care less how much people make. You know that. I just want to be happy."

She laughs. "We all do, Chloe. We all do. So, you like this guy?"

"I think so. We'll see what happens. In the meantime, I plan to meet more people."

She sighs. "You've been doing this online thing for months. Seems like a crapshoot, just like meeting someone at the grocery store or the library. You should just save your money and admit to yourself that you're just too damn picky. Should we open some presents?"

Now it's my turn to sigh. What's the point of even trying to convince her that she's wrong?

chapter forty-six

The next morning, I wake up on the sofa in my parents' basement. We played mahjong with a friend of my mother's all Christmas afternoon. I intended on going home after dinner, but my mom was so sad after talking to James and Sarah that I decided to stick around. After a couple of movies, I retired to the basement to check my Personals account.

Lately, when I log in, there are only a few new faces added to my list of matches. It seems like most of the same people continue to show up week after week. I even still come across Scott's profile once in a while. He's on his third screen name—that I know of anyway. Either people are too busy to date around the holidays or online dating is not going to take off the way some people think it is.

My reason for logging in last night was not to check for new matches though. As stalkerish as it sounds, I wanted to check again to see if Paul had been active. A sense of satisfaction washed over me when I saw that he hadn't logged in for at least two weeks. The way I feel about Paul's inactivity has hypocrite written all over it though, because after checking his account, I wrote down a guy's phone number and messaged him to say that I would call to schedule a date sometime next week.

Besides perusing my Personals account, I also checked my email. Jess and I exchanged Christmas greetings over the phone during the day, but Shelly still hasn't called. I was hoping she might have sent a message—even if it was just to say Merry Christmas. Part of me is ready to cave and call her, but I keep reminding myself of the argument we had in Tom's basement. I don't know if I'll ever be able to forget her insinuations. And now that she's officially dating Craig, it seems like I'm no longer an important part of her life. I feel like an expendable friend who's no longer on the same acceptable path.

After brunch at my parents' house, I head home. My phone rings as I'm driving, but it's in my bag in the backseat so I can't answer. Today is going to be my cleaning day. Then I have time to curl up with a book until later, when I said I would meet Jess and Ned out for a few drinks. Ned's friend is a bartender at the bar where we're getting together. It's a total dump loaded with potheads, but it does have shuffleboard. It's also kind of perfect that it's the type of place where I don't have to worry about what I wear or what I say because no one is really in a state to notice or care anyway.

I'm all for a little less introspection these days.

∼

I'm lying in the bathtub reading when I realize I never checked my phone to see who called. Maybe it was Jess calling to cancel for tonight. I hop out of the tub and throw on a robe.

"Chloe, it's Paul. Just calling to let you know I'll be hitting the road soon. I should be back in town by four. I'd really like to see you. How about dinner tonight?"

It's nearly four now, and I'm supposed to meet Jess and Ned at seven. Maybe I can have dinner with Paul *and* meet up with Jess and Ned. Before returning Paul's call, I have to see if it's okay with Jess for him to join us.

"*He*-looo," she sings into the phone, sounding chipper for the first time in a long time. Things must be going well with Ned.

"Wow. Someone's in a good mood."

"Wait until you see what Ned gave me for Christmas," she says, her voice giddy.

"Oh no," I mumble.

"Nooo. I know what you're thinking. It's not *that*. Don't worry, you'll know before it happens if he ever plans on proposing to me.

He would ask my step-dad first, and there's no way my mom would be able to keep it a secret."

"Phew. That's a relief."

"Very funny. What's up?"

"Well, Paul is wondering if I'm free for dinner tonight."

"Yeah, so? You have my permission to go."

"Ha ha. I'm actually wondering if it's okay with you if I bring him with me tonight?"

"Of course it is. Is this your third date?"

"Fourth actually. I forgot to tell you he stopped over on Wednesday night before he drove to his parents' house."

"Oh *really*? How dare you not kiss and tell."

"We didn't kiss."

"Are you serious? You still haven't kissed him?"

"No. After what happened with Sean, I'm making it a point to take things slow this time."

"Why? How can you tell there's chemistry if you don't kiss him?"

"Trust me, I can tell."

"So, are you still seeing other people? I can't imagine how exhaustingly boring it would be to just date a bunch of people and not be getting any action."

"Not at the moment. I'm supposed to give this new guy a call to set up a date though."

"Good. You deserve to have some fun."

"Yeah, it's been real fun."

"Oh, stop. This is what dating is all about. Ups and downs and twists and turns."

"I know, but I've been thinking lately about how all of this drama probably isn't worth it, especially if there's already a master plan for our lives."

"What do you mean? Are you still hung up on that psychic? Or is this because you made your biannual trip to church?"

"Wow, you're a real hoot today."

"Chloe, if you believe God really has your life all mapped out, then that's all the more reason to let loose and enjoy yourself. It would be part of the plan."

I roll my eyes even though she can't see me. "Anyway, I'll see you later. And can you please ask Ned to refrain from being a dick if Paul is with me?"

"Not nice, Chloe. But yeah, I'll just tell him to keep his opinions to himself."

"Thanks. I don't want him scaring Paul away. According to the Angel Lady, he *is* my future husband, you know?"

～

"Hey, Chloe. I was just about to call you again." I smile at the sound of Paul's voice.

"Yeah, sorry I'm just getting back to you now. I was driving when you called and completely spaced on checking for messages when I got home. How was your Christmas?"

"It was great, but I have a confession to make . . . I couldn't get you out of my head. But not in a creepy way, of course."

"Good," I say with a laugh. "I thought about you too."

"Perfect," he says with a sigh. "So, are you up for dinner?"

"I am, but one thing. I already have plans with my friend Jess and her boyfriend. Are you fine with meeting them out?"

"I'm fine with anything as long as I get to see you."

"I can be ready in twenty minutes."

"I'll be there in thirty."

chapter forty-seven

Dinner with Paul could not have gone any better. He brought me flowers again and took me to my favorite sushi restaurant in Milwaukee's Third Ward. It seems as though our attraction to one another has only grown since the last time we saw each other. Maybe it has something to do with my decision to take things slow. Then again, maybe it's a result of my obsession with the Angel Lady's notes. Somehow, I can't help but wonder every time Paul touches me (or even looks at me) if he's the guy she was talking about. I've had to consciously push the thought out of my brain numerous times.

We're on our way to meet Ned and Jess, and I may be rambling just a bit. ". . . And one more thing. I've only been to this bar a few times. And only because Ned's friend was bartending those nights."

"Chloe, relax. Do you think I've never been to a dive bar? Don't worry, I'm not going to judge you based on the décor or clientele of this bar."

"Oh, and just keep in mind that I disagree with ninety-five percent of the things that come out of Ned's mouth."

He chuckles. "Okay. I'll remember that."

Smoke envelops us when we step inside the bar. Paul wrinkles his nose. "Is that what I think it is?"

"Probably," I say.

I lead him to the far corner of the bar. Ned is seated on the same stool he always sits on, and Jess is standing behind him rubbing his back. The sight makes me gag.

"Hey, you two," I say.

"Chloe!" Jess hugs me. Then she approaches Paul with open arms. "You must be Paul."

"And you must be Jess," he says, looking at me over her shoulder.

She releases him and then pulls him over to Ned. "Paul, this is my boyfriend Ned."

They shake hands and Paul says, "Good to meet you."

Ned sizes Paul up first. Then he says, "You're taller than the last guy she dated."

"Oh, yeah?" Paul replies.

I smile because Paul doesn't play into Ned's little game. He tends to say things in an attempt to make people feel uncomfortable. My best guess has always been that it must make him feel better about his own pathetic self to see others squirm. In this case, his target doesn't show the slightest sign of discomfort. Paul actually looks amused.

"Yeah. Do you want a beer?"

"Sure. And Chloe would like an Absolut Mandarin and seltzer. Thanks."

"Anyway," Jess says, "do you guys want to sit over at that table so we can talk?"

"Sounds good," I say.

She looks to Ned for an answer. He sighs. "You guys go. I'll wait here for the drinks."

Paul steps up though, "Go ahead, Chloe. I'll wait with Ned."

Jess is smiling at me when we sit down. "You guys do have a certain chemistry. I can see it."

"You can?"

"I can, but don't let that dissuade you from dating other people. You haven't even kissed him yet."

When Ned and Paul join us, they are in a heated discussion about politics. But, to my surprise, Ned seems to be enjoying Paul's company—so much that he even agrees to play shuffleboard. Jess and I kick their butts, of course.

It's around eleven when I realize how tired I am. Ned and Jess are at the bar getting another round of free drinks, and Paul and I are sitting at the table bouncing quarters into a cup. "Ready to call it a night?" I ask.

"I'm ready when you are. This is fun though. Jess is nice. And Ned's not so bad."

I consider his statement about Ned. "You know, he usually isn't this pleasant. He seems to really like you though. Maybe he'll ask you out."

Paul laughs. "He'll have to get in line."

Get in line? Does that mean Paul is dating a lot of other people? I suppose just because he hasn't logged into his Personals account doesn't necessarily mean he doesn't already have a slew of dates on his calendar.

"You being at the front of the line, of course." He grins at me.

"Paul?"

"Yes?"

"I just want you to know that I don't mind if you continue dating other people. I mean, I really like you, but I still want to date other people too."

"Okay." The grin on his face doesn't change one bit. "That sounds like a good plan."

"It does?" I expected him to at least show a little bit of jealousy or concern, but he seems just fine.

"Of course, that's why it's called dating." He nudges his shoulder against mine. Then he gently takes hold of my chin, turns my face toward his and kisses me.

My heart palpitates, and all of the background noise disappears as I enjoy the moment. Unfortunately, the moment of bliss is interrupted by a deliberate coughing sound.

"Sorry to interrupt you two," Jess says.

Ned nods toward the bar, "Don is asking if we want a round of shots on the house."

"Actually, we're both feeling kind of tired. I think we're going to get going," I say.

"Noooo! You guys can't leave. We're having such a good time," Jess whines.

Ned looks around. Then he pulls a small vial of coke out of his pocket and holds it out in front of us. "Do you guys need a pick-me-up?"

"What the hell, Ned?" I stand and start putting my coat on.

"Ned, put that away. *Now*," Jess says.

"What? I was just trying to be helpful." He throws his arms up and returns to the bar.

"Sorry about that," I say to Paul. "You ready?"

"Sure. Let's go. It was nice to meet you, Jess."

"You too," she says as she gives him a hug. Then she hugs me and whispers, "I really like this guy. That's *two* good ones from online. I stand corrected."

～

Paul and I don't talk much during the drive to my place. Instead, he puts in some new CD he received for Christmas and we just enjoy the music. When we arrive, I don't even think twice when he turns the car off and walks with me to the door. In fact, I expect him to come in this time. But when I unlock the door and step inside, he stays outside.

"Aren't you coming in?"

"I don't know. I'm pretty tired."

"Well, you certainly wouldn't want to risk falling asleep behind the wheel now would you?" I laugh at my own joke, but Paul remains straight-faced and looks in the direction of the road. "Paul? What's up? Is something wrong?"

"No, nothing. I guess I can stay for a little bit."

"Okay. Come on in."

Walking upstairs, I wonder if he was lying when he said nothing was bothering him. But as soon as we enter my apartment, he pulls me in for a kiss, immediately reassuring me that he must have been telling the truth.

～

I wake up the next morning expecting to find Paul still in bed with me, but he isn't. "Paul?" I crawl out of bed and quickly change out of my smoky clothes from the night before. Then I check the bathroom. He's not there either. "Paul?" Even before I check the kitchen and living room, I fear that he's already gone, and I am right. *What the hell? Why would he leave without saying goodbye? Wait, today is Monday. I'm still on winter break, but did he have to work? No, I swear he told me he was still off today.*

I grab the phone, intent on calling him for an explanation, but I dial Jess's number instead.

She answers sounding groggier than ever. "Why are you calling so early?"

"Sorry. I don't even know what time it is."

"Why would you call when you don't even know what time it is?"

"Well, I assumed it was late enough for you to be awake based on how sunny my apartment is right now."

She moans. "Can you just tell me why you're calling so I can go back to sleep?"

"Paul left this morning without even saying goodbye."

"Ohhhh," she coos. "How was it?" Suddenly, she sounds wide-awake.

"How was what?"

"Well, I assume you slept with him, right?"

"*No.* We just made out until both of us passed out."

"Well, then who cares if he left without saying goodbye. He probably had somewhere to be and didn't want to wake you. That's actually pretty polite. You know, *to not want to wake someone.*"

"I don't know, Jess. He's not the kind of guy who would just up and leave without a word."

"Apparently, he is that kind of guy. But honestly, I think you're getting worked up over nothing. Why don't you call him?"

"Because I think that would seem weird, me calling first thing in the morning. Don't you think I should wait another hour or two?"

"Yes, that sounds like a plan. Now, I'm going back to sleep. Call me later. But *not* until noon at the earliest."

"Fine."

chapter forty-eight

It's been two days, and still no word from Paul. I drew the line at leaving two messages, afraid of turning into someone else's Cliff or Drew. Instead of continuing to obsess over why he has vanished, I've decided to take Jess's advice and move on. Besides, unless he's dead, there's no good reason for someone to just disappear for so long.

I haven't heard from Shelly either, which is really starting to wear on me emotionally. I know she had plans to spend a few days at the Mall of America with Craig after Christmas, but it takes five hours to get there from Milwaukee. That's certainly enough time to call. Maybe I should just call her. I glance at the clock. Four fifteen. Tonight is Home Bar night, so she's probably getting ready to meet Craig for a BAB. Maybe instead of calling, I will just show up for a BAB myself. If they are not there, I can always talk to Chris for a while. Jess thinks Shelly is just jealous because I'm out having fun meeting new people while she's stuck in a relationship. I told her that if that were the case, Shelly would have no problem cutting Craig loose—at least I don't think she would. But if there's any truth the Jess's theory, then why would Shelly encourage me to date freely? Friendships should not be so complicated.

I finish up a post-workout stretch and hop into the shower. It's time to end this feud with Shelly once and for all.

∼

"Welcome Home!"

I wave at Chris and spot Shelly and Craig in their usual stools at the far end of the bar. Shelly and I lock eyes. Then she looks at Craig and says something. He stands as soon as I'm next to them and says, "Hey Chloe. Long time no see. I'm going to play some tunes. Anything you want to hear?"

"No. Thanks, though."

Shelly and I watch Craig as he heads toward the juke box. Then I climb awkwardly onto his stool. Seconds later, Chris plops a drink down in front of me.

"So," I say. "How was your Christmas?"

"It was good. How was yours?"

"Fine. It was just my mom, my stepdad and me. Oh, and my mom's friend stopped over for a few hours."

"Well, we went to my parents' for breakfast. Then we went to Craig's parents' house for lunch. And then we went back to my parents' for dinner. It was exhausting."

"Did you guys go to the Mall?"

"Yep. Just got back into town. Did you know Minnesota doesn't tax clothes?"

"Really?"

"Really. We should take a road trip there in August to buy clothes for work."

"You mean to go *school* shopping?"

She giggles. "Yeah. That was one of my favorite times of year growing up. The end of summer when my mom would take me school shopping."

"I know. Me too."

We stare at each other, and then both of us start talking at the same time. We both laugh uncomfortably, and then I take a deep breath and ask, "I'm sorry, what were you going to say?"

"Just that, I'm sorry I haven't called you. Last week was just really busy. And you know how crazy the kids are right before break."

"Yeah, tell me about it."

"And then it was Christmas . . . and . . . you know."

"Why didn't you call while you were driving to the Mall?"

"Because, Chloe, I didn't want to talk about any of this in front of Craig."

"Any of what? We haven't talked about anything that happened at Tom's house."

"I know. Look, can we just forget about that? It was two weeks ago. I should have called you. I'm sorry."

"Shelly, I don't need an apology from you for not calling. I need an apology for the things you said to me."

She gives me a confused look. "I really don't think I have anything to apologize for—unless you want me to apologize for being honest? But isn't that what friends are supposed to do? Provide an honest opinion when it's needed?"

"You're kidding me, right? You basically called me a slut. And even if I was a slut, a real friend would not call me that."

"I did *not* call you a slut. I simply stated that you should be *dating* people, getting to know them, *not* sleeping around."

"Shelly, I am *not* sleeping around. I had sex with one guy I met online. *One*."

"Yeah, well, I have a feeling if I hadn't said anything you would have ended up hopping into bed with Paul, too. Or who knows, maybe you already have. Tom told me he's a real ladies' man."

"What is your deal? Why are you acting like this?"

"Because it's time to grow up. I know, I know. I'm the one who told you to stop acting like an old biddy when we were in college. But that was *college*. We have careers now."

"This doesn't make any sense. Maybe Jess was right."

She laughs. "Jess? Oh please, what did she say? That I'm just being a judgmental bitch?"

"No. She said maybe you miss being single. That maybe you're bored."

"Well you can tell Jess that I'm not bored. And the reason I'm not bored with Craig is because we were friends first. Trust me, if I was bored with him or if I knew he wasn't the one, I would break up with him. And I wouldn't need my friends to tell me what to do. I also would not try to satisfy myself by sleeping around behind his back the way Jess did with Ned. And I wouldn't go around kissing women when I know I'm not a lesbian!"

"How is that even relevant to this conversation?"

"I don't know. I'm just frustrated, and I'm starting to think that you and Jess have a lot more in common than we do. Not the kissing women part, but you know what I mean. I'm just so tired of all the drama."

There are a million things I want to say to her, but I can't narrow my response down to just one thing. Instead, I say nothing and sip my drink.

"Everything okay here?" Craig asks.

"Fine," Shelly says.

"Yeah, fine." I finish my drink with one long sip, and hop off of Craig's stool. "I'm gonna get going. You guys have fun."

Shelly looks surprised. "Chloe, you don't have to leave."

Craig looks at Shelly. "I thought everything was fine."

Before Shelly can respond, I jump in. "It is. I got exactly what I came here for. I'm good."

Chris stops me as I'm opening the door to leave. "You coming back, hon? Should I make you another drink?"

"Nah. I'm not up for drinking tonight. Thanks though. Maybe I'll see you next week." But I know deep down that I probably won't be returning to the Home Bar anytime soon.

~

By the time I get into my car, my face is covered in tears. Luckily, I have a healthy supply of Starbucks napkins in the glove compartment. When my sobbing slows to an occasional quick breath, it occurs to me that I haven't cried so hard since my grandmother died. The last time before that was when I was fourteen and my dad told me I could not live with him. Both times, I felt abandoned. I guess that's how I feel about Shelly—like she's abandoning me. Maybe that's why I like the idea of being in a relationship, but can't seem to go the distance with anyone; I would much rather be the abandoner than the abandonee.

The thing is, don't I have to get over that eventually? I hate the way Shelly talked to me. I hate how judged she made me feel. I even hate that she's been giving me conflicting messages about what she thinks I should do since the day we met, without ever really seeming to think I might deserve an opinion of my own on that front. But . . . maybe she was right about one thing. Maybe it's time for me to grow up.

Maybe I need to stop being so afraid of being abandoned, and open my heart up to the possibility of finding something real.

But I'm not so sure Internet dating is the place to find it anymore.

Since I didn't have a BAB, I head straight to my parents' house for leftovers. They are at the local casino, so I won't have to explain why I've been crying.

Wanting to get in and out as quickly as possible, I take my plate of Christmas leftovers into the basement. That way I can check my Personals account while I eat. Even though I have a date scheduled for tomorrow night, I've decided to cancel my account. From what I understand, canceling a Personals subscription doesn't mean you stop receiving new matches. It just means you are not able to initiate communication with anyone. That way, if someone catches your attention, you are tempted to reenroll. I'm not just canceling though. I'm done with online dating, period. No more perusing through matches. No more analyzing stats or trying to find hidden meaning in introductory paragraphs. No more deciding whether I should send an icebreaker or a message or whether I should respond to icebreakers and messages. My only reason for logging in tonight is to satisfy a few curiosities. The first profile I look up is Frank's, the single dad who couldn't handle my crazy exes. It's exactly the same, and he has not been active for a month. I hope this means that he found someone perfect for him, because he deserves it.

The next profile I click on is Sean's—another guy I wish nothing but the best for. He has been active within the last two weeks. Last, I click on Paul's. When I see that he has logged in within the last twenty-four hours, I feel sick. Now I know why he was too busy to call. The least he could have done was provide an explanation for his Houdini act, but then again, maybe it's better if I never know why he suddenly changed his mind about me. I probably couldn't handle the truth.

No longer hungry, I push my plate away and navigate to the Account Settings page. A few clicks later, I have notified Yahoo! Personals that I wish to cancel my account.

chapter forty-nine

I'm meeting my final online suitor at a German bar called Von Trier. As I drive, I make a pact with myself to stay for at least an hour before telling him I'm not feeling well. Considering the crappy mood I'm in, a direct result of the argument I had with Shelly yesterday, I probably should have canceled. But I decided to be a good sport and meet this one last person. In an attempt to lighten my state of mind, I turn on a more upbeat station in lieu of the melancholy lyrics of Norah Jones. The change in music makes me feel a little better until I realize I can't find a parking spot. Then I remember why the streets are so crowded. It's not just my winter break; it's also winter break for all the local college students. Why the hell did this guy have to choose a bar right in the middle of everything?

When I finally find a spot, it's four blocks away and I'm five minutes late. Since it will take me at least ten minutes to limp to the bar, I debate hopping back into my car. But then I think about how terrible I would feel if someone stood me up and begin the long trek.

The walk makes my ankle throb, so I have to rest against a wall as soon as I enter the bar. The place is crowded and I don't remember what my date looks like all that clearly. At least if I can't find him, I won't have to feel bad for leaving. I look at my watch and vow to search the crowd for ten minutes before calling it quits.

Five minutes into my lackluster attempt at finding HistoryGuy1976, a woman taps me on the shoulder. "Excuse me. Are you Chloe?"

"Yes."

"Tony is a friend of mine. He's in the other room waiting for you."

"Oh. Okay. Thanks." I bypass the bar and make my way into the next room, but all I see are groups of people. Then I feel another tap on my shoulder.

"He's right over there," says the same girl from before. "Come on, I'll take you over."

This is ridiculous. Why is this guy here with a table full of guys and girls?

"Hey, Tony," the girl says loudly.

HistoryGuy1976, also known as Tony, looks in our direction along with everyone else at the same table. Tony looks from the girl to me. "What?"

"You idiot. This is your date."

"Oh. All right." He rises and walks over to us. The girl pats my shoulder once again, and sits down in Tony's empty seat. "So, you're Chloe?"

"Hi. Nice to meet you."

"Yeah, you too. You didn't get yourself a drink?"

"Uh, no. I'm not really in a drinking kind of mood." But clearly if I was, I would be getting it myself.

He sticks his hands in his pockets and nods but doesn't say anything.

"So, these are all your friends?"

"Yeah. Most of us live a few blocks from UWM, so we hang out here pretty regularly."

"So . . . Tony, right?"

"Yeah."

"Your profile says you're a teacher."

"I'm actually student teaching now. Graduating in May."

I'm so annoyed. "Why did you say you were a teacher then?"

"I don't know. What's the difference? Teacher. Student teacher. I'll have my own classroom soon enough, right?"

I limped four blocks for this nonsense? I have to get out of here. But first, I have to pee, and the bathroom is five feet away.

"Can you excuse me? I have to use the restroom."

"Yeah. Go for it."

I can feel his eyes on me as I limp away.

When I return, Tony is sitting with his friends again. I feel extremely awkward as I approach, especially when a few people look up to watch.

"Hi," I say aloud.

A few people wave, some just smile and others don't even notice I'm there. Tony stands to talk to me again. "Do you have some sort of . . ." he points to my leg. "Some sort of . . . deformity or something?"

"Excuse me?"

"You have a limp."

"I know. I hurt my ankle a few weeks ago, and I had to walk four blocks to get here."

"Oh," he sighs, as if relieved to find out I'm not handicapped. "Well, that sucks."

"Yeah. It sucks. So, I feel . . ."

"Hey, what's your ethnicity?"

"Why do you ask?"

"Well, my buddies and I have a little wager on it. Are you Korean?"

"No."

"Damn. So, what are you then?"

"Taiwanese."

He slaps his thigh. "I knew it was something chinky."

"That's it. I'm leaving. I wish I could say it was nice to meet you, but, honestly, it wasn't."

I walk as fast as I can through the crowd, and I faintly hear one of Tony's friends say, "Damn, what's her problem?"

Well, at least I'm getting out of here in less than an hour. I look down at my watch. *Heck, less than thirty minutes.* When I look back up, I nearly crash into a couple heading toward me. I want to disappear when I realize one of the pair is Paul, and I want to shrivel up and die when I realize he's holding hands with the woman beside him.

"Chloe?"

"Uh . . . Hi," I say to him. Then I look at his date and extend a hand. "I'm Chloe." I search her face for a hint of recognition, but nothing appears to register.

"Hi, Chloe. Nice to meet you. I'm Alice." She looks at Paul, clearly curious about who I am.

Finally, Paul says, "Chloe is an old friend." He looks at me with pleading eyes—the same pleading eyes he had after our second date when he tried to weasel his way into my apartment. Only this time he's trying to weasel his way out of Alice finding out who I really am. Or at least how terribly he ended things with me.

"Yep, that's right, old friends," I say as I walk right in between them and out the door.

If Alice is smart, she'll nag him about my reaction to his claim. And if she's really smart, she won't let up until he caves and tells her the truth.

Now I need a drink.

chapter fifty

As soon as I get home, I uncork a bottle of wine. What a couple of days. First Shelly, then the rude frat boy, and then, like some kind of cosmic kick when I'm down, Paul. My apartment is spotless since I've been off all week, so there's nothing to clean. I walk around, holding a glass of wine, and try to find something that needs straightening, organizing or even reorganizing. When I arrive in my bedroom, I know exactly what will take my mind off of everything: a wardrobe purge. I turn on my clock radio and get to work.

Two hours later, the final drops of wine have been poured and I'm feeling much better. Numerous items have been bagged, including the hideous purple chenille sweater that I was only holding onto because James had given it to me. It was a struggle, but I also forced myself to part with my ratty old gym T-shirt and shorts —I even threw them in the kitchen garbage and topped them with some ketchup to avoid the temptation of retrieving them.

As I'm in the final stage of putting my closet back together, my cell phone rings. I pick it up off of the nightstand. *Well, well. Look who finally decided to call.*

"Hello?"

"Hi. It's Paul."

"I know. Cell phones have this great thing called caller ID."

"Okay. I know. You have a right to be pissed."

"What about Alice? Is she pissed, or does she still think I'm an old friend? And does she know about all of your other *old* friends?"

"Chloe, can you please let me explain?"

"Why do you need to explain anything to me? I already know what's going on. I should have listened to Tom."

"Look, Alice and I dated for years—all through college. Then we decided to take a break. It was mutual. I started dating other people and all of a sudden, I ran into her last week when I was visiting my parents. She asked me to think about giving us another chance and, well, to be honest with you, I was confused. Then when I returned and had dinner with you, I thought I knew what I wanted to do, which was say goodbye to her for good. But then Ned brought out those drugs, and I freaked thinking that maybe you do that stuff too. Chloe, I can't be around someone who abuses drugs. Anyway, I bolted on you, and I'm sorry."

"So, you ditched me because *Ned* does cocaine once in a while? And now you're back with Alice?"

"No, I'm not back together with her. We're just seeing what happens. She knows I've been online dating. I don't know why I said you were an old friend. I just froze."

"Why are you calling now Paul?"

"I just think it's only fair for you to know why I flaked out on you. And to be completely honest, Alice encouraged me to call."

I take a deep breath. "Okay. So, now what?"

"Well, now I'm going to take a break from online dating while Alice and I figure out what we're going to do. I already put in the request to cancel my subscription. I'm sorry."

"Forget about it. Don't be sorry. I think I understand. Good luck with Alice, I guess."

"Good luck to you too, Chloe."

Before we say goodbye, another call comes in, so I click over without another word to Paul. "Hello?"

"Chloe?" Jess sobs. "It happened again."

"Jess? What happened again?"

"Ned caught me with Brant."

"The pilot?"

"Yes." She continues sobbing heavily.

Suddenly, I'm even angrier with Jess than I was with Shelly or the idiot frat guy or Paul. "Jess, why the hell do you keep on doing the same stupid bullshit over and over and over? Either you want to be with Ned or you don't. It's that simple. But you can't just cheat on him when you feel neglected or when you're bored with him. What is wrong with you?"

The line is silent for what feels like an eternity. I almost hang up, thinking Jess has already hung up on me, but then she blows her nose and says, "I think I'm just scared."

"Well, you *should* be scared—scared that you're going to end up alone if you keep cheating on your boyfriends. You know what though? I'm actually glad you cheated on Ned this time. You want to know why? Because he screwed up any chance I had of continuing to date Paul."

"Chloe, what are you talking about?"

"The coke, Jess. Paul thinks I'm probably a coke head too."

"Well, that's absurd—him thinking that you would do coke *and* you blaming Ned for ruining your chances with him. Both of those things are just plain dumb."

"Dumb? Look, Jess, I've had a really shitty night. I want to be here for you but we should probably end this call before I say something I might regret. I'm just not up for this kind of drama tonight."

"Gee. Thanks for the support, Chloe."

Her tone fills me with guilt, but I'm too buzzed to back down from the combative stance I've already taken. And I'm riddled with angst over the things Shelly said about Jess and me. Maybe Jess's dramas combined with my own have contributed to my own fear of commitment. As the saying goes, misery loves company.

"Jess, I just think it might be better if we talk about this tomorrow. Are you going to be okay?"

"Yeah, I guess so."

"I'll call you tomorrow then. Just try to get some sleep."

She sniffles. "Okay. I'll talk to you then."

Within minutes of hanging up, I turn off the lights and fall into a deep, wine-induced sleep.

chapter fifty-one

Usually when I fall asleep upset, I wake up the next morning with a fresh outlook. Not today, though. The first thing on my mind is Jess. I wish I had talked to her instead of pushing her away when she needed me. Still lying in bed, I grab my phone and dial her, but she doesn't answer. Hopefully she's okay. Next, I think about Shelly, and search my heart for guidance on what to do about her. But, to my surprise, I feel nothing, telling me that maybe it's time for Shelly and me to take a break from each other. Or maybe we should just part ways for good this time. My next thought is of Paul, which disgusts me, so I reach over and turn on my clock radio, hopeful that some background music will boost my mood. Instead of music, a commercial for New Year's Eve drink specials at a club downtown is playing. *Oh my gosh. That's right. It's New Year's Eve.* How depressing.

Instead of feeling sorry for myself for being a total loser who has no plans on New Year's Eve, I decide to sweat my sorrows away. Halfway through Tae Bo Live, my home phone rings. The answering machine is loud enough for me to hear my mother's message.

"*Chloe? Where are you? Are you still sleeping? Helloooo! If you're there, pick up . . . mumbling . . . Well, I don't know where you are, so call me back. Glen is setting up the grill in the garage. We're grilling a turkey and some ribs for tonight. You probably have plans, but why don't you stop over for an early dinner?*" Click.

∾

It's early afternoon when I pull into my parents' driveway. The garage door is open, and Glen is lounging in a lawn chair in between two charcoal grills. He's holding a beer.

"Hey, Glen. Something smells good."

"Hi, Chloe. Are you staying for dinner?"

"Actually, I think I'm going to hang out here tonight if you guys don't mind."

"Really? That will make your mother very happy. She's in the bathroom washing her hair."

"All right, thanks."

More delicious aromas excite my taste buds when I enter the house. The kitchen counter is filled with empty serving trays waiting to be filled with appetizers, bottles of liquor and champagne, and party favors.

"Mom! I'm here," I say as I make my way down the hallway to the first floor bathroom.

"Chloe? I'm washing my hair!" she yells just as I arrive in the doorway.

"I know. Glen told me. Wow. Are you guys having people over tonight?"

"Eh. Just the usual. You know."

By the usual, I assume she means the same friend who joined us on Christmas and possibly Glen's mom and brother.

"Well, I think I'm going to hang out here tonight too."

She stands upright, her hair hanging in her face and dripping. "What? It's New Year's Eve. Why aren't you doing something with your friends or with one of those Yahoo! guys?"

"I don't know."

"What do you mean, you don't know? What's going on?"

For some reason, the look of concern on my mother's face makes me burst into tears. She wraps her wet hair in a towel on top of her head, and we sit on her bed while I tell her everything.

"You know, Chloe, I was your age when I met your father. I liked him so much, but I wasn't sure if I wanted to leave my country to live here in America with him." She leans in close and whispers, "I'm going to tell you something I've never told any of you kids—even though you could all probably figure it out if you wanted to. I was pregnant with your brother when I was deciding whether or not to come here." She backs away, looking ashamed by this admission.

"You were?"

"I was. So as you can imagine, the decision was even more difficult than if I wasn't pregnant because I wasn't just deciding my own future. I was deciding the future for your brother too."

"That must have been really tough. So how did you decide?"

"Well, I had a lot of family and friends telling me what they thought I should do. My family told me not to go. They said your father would leave me. But my friends, well, they all told me to go. They were excited for me. They said America would open up a world of opportunity for your brother and me. I listened to my friends because the scenario they helped me imagine seemed so much more plausible at the time than the warnings from my family. I think young hearts too often have tunnel vision. Anyway, you know how it ended."

"So, are you saying you wish you had listened to your family and never come to America?"

"No. Because then I never would have had you or your sister. And your sister would never have had Simon and Sadie. And your brother would never have gone into the Navy. And I never would have met Glen. Chloe, you can't let other people decide how you should do things or how you should feel. Things will turn out exactly the way they are supposed to just by you being you and doing things the way you do them. My heart happened to agree with my friends when I was deciding whether to come here or not. And you know what, I know I say mean things about your father sometimes..."

"Sometimes, mom?"

"Okay, okay, I say a lot of inappropriate things about your father, but I have to admit, him following his heart worked out perfectly for both of us. Now he has Nancy..." *What's going on here? She didn't say* 'that woman'. "... and I have Glen. We're all much happier because of it. As for your friends, I don't really know what to tell you about them. They sound much more bossy and negative than mine ever were. I suspect they care about you, but remember, that doesn't mean they know what's best for you. You have to decide for yourself how you live your life—with my input, of course."

I roll my eyes. "Okay, mom."

She laughs. "Seriously, Chloe, if you want to stop online dating, stop. If you want to stop dating all together, then stop dating. Things are going to end up the way they are supposed to be regardless."

"No offense, mom, but then why do you still give me a hard time about Matt?"

"I shouldn't. And I won't anymore."

∼

The unexpected heart to heart I had with my mother has inspired me to drive over to Jess's. The way I brushed her off when she called last night doesn't make me feel very proud of myself. And it certainly doesn't make me feel like the kind person that my mother seems to think I am. Do I think Jess should be cheating on Ned? Absolutely not. Do I think Ned is a jerk to Jess and that she deserves better? Absolutely. But do I think it's up to me to tell Jess how to navigate her love life? No. I can't even figure my own out. I'm supposed to be her friend and confidant, not judge and jury.

The main entrance to her building is open as usual, so I let myself in. When I get to her apartment door, I know she's home because I can hear the sounds of Paul Simon coming from inside. I knock loudly, but there's no answer. After knocking one more time, I try the doorknob. It's unlocked, so I let myself in again.

"Hello? Jess?" I walk slowly through the dining room and into the living room where the music is coming from, but she's not there. Then I make my way toward her bathroom. As soon as I turn the corner, I come face-to-face with Jess wrapped in a towel.

"Ahhhhhh!" she screams.

I jump back, startled by her reaction. "Jess, Jess. Calm down. It's just me."

"Chloe! What the heck? You scared the shit out of me."

I laugh. "I'm sorry. I heard the music and figured you couldn't hear me knocking."

"What are you doing here?"

"Can we sit down?"

"Sure. Let me get dressed real quick. I just made some muffins. Help yourself."

I'm relieved by Jess's demeanor. She actually seems okay despite the state she was in last night when I talked to her. I grab a muffin from a plate on the stove—banana chocolate chip. Then I sit down at the table and think about what I want to say to her.

I hear Jess enter the room from behind me. "So, what's up?" She asks, grabbing her phone off the counter and examining it. "Did you try to call?"

"No. I just decided to come over so we could talk in person."

Jess grabs a muffin and takes a seat next to me at the table. "I'm sorry for calling you last night about more Ned drama. You're right. I need to get my shit together."

"Don't be sorry. I'm the one who needs to apologize. I should have been there for you regardless of the kind of day I had."

"No, Chloe, just because you're my best friend, that doesn't mean you should have to put up with hearing about the same stupid mistakes I make over and over."

"Well, I'm sorry anyway. So, what happened?"

"Oh, you know, the usual. Ned was being a dick, so I got pissed at him and called Brant. And you can imagine the rest. What happened to you?"

I fill her in on the unfortunate events of the day before. I see a the hint of a grin on her lips when I start telling her about Shelly, but by the end of that recount, the look on her face is far from amused. When I tell her about the guy who said he knew I had to be something "chinky," we both laugh. And then Paul shifts us into somewhat somber moods.

"So, it wasn't Ned's fault?" she asks.

"No. I shouldn't have led you to believe that. He did mention the coke, but that really had nothing to do with why we won't be seeing each other again. I'm sorry I said it was Ned's fault. That was pretty lame of me."

"It's okay. I figured you had a good reason for being such a bitch. You always do." She smiles.

"Whatever. So, what are you doing tonight?"

"I don't know. I was thinking about going out to Jannigan's. Do you want to go? It *is* New Year's Eve."

"Why don't we try something different this year?"

"Like what?"

"Do you feel like going to a low-key party?"

"Where?"

"Well, it's where they're going to have grilled turkey, barbecued ribs, lots of appetizers and all the champagne you can drink. Oh, and there might be a heated mahjong tournament going on."

"You're not talking about your parents' house, are you?"

"Maybe."

She grins and rolls her eyes. "Gee, that sounds like a real hoot."

"Come on Jess, it might actually be more fun than ringing in the New Year with a bunch of drunk strangers."

"Maybe you're right. I don't know."

"Well, think about it," I say as I stand. "I have to get going because I told my mom I would help her with the appetizers. I hope you decide to stop over, but if not, be sure to call me when midnight rolls around."

"Okay. I'll call for sure."

Before I leave, we give each other a hug, and Jess holds tight a little longer than usual. I can sense that she might be ready for some much needed change, which is good, because I am too.

Shortly after my mom and I get all of the appetizers on the dining room table, there's a knock at the door.

"Hey, Glen, can you get the door?" my mom yells. Then she says to me, "That Betty always has to come early, and then she wonders why we're not ready to eat."

But instead of Betty, Jess enters the room.

"Jess!" My mother exclaims. "I haven't seen you since I busted you and Chloe with wine coolers in her room."

"Yeah, it's been a long time Jan."

They give each other a hug.

"I'm glad you decided to come," I say.

"Yeah, it's probably time for me to make a few changes in my life. When better to start than tonight?"

I give her a hug. "Agreed."

chapter fifty-two

It's my first Friday back at work. I'm sitting at my desk during lunch, peanut butter and jelly sandwich in hand. A brief phone call to my credit card company has just confirmed what Jess warned might happen: I've been charged for another month of services by Yahoo! Personals. Apparently, when Jess's redheaded co-worker thought she had canceled her subscription, she later found out that her credit card was still being charged for the service months later.

"Hello. This is Dana with Yahoo! Personals. How can I assist you today?"

"Hi, Dana. I canceled my account last week, so my credit card was not supposed to be charged for this month. However, I just checked, and it was."

"Well, ma'am, I apologize for your inconvenience. I just need to get some information from you in order to pull up your account. Can you please spell your first and last name?"

"Yes. It's Chloe—C, H, L, O, E—Thompson—T, H, O, M, P, S, O, N."

"Thank you, Ms. Thompson. And to make sure I have the right Chloe Thompson, can you please confirm your birthday?"

"Sure. It's February 3, 1976."

"Thank you. Hm. Okay. I see here that you put in the request to cancel your account on the twenty-ninth of December. However, cancellation requests must be made prior to the twenty-fifth of any given month to avoid being charged for the next month."

"Well, isn't there something you can do? I've decided to quit online dating."

"Hm. Tell you what, I can go ahead and reverse this charge for you. Consider it a late Christmas gift."

"Thank you so much. I really appreciate it."

"You're very welcome. By the way, Ms. Thompson, since your card was already charged, you will continue to have communication access with matches through the end of January. Maybe one more connection is all you need."

"I doubt that, but thanks anyway."

"Okay, ma'am. Well, you have a great day and a happy new year."

"Thanks. You too."

I take another bite of my sandwich and glance at the time. Twelve twenty. I still have nearly twenty minutes before I need to pick my students up from the lunchroom. My computer screen is open to the Yahoo! homepage, and out of habit, my eyes are drawn to the Personals link. *What the hell? Why not take a peek?*

The last time I logged in was over a week ago when I put in my cancellation request. Since then, dozens of new matches have been added to my list. The very first one displays the screen name Captain4408. In his profile picture, he's standing in front of large evergreen trees and wearing an army uniform. I can't resist clicking to read the entire profile.

~

Captain4408 – 27
Location: Milwaukee
Committed Gentleman

Relationship Status: Never Married
Kids: No
Want Kids: Yes
Ethnicity: White / Caucasian
Hair: Brown
Eyes: Brown
Body type: Athletic
Height: 5' 10"

Religion: Catholic
Politics: Conservative
Smoke: No
Drink: Social Drinker
Pets: No
Education: Bachelor's
Employment: Distribution Management
Income: 60,000-80,000

∼

His profession has nothing to do with education, and based on his profile picture, he has clearly served or is still in the military. Something compels me to click the *Send Icebreaker* button. As soon as I do so, the phone rings, prompting me to close out of my account.

At the end of the school day, I already have a message from Captain4408. In it, he has provided me with his phone number and has requested that I give him a call tomorrow if possible. His name is Daran. I'm still convinced I'm done with this whole online dating thing, but for some reason ... I jot down his number.

∼

It's Saturday morning, around ten—cell phone in my right hand and Daran's number in the left. I try to recall stats from his profile, but then I remember how silly it is to rely on stats. Stats simply can't predict compatibility. Then his profile picture comes to mind—the military uniform, the beautiful scenery. I've never dated anyone in the military before, yet my dad, my brother and my uncles on my mother's side all served.

"Hello?"

"Hi. Is this Daran?"

"Yeah, is this Chloe?"

"It is. I wasn't sure if it was too early to call on a Saturday, but then I remembered your profile picture. Military guys are used to getting up early, right?"

"That's right. Up at the crack of dawn for a ten-mile jog. And I just got done perfecting the hospital corners on my bed." He laughs.

"So, if you're in the military and live in Milwaukee, where are you stationed?"

"Well, to tell you the truth, I just got into town a week ago."

"Really? Where did you move from?"

"Virginia. I was stationed at Fort Eustis, but now I'm getting out of the Army."

"Why is that?"

"Because I'm ready for the next stage of my life. You know, a family."

"Are you originally from the area?"

"No. I'm from Vermont."

"So, you grew up in Vermont, and you just moved from Virginia?"

I make my way to the stationery box in my nightstand as I speak.

"That's right. What about you? Are you from the area?"

"I am. I grew up in a suburb of Milwaukee. And now I teach for Milwaukee Public Schools, so I'm required to live in the city."

I unfold the sheet of paper from the Angel Lady.

"That's right, you're a teacher. I actually got my undergraduate degree in secondary education. I was in ROTC."

I stare at the scrawled notes, mouth ajar. *Vermont. Virginia. Background in education. Two years older. Two boys.*

"Hey, Daran?"

"Yes?"

"How old are you?"

"Twenty-seven. How old are you?"

"Twenty-five."

"Okay. What else do you want to know?"

Near the end of our three-hour conversation, Daran mentions

how much he's enjoyed talking to me and then he says, "So, I guess I should clear one thing up before we meet. How many children do you want? How does two boys sound?"

"What did you just say?"

He laughs. "I was just kidding."

"I know. But did you say *two boys*?"

He laughs again. "Yeah, two boys. I once had a psychic tell me that I would marry a girl from the Midwest, and we would have two boys. Maybe you're the girl."

I smile to myself. "Who knows, maybe I am."

more. *books*. by k. j.

Click Date Repeat Again

Don't Call Me Kit Kat

A Case of Serendipity

Visit kjfarnham.com for more information.

ALSO AVAILABLE BY K. J. FARNHAM

click. date. repeat.
again.

Never in her wildest dreams would Jess Mason ever imagine herself being a part of the online dating hype. Yet here she is smack-dab in the middle of it all. And she's dated her fair share of online crazies to be a new connoisseur of all the weirdos out in the cyber world. After a slew of bad dates and pussy (cat that is) pictures, Jess knows that she needs to finally commit to something—or someone. And suddenly there he is, a man she can actually imagine herself with.

But when Jess is faced with an undeniable attraction to a handsome, unavailable co-worker, she's conflicted about continuing her quest for Mr. Right-At-Her-Fingertips. Now, it's feast or famine—and she's not willing to starve. She certainly can't have both--that wouldn't be right. After all, that's the "old Jess." The new Jess is ready to start clicking with someone special and make a real love connection.

about.*the*.author.

K. J. Farnham was born and raised in a suburb of Milwaukee. She graduated from UW-Milwaukee in 1999 with a bachelor's degree in elementary education and went on to earn a master's degree in curriculum and instruction from Carroll University in Waukesha. She then had the privilege of helping hundreds of children learn to read and write over the course of twelve years. Farnham now lives in western Wisconsin with her husband and three children.

Connect with K. J. at kjfarnham.com

CPSIA information can be obtained
at www.ICGtesting.com
Printed in the USA
LVHW091725220519
618749LV00005B/792/P

9 780692 113349